Praise for the Author

"Walsh has penned another endearing novel set in Loves Park, Colo. The emotions are occasionally raw, but always truly real. Readers will root for the characters to discover their potential and realize that love is right in front of them. It takes a little long to get to the point, but the journey is enjoyable."

—*RT Reviews*, ****

"Walsh (*A Sweethaven Summer*) pens a quaint, smalltown love story, complete with an overbearing mother, an unscrupulous business partner, and a group of busybodies whose hearts are in the right place even if their actions are questionable. While certain elements are predictable, Walsh develops enough plot twists to make this enjoyable to the end."

—*Publishers Weekly*

"Heartwarming! *Paper Hearts* is as much a treat as the delicious coffee the heroine serves in her bookshop. Courtney Walsh's warm author's voice tells a story of a doctor and a bookstore owner, both living in a town centered on romance, yet both disillusioned by love. Like the matchmakers that surrounded the couple in the novel, I couldn't help cheering them on. A poignant, wry, sweet, and utterly charming read!"

—Becky Wade, award-winning author of *Meant to Be Mine*

"Delightfully romantic with a lovable cast of quirky characters, *Paper Hearts* will have readers smiling from ear-to-ear! Courtney Walsh has penned a winner!"

—Katie Ganshert, award-winning author of *A Broken Kind of Beautiful*

"Walsh's touching debut will have readers longing for a visit to the idyllic vista of Sweethaven, Michigan. The touch of mystery, significant friendships and a charming setting create a real treasure."
—*Romantic Times*, ****

"This book captivated me from the first paragraphs. Bittersweet memories, long-kept secrets, the timeless friendships of women—and a touch of sweet romance. Beautifully written and peopled with characters who became my friends, this debut novel is one for my keeper shelf—and, I hope, the first of many to come from Courtney Walsh's pen."
—Deborah Raney, award-winning author of the Chicory Inn series and *A Vow to Cherish*

"Courtney Walsh puts the sweet in Sweethaven. If you're looking for an uplifting, hope-filled story filled with characters you'll feel like you know, *A Sweethaven Homecoming* has it!"
—Marybeth Whalen, author of *The Mailbox* and *The Things We Wish Were True*

Hometown Girl

ALSO BY COURTNEY WALSH

Hometown Girl

COURTNEY WALSH

Waterfall
PRESS

Published by Waterfall Press, Grand Haven, MI.

www.brilliancepublishing.com

Amazon, the Amazon logo, and Waterfall Press are trademarks of Amazon.com, Inc., or its affiliates.

ISBN-13: 9781542045636
ISBN-10: 1542045630

Cover design by Janet Perr

Printed in the United States of America.

For my dear friend Natalie Emenecker, with whom I share a love of Jesus, kids, theatre and romance. And who was gracious enough to share the name of her family farm for my fictional purposes in writing this book. Your real-life Fairwind Farm is full of the peace and simplicity this old soul needs.
Thank you for sharing it with me and for being my friend.

Chapter One

Beth Whitaker hated flowers.

Sure, they were pretty, and some of them even smelled good. The right assortment could dress up a dinner table, and she could appreciate how each one was different. But flowers were a sign of weakness.

And death.

People brought flowers to gravesites and hospital rooms. One of her earliest memories was being pulled out of kindergarten to attend her great-grandmother's funeral. She didn't remember the way Grandma had looked in the casket or who else had been there, but she distinctly remembered the smell of the flowers.

It was the same smell that had filled Mom's hospital room ten months ago. Floral sympathy left as sour a taste in her mouth as floral courtship. Pining over some man, waiting for him to bring flowers for no reason.

Weakness.

Now Beth sat in the small exam room, waiting for Dr. Berry to check on her mother. The checkup they'd been waiting for, the one that told them her mom had recovered from her stroke.

But Beth knew better. After all, she was the one taking care of her mom on a daily basis.

"Would you stop doing that?" Her mother's brows matched her mouth, turned down like blankets in a fancy hotel.

"What am I doing?" Beth's own wrung-out hands drew her attention to her lap. "Sorry. I'm nervous."

Her mom waved her off. "I'm fine. I feel great."

"I just hope it's not the calm before another storm."

"You are so negative, Beth," her mother groaned. "Is this how I raised you?"

Beth shot her a look. It was, in fact, exactly how she'd raised her. The difference was that her mom's near-death experience had given the elder Whitaker a new, cheery outlook on life. One she flaunted like a child wearing a new dress.

"You've gotta realize one of these days that life is short. It's time you get back to your own life and let me worry about mine."

Beth stood. "What is taking so long?"

Despite her mother's protests, Beth opened the door and started down the hall—more to get away from her mother's lecture than to search for Dr. Berry. The nurses' station around the corner might provide an escape, or at least some answers as to what was holding up the good doctor.

But when she reached the end of the hallway and overheard someone say her name, Beth stopped.

"I guess Miss Most Likely to Succeed is just a commoner like the rest of us," a woman's voice mocked. "Didn't she always talk about getting out of this dead-end town?"

"Tandy, stop. Her mom had a stroke."

"Ten months ago. She had plenty of time to get out of here before that. Years, in fact."

From where she stood, Beth heard papers rustling and fingers clicking on a keyboard.

"Give her a break," the other woman said.

"Sorry. I just can't stand these rich girls who think they're better than everyone else."

"It's not like everything's come easy to her, Tandy. She's had a rough few years."

There was a pause then—for effect? An eye roll? Beth could only imagine.

"If you're talking about Michael, she should've known."

Beth tensed at the mention of his name.

"I mean, everyone else did."

"I think it's sad," the other nurse said. "If the homecoming king and queen don't stay together after high school, what chance do the rest of us have?"

"You can't be serious."

"Why not?"

"You voted them Cutest Couple, didn't you?" Her voice dripped with sarcasm.

"Why are we still talking about high school, Tandy? The rest of us have moved on, including Beth Whitaker."

"Yeah, she moved straight out of her college dorm and into her parents' house. Guess the black hole of Willow Grove sucked her back in with the rest of us."

The nurses laughed. Hometown girls, no doubt—the kind who'd always wanted out of Willow Grove but never left.

Who was she kidding? She'd just described herself. She wasn't supposed to still be here. That was never the plan.

"Just a temporary gig," her father had told her when he'd hired her at his company. "You're different, Beth. You can get out of here and do so much more with your life."

The job at Whitaker Mowers turned out not to be a temporary gig. And she'd turned out to be a major disappointment. When she thought of how much she had cost him, her stomach tied itself into a thick knot.

"Beth?"

One of the nurses—Jillian, her name tag said—had turned the corner and now stood in front of her, and Beth felt weak and helpless all over again. It was getting old. She wasn't the kind of person who should feel this way.

"What are you doing out here?"

Beth could tell by the look on her face—the nurse knew she'd heard the conversation. She should tell Jillian and her friend exactly what they could do with their high-and-mighty attitudes. She should—but she wouldn't. She didn't have the courage or the energy, so she chose to ignore it. Never mind that its sting had already done its damage.

"Sorry, I was just looking for Dr. Berry."

"He's back with your mom."

Beth straightened. "Thanks."

"We're all pulling for her," Jillian said. "We're hoping for good results."

Beth started back down the hall, trying not to think of the day her perfectly planned-out life had taken a turn for the worse. The very worst.

Some days she wished she was still blissfully unaware of the truth about the man she'd devoted so many years to. Her first—and only—love had broken her heart.

She wondered if she'd ever find all of the pieces.

She could practically smell the tulips he'd sent in an effort to win her back. Cards attached to bouquets had gone unread and were thrown away until finally, one day, the flowers stopped coming.

He'd gotten the hint.

And it was on that day Beth realized she'd wasted years of her life building a relationship with a man who could never really love her. The only person Michael really loved was himself.

When she reached the closed door of her mother's exam room, Beth barged in on Dr. Berry talking in hushed tones the way doctors always seemed to do.

"What's wrong?" she said as soon as she opened the door.

The doctor turned to her, a puzzled look on his face. "Hi, Beth." He smiled. He had a fatherly way about him with his gray hair and glasses. He wore a blue dress shirt rolled at the sleeves and a nice gray-and-blue tie. He was handsome with caring eyes, the kind that danced a little.

"Sorry," Beth said. "I just assumed . . ."

"She assumes a lot, Dr. Berry. It's not her best quality." Her mom tossed a smile over her shoulder toward Beth—a smile that faded in a reprimand as soon as their eyes met.

Beth sat, shaking off the effects of the conversation she'd overheard in the hallway.

She'd been so confident once. A high performer, an overachiever. She'd grown up believing her father when he'd told her, *"Beth, I don't care if you're a woman in a man's world. You were born to lead."*

Michael had taken that from her.

Leaving should've made her stop loving him. It sickened her to think of how many times she'd wished she'd never found out the truth. It would've been easier to go on believing everything was fine.

Her own weakness disgusted her. She'd never been this woman before. Or maybe she'd never had occasion before for her weakness to show through.

But here she was. Still running the office at Whitaker Mowers. Still living in Willow Grove. And still completely unwilling to even consider putting herself out there again.

Most days she was fine with the way her life had turned out, but lately—and always when she ran into old friends from high school, especially the ones who'd moved away—she had this disheartening sense of discontent.

She should've made more of herself by now.

And now she was stuck. Her father's death had left her with a responsibility to carry on the family business. Did it matter that she didn't love it? No. She didn't get to be choosy after the mistakes she'd made.

Still, sometimes it gnawed at her—this idea that maybe she'd lost herself along the way. Had she become the opposite of what her father had wanted her to become?

Had she become the kind of woman who wanted a man to bring her flowers?

She shook the taunting thoughts away. She didn't want to think about her poor judgment right now.

Beth forced herself to focus on Dr. Berry's assessment of her mother's condition. The words "miraculous recovery" and "near 100 percent" caught her attention. Did Dr. Berry know that her mother hardly moved from her chair in the living room? Did he know she still required help in the shower? Mom still needed her. Otherwise, Beth would've moved out and into her own apartment. Maybe even finally found a job in the city like she'd always intended.

Wouldn't she have?

In the car on the way home, a soft smile rested on her mother's face.

"You look happy," Beth said.

Her mom glanced at her. "Why does it sound like an accusation when you say it?"

Beth kept her eyes on the road. "Obviously the doctor was a bit optimistic, don't you think?"

She could almost hear her mother frown. "No, I don't. I agree with everything he said."

"Near 100 percent? Mom, you still need help walking around the house. That's not a full recovery."

Her mother was quiet for a long moment. "Have you ever thought that maybe I don't actually *need* help? But that I'm not going to turn it down if you offer it?"

"I don't understand."

"You heard Dr. Berry. I'm better, Beth. A little slow, maybe, but the day of my stroke, we didn't even know if I'd be able to speak again."

Beth remembered. She'd been so filled with panic, so full of guilt. She couldn't help but think that if her father were still alive, none of this would've happened.

And she couldn't help but think that her father *would* still be alive if it weren't for her.

"Well, I still think you've got a ways to go." Beth turned onto their road, a private, tree-lined drive that took them to the front of the large white house out on the edge of town. Daddy had done well for himself and continued to take care of his family even after his death.

What she wouldn't give for just one more conversation with him. Would he have still pushed her toward the big dreams—the city life— if he'd known he wasn't going to live? Or would he have changed his tune, telling her to take care of their family business, to watch over everything he'd spent his life building?

Beth killed the engine in front of the garage, but before she could get out, her mother rested her hand on Beth's.

"Are you happy, Beth?"

She hated it when her mom took on this serious tone. It seemed like Lilian Whitaker was plenty lighthearted with everyone except Beth these days.

Beth made her mother's brow furrow.

"Of course, Mom." She laughed the question off.

"When was the last time you felt genuine happiness?"

Beth's mind spun, trying to recall a moment of pure joy. How sad that she came up empty. "My work makes me happy. I like knowing I'm carrying on the Whitaker name."

"In a job you've never loved."

"Where's this coming from, Mom?"

Her mother gave a soft shrug. "I guess I have a new perspective is all. A new lease on life. And I don't like seeing you this way."

"What way? I'm fine. I have responsibilities here." *I have to make up for the things I ruined. I owe that to him.* "Don't you want Dad's legacy to go on?"

"Not at the expense of your happiness."

"I'm fine. I just—"

"You're not happy. And you haven't been for a long time. The life you used to dream of—it's not the one you're living. And that concerns me."

Beth looked away. Her mom didn't get it. Things changed. People, plans, dreams—they all changed. Once upon a time, Beth had dreamed of art school and paint-covered hands. A healthy dose of reality had changed her. What was to say that hadn't happened again?

"Don't use my health as a reason to stay here, Beth. Not if this isn't what you love."

Beth sighed. "I can't imagine leaving you now, Mom. I don't care what Dr. Berry says, you're not strong enough."

Her mother's smile waned. "I appreciate that, and I appreciate you helping me, but I'm getting stronger now. It's time for me to get on with my life." She stilled a moment. "And time for you to get on with yours."

Her mom squeezed her hand, then turned toward the car door.

"Here, let me—"

"No, Beth." Lilian stared at her own hand on the door handle. "I need to start doing things for myself again."

Beth watched as her mother opened the door gingerly, still in pain. But she didn't jump in to help. Instead, she sat in the car while her mom inched her way out, closed the door and then walked toward the house, a smile lighting her face.

A smile that was less optimistic and more triumphant.

A smile that told Beth that while she'd been trying to help her mom recover, what she'd actually done was get in the way.

Her mother's words hung in the stale air of Beth's closed-up Audi. Her mother didn't understand. Beth had tried to be genuinely happy once, and it hadn't panned out. And now, the only thing on her mind was making amends for the things she'd done.

Happiness wasn't in the cards.

Chapter Two

"My horse won't go faster."

The whine seeped under Drew Barlow's skin. He'd led a lot of trail rides, and he could usually tolerate the complaining, but if this kid dug his heels into Juniper's sides one more time . . .

"The horse isn't supposed to go faster, kid," Drew said. "She's trained to stay behind mine."

"This is boring."

Drew blew out a stream of hot air. He took in a fresh breath and cast his eyes toward the Rockies. There. That was the reason he stayed on at the dude ranch every year. That and the seclusion of the off months.

"Are we almost done? My horse is broken."

Lucky for the kid, they *were* almost done. Otherwise, Drew might've swatted Juniper on the backside and sent her off to show him how not-boring horseback riding could be.

Up the hill and around the bend, Elkhorn Ranch came into sight. Elkhorn had been his home now for four years, and the owners, Doug and Cheryl McClain, liked Drew so much they made room for him year-round. He didn't make much money, but he didn't need much. He enjoyed managing the rest of the staff, he loved the horses, and his room and board were part of his salary. Every now and then, he even enjoyed the guests, though sometimes Drew wondered if he'd do better to find a profession where he didn't have to talk to anyone at all.

Quiet suited him just fine.

They reached the stable, and the other ranch hands met them and helped return the horses to their stalls.

"Tough ride, Boss?" Dylan Hauser took the reins as Drew removed his cowboy hat, ran his hand through his hair and sighed.

"That obvious?"

"I had that kid in a private lesson yesterday." Dylan shook his head and led Mabel, Drew's favorite horse, into her stall. "He's a pistol."

Mabel whinnied.

"That's one word for it. I'm assigning out all of his activities from now on."

"I'll clean up here," Dylan said. "You've got a visitor up at the lodge."

Drew frowned. A visitor? Anyone he considered a friend was there on the ranch with him.

"It's your mom."

His heart dropped. "My mom?" He hadn't talked to his mother in months. She'd give him the guilt trip, then the lecture, then ask him to imagine a world without her in it. He hated to admit it, but he didn't miss their chats.

Dylan shrugged. "She didn't exactly look comfortable when I left her. Good luck, buddy."

Drew walked through the stable and past the guesthouses until he reached the lodge. His mother sat on the porch, clutching her purse, looking exactly like what she was: a former beauty queen on a dude ranch. How long had she been waiting?

She stood at the sight of him, and a forced smile washed over her face. "You look rugged and handsome," she said, holding her hands out. She pulled him into a hug, clapped him on the back a few times and then stepped back to look at him. "And maybe a little bit dirty."

"I'm surprised to see you here."

"I would imagine so. It's been so long since I've heard anything from you. I had to make sure you were still alive."

And it began.

"So you drove two hours into the mountains? Why didn't you just call?" He sat down on the stairs of the lodge.

"I did." She faced him. "You never called back."

He vaguely remembered that.

"Well, you're here now. You want to get some dinner?"

She scrunched her nose. "Here?"

"We have a five-star chef, Mom. It's not like we eat C rations out of a tin can."

She drew her lips into a thin line. "I admit that is a little more what I imagined."

He secretly hoped she'd decline his offer. He didn't much care for small talk, and with his parents, that's all it had ever been.

"I won't keep you, Drew. I'm sure you've got other things to do."

Shower. Eat. Go for a run. Sit in front of the television. Sleep. Same as every other night.

"I just came because I wanted to show you this." She handed him a newspaper clipping. "Harold Pendergast died last week."

Drew looked at the obituary, the photo of the man—a lot older than Drew remembered and with sadder eyes, but still the same man they'd known all those years ago. He glanced at his mom. "That's too bad."

Why did his mother think he'd care whether Pendergast was dead or alive?

"I was hoping it'd bring you some closure, maybe."

Drew looked out over the yard and up toward the mountains. He knew every square inch of those foothills, almost up to the peaks. He'd put his past behind him—why'd she have to come out here and dredge it all back up?

"I'm doing fine, Ma."

Her eyes had filled with tears.

This is why he stayed away from her. The emotion she carried so close to the surface made him uncomfortable. She swiped away a tear. "You think you're fine, Drew, but you're not."

She was convinced of his brokenness, but how would she know? She could only assume what he thought—he'd never let her into that part of his mind.

"You're living in some strange denial of what happened, and I think it's kept you from ever really enjoying your life." She hugged her slick black bag a little tighter. "You seem to keep everyone at an arm's length, and I'm worried about you. Worried you're going to end up alone."

Had she practiced this speech in the car? Something about it felt rehearsed.

"When was the last time you went out on a date? And do you have a single person in your life you'd call a friend?"

He stood, filled with the sudden urge to get as far away from her as possible. "What makes you think I'm not enjoying my life?" He had Mabel and Juniper and the other ranch hands. He didn't need society's idea of a good life in order to be happy.

His mother laughed. "You've got yourself so far removed from anything real—what kind of life is this, hiding away up here in the mountains, living in a dingy old cabin? It's not a real job, and it's not a real life." She looked at him and sighed. "Don't you see I'm worried about you?"

Worried or disappointed? Because he felt nearly certain that was disappointment all over her face.

Drew resented the words. She'd never understand his career choices—never understand why he didn't want to live in some big city or wear a suit and tie to an office every day. If she expected those things from him, she didn't know him at all.

She made assumptions about him, and for that, he stayed away. He didn't have the energy to dissect his every choice. He came to the ranch because it promised him the one thing he wanted more than anything else—peace. His family would never understand that.

His mother cleared her throat. "Drew. You've been running away your whole life. How much longer are you going to hold on to this?"

She thought he should be over it by now. But time didn't heal all wounds, did it?

Drew handed the newspaper clipping back to her. "This doesn't change anything, Ma. I'm doing fine out here. I don't need you stirring up the past."

The sound of laughter drew his attention. Two of the other staffers rounded the corner. "Hey, Drew," one of them said. "You heading in for dinner?"

Drew glanced at his mom, then back at the girls. "Yeah, I'll be right there."

His mom stood, still clutching her purse. "Go. It's fine. I said what I came here to say."

"You sure you don't want to stay?" He didn't mean it. Surely she'd sense that.

She put on a phony smile. "I have to get back." She set a hand on his shoulder and squeezed. "Take care of yourself, sweetheart."

He watched her get in her Lexus and drive away.

As was customary after a conversation with his mother, Drew now had a pit in his stomach that rivaled the Grand Canyon.

He didn't feel much like socializing. Inside his cabin, Roxie sat at attention. He rubbed the German shepherd behind the ears, and she stood as if she knew something was wrong.

"Why do I need friends when I've got you, Rox?"

She licked his hand.

"Let's go for a run. You're looking a little hefty in the middle."

She lay back down, letting out a soft growl as Drew changed into a pair of loose athletic shorts and a T-shirt, pulled on his running shoes and opened the cabin door.

"You comin'?"

Roxie, always quick to forgive, ran outside toward their favorite running trail. Drew preferred to run without music, focusing instead on the sounds of his breathing and the great outdoors. He'd grown to love the ranch and everything it had taught him. He oversaw the daily operations and managed the staff, but he'd worked the schedule out so he could also spend time alone. That time had never haunted him until today.

With every familiar tree he passed, the memories crept closer to the surface of his mind—memories he'd buried long ago in the hope of never reliving them again.

Drew turned a corner and ran along the creek at the back of the ranch property, his mind spinning. *Closure.* His mother made it sound like it was something he could buy at the drugstore. He knew better. It had been twenty years, and he'd never found it.

Revisiting Fairwind, dredging up the past—it couldn't bring him what he needed. The ranch, Colorado, his long runs—those were peaceful. Why did his mom seem to think he was still searching for something he'd found long ago?

And yet, as he weaved to the right to avoid a dip in the trail, he knew peace was about more than a quiet environment. He'd come here in search of something specific, but if he was honest with himself, he was still looking for it.

His spirit wasn't at peace, and the realization irked him.

Some men pursued women or money or fame or power. Drew asked for so little compared to them, yet *peace* seemed more elusive and much harder to attain.

Roxie quickened her pace to keep up, panting a little harder than usual. Drew's mind wandered to the photo in Harold Pendergast's obituary. He'd grown to see Harold mostly as a nuisance, what with his regular calls begging Drew to come back to the farm. Drew had stopped answering those calls a long time ago. Harold always left messages, but Drew never called back. Then the old man started sending letters filled with new, crazy ideas about the case, and he always listed the reasons why returning to Fairwind might help Drew, not to mention possibly give them the lead they'd been waiting for.

Son, I'm not asking you to spend a whole summer here like you used to, just a few days to jog your memory. See if anything shakes loose when you walk the grounds. It's important. Don't do it for me. Do it for Jess.

But Drew had never gone. He'd resisted every attempt to reconnect with Fairwind and the old man. Why was he spending even a second thinking about it now?

Sticks snapped underneath his feet. He inhaled the scent of pine trees, and Jess's face swept through his memory.

All these years, Harold had been the one fighting on her behalf, but who would do that now that he was gone?

As soon as the thought entered Drew's mind, another one replaced it: *This is not your problem.* He'd been telling himself that for years now, and he believed it. So why the sudden urge to drive to Willow Grove, Illinois, and see what had become of Fairwind?

Why now, after all this time, did it feel like maybe Harold had been right? Maybe Drew would remember something or find the closure he'd been craving.

He stopped and doubled over, winded—a punishment for failing to focus on his breathing. He'd been running too fast. He'd been running too hard and too long.

Roxie slowed, doubled back and sniffed his face.

He stepped off the path and sat on a boulder next to the water, watching as the current lapped over the rocks on the creek bed. He could see straight to the bottom. Everything here had always felt cleaner—clearer. Did he really want to go searching through the mess that Harold had left behind?

Drew had done such a good job of pushing everything down and away, into little boxes he'd neatly stacked at the very back of his mind, but Harold's death was chipping away at that tidy pile.

His breathing finally slowed. He stood back up, still inhaling deeply, and stared up at the bright-blue sky. He'd been here at this ranch for years, and for the first time in as long as he could remember, he felt an undeniable push to do the one thing he'd been avoiding.

He had to go back to Fairwind. Not for long—just to walk the property. To revisit the place where his entire life had changed. He needed to prove to himself that there were no hidden memories locked up somewhere in his mind.

He needed to prove he couldn't have been the one to provide justice for Jess.

He just didn't have the answers everyone was looking for.

"Let's go, Roxie." He ran home, showered and changed, then called his boss to make arrangements for a short vacation.

"It's the start of the busy season, and we're booked solid," Doug said. "Be awfully hard to have you gone now."

"Have I ever missed a day in the four years I've been here?" Drew paced the small living room of his cabin, walking its full length in just a few short steps.

"No, you haven't."

"Then you know it's important. I wouldn't ask otherwise."

There was a pause on the other end, followed by a sigh. "How long are you thinking?"

"Maybe a week?"

"Make sure everything is lined up here, and we'll see you when you get back."

Drew threw some clothes into an old duffel bag. It had been years since he'd packed to go anywhere—most of his journeys only led him the few miles into town or, occasionally, down to Denver. Usually, though, he just stayed here. Elkhorn Ranch was his home now, and he was fine with that.

After he finished packing his things, he went outside and slung the bag into the back of his truck along with a half-eaten bag of dog food for Roxie. The dog had followed him outside and now sat just below the front stoop, staring at him with a tilted head.

"Come on, Rox." He opened the door of his pickup truck.

She stood and barked but didn't move.

"You're riding shotgun, girl," he said. "Let's go."

She barked again, then finally jumped inside the truck, turning around once before sitting on the passenger-side seat. She stuck her head out the opened window, and he gave her snout a rub.

"You ready for this, Rox?"

She whined. He moved around to the driver's side, got in and inhaled a very deep breath.

This was going to hurt a little.

Who was he kidding? This was going to hurt a lot.

Chapter Three

The following day, Beth arrived at work promptly at 8:00 a.m., same as always.

She'd worked at Whitaker Mowers throughout high school, but she'd never expected to stay around Willow Grove after college. After she'd been passed over for a job in the city, she'd graduated and come back home to get her bearings. Then she'd found out about Michael.

Her dad had reluctantly made room for her at Whitaker—to proofread ad copy, get coffee and restock the office supplies. By all accounts, she was a glorified secretary.

He'd been against the idea from the start.

"She needs to move past this or it's going to define her," she'd overheard him telling her mother. "She should move into the city and find a job there. Willow Grove is too small for someone like Beth."

He'd wanted so much more for her. More than struggling as a starving artist. More than a small, simple life. Never mind that he'd chosen this life after years of working in downtown Chicago himself. Somehow, he'd convinced her she needed the big-city experience to really learn what she needed to know.

But she was twenty-nine, and so far none of that had happened. What was she waiting for?

Still, she wasn't miserable. Whitaker Mowers had been good to her. She'd moved her way up quickly. Little by little, her dad had begun to accept she could be part of the next generation at Whitaker—not Ben, and certainly not Seth. Her brothers had no interest.

Beth had a knack for running an office. With her dad's help, she'd learned all she needed to know about this world—a world he'd all but conquered well before his death. Almost daily for the first two years, he'd asked if she was sure this was where she wanted to be.

"I think I could help, Dad," Beth had said. "I think I'll be great for Whitaker. I'm smart. I'm capable. I have a degree in business."

"I just pictured you doing something different," he'd said. "Something, I don't know—bigger?"

"Maybe someday," she'd told him. "But this is good experience for me for now."

He let it drop—for a little while, anyway. Months later, he asked again. "You think any more about applying for a job in the city?"

"Are you trying to get rid of me?"

He laughed her off, but she could see the disappointment behind his eyes. "Just never thought you'd stick around Willow Grove. You couldn't wait to get out of here."

"Things change."

She'd tried not to think about how much they'd changed or how she'd all but abandoned her self-confident, dream-seeking courage, leaving it sitting on a roadside somewhere between here and Chicago.

Months later, he checked in with her again, but by that time, she'd made herself indispensable to the company. She'd had a hand in rebranding their line of riding mowers. She'd even made several improvements to the machines over the years. Added a line of snowblowers and launched a successful ad campaign. Somewhere along the way, she'd stopped thinking about moving out of Willow Grove and fallen into a comfortable pattern of working and living in the town she'd always known.

And yes, she often felt like a failure for it. After all, it had never been her dream to go into the family business and live in a small tourist town in Illinois, even if it was home.

Yet somehow she'd grown content with the monotony of it all. And now, as her Keurig spit to life and her assistant pulled into the parking lot, she prepared for another day that was nearly indistinguishable from the last.

She arrived at work early on purpose—she liked to start the day with a little peace and quiet. But as she sat down to enjoy her cup of coffee, her cell phone buzzed in her purse.

She pulled it out and saw Molly's name on the screen. It shocked her that her sister was even up before nine o'clock. Beth's stomach dropped—had something happened to Mom?

"Hello?"

"Hey. Are you busy right now?"

"I'm working."

"So that's a no?"

Molly probably wanted her to go junking again. Or to go to the animal shelter or some estate sale hundreds of miles away. No matter how many times Beth refused, her little sister seemed to believe Beth could leave work whenever she wanted. After all, it was the family business, which apparently meant Beth could throw all the rules out the window.

But then, that was the difference between the two of them, wasn't it? Beth stayed in her office and ran the business while Molly booked trips to Europe, started dog-walking businesses and ordered a car off the Internet.

"I've got a meeting this afternoon, and I need to look over my notes."

"But right now in this moment, you're not busy, right?"

"Molly, I've got work."

"It'll be there when you get back."

"Back from where?"

"I need you to meet me somewhere."

Beth stifled a groan. Molly's excursions didn't always go as she planned. Beth's impulsive little sister rarely thought things through. Beth pictured her stranded on the side of the road outside the Superman Statue in Metropolis or at the top of the Ferris wheel at Navy Pier.

"Come on, Beth, it's something really cool."

"I have a lot to do today." She glanced down at the planner on her desk. In fact, the whole day was wide open with the exception of one meeting, which Beth knew would take maybe thirty minutes. She'd all but delegated herself out of a job. Most business owners would love the freedom she now found in her schedule, but a part of her felt unchallenged. Maybe even a little bored.

Still, this was her career, whether she'd intended it to be or not.

"It won't take long, I promise."

Beth groaned. Maybe mixing up her day was a good thing. "Fine. Where?"

"Fairwind Farm."

Images from childhood turned through her mind like a slideshow of her favorite memories. Fairwind had been a weekly event for the Whitaker family—and for many families in Willow Grove.

In the fall, they'd fill bushel baskets with handpicked apples, play family-style games in the meadow and, on occasion, spend an evening around the magical bonfire. Beth had sworn there was pixie dust on the falling embers of those flames.

It was as if Fairwind had been frozen in time. There, everything was perfect. No cheating boyfriends. No sick parents. No panicky guilt.

In the winter, they'd trudge through the snow out behind the barns to locate the perfect Christmas tree. Every spring and summer, they joined their neighbors for picnics and a countywide flea market that had put Willow Grove on the map.

But that was years ago. The farm had closed and, last she heard, was now in complete disarray.

"Why do you want me to meet you there? You know we can't trespass on Old Man Pendergast's property."

"Trust me, it's fine."

Wes Simpson walked by Beth's office. The awkward thirtysomething had a knack for hanging around outside her door, just waiting for a chance to come in and make small talk with her. She knew he was working up the courage to ask her out, and judging by his nervous pacing, she thought today might be his day.

"Okay, when do you want me to meet you?" she asked, turning her attention back to her sister.

"Now. I'll be waiting." Molly hung up.

Beth glanced up and met Wes's gaze. His eyebrows popped up, and he smoothed a hand over his balding head.

As much as she didn't want to get pulled into another of Molly's ridiculous schemes, she didn't want Wes to ask her out even more.

She stood, phone still pressed to her ear. "I suppose I can make that work." Nodding, she pretended to listen to a nonexistent person on the other end. Then she picked up her purse, slung it over her shoulder and walked out into the hallway, closing her door as she mouthed an "I'm sorry" to Wes.

He held up a hand to excuse her, and she mumbled a quiet "mm-hmm" as if still talking to someone on the phone.

Outside, she drew in the crisp spring air and stuffed her cell back into her purse. Several employees were just making their way to work, many of whom she barely recognized. She spent more time in her office staring at the wall than socializing with the rest of the Whitaker team.

"Love your people, Beth. That's rule number one." Her dad had been so good at that. Why hadn't he passed that on to her?

Beth drove out to the edge of town, then down a string of country roads that would lead her to Fairwind Farm and Orchard. Gravel kicked up underneath her tires, and a trail of dust followed her to what used to be the old farm's parking lot.

Her memories of Fairwind had deceived her. In her mind, the farm was something grand, teeming with excitement and joy, but what she saw before her was a lonely spot of land that had long been forgotten.

A huge white barn sat at the front of the property. Back in the day, it had been a store, a place to buy apple pie, apple cider or any one of ten different kinds of fresh-picked apples, among other things. And one glorious day in late spring, there had been tents set up outside where locals hosted the county-famous barn sale, the Fairwind Farm Market. Artisans and farmers and vintage collectors sat under white pop-up tents selling their goods and greeting the droves of tourists that spent the day exploring Willow Grove and the farm. People would drive hours to visit Fairwind—made it an annual ritual.

When had that changed?

Outbuildings dotted the land, and behind them, rows and rows of trees. The apple trees. The evergreens. How had they fared all these years? She drove along the perimeter, where weeds had grown up into the parking lot. She could almost see the families flocking toward the main entrance, excited to spend their day picking their own apples, the smell of sweet apple-cider donuts filling the air. Children would squeal as goats and sheep and llamas ate from their hands.

She remembered being one of those children.

Up ahead, she saw the main house—set apart from the orchard, barns and public grounds. She remembered thinking how lucky the Pendergast family was to live in a place everyone wanted to visit. How quickly that blessing had turned into a curse.

In the driveway, Molly's green VW Bug sat, her sister not far away. Never had she known a car to suit someone so well.

Beth parked and got out, still not sure what she was doing there but certain that romanticizing this old orchard was just about the last thing she needed to do right now. She should be sitting at her desk, working.

"Isn't it spectacular?" Molly was at her side before she even emerged from her car.

"You can't be serious." Beth looked around, saddened by what had become of this place. It had been such an important part of their lives growing up. Now, weeds pushed their way through the earth, overtaking what might have been nice landscaping. The main barn and two visible outbuildings needed paint and some obvious repair. The big white farmhouse off to the left still boasted a grand wraparound porch, but Beth could tell, even from a distance, the old house had been all but forgotten.

It was weatherworn and uncared for, and it showed. Maybe the rumors were true—Harold Pendergast had gone mad and given up completely.

"Look around, Beth, don't you remember this place?" Molly sounded like a kid, all wonder and excitement. Did she really not see how run-down Fairwind had gotten? Beth walked toward the main barn and stopped, taking it all in with a wide smile and a deep breath.

"I do remember this place," Beth said. "That's what makes it so sad to be here now." Really, truly sad. This was somewhere they'd all come as a family—before her mom's stroke, before her dad died, before Seth became the black sheep and moved away. It broke her heart to think about her youngest brother—out there on his own, still holding on to old grudges as if he needed them to live. All attempts to reach him had gone unanswered, and while Beth and her siblings had found a way to get on with life, she knew it devastated their mother.

"It just needs some TLC," Molly said, turning back toward the main barn and pulling Beth out of the past.

"It needs a lot more than that," Beth scoffed.

"Think about how great it could be. I mean, really, just picture it for a minute—I can practically hear the folk band playing. I can smell that glorious scent of apple-cider donuts filling the air. I can see the rows and rows of pumpkins out back—kids trudging through the fields to pick the perfect one." Molly squinted toward her, shielding her eyes from the sun with her hand. "We were those kids."

"That was a long time ago." Beth followed her sister toward the barn.

"What if this place could be restored?" Molly turned and faced her, walking backward. "How great would that be?"

"It would be a lot of work. A lot of time. A lot of money." Beth crossed her arms as she plodded through the unmown grass.

"But it would be great. Admit it." Molly stopped walking, so Beth followed suit.

She said nothing.

"Admit it, Beth. It would be great."

Beth shrugged. "I guess it would be great."

"Ha. I knew you'd agree." Molly practically jumped when she said it, like a lawyer who'd just made a critical point for her case.

"We're talking hypotheticals here, right?"

"Think about it for a minute. Everything moves so fast nowadays. Even the tourists here—they're all so busy. It wasn't like that at Fairwind. Things were slow and relaxed. It was the perfect escape." She shoved the barn door open, and they both stared at what had once been a gathering place for all of their friends and family.

This space had been a little shop filled with homemade jellies and jams. They'd sold easy lunches and bags of freshly picked apples. There'd been a homemade-fudge counter off to the side and a whole separate space for the bakery. The smell of apples and cinnamon had always lingered in the air.

How full of life that old barn had been.

But now, the empty space was just a shell of its past glory. Tables and chairs caked with dust had lost their rustic charm. The shelves along the walls stood dull and lifeless, and the counter where friendly cashiers had handed out the occasional free piece of candy had all but fallen apart.

"I don't think anyone would see this as an escape."

Molly crossed her arms over her chest. "I think you're wrong. You have to see the potential here."

"It was a different world back then. People are too busy to come to a place like Fairwind." A stray cat ran into the barn and darted through the half-opened door of a storage room. "Besides, from what I've heard, Old Man Pendergast is not interested in selling Fairwind. If he catches us out here—"

"He's dead."

Beth frowned. "He is?"

"Yes, and he didn't have any family and he didn't have a will."

Beth stared at her sister, recognizing that gleam in her eye. "No way. Molly, this is a bad investment."

"Beth, listen, you're a businesswoman. This is what you're trained for—to walk into a business and figure out how to make a go of it. You must be able to recognize a gold mine when you see it."

"This is not what I was trained for. This is—" A mouse scurried across the floor and Beth recoiled. "This is something else entirely." She turned and walked out of the barn.

"Look around. Breathe in that fresh country air. Picture what this place could be again if the right people got their hands on it."

Beth had been here before—carefully balancing Molly's sensitivity with the need to speak the truth. This was not a good idea. Anyone could see that.

Anyone, that is, except Molly.

"You trust me, right?" Beth asked. "You know I wouldn't steer you wrong?"

"Of course, but you're kind of closed-minded."

"No, I'm pragmatic. And that's why I can tell you in no uncertain terms that this farm is a money pit. Everywhere I look, I see things falling apart."

"I bought it."

Beth spun around to face her sister. "You did what?"

"There was an auction this morning, and I was the only bidder. I got it for a steal." Molly beamed.

Beth shook her head, starting back up the hill toward her car, Molly close on her heels.

"Would you stop with that look? I brought you out here because I want us to do this together."

Beth didn't slow her pace. "This is crazy, Molly. I know you're impulsive, but *this*! Buying a *farm*?"

"Would you at least hear me out?"

"No, I don't need to hear anything, because there is no way I am going to be a part of something so ridiculous." Beth pulled open her car door. "You always do the stupidest things!"

Molly's face fell. She stood, unmoving, just a few feet away from the car.

Beth dropped her gaze to the ground and let out a heavy sigh. "I'm sorry. I didn't mean that."

"Yes, you did. I know what you think of me. What all of you think of me. I know Dad never thought I could do anything big and important— he saved all those dreams for you."

Yeah, and look at me now.

"You're right," Molly said. "I've done some stupid things. I went to cosmetology school, and I don't like to touch other people's heads. I bought that car last year that didn't have an engine in it. I make decisions based on how I feel."

Beth glanced at Molly. All this time, she'd assumed her sister didn't know those things were foolish.

"But you're the flip side of my coin, Beth. You don't do anything based on the way you feel. Everything is planned out and calculated, and you never allow yourself to have a single emotion without a checklist of pros and cons."

"That's not true."

"It is. That's why it threw you for such a curveball when your perfectly laid plan fell apart. That was six years ago—and you're still here, working in Dad's company, in a job you hate."

"I don't hate it." *And I have to stay. I have to make it up to Dad.*

"Tell me this is what you always dreamed you would do."

Beth searched for a reply but came up empty.

Molly softened. "You need a change, and so do I. Fairwind can give it to us."

Beth shook her head. "I can't even believe what I'm hearing."

"Think about it. Remember what it was like here."

Beth didn't want to remember. Recalling how it felt to have no worries or no cares—it would make her long for something she'd never have again, and what would be the point of that? She wasn't a fan of self-imposed torture.

Molly turned away, eyes scanning the forgotten land in front of her.

"I can still remember every time we came here, before we went home, Daddy would make us all head over to that little stand at the edge of the flea market. They had fresh-made kettle corn—"

"And lemon shake-ups," Beth said. "I remember."

"What if we could bring that back to Willow Grove? Tourism is still big here. Why shouldn't we introduce Fairwind to a new generation?"

Beth shut the car door and leaned back against it. A part of her wanted that more than anything—to go down an unexpected path, one she'd never considered before.

Molly stared at her. "Every single day of your life has been exactly the same for at least the last five years. Aren't you bored?"

Thoughts ran around in Beth's mind like a toddler with scissors. Dangerous. Chaotic. She didn't like thinking about change when she was stuck where she was.

"I've done something amazing here, Beth, and I'm offering you a chance to get on board. Be a part of this—for us, for this town, for this place. Doesn't it deserve to be restored?"

Beth drew in a deep breath. "Of course it does. But we're not equipped to do it. We know nothing about apple orchards or farms or pumpkin patches."

"But we're smart. And we learn fast. You know business. And I'm great with people. We can do this. Together."

Beth looked at her sister's pleading eyes. Molly was desperate to make a go of this plan. But this was the same sister who only last year had been convinced she wanted to drive a food truck. Never mind that Molly wasn't a chef. She'd never even worked in food service. She'd gotten so far as to test-drive an old, falling-apart food truck, only to decide—at the very last minute—she didn't like the way she looked driving such a big vehicle. The next day, she'd gone out and bought her VW Bug, and the food-truck idea went to the place all of Molly's grand plans went: the idea graveyard.

It would be only a matter of time before she lost interest in Fairwind Farm too, and Beth would be left to pick up the pieces.

"Look, I know what you're thinking," Molly said.

"Oh, do you?" Beth hoped not.

"Yes, you're calculating all the reasons this is a bad idea. But just promise me you'll sleep on it for one night. Isn't that what Dad taught us to do? Sleep on every big decision?"

"Did you sleep on this one? Did you pray about buying a run-down farm?"

"Yes, actually, I did." Molly stared off into the distance. "In my own way."

Beth stuck her hands on her hips and studied her own feet, her sensible pair of shoes.

"It's different this time, Beth. I promise." Molly's eyes begged. "Just spend one night thinking about it, please?"

How could she say no?

"One night. If my answer doesn't change—and I don't think it will—then I'll try to find a way to help you get out of this deal."

Molly frowned. "I don't want out, Beth. If you decide not to do this with me, I'm going to do it on my own."

The words, spoken with such conviction, worried Beth. What if this was the one time Molly stuck with a project so long she didn't give herself an exit strategy? And worse, what if there was no one there to bail her out this time?

How would their mother respond if Beth didn't jump in and save her then?

Chapter Four

Whitaker family meetings were reserved for important family events. Dad's will. Mom's care. Their trusts. They weren't typically called to discuss individual life events, but the day after Molly had summoned her to Fairwind Farm, Beth decided to call their oldest brother, Ben, to get everything out in the open.

Ben rarely made it back to Willow Grove. After his career in professional baseball had ended, he'd made a life in the city—and he didn't like the attention he got when he was home. But this was an emergency, and Beth needed his support.

"Is it too much to hope you've called this meeting to tell me you're in on my new plan?" Molly's eyes practically sparkled with expectation.

"I told you it wasn't likely I'd change my mind." Beth pulled two cans of beans from the cupboard.

Molly stared at her sister. "Why do I feel like you tattled on me?"

"I didn't tattle, Molly. I just thought it would be good to have Ben's input."

"And mine." Their mom sat at the table with an afghan over her legs, knitting another scarf. As if the fourteen in the other room weren't enough.

"I'm getting a head start on Christmas," Lilian had said when Beth noted the pile of scarves she'd amassed these last few months. Beth was pretty sure her mother didn't know fourteen people who would wear a hand-knitted scarf, but Beth wasn't going to be the one to tell her.

"What's the big deal? We haven't all been together in weeks. It'll be good to catch up." Beth knew they would all see through her excuse, but she pretended the words were satisfactory.

"How'd she even get you here, Ben?" Molly popped an olive into her mouth.

"She promised me a home-cooked meal." He leaned against the counter, arms folded midtorso.

"You don't look like you've been starving lately." Molly dunked a baby carrot in the dip and crunched it in half. She was right. Their brother had always looked like he'd stepped out of a Calvin Klein ad, but he looked older and more filled out now.

"Ben, can you go start the grill?" Beth pulled five burger patties from the refrigerator.

"You never said I was going to have to cook the meal." He didn't move.

Dad had always manned the grill.

Silence hung in the air, as if they'd all remembered at the same time. Ben gave one quick nod, then strode through the kitchen and out onto the patio.

"Can't believe you're getting Mom and Ben involved in this." Molly sat on a stool on the other side of the counter.

"This concerns everyone, Molly."

"Hardly. You just want to bulldoze my idea."

Beth ignored her. She'd called Ben yesterday on her way home from the farm and filled him in, hoping he could talk some sense into their sister. The two of them had always had a special bond. If anyone could get through to Molly, it was Ben.

Beth put together a salad and a dish of baked beans while Ben grilled burgers and Molly sulked. Their mom hummed to herself quietly, knitting away as if she had nothing else to do.

When Ben returned with the cooked burgers, they gathered at the kitchen table.

"Is your boyfriend coming?" He raised an eyebrow as he peered down at Molly.

"If you're referring to Bishop, no. He's working. And he's not my boyfriend."

Bishop had been Molly's best friend since grade school, with the exception of a small separation somewhere around junior high when they each realized, as if for the first time, that they weren't the same gender. He now worked at the Willow Grove Police Station, where Molly's VW Bug was frequently seen in the parking lot. Everyone knew it wasn't a matter of if but *when* the two would get together—everyone, it seemed, except the couple in question.

Molly moved from her stool to the chair next to their mom and shot Ben an annoyed look.

"Uh-huh." Ben looked to Beth to join him, but she couldn't get on board with teasing Molly about her denial of Bishop's feelings for her— or hers for him, for that matter. She just wanted to talk through Molly's latest disaster of an idea and come up with a plan to make it go away.

They said grace, filled their plates and tried to pretend the silence wasn't awkward.

"Well?" Molly glared at Beth. "You called this meeting, so let's get it over with."

"Don't be like that." Beth wished there was a good way to tell someone they'd just made another terrible mistake. It seemed to be a pattern with Molly, and Beth always seemed to be the one who had to point it out.

Molly looked away. "It's a good investment, Beth." She glanced at their mother, who ate smaller bites now. "Tell her, Mom."

Lilian held both hands up. "I don't pretend to understand anything about investments. But I did think it was an interesting idea."

"It is an interesting idea," Ben said. "But it's not very practical."

"Thank you." Beth knew she could count on him.

"But you agree it's interesting." Molly took a bite of her burger. Leave it to her to hear only what she wanted to hear.

"But not practical," Beth said. "That's the point."

"Practical isn't always best," their mother said.

"You don't really support this idea, Mom."

"I just said it was interesting. And I can tell you that when your dad started his business, his parents told him he wasn't being practical either."

"I can't believe what I'm hearing," Beth said. Why was their mom encouraging this? "Do you know what kind of debt you're getting into?"

"Well, that's my business, isn't it?" Molly dropped her fork on her plate with a clank.

"And now it's mine. Because you're asking for my help."

"Fine, Beth. I won't ask for your help, but if you'd shut up and listen to me for five seconds, you'd know this is a good investment."

Ben glanced at Beth but didn't say anything.

Beth set her fork down. "Fine. I'm listening."

"Maybe you should start with what possessed you to buy the farm in the first place." Ben piled a second burger with tomatoes, onions, lettuce and pickles.

Molly frowned. "Are you kidding? When I heard about Mr. Pendergast, I felt something go off inside me. Like, finally! The thing I'd been waiting for was right in front of me."

"You've been waiting for the man to die?" Beth took a drink of her lemonade.

"You know what I mean. I've tried to get excited about hundreds of business ideas—this is the only one that's got me completely jazzed."

"I seem to remember you being pretty jazzed about the mobile-dog-grooming business." Ben wiped his mouth with his napkin.

"And the frozen yogurt café," their mom added.

"And massage therapy school," Beth said.

Molly stared at them, that wounded-animal look on her face.

They did this sometimes—pointed out Molly's mistakes. Laughed at her expense. Nobody ever meant to be hurtful, but Beth could see by her sister's expression that they had been.

She expected her to push her chair away from the table, throw her napkin on her plate and storm off. That was classic Molly.

But she didn't. Instead, she drew in a deep breath and leveled her gaze at Beth. "I knew Old Man Pendergast didn't have any family left, so that meant Fairwind was going to go up for auction. I went to the bank and talked to Jerry. He looked over my financials and said with the right down payment, they'd approve me for the loan."

"Jerry Harris?" Beth asked. "That's how you got the loan?"

"So?" Molly steeled her jaw.

"He would give you his kidney if you asked, Molly. He's been in love with you since the eighth grade."

"That doesn't mean he didn't think this was a viable business option. He couldn't have given me the loan if I was too much of a risk." She sounded like she was trying to convince herself.

"So you got the loan and then what?" Clearly Ben had no interest in the drama of the thing.

"I went to the auction. It wasn't as exciting as I thought it would be. Not many people, and I didn't even get one of those little paddles. I knew how much I had to spend, so I put my bid in, and I got it."

"Just like that," Beth said. Maybe now their mother would see the problem.

"Just like that." Molly grinned. "Like it was meant to be."

Oh, Molly, always superstitious and never sensible.

Beth waited for her to go on. Waited for Ben to respond. Waited for Mom to add her two cents. When none of those things happened, Beth searched for something to say. She admired Molly's intention—it would be wonderful for their community to bring Fairwind back to life. But she couldn't pretend she thought this was a good idea. Especially for someone who lacked both the business and the physical skills to be successful.

"Say something."

"I don't know what you want me to say, Mol. I'm sure there's a way we can you get out of the contract."

Molly's face fell. "I already told you I don't want out. This is what I'm supposed to do. I can feel it."

"You can feel it?" Beth shook her head.

"Yes, Ice Queen. If you had any emotions, you'd know what that meant." She threw her napkin onto her plate of half-eaten food.

"Molly," their mother warned.

It stung, that particular insult. Beth did her best to ignore it, despite the fact that it threatened to open an old wound. "I'm not going to apologize for having my head screwed on straight."

"And I'm not going to apologize for having feelings," Molly snapped.

"Well, your *feelings* have done nothing but get you into trouble—and this is your worst idea yet. I don't think you have any clue what you've gotten yourself into."

Molly looked at their mom and raised her eyebrows. "Told you."

Beth's eyes darted to her mother. "Told her what?"

"That this is how you'd react. She actually argued with me. Said maybe you'd surprise us. But of course this is what you'd say—you're always finding ways to shoot down my ideas."

With good reason.

Lilian folded her hands in her lap. "Girls, please. You know I hate it when you argue."

Beth glanced at their mom, the memory of her stroke flooding her mind. Beth didn't approve of Molly's plan, but she had to keep it together—for their mother's sake.

"I said I thought the idea was interesting, and I do," Lilian said. "I hadn't thought of including Ben, but that's just brilliant."

Ben nearly choked on his burger. Maybe now Beth would get a little support.

"It *is*, Ben," Molly said. "You are a landscape architect, after all."

Beth shook her head. "Why would you think I'd have any other reaction to all of this than the one I'm having?"

Their mother's face fell. "It's like I told you before, Beth. You just don't seem very happy. And you haven't for a long time."

Molly glanced at Beth. "See? I'm not the only one who thinks so."

"So you guys have been talking about this?"

"No, of course not," their mom said.

"I think you like it here, but I don't think you like your job," Molly said. "And maybe you just need someone to tell you there's no shame in not wanting to move to Chicago and have some big, fancy life like Michael."

Beth shifted at the mention of his name—a name that still held far too much power over her. It had been six years since she'd left Michael, and she still nursed her broken heart. The really sad part was, if she hadn't caught him that day, she'd probably still be with him, waiting for the ring, the wedding, the big, overpriced house.

In some ways, she still was. Waiting for her life to begin.

But she didn't like being reminded of it. At all.

"We can do this together." Molly smiled. "It'll be fun."

Beth met her sister's eyes. "And that is the problem. You think this is going to be fun."

"What? It could be." She dropped her napkin on her plate and stood.

"It's going to be expensive and hard and frustrating. Do you know anything about running a farm?"

"Well, it's not a *real* farm. It's not like I'm going to be milking cows at dawn or something, though I would like to get a pair of wellies. You know those rubber boots you wear in the mud?" Molly walked to the window and stared out across their parents' backyard. "It'll be like it was, you know, when we were kids."

Beth could see the sadness in her sister's hunched shoulders. None of them talked about it much, but they all missed their dad. He'd always had a way of pulling them together. Beth understood the desire to put everything back the way it used to be, but despite what Molly thought, Beth didn't crave the simple life. She'd fallen into it by accident—and, she supposed, had never found the courage to leave.

But Molly? She didn't seem to have any plans for something more. Ever. She was a hopeless romantic—and her perfect love stories were always set in their small midwestern town.

Beth met her sister at the window and followed Molly's gaze to the old oak tree in the backyard. The lonely tire swing hung below, moving ever so slightly in the spring breeze. How many days had they spent out in that yard, waiting for their dad to come home and push them on that swing? He'd make up silly songs while he pushed, and their mom would watch from the porch. It was like something out of another time, as if the world outside Willow Grove had moved forward and they'd all stayed happily rooted in the past.

"Molly, I know you're looking for your place, trying to figure out how to spend the rest of your life, and I'm not trying to discourage you from doing that."

"Aren't you?" Molly turned to her. "You hated the idea before I got the words out of my mouth. You won't even consider that this could be exactly what we've been waiting for."

Beth shook her head and stared at the swing. "I haven't been waiting for anything except for Mom to get better."

Molly wrapped her arms around herself. "Then go, Beth. Go to Chicago and find your own impressive job and make a ton of money. Tell me that's really what you want."

"I didn't say that's what I wanted." Beth could feel her jaw tighten. It was, though, wasn't it? Or maybe not what she wanted, but what she thought she should do. Yet she couldn't—and she would never tell Molly why.

She stared at her sister for a few long moments, and then Molly grabbed her jacket from the back of the chair and sighed. "I should've known better than to tell you. You've always been the first one to throw cold water on my dreams."

Beth spun around, but her sister was already gone.

Ben stood. "I'll get her."

"Be kind to her," their mother said as he left.

Beth met her mom's eyes—eyes that challenged her. Eyes filled with an emotion Beth couldn't quite place. Disappointment?

"She is so dramatic." Beth shook her head and sat back down. From her mother's pursed lips and raised eyebrows across the way, Beth could tell she had words. "Fine. What are you thinking?"

Her mom's thin lips drew into a knowing smile. "I didn't say anything."

"Please. Your face says it all."

Her gaze fell to her mom's lap, where two small, feeble hands Beth hardly recognized rested. Everything about her mother seemed frail, in spite of Dr. Berry's claims of recovery.

"Molly is too impulsive," Lilian said.

Beth scoffed. "That's an understatement."

"But you are too pragmatic."

Beth shifted. "Really? I didn't know there was such a thing."

"I worry about you, Beth." Her mom inched forward, each movement slow.

"Of all of your children, I'm the one you need to worry about least." Beth stood, waiting as her mom struggled to get to the edge of her seat. "Where are we going here?"

"Up. Out. Away from the chair." She grabbed Beth's arms and did her best to lift herself up, but she needed help—more help than she should if she was going to live on her own again.

"Do you want to walk around the block?" It was their usual evening stroll. Her mom hadn't done it unassisted since the stroke, and she still got winded before they circled back to their driveway.

"Sure. Let's do that." She took Beth's arm.

Another reason to do what was smart—their mother needed stability right now. Beth couldn't dive into Fairwind Farm any more than she could dive into a job search in Chicago.

Still, so much time had already passed. Did she really want to waste another year in Willow Grove?

I was made for more than this.

The words nagged at her, unwanted. She dismissed them, wishing for a fleeting moment that the little things could keep her content. Wishing, she realized, for just a smidge of Molly's optimism.

Outside, the evening had turned brisk, as spring in Illinois often could. The sun had started its descent, and a chill was in the air. Still, it felt good to inhale spring after too many months of winter.

Lilian wove her arm through Beth's and clung to her with both hands as they shuffled down the driveway and away from the house. Beth had been taught to move quickly—to walk quickly, work quickly—but she'd grown accustomed to moving at her mother's pace.

"Are you going to tell me what you're thinking?" Beth asked, not sure she wanted to know.

"What makes you think I'm thinking something?"

"You're always thinking something." Beth glanced at her mom, who kept her gaze on the tree-lined road in front of them.

"Yes, but telling you what I think doesn't usually result in the outcome I'm hoping for. You're too much of an independent thinker. You like to have your own ideas. As soon as someone tells you what they think you should do, you do the opposite just on principle. Your father was the same way."

Beth didn't deny it. She didn't like being told what to do. Still, for some reason, she wanted her mother's opinion.

"You don't think this is the stupidest thing she's ever done?"

"Darling daughter, you forget the time your sister *walked* through the automatic car wash."

Beth laughed. "Okay, the second stupidest."

Her mom squeezed her arm. "I think on her own, she can't make this happen. A farm is a lot of work, especially one that's also a tourist attraction."

"Right. And an apple orchard, retail store and pumpkin patch. What is she thinking?"

"You didn't let me finish." Lilian wore a slight smile. "I admire her dreams. They're absolutely crazy, but they're also . . . inspiring."

"Inspiring?"

"You're a thinker, Beth. Logical. Focused. Your father made sure of it. These are wonderful traits, especially in the corporate world."

"I hear a 'but' coming on."

"But you never pay attention to your heart."

Beth sighed. "A heart can be very misleading."

"And it can be empowering." Lilian squeezed her arm. "You know you and your dad always had this special language only the two of you could understand. Somehow he always connected best with you and vice versa. I told myself that was fine. He was doing a fine job of raising you—but what I've realized is you got all of his good qualities and none of mine."

Beth stilled. She'd never looked at it that way. She and her mother didn't have the same bond she'd had with her father. Only now did she wonder how that made her mom feel.

"Your sister is the opposite. She's all heart and very little logic." Lilian stopped walking and looked at Beth. "Imagine what the two of you could accomplish together."

Beth could feel the words settle on her shoulders with more weight than they should, as her parents' words always had. They'd been so good about steering her in the right direction without controlling her life. It was how she'd learned to think for herself. But her mom was right.

"I never expected to work at Whitaker for this long. That was not in my plan."

"I know." They came to the end of the street and made a loop, heading back toward the house the way they had so many times before.

"And I'm not getting younger, so if I'm going to get out and make a difference in the world, I should probably do that now."

"You're talking about moving away."

Frustration wound its way inside her. She didn't get to run away from the mess she'd made—not when it hadn't been completely cleaned up. Not when she was still keeping the truth hidden. "No, I can't."

"But it's what you always wanted to do."

"Yes."

"Then what's stopping you?"

So many things were stopping her. Molly's idea, however, was not one of them.

In that moment, she had the briefest flashback to their family—all six of them—racing through the pumpkin patch in search of their perfect pumpkin. Seth had hauled a huge, half-rotten pumpkin to where their parents stood, and dropped it at Dad's feet, claiming it was the one he wanted. The look on Dad's face was caught in Beth's memory like a photograph.

She didn't disagree that Fairwind needed to be restored, that new generations of families needed to experience it for themselves.

She just disagreed that she and Molly were the ones to do it.

"You're thinking about it, aren't you?"

"What?"

"The farm. Molly's proposal."

"I would hardly call it a proposal. She got as far as 'I bought Fairwind Farm' and stopped."

"But you *are* thinking about it. I can see it on your face." Her mother's lips settled into a soft, contented smile as she squeezed Beth's arm. "I feel like I'm living with a bird in a cage. You've got wings, my darling daughter. Use them."

"But shouldn't I use them to create the life I've wanted instead of building a new one here with Molly?"

Lilian stayed quiet for a few long moments. "I suppose. If that's what you really want."

Beth sighed. "It's like a conspiracy around here."

"I assure you, it's not." Her mom's tone stayed soft. "You just get these ideas in your head, Beth. The way things are supposed to be. The things you're supposed to accomplish. I wish I could erase all of that and help you figure out what your heart wants."

Beth shook her head. "That's not how I'm wired."

Her mother stopped shuffling. "That's not how you *think* you're wired."

"I can't believe we're even having a conversation about this. What are you saying? You think I should join Molly in this crazy, doomed project?"

"You need a change."

"I'm fine." Beth stared off toward the house.

Lilian ignored her. "Can you think of a more exciting change than this?" Her eyes almost sparkled in the light of dusk. "For once in your life, what if you did something completely unexpected? What if you even surprised yourself?"

"Anything in Willow Grove isn't exactly my idea of a surprise."

"Beth, you *live* here. And there's nothing wrong with that."

Then why did it feel wrong?

She needed to stay focused on what really mattered. Making things right at Whitaker Mowers. Taking care of her mom. Being smart with her money.

And yet, as she drifted off to sleep that night, the image of a big white barn floated through her mind.

Chapter Five

Butler's Bake Shop sat smack at the center of downtown Willow Grove. On either side of Town Hall Road, visitors perused boutiques, antiques and historical buildings. Cafés and sweet shops, like the old-fashioned ice cream parlor on the corner, drew tourists in from the city and beyond. But the locals preferred Butler's.

It was quaint without being overly charming, the kind of place the hometown crowd could appreciate.

And for Beth, Butler's was chock-full of memories. Being the best friend of the owners' daughter, she'd practically grown up sitting on the last bar stool, closest to the kitchen, a plate of freshly made french fries between her and Callie. They'd watch Callie's parents, JimBob and Verna Butler, maneuver their way from the kitchen to the main floor, chatting up their loyal patrons.

If Beth didn't know better, she'd almost think JimBob and Verna had no interest in appealing to tourists. They'd done little to keep the place updated, and they didn't even have a website. In many ways, they were Willow Grove's best-kept secret. After all, they made pot roast and mashed potatoes that would rival Paula Deen's.

The morning after the disaster of a family meeting, and after a restless night of practically no sleep, Beth walked in and spotted Callie waiting on someone near the back set of booths.

Beth made a beeline for the same booth near the back that she'd claimed since she was twelve years old, which was about the time the bar stool became "uncool." Callie gave her a quick nod, then turned her attention back to her customer—a handsome stranger Beth hadn't seen before.

Odd. He must've wandered in. Goodness knows he couldn't locate Butler's on his iPhone.

"I'll be right back, Beth," Callie said, then whisked off toward the kitchen.

Before Beth could respond, Dina Larson locked eyes with her from a table right in the center of the room.

And this was the downside of strolling into places where only the locals seemed to gather. Dina had moved out of town not long after high school, and Beth would've lost track of her if it weren't for Ginny Larson, Dina's grandmother. Ginny had a way of broadcasting Dina's latest.

"Did you hear about Dina's engagement party? It happened on a yacht right next to Navy Pier. It cost a fortune, but her fiancé is R-I-C-H rich, and he said, 'Only the best for my Dina.'"

Beth forced a smile and reminded herself to be nice.

Dina's smile widened as she approached, and Beth noticed the woman's teeth were perfectly straight and blindingly white. Beth's smile faded as she felt suddenly self-conscious and worried that her teeth weren't bright enough.

"Beth Whitaker," Dina said. "I haven't seen you in ages. My grandma told me you were still in Willow Grove. I must say, I was a little surprised."

As Dina talked, Beth thought she detected a southern accent, which was odd since she and Dina had both been born right there in Northern Illinois.

"Oh?" Beth took a drink of water.

"Weren't you the one leading the charge straight out of town senior year? I thought for sure you'd be a big-city girl by now. But then I never thought I'd be one, and just look at me."

"Yeah, I think I heard you were living in Chicago now."

"I am. I have my own ad agency." Dina flashed her brilliant smile. "I run into Michael sometimes. He's still there, you know." She rolled her eyes. "I swear, that man is a complete idiot for what he did to you."

Heat rushed to Beth's cheeks.

"Oh, I'm sorry, Beth. I'm trying to stop being so blunt all the time. My husband says it's off-putting." As if on cue, Dina flipped her left hand in the air just long enough for the large diamond on her ring finger to catch the light.

"Anyway," she went on, "I actually came over here because I heard you bought Fairwind Farm and I just could not believe it. I mean, there's living in Willow Grove, and then there's putting down roots in Willow Grove. Sounds like you're in it for the long haul."

Beth looked around to make sure no one was listening. She did not want anyone—least of all Dina Larson—thinking she'd done something as stupid as buying a dilapidated farm in Willow Grove. She needed to get as far out of town as she could, and fast.

"I tell you what. It's brilliant. Absolutely brilliant," Dina said, cutting off Beth's mental gymnastics.

Was that sarcasm?

"I told my husband all about it, and he said we should try and buy it from you." She let out a loud, ill-timed laugh, then studied Beth as if her statement warranted a reply. Beth couldn't have conjured one if she tried.

"I should've known you had a plan, living here all this time. No way you were just hiding out here because some guy dumped you." She grinned. "That is not the Beth Whitaker we know and love." She punctuated every other word of her last sentence with tiny swats on the shoulder.

Beth stuttered, noticing a few errant stares in their direction. She supposed everyone knew about her and Michael. They were the homecoming king and queen. That made them Willow Grove royalty. Practically. And it also seemed to give everyone in town a right to have an opinion about their relationship.

"After all, it was you who pushed me to do better during high school. If it weren't for you, I might not have gotten my scholarship to Northwestern, and then I never would've gotten the job at Pierce Advertising, and if I hadn't gotten that job, I wouldn't have met my husband and we wouldn't have started our own agency." She paused and looked at Beth. "It's like I owe all my success to you."

Well, at least she could take solace in that.

"Anyway, I knew you were just biding your time, waiting for the right opportunity to come along. Obviously. I told my granny that, and she didn't believe me. Said she was sure you were the latest victim of the Willow Grove vacuum. You know how this town is, sucking people back in to watch their lives slowly rot away. You can't chase dreams here, Beth. It just doesn't work that way."

Beth didn't respond.

"Unless, of course, you have a genius idea like this one. Get yourself a piece of the tourism pie—and then, after you get it up and running, you can add it to your résumé and get out of Dodge. The place will practically run itself if you hire the right help."

"I didn't buy—"

"It's impressive, Beth. Smartest thing ever. Seriously, my daddy always said that old farm was what started it all. Said Fairwind put Willow Grove on the map. People just loved that place when we were kids."

Beth smiled. "They did."

"Well, I can't wait to see what y'all do with it. We'll be sure to keep checking in on your progress."

Beth had no doubt.

"And if you do decide to sell . . ." She pulled a small white business card from her purse. "Smell that. I sprayed it with this really expensive perfume my husband brought home after his last trip to Paris."

Beth touched the card to her nose absently.

"Isn't it the most delicious thing you've ever smelled?"

"It's nice," Beth said.

"Okay. Good to see you again, Beth." Dina leaned over and pulled her into one of the top most awkward hugs of all time, then sauntered away.

As she did, she revealed Callie standing behind her, wearing a dirty apron and an exasperated look. "You did what?" She sat down next to Beth, setting a tray of undelivered food on the table in front of her.

Beth glanced at the handsome stranger, who eyed the food. Callie seemed oblivious.

Beth picked up the tray and walked toward the guy. "I take it this is yours?"

The man looked up at her. He had the bluest eyes she'd ever seen, complemented by dark-brown hair. "Egg-and-cheese sandwich?"

Beth looked at the plate. "Side of home fries."

"Yeah, that's mine." He didn't smile, but he didn't frown either.

"Sorry about my friend. She's usually a much more attentive waitress." Beth set the plate in front of him. "Did you need more coffee?"

"That'd be great. Long night."

She grabbed the pot from the counter and poured him a fresh cup, resisting the urge to ask him why his night had been long, who he was and how he'd managed to find himself here in Willow Grove. "Anything else?"

"Have you done this before?"

She laughed. "Not for a really long time."

"Well, thanks."

"If you need anything . . ." She pointed at the booth where Callie still sat, anxiously waiting for Beth's return and far too happy to allow her friend to do her job for her.

"I know where to find you both." He smiled. Not just any smile. The kind that could make a girl want flowers.

Beth smacked that idea away like a pesky fly and forced herself to smile back, begging herself to play it cool.

But photoshopped-blue eyes. Messy dark hair. The perfect amount of facial hair to accent chiseled cheekbones. "Cool" wasn't an option.

"Beth, stop gawking and get over here." Callie's voice—too loud, too embarrassing—pulled her back to the counter, mortified.

"Gawking? Really?"

"What? I was gawking too. He's almost as cute as your brother."

Beth rolled her eyes.

"I cannot believe you bought a farm and didn't tell me. And Fairwind of all places. Didn't you have your first kiss in one of those barns?"

Beth gasped. "I had completely forgotten that."

"You forgot?" Callie looked horrified. "How could you forget Tim Porter"—she said his name with a breathy sigh—"taking your hand and leading you away from the rest of the class"—back to the wistful voice then—"gently leaning you against the wall and covering your lips with his?"

Beth stared at her.

"How could you forget? The rest of us were so jealous."

"I'm not the one with the faulty memory," Beth said. "Class field trip. Ninth grade. Tim Porter dragged me behind that stinky barn *on a dare* and planted the wettest, most awkward and disgusting kiss, half on my lips and half on my chin." She shuddered at the memory. "I swore I'd never kiss anyone again."

When Callie shook her head, the messy brown bun on top of her head bobbed from side to side. "That's not how I remember it."

Beth glanced at Mr. Handsome, surprised when their eyes met and she detected the slight trace of a smile on his face. Great. He'd overheard that whole thing.

How red were her cheeks?

"Can you get me a vanilla latte to go?" Beth asked.

"Not until you tell me what on earth Dina was talking about. Also, it's sort of pathetic that you were in the ninth grade before you had your first kiss."

"Dina's got her facts wrong," Beth said. "And I can't help it if I was a late bloomer. Besides, who are you to talk? Summer before ninth grade is hardly any better."

"So you didn't buy Fairwind?" Callie frowned. "And I was holding out for your brother."

Beth shook her head. "Molly did. She's trying to get me to invest or take on this project with her or something. Terrible idea, but you know Molly. And I know. Ben's an idiot for not realizing how awesome you are."

Callie slapped a hand over her gasping mouth. "Molly bought Fairwind Farm?" She did nothing to hide her excitement.

"This is not a good thing, Cal."

"Are you kidding? Finally Willow Grove can have its farm back." Her shoulders slumped. "And yes, your brother is an idiot. Too bad he's still so hot."

Beth shook her head. Leave it to Callie to get wrapped up in the nostalgia—and the romance—of a thing. "Callie, please. I'm trying to find Molly a way out of this mess."

"What mess? Even Dina thought it was a great idea."

Beth scoffed. "What does that woman know?"

But she could tell by the look on her friend's face that whether Beth wanted to believe it or not, Dina *did* know business. They'd competed all through high school and, thanks to their relatives, through college too. But then Beth had done the unthinkable and stayed in Willow

Grove while Dina carved out a life for herself in the city, complete with a rich husband, booming business and, apparently, teeth whiter than freshly fallen snow.

"Maybe you should think about it?"

"Are you kidding? You know how my sister is with these crazy ideas." Beth shook her head. "If I'm going to do something crazy, I'm not doing it here."

Callie's eyes fell. "But it's not a bad place to live."

"Of course it's not. But it's too . . . simple . . . for me."

"A lot of people like simple." She stood. "I'll get your latte."

"Cal, I didn't mean—" There she went again, not understanding the emotions of those around her.

Callie stood behind the counter, going through the motions of making Beth's favorite drink. Beth watched as a couple purchased two of Callie's famous pies—something her friend had fought her father to sell. The place was called Butler's Bake Shop, for heaven's sake, but they'd been more of a café than a bakery, and JimBob Butler wasn't open to change.

Beth had been the one to help Callie with a presentation—loaded with facts and figures and projections and visual aids—to convince her parents to expand their menu with the baked goods Callie loved to make. Waiting for JimBob to respond had been agonizing, but finally, he'd given one stern nod, while Verna simply shook her head.

"I hope you know what you're doing," she'd said.

"No risk, no reward, Mama." Callie had beamed.

She'd been so excited that day. So excited to have a little piece of something that was all her own. And look at her now. Her baked goods were the talk of the town.

In fact, people said the pies were just like the ones you could buy at Fairwind Farm all those years ago.

No risk, no reward.

No. It was not a good idea. None of it.

And yet, what if . . . ?

When Callie returned to the booth and set her latte down without a word, Beth couldn't help herself.

"You really think this is a good idea? This Fairwind Farm thing?"

Callie had been intent on pouting, and it showed on her face, but they never could stay mad at each other for long. "Yes. For once, I think your sister got it right." She slid back into the booth. "And you think so too, don't you? But you don't want to admit it."

Beth pressed her lips together. "No, of course not. It's really, really stupid. And really . . ."

Callie leaned in closer. "What?"

"A ton of work."

"Since when has hard work scared the invincible Beth Whitaker?" Callie's raised eyebrows offered a challenge.

Before Beth could respond, a woman behind them let out a squeal, stealing their—and half the diner's—attention. Beth turned and found Marion Proctor, with her bottle-dyed fiery-red hair, heading straight toward her.

"Little Whitaker!" Marion said, obviously confusing her with Molly. "My husband told me you bought the Fairwind Farm!"

Beth shook her head, begging the old lady to lower her voice, but she could almost see the gossip ripple through Butler's like the water in a pond after skipping a stone.

"It's about time. Poor Harold, after all he went through—that terrible tragedy—he should've moved away years ago, before the farm fell to ruins the way it has. But I speak for many, many people when I say we will be there to help you with whatever you need."

"I'm sorry, Marion, I think you have me confused with my sister—"

"Some of my very best memories are from our trips to Fairwind," Marion said, ignoring her. "Verna!" She called to Callie's mom, who stood behind the counter. "Did you hear the Whitaker girls bought

Fairwind Farm? They're going to renovate it. We get our farm back!"
She clapped her hands like a little girl about to get an ice-cream cone.

Verna rushed over. "Why didn't you tell me this, Callie?" She swatted her daughter on the arm with a dish towel.

"I just found out, Mom." Callie's raised eyebrow told Beth her friend wasn't happy she'd found out the way she had.

Verna sighed one of those nostalgic, overly romantic sighs. "I can still remember all of our families meeting out there for those big summer bonfires at Fairwind."

Marion clutched Verna's arm. "I remember. Everyone would gather around the fire and sing and make s'mores. Sometimes it felt like the whole town was there."

"It was so good for our little community. Kept everyone together. It hasn't been the same since."

Beth had loved those bonfires. Her parents had often led the group in some of their favorite church songs. She and her friends would look forward to those nights because they got to stay up way past their bedtime, catching fireflies and eating toasted marshmallows.

The women prattled on, and a buzz shot through the diner as the locals picked up on the news, albeit faulty, that Beth and Molly had purchased Fairwind Farm.

She would've expected them to drone on with their opinions on how things should be run, but in every bit of conversation, she picked up nothing but excitement at the prospect of Fairwind coming back to life. Maybe none of them had realized how much they missed the old orchard until someone mentioned the possibility of getting it back again.

If that was the case, she had to wonder if maybe this little town really did have what it took to support Molly's harebrained idea.

How had Molly predicted this when Beth had so obviously missed it?

"Ma'am?" Mr. Handsome's voice cut through the chatter, and everyone paused.

"Oh, my," Marion said. "Aren't you good-looking."

Callie pushed through the others. "I'm sorry. Are you ready for your check?"

He nodded.

"Follow me this way. I'll get you taken care of."

Before he left, Mr. Handsome tossed one more look toward Beth, and she found herself helpless to look away.

"Normally our service is a lot better than this," she heard Callie say as she led him toward the register. "There's not usually this much excitement."

"Little Whitaker, you should get his number." Marion literally did gawk at the man, whereas Beth had just *looked*.

"Don't be ridiculous." Beth stood. "I'm perfectly happy being single."

"And I'm perfectly happy being thirty pounds overweight." Verna and Marion laughed.

"Will we ever marry these girls off?" Verna said as Beth pushed her way past them. "At this rate, I'll be dead and buried before Callie has a serious relationship."

Their voices didn't seem to quiet even as Beth put distance between them. She waved to Callie, who had just made change for the handsome stranger, and walked out the door. She needed to clear her head—and she certainly couldn't do that with half of Willow Grove prattling in her ear.

Oddly, when she got in the car, she found herself driving a familiar road—one that led to an old, worn-down farm that seemed to beg for a second chance.

Chapter Six

When Drew had wandered into Butler's Bake Shop, he'd hoped for a quiet breakfast to collect his thoughts. He quickly realized he'd picked the wrong place for that.

According to the town gossips, Fairwind had already been sold.

Worse, it had been sold to two nostalgic sisters who wanted to restore the old place and "give the town back their farm." For a minute, he'd almost felt like he'd been at a Save Our Farm rally, the way they were carrying on.

But all he could see was the potential for danger. The idea of Fairwind reopening, bringing in busloads of unsupervised children, set something off inside him. Panic? Everyone seemed intent on remembering Fairwind before tragedy had hit. Had they all blocked out the reason the farm eventually went under?

He found Roxie patiently waiting for him in the passenger seat of his truck.

"You wanna walk, girl?" He hooked a leash onto her collar, much to her dismay. "Sorry, Rox. City rules are different than country rules."

As if he could call Willow Grove a city.

The fifteen-hour drive from Colorado to Illinois had taken Drew, well, a lot less than fifteen hours. It helped that he didn't require many stops, he'd packed a cooler and he routinely drove twenty miles over the speed limit. He'd been so amped up when he arrived, he'd checked into a landmark hotel downtown and headed straight for the diner.

Now, the tiredness he'd been ignoring landed right behind his eyes, but Roxie needed some outdoor time. He owed her that much for ripping her away from home and forcing her to put up with an impromptu road trip.

Drew crossed the street, heading toward what looked like open grass for Roxie to run. He hadn't been back here since he was what, nine? Ten? And yet, something about this place was exactly as he'd left it, as if the town had been frozen in time. He supposed that's why the locals wanted Fairwind back. Everyone wanted that little piece of Mayberry.

Which meant this place was completely unprotected.

The downtown looked like an old postcard with red brick buildings on either side of the road. Each doorway was adorned with an overhead sign that jutted out perpendicular from the side of the building, giving a name to whatever occupied each space. An ice cream parlor. A jewelry store. A bank. A general store. Antiques and vintage markets. Restaurants and coffee shops. They all coexisted right there downtown.

Old-fashioned lampposts dotted the street, and on the corner sat a horse-drawn carriage. It wasn't quite tourist season yet, but there were plenty of people out enjoying the spring sunshine.

Then there was the historical side of this place. Once the home of two different US presidents, Willow Grove had all kinds of stories to tell. And tell them, it did. There were museums and house tours and reenactments—a school field-trip destination for elementary kids within a two-hour drive in any direction.

As Drew reached the other side of the street, someone shoved a piece of paper at him.

"Community Work Day out at Fairwind Farm this weekend. Hope to see you there." The young woman handed a flyer to another passerby and repeated the same words.

He watched as she handed out another flyer, then another, each time saying the same thing. He stared at the paper. Even the image of the old farm stirred something inside him.

The girl—tall, thin, brunette, probably mid-twenties—smiled at him. "You're not a local, are you? Sorry." She snatched the flyer out of his hand, then glanced at Roxie. "What a beautiful dog."

"Thanks." He felt out of sorts after his night of no sleep. Or maybe it was hearing the whole town cheer over the thought of reopening Fairwind Farm. Or maybe it was the photo on that flyer.

The girl squatted in front of Roxie and let the big dog sniff her face. "What a sweetheart," she said. "What's her name?"

"Roxie."

"I love it."

Drew shook his head as he watched Roxie revel in the attention. "She seems to like you." He motioned to the flyer in the girl's hand. "Do you mind?"

She gave Roxie one more head pat and stood. "Not at all."

He scanned the flyer. "So, are you the new owner of Fairwind Farm?"

She grinned proudly. "I am." She thrust her hand at him, and he shook it. "Molly Whitaker."

"Drew Barlow."

Molly continued to hand out flyers to passersby.

People liked friendly people. He'd try to be one of those. "What's your plan for the old place?" He reminded himself to keep his tone light. He wanted to get in there and take a look around, but he didn't want to come off as a creepy stranger trespassing on someone else's property. It'd be so much easier if she'd let him in.

"You know Fairwind? I've never seen you around here before."

"I used to come here with my parents when I was a kid."

Molly hugged the flyers. "Wasn't it special? That's what I want to make it again. I thought we'd start with a Community Work Day.

Willow Grove loved that old farm once upon a time. I just know they'll love it again."

Drew saw an opportunity. "Maybe I can help."

"Really?" She grinned, and while he certainly didn't presume to know either of the Whitaker sisters, they seemed about as different as they could be. He hadn't purposely eavesdropped back at the diner, but no one in that place was exactly quiet. The other sister seemed uptight, like she'd spent too many days in an office.

Judging by her conversation with the loud woman who'd practically accosted her and then the waitress, she already had her ticket out of town in her back pocket. This sister, on the other hand, could've been Willow Grove's spokeswoman.

"Do you have experience with any of this construction-type stuff?" She still smiled at him.

"I have a little bit."

"But you're not a local. You don't have to put in a full day of work in a town where you don't even live."

"I know I don't have to," he said. "I want to."

"Well, okay then. We'll see you Saturday."

He nodded as she gave Roxie another quick ear rub and walked away.

Molly was an idealist, but before long, she'd realize she was in over her head. He almost felt sorry for her.

But she wasn't his concern. He had a clear goal: get into Fairwind, dig around, see if the visit shook loose any old memories and get back to Colorado.

He glanced at the flyer, a simple photo of the old farm with the words "Community Work Day" handwritten above it. The details were listed below, also handwritten. Simple, the way they did things here, not unlike the way he did things back at Elkhorn—but with a whole lot more baggage.

The work day provided the perfect opportunity to get into the old barn and explore.

If only he knew what he was looking for.

Maybe being back at Fairwind would fill in the gaps of his spotty memories, not that he was too anxious to relive that dreadful day. But if this is what it took to find that elusive closure, he'd do it.

Besides, he owed it to Jess.

Chapter Seven

Beth sat at her desk, latte in front of her, and prepared for another monotonous day at Whitaker Mowers. She didn't often stop by Butler's on her way to work, and she certainly didn't drive to the office by way of Fairwind Farm, but after the week she'd had, she'd wanted to indulge herself a little.

Instead, she'd been accosted by craziness.

Darren Sanders, her father's right-hand man, strolled through the office and stopped at her door.

"Beth. You got a minute?"

She glanced down at the sketch she'd been absentmindedly doodling in her notebook. The hand-drawn image of a large farmhouse with a wraparound porch stared back at her. Surely she'd lost her mind. "Sure."

He closed her door and sat down across from her. "How are you?"

She'd been fine before he walked in, but now she felt uneasy. In all the years she'd been working at Whitaker, Darren had never once sat down in her office. "I'm fine, sir."

"Mother's doing better, I hear?"

"She's recovering, yes."

"Good." He looked away, but only for a second. "Listen, there's something I've been meaning to talk to you about. You know it's been challenging to get everything in order after we lost your father."

Beth studied her folded hands.

"But we've had time to sort through everything, and, uh . . . a few things have come to light."

Her stomach dropped. "Oh?"

He pressed his lips together, like a father having a hard talk with his kid. "I think you probably know what I've uncovered, Beth."

Her throat went dry.

"You can imagine what an awkward position this puts me in."

"Sir, I can explain—"

"The truth is, I've been trying to figure out why we've been hemorrhaging money, and now that I know, I've got to plug the leak."

"What are you saying, sir?"

"I respect you. I respected your father. He was one of my best friends, but my job is to look out for the good of this company."

"My father's company."

"He left me in charge, Beth. He had a lapse in judgment when he tried to cover this up for you." His eyes were sad, and she could see he took no pleasure in this conversation.

"Does my mother know?"

"Nobody else knows. I can keep it that way if you agree to quietly resign from your position."

Beth's fingers tingled, and she felt like the oxygen had been sucked straight out of her lungs. "I've been working on making this whole thing right. It's all I do, Darren. You have to know that."

"I know, but I think we can handle it from here."

"But this is my family's business."

"And it still will be. It will just be run by other people."

"And my mother?"

"Your father left very clear instructions to make sure she's taken care of. Your mom will be fine. And so will you."

She wasn't so sure.

He stood. "Beth, your dad always thought you had one foot out the door. I think he hoped for it, actually. Maybe it's time to think about that."

She didn't respond.

He said something about getting exit papers ready and walked out of her office, leaving her sitting in a puddle of sorrow and confusion.

She knew it had only been a matter of time before someone found out what she'd done. Ordering materials from a new supplier for the parts Whitaker Mowers manufactured had looked so good on paper, but she hadn't done her homework, not really. When the cheaper materials turned out to be defective (like her father said they would be), it had landed Whitaker Mowers on the wrong side of a lawsuit.

It had cost Beth her father's respect. It had cost him his reputation. And sometimes—often—she thought the stress of it all had cost him his life.

She needed to get out of there—to clear her head. To figure out why her life had just fallen apart. Again.

She picked up her purse and her latte, walked outside, got in her car and started driving.

Ten minutes later, Beth pulled into the parking lot of the run-down farm, unsure of what drew her there. Especially since she'd felt so silly driving by only half an hour before. What was she doing here?

She made her way to the porch of the old white farmhouse and surveyed the acres that had once brought in kids by the busload. She'd picked apples right off those trees. She'd worked up the courage to feed a goat at the petting zoo and got lost in the corn maze, only to have the wits scared out of her by her hidden brothers.

Something inside her longed for those days again.

But the amount of work it would take to host even one visitor? Not to mention the money. What was Molly thinking?

But then, who was she to criticize? She'd just been asked to resign from her own father's company.

Dina's words tumbled around in her mind. *Brilliant,* she'd said. She wished she'd thought of it herself. And the rest of the locals in the diner—they were all on board. It seemed everyone loved this idea. Everyone except Beth.

She hadn't even considered—not for a second—that it could work. She'd dismissed her sister out of hand. Written off the whole idea before Molly could even finish telling her what she was thinking.

Beth couldn't deny the excitement she'd felt listening to Marion and Verna reminisce about the old place. This little town had supported Fairwind loyally back in the day. Was it possible that could happen again? Did it matter that everyone's lives were so different now, so busy and high tech?

Molly's car came into view in the distance, and Beth sighed. She'd wanted to be alone with her humiliation, but she couldn't overlook the fact that she—not Molly—was trespassing.

Beth met her sister in the yard near the worn-down parking lot and tried not to calculate the cost of repaving the entire thing.

"I didn't expect to find you here," Molly said, a lousy smirk on her face. She got out of the car.

"Don't get any ideas," Beth warned, heading back toward the farmhouse. "I just wanted some peace and quiet."

"Which you could have every day if you do this with me." Molly followed her back to the house.

Beth sat on the rickety old porch steps and inhaled the smell of late midwestern spring. Grass and dirt mixed with the quiet, still-cool breeze, the sound of cicadas humming in the trees.

"It's bonkers, what you're doing. You know that, right?" Beth shook her head. "There are a million reasons why this is not a good idea."

"But Daddy always said 'go with your gut.'" Molly sat down beside her. "My gut has never spoken this loudly, Beth."

Their father had been a brilliant businessman. He'd taught Beth everything she knew. Most of what she'd learned about leadership was a direct result of working for her father. And Molly was right, his business had been governed not by logic or common sense—not entirely, at least—but by this crazy gut feeling he'd never quite been able to explain.

Why couldn't he be here now to tell her what to do? Why couldn't he give her permission to do something out of character just because she was curious what might become of it? Molly hadn't gotten Daddy's business sense. She'd gotten his sense of adventure.

Envy rose up inside her. She tried to ignore the feeling, but she was jealous—of Molly's ability to take risks, of her lack of concern for what anyone else thought of her.

Beth had none of those things. And now, thanks to her own poor judgment, she didn't have a job either. If only she'd listened to her father, she wouldn't be in this mess at all.

"You know, Beth, this could be your next great conquest," Molly said.

Beth laughed. "Why do you think I need a conquest?"

Molly tilted her head and studied her. "Because you've always needed to prove something. You've spent your whole life climbing a ladder, collecting newspaper cutouts of your accomplishments. Everyone knew you were going to amount to something." She held up her hands and affected a deep, announcer-type voice: "Big things were in store for Beth Whitaker." Molly stopped. "And that's great. Why can't Fairwind be the next big thing? I mean, what else are you doing, really? You can't tell me it's really what you want."

It didn't matter anymore, did it? Her job wasn't an option now that Darren had uncovered the truth.

"Is it what you want, Beth?"

She didn't know what she wanted. She only knew her life wasn't supposed to turn out like this.

But life didn't dwell in supposed tos. And things didn't often go as planned. As emotionally detached as she appeared to be, something was still broken deep down inside her. And that made her feel weak.

Beth started off toward the main barn. A barn once filled with hundreds of people every weekend had become a mere skeleton of what it once was.

She and that barn had a lot in common. Somewhere along the way, Beth had lost her drive, her ambition. She'd lost her resolve. Or maybe she was starting to realize there was more to life. It seemed selfish to ask for more, but here she was, asking.

"You think I don't know what I'm talking about, but I probably know you better than anyone." Molly was close on her heels. "And these last ten months since Mom's stroke, I've spent more time with you than anyone."

Beth pulled open the oversized barn doors and let the light penetrate the darkness.

"And I've loved it. It's like, finally, after all these years, I have a sister."

Beth turned and saw tears in Molly's eyes. She had a wild look about her, like someone had cracked her top open and she was about to overflow. "I never felt like I was good enough for you. And because of that, I never even tried to do anything great." Molly turned away. "Dad told me once I had to let go of your shadow—that I was the one who put myself in it. I got mad and tried to blame him and Mom, but he was right. I always thought he wanted me to be silly little Molly. He knew God gave me this big heart for a reason. He told me I was fearless." She laughed as a tear trickled down her cheek. "Do you believe that?"

Beth turned and put a hand on her sister's arm. "Yes. I've always admired that about you."

Molly's face puckered as she tried not to cry. "I didn't know that."

"He told me once I worried too much. To stop trying to always find the 'best way.' That sometimes it's okay to be wrong." Beth swallowed the lump in her throat. "I guess if this is a mistake, it just feels like it would be a really big one."

Molly stilled. "But it's our mistake to make, Beth."

Beth couldn't afford another mistake. Her last one had cost her so much.

"And who knows? Maybe we'll fall flat on our faces. But that's okay. I mean, if we're going to fail, let's fail gloriously."

The image of Darren's disappointed expression rushed back. Beth squeezed her eyes shut. "I don't know if I can do that."

"I know. Because you've never failed at anything in your life."

Beth thought about setting the record straight—telling Molly everything—but she couldn't. She couldn't stand the thought of everyone knowing what she'd done.

"I'm an accomplished failure," Molly said, "and I can tell you, if this is a disaster, we'll bounce back."

"This is a terrible sales pitch."

Molly reached over and squeezed Beth's hand. "And if it's a success, it could be the best thing we've ever done in our lives. It's like we get a second chance to do something really amazing."

"Did I miss our first chance?"

"Everything before today was our first chance." Molly smiled. "Today is a brand-new day. I remember a version of you that wanted to be an artist. You were good, Beth. And you gave it up because Dad convinced you it wasn't practical."

"It wasn't," Beth said. "And he didn't convince me. I came to that conclusion myself." She'd known better than to pursue something so unsteady. It wouldn't have suited her the way it might have suited Molly. Besides, her father had been right—she did have a head for business.

Her sister let out an exasperated sigh. "Does everything have to be evenly measured? Life isn't all about dollars and cents. There's so much more to it than that."

Beth waved her off. "It doesn't matter. That was a long time ago."

"Yeah, before you started letting your head make all the decisions."

Beth stilled. Every major decision she'd made, from where to go to college to what internships to apply for to how to manage the office staff at Whitaker Mowers, had been accompanied by lists of pros and cons. She was a rigid planner, but what if Mom was right? What if she and Molly really did make a good team? What if they filled in each other's gaps?

What if they could bring Fairwind back to life? She drew in a deep, long breath and closed her eyes. This was crazy. Absolutely, 100 percent, off-the-charts crazy.

And going into business with her sister was perhaps the most foolish part of the whole idea. She hadn't made a pro–con list for this yet.

But for once, she wondered if she could follow her heart instead.

"Fine," Beth said, rushing the words before anything could make her change her mind. "I'm in."

Molly clapped her hands over her mouth but failed to contain a noise that could only be described as part squeal, part scream. "You're in." She gasped.

"But there will be conditions," Beth said, moving away. "Terms. A written business plan. And I'm not here for good, Molly. Just long enough to get things off the ground, and then I want to become more of a silent partner. I'll have to take a leave at work and figure out what to do about my plans and everything else." She waved her hands in the air, the weight of her deception and her decision pressing on her shoulders. "We'll need capital. More than we have."

"What about Mom?"

Beth frowned. "That wouldn't be my first choice." She didn't want the risk of this venture to threaten their mother's bank account. "I'll talk to Ben first. Let me see what I can do."

Molly nodded, hands still covering her mouth. A smile worked its way up to her eyes. "You're in."

"And you won't make any decisions without consulting me first."

"Can we get a dog?"

Beth groaned and walked out of the barn. "I already don't have a good feeling about this."

Chapter Eight

Drew ran at breakneck speed down the hill and into the barn. He could hear Jess behind him, laughing. "I'm gonna get you, Drew Barlow!" She'd never find him in here. She hated climbing the wobbly old ladder.

The smell of hay and earth met him, but he barely noticed. Ran for the ladder and pulled himself up into the loft, where he ducked out of sight and waited for her to appear in the doorway below. At the sight of her shadow, he ducked lower, peering down at her from behind the bales of hay.

"Drew, no fair! You know I don't like this barn."

He stifled a laugh. He had her now. No way she'd win this time.

She moved through the dusty space, searching in each stall, and then he heard it. A car door right outside.

"Drew?" Fear echoed in Jess's voice. Another shadow appeared in the doorway, and Drew stood.

"I'm up here, Jess." He rushed down.

Before he could reach her, something came at him from behind, knocked him to the ground. The smell of hay and earth filled his nose again. Then he heard the scream. The car door. The engine.

Then . . . blackness.

Drew shot up, sweat drenched and out of breath. He looked around, a few long seconds of panic passing before he remembered where he was.

The Dulles Inn. Willow Grove. Only a few miles from Fairwind.

He rose and walked to the sink, stuck his head under and took in a few long drinks of water.

He hadn't had the nightmare in months. Hadn't thought about it in months. He'd finally put it to rest, focused on work—finally felt like he could live a normal life.

And then his mom showed up with her guilt trip and the promise of something he'd chased for years, whether he cared to admit it or not.

Closure.

Something he'd never have. Without justice, there would be no closure.

Even then, he had doubts such a thing existed.

Drew pulled on a long-sleeved shirt and walked out onto the balcony, stared out over the sleeping town. Nestled on a hill, the Dulles provided a vast panorama of Willow Grove—a place he'd tried for years to forget.

Why had he come back here? He loved his life. Loved the horses. Loved the ranch. Loved working with his hands. Loved the solitude. He'd picked up so much knowledge in his years at Elkhorn. He'd learned to cook. He had his own garden. If something needed fixing, he fixed it. He liked being useful, and he liked being worlds away from the past.

What he didn't like was small talk. Or questions. Or thinking about Jess.

He closed his eyes, and the dream rushed back at him. Too familiar, it had recurred off and on for years. A therapist would probably have a field day with him, but he'd never told a soul about his nightmares. They always ended at the same part, and they always felt unfinished. Something was missing.

Something he'd forgotten or blocked out. Something . . . Drew shook it off. No. He wasn't going to do this. The past was the past. He didn't need this—didn't need to dig it all up and lay it out on the table.

He should go back to Colorado where he belonged.

But that laugh. He could still hear her. It taunted him. Even in the dream, it had been so vivid. She had been so vivid. Jess had one of those bubbling-over-from-the-gut laughs. Infectious.

Harold's face flashed in his mind. The photo from his obituary. His face had hardened and gained deep wrinkles, the kind that come from a lifetime of worry. He'd called Drew every few months for years—and then one day, he'd just stopped. Why? Had something happened to make the man stop begging him to come back for "just one more look around"?

Had he finally accepted the fact that this side of heaven, he'd never know the truth?

But without Harold as her mouthpiece, Jess had no one. No one left to fight for her. Everyone else was gone.

Maybe it was the chill in the air or the suddenly unsettled feeling in Drew's gut, but he knew he couldn't leave here without at least trying to finally do the right thing.

It didn't matter how much he hated it.

After a nearly sleepless night, Drew got up early. He was used to early mornings, but usually he had at least six hours of sleep before getting out of bed.

Not today.

He showered, dressed, grabbed a cup of coffee from the lobby of the hotel, then made his way out to Fairwind for the Community Work Day. He wasn't part of the community, but if they were opening the doors to the place, he'd do his part—anything to get a chance to look around and get back to Colorado.

Even annoying kids were better than this torture.

He drove the country roads out to the farm, surprised to discover a line of cars waiting on the old orchard grounds. The lot was already full, and people had taken to parking on the grass.

The activity seemed concentrated right in front of the main barn. He could still remember hiding out in the kitchen, stealing pieces of broken apple-cider donuts when the workers weren't looking. He and Jess had had their run of the place.

As he parked the truck and scanned the property, his heart kicked into high gear, pounding in his chest like the bass drum in a band.

Deep breath in. Deep breath out.

Why am I here? I shouldn't be here.

Again, Jess's laugh echoed through his mind. He had to do this—for her.

"Just look around, Drew," Harold had said in a particularly long voice-mail message. "That's all I'm asking."

Drew hadn't bothered to respond. He could've at least called back to decline.

Guilt nipped at him like an untrained poodle. He'd been so selfish.

Still, sitting here on the lawn of Fairwind Farm, he didn't know how to move forward. In his head, he was willing, but the ramifications would be great. Was there a way to jog his memory without actually reliving that day? To preserve his sanity?

He knew Harold had been collecting details on the case. The old man likely had a larger file than the police did—Drew would have to find it, assuming no one else already had. What if Harold had unearthed something new? What if there was something that filled in the blanks of Drew's nightmare?

Could he even handle such a thing?

Twenty years had passed, and Drew had never spoken a word about that day. He wasn't even sure he'd be able to speak up if he did remember something.

He had no time for shameful thoughts today. He got out of the truck and watched for a few long moments as people flocked toward the barn. Probably many of the same people who'd been there that day—had they all forgotten the horror? Sure, most of them hadn't been as close to the front line as he had, but they'd been there. They'd seen the heartbreak it caused. There had never been justice—why weren't they demanding it?

Instead, they were scurrying around with their to-go cups of coffee and their lawn equipment. They moved in groups toward the main barn, which bore almost no resemblance to the image in his mind. The paint was peeling, and the weeds had nearly overtaken the place. It was almost summer—surely these sisters didn't hope to have Fairwind up and running by early autumn, did they? They had no idea what they were up against.

Drew glanced at the clock. Almost half past seven. The flyer said to meet in the main barn for pastries and coffee, and while an urgency to explore Fairwind bubbled inside him, he'd skipped breakfast. After his sleepless night, more caffeine was in order.

Besides, he was a stranger. He couldn't bypass the meeting and snoop around like he owned the place.

Outside, the sun shone but the air was still crisp. Pretty perfect weather for a Community Work Day. Almost like God was smiling down on Fairwind.

Why did the thought irritate him?

Wooden folding chairs, probably left over from long ago, had been set up in rows like a church in the center of the barn. Old tables had been pushed to the edges, and the brunette he'd met on the street appeared to be serving pastries and coffee off to the side. She smiled a kind smile, happy, like she had an excitement inside her she couldn't contain.

He didn't remember if he'd ever felt that way about anything.

People filtered to their seats, and Drew made his way over to the coffee. As he poured himself a cup, he glanced up and saw the blond sister—the uptight one—standing on the other side of the table, staring at him.

"What are you doing here?" she asked.

"Getting a cup of coffee."

"No, I mean, you don't live here. I didn't think I'd see you here." She seemed nervous, but he didn't know if it was because of him or because she and her sister had so obviously taken on more than they'd bargained for.

"Does that mean you thought about me?" He took a sip of his coffee.

Her face reddened and she stuttered, but before she could respond, the girl from the street—Molly—appeared beside her. "I can't believe you showed up." She grinned, then looked at the blond one. "Do you two know each other?"

Drew took a bite of a donut and shook his head. "Nope."

"I saw him at Butler's the other day, that's all."

"She brought me my food."

Molly frowned. "You waited tables? That doesn't sound like the Beth Whitaker I know and love."

The blond one—Beth—stiffened. "I was helping Callie." She turned to Drew. "All I meant was, I thought we'd only see locals today."

"He used to come here with his parents," Molly said. "So he's practically local."

Beth raised her eyebrows. "That so?"

He finished the donut and took another drink. "It was a long time ago."

"So, what? You're here for nostalgia's sake?"

He shrugged. "Something like that."

Molly's eyes darted back and forth between the two of them. "We should start, Beth."

She grabbed her sister's arm and pulled her to the front of the barn, where a makeshift stage had been created. He scanned the space. They might be in over their heads, but they knew how to get people excited. From the looks of it, most of the town was there.

The building had seen better days, but there were flowers on the tables and plenty of pastries and coffee to keep anyone from complaining. He had to admit, he might've underestimated the plan to revive the old farm, although donuts weren't going to rebuild ramshackle barns.

Drew sat in the back row and waited for the room to quiet down. The sisters intrigued him. The younger one reminded him of a girl who'd worked at the ranch for a summer. Amanda had been excited about everything and willing to learn, but she'd also had unrealistic expectations and about as much common sense as a ball of lint. He didn't have the right to judge Molly based on their two brief interactions, but he couldn't ignore the similarities.

The older sister, though? She remained a mystery. She was pretty, if a little plain. Blond. Big blue eyes that seemed to look right through him. Probably wondered, even more than she let on, what someone like him was even doing here.

If he had his way, she'd never find out the truth about that. No sense dragging her into the sordid past that followed him around wherever he went, whether he liked it or not.

She stood at the front of the room, elevated just a few inches off the ground. He couldn't say for sure, but it almost seemed like she was trying extra hard not to look at him. Twice their eyes met, and both times, she quickly looked away.

And that was just fine with him. He didn't need a connection with a pretty girl who lived in Willow Grove, after all; he wasn't there for social reasons.

And yet, as she cleared her throat and avoided his eyes, he found himself helpless to ignore a nagging curiosity about Beth Whitaker. And as she began to speak, he kept his gaze firmly on her, oddly hopeful that their eyes would meet again.

Chapter Nine

Beth stood in front of the crowd that had gathered in the old barn, looking out over a sea of friendly, excited faces. She wiped her sweaty palms on the sides of her jeans, realizing she was more nervous than she should be.

She'd lived in Willow Grove her entire life. Most of these people had known her that long—but maybe that was part of what made her pulse race. Would anyone take them seriously if they'd known them when they were little kids running around the playground at Page Park?

Worse, what about the people (person) who didn't know her then? What was Mr. Handsome from the diner doing here? He sat in the back row, quiet, unassuming. She could feel him watching her, studying her. It made her feel wobbly.

"He's totally into you," Molly said as she passed behind her.

"Will you stop it?" Beth waved her off. "We need to start."

"You're the pro." Molly motioned for Beth to take the stage. "His name's Drew, by the way."

Beth glared at her. "Focus."

They'd been up almost the entire night attempting to make the barn presentable and solidifying their plan, but their work was only a reminder of what Beth had known all along. They couldn't do this on their own. Hiring out all the help would be too expensive, and while she and Molly were willing to get their own hands dirty, she knew they lacked the sheer strength it would take to do what needed to be done.

And, for the first time in her life, Beth felt like she needed someone to tell her what to do. She hated that feeling. She hated knowing that she didn't know something. She liked being in charge, and she liked feeling competent.

At Fairwind Farm, she was neither of those things.

In her panic, she'd called Ben, not realizing it was the middle of the night. He wasn't exactly happy about that, but he did agree to come out for the Community Work Day. Ben's business kept him busy most of the time, but Beth knew he could at least get them on the right track. As a landscape architect, his expertise would be invaluable. The only question was how involved he would be.

Agreeing to come at all was a big deal for her brother. He didn't like the attention he got when he was home. Probably why he hadn't shown up yet. He'd make a late entrance and slip out unnoticed—or try to, anyway.

He wasn't the kind of guy who often went unnoticed.

Beth took a deep breath and reminded herself she was a professional. It didn't matter that the barn was filled with people who had watched her grow up. If they had any hope of restoring Fairwind, they needed these people. And these people were obviously excited about the idea. All she had to do was tap into their nostalgia, inspire them to get on board. That would be her focus.

She said a silent prayer, cleared her voice and reminded herself not to meet the gaze of the handsome stranger in the back row.

"Hi, everyone." She waited for people to quiet down. Across each row, familiar faces turned toward her and smiled, excitement dancing behind their eyes.

Beth smiled back. "For those of you who don't know us, my name is Beth Whitaker, and this is my sister, Molly."

Molly waved at the crowd, wearing a smile that made her look younger than her twenty-seven years.

"You've probably heard that we are the new owners of Fairwind Farm."

The crowd erupted in applause, the kind she'd heard at Little League games every summer when she was growing up—celebratory, if a little rowdy.

Beth glanced at Molly, who grinned, reached for Beth's hand and squeezed. Maybe it was lack of sleep or caffeine (or both), but the whole scene stirred something inside Beth, and she worked to swallow the lump that had formed at the back of her throat.

Molly leaned toward her. "I told you people would love this."

Beth blinked several times in quick succession, willing away the unwanted emotion.

Obviously Molly understood something about these people that Beth didn't. They'd gotten up at dawn to spend the day doing manual labor for edible payment and they were cheering? For them?

Something like a laugh rose inside her, and she gestured to the crowd that their applause wasn't necessary. Finally, they quieted down.

"Wow," she said. "You guys made me forget what I was going to say."

Laughter scurried through the group, giving Beth a chance to pause.

"Here's the truth," she said. "When Molly came to me with this idea, I thought she'd officially lost her mind."

More laughter.

"I have no idea if we can pull this off. We're working on a business plan, and Molly has a notebook full of big, crazy dreams, but we've never done anything like this before." She tried to make eye contact with as many people as she could. "One thing is certain. Without your support, we'll never make any of those dreams come true. But with your support, with your excitement about Fairwind, I feel like we—all of us—just might see Fairwind flourishing again." She glanced at her feet, then back to the happy faces in front of her.

Molly inched closer and wrapped an arm around Beth's shoulder. "My sister is a brilliant businesswoman, as most of you probably know."

Someone let out an embarrassing "Woot!"

"But she has trouble taking risks that don't make much sense on paper."

Beth nodded. "And Fairwind Farm makes no sense on paper."

A murmur made its way through the crowd.

"Maybe not," Molly continued. "But it makes sense in here." She put her hand on her heart. "I don't have to tell you all how much Fairwind Farm meant to Willow Grove for so many years. For most of us, it was one of the best parts of our childhood. How many of us walked the orchard with our bushel basket and filled it up with the very best apples we'd eat all year? How many nights did we spend out around that bonfire singing songs and roasting marshmallows? How many of us chopped down the perfect Christmas tree right out in that field?"

Beth noticed the sweet expressions on everyone's faces as they nodded and reminisced along with her sister.

"We want to bring that back. The simple joys that kept our families strong. I've done my share of traveling . . ."

She had. Beth envied her that. Beth had lived a confined life while Molly saw the world. It had changed her sister, certainly, but deep down, she was, and always had been, Molly. It was like she never questioned herself. While that sometimes got Molly into trouble, Beth was often paralyzed by all her own second-guessing.

Not her best trait.

Molly went on. "I really believe there's no place in the world like Willow Grove, and we want to be a part of this community in a memorable and important way. And we will be, for as long as you'll have us."

The crowd applauded again as Beth tried not to think about the ramifications of another professional misstep.

"So, why don't we talk through the way today is going to work?" Molly sounded like she was leading a pep rally, and the people in the barn responded with a cheer.

Beth wondered if they'd all be this excited *after* they got their work assignments for the day.

She took a step back as Molly started outlining some of the jobs that needed to be done. Only then did she dare a glance in the direction of the good-looking stranger. She was surprised to find his eyes focused squarely on her. This time, instead of pulling her eyes away, she challenged his look with one of her own, locking onto his gaze and wondering if it would set him off balance the way it did her.

She doubted it, but when she detected the slightest lift in his eyebrows, she almost lost her resolve.

Was she flirting?

How ridiculous. She pulled her eyes away and focused on Molly, who was explaining what needed to be done. They'd consulted with Ben on this part too, just to get a list going, but secretly Beth hoped someone would take charge of the whole day and instruct all these people in the tasks that were most pressing.

"There's weeding, yard work, sweeping out the barns. The barns will need some serious attention, and we haven't even started talking about the orchard or the trees."

Already Beth felt overwhelmed. Ben had warned them not to expect anything to look much different at the end of their work day, and she knew he'd never leave his business to give them the kind of help they probably needed. He just couldn't—he'd worked too hard.

Still, she wished someone with some know-how would come forward and take a bit of the guesswork out of this whole project. Beth felt like a child who'd just been thrown into the deep end of the pool without a life preserver.

"We have to clear out the old before we can bring in anything new," Molly told the group of willing workers after assigning them to various tasks. "And don't forget to head back here for lunch at noon. We'll be grilling hot dogs and burgers, and several of the ladies from Willow Grove Community Church brought dishes to pass. We promise they all have clean kitchens."

The crowd laughed, and once Molly was finished, they dispersed to their respective jobs. Mr. Handsome sat for a long moment as the others shuffled out around him. He took what seemed to be the last drink of his coffee, stood and walked straight toward her. Beth stiffened—like a junior high girl at her first dance. *What if he talks to me?*

Her mouth went dry.

He met her eyes as he threw his coffee cup in the trash can right beside her, then quietly strolled out of the barn. Holy smokes. She needed to get ahold of herself. Beth Whitaker was not one of those girls who went weak in the knees over a guy. No matter how good-looking and mysterious he was.

She felt foolish that she'd half expected him to talk to her, when really he was just looking for the garbage can.

Get a grip.

She turned and found Molly and Callie staring at her. "What?"

"What was that?" Callie's eyes were wide.

"What?"

"Whatever that long, sexy gaze was between you and Drew the handsome cowboy," Callie said.

"He's a cowboy?" Beth didn't date cowboys. She'd always gone for guys in suits and ties. Guys like Michael. Of course, look where that had gotten her.

Molly shrugged. "Looks like a cowboy to me. A cowboy in a baseball cap."

"I don't know what you're talking about."

"You're smitten with him, aren't you?" Molly waggled her eyebrows, looking every bit the little sister she was.

"Don't be ridiculous."

"I think the feeling is mutual," Callie said.

"What feeling?"

Ben. Thank God.

Callie snapped her jaw shut at the sound of his voice. She'd had this *thing* for Beth's oldest brother ever since they were kids, and he seemed either uninterested or unwilling to notice. Beth had barely touched on the subject with Ben, whose own heartbreak had taken him out of the dating game years ago. They'd only spoken in generalities, but he clearly wasn't ready for romance. Not yet.

Her thoughts briefly turned to Michael. Had their relationship put Beth's whole life on hold the way Ben's heartbreak had done for him?

God, I don't want to be as closed off as my brother. Please help me get past this.

She'd prayed this so many times over the years. It never seemed to stick. But then, maybe she hadn't meant it before. Something about seeing Ben unknowingly standing next to someone who would love him unconditionally pulled a sadness through her soul—not only for her brother, but for herself.

Neither of them needed to keep living in the past.

She pushed the thoughts aside. "It's nothing. What'd you do, sneak in the back?"

Ben pulled his tattered baseball cap down even lower. "I think I was undetected, if that's what you're asking."

Molly rolled her eyes. "You could've helped with our sales pitch, you know. Having a baseball celebrity on our little stage would've given us some street cred."

"*Former* baseball celebrity," Ben said.

"Around here, you'll always be a celebrity." The words seemed to have escaped Callie's lips without her permission. She stared at Ben with that faraway look in her eyes. And he seemed as oblivious as he always did.

"Cal, how about you get started prepping lunch, and we can go pick Ben's brain for a while." Beth had gotten used to keeping her friend from making a fool of herself. She considered it her duty.

Callie sprang into action without a word, and the three Whitakers headed outside.

"Can't believe how many people showed up," Ben said. "That's a good sign, I guess."

"You guess?" Molly didn't hide her annoyance. "Five years from now when this place is back on the map, producing apples and pumpkins and landing on the cover of *Country Living* magazine, you're both going to have *me* to thank for it." She stomped off toward Bishop, who looked about as awkward holding a hammer as Molly would've in a power suit. Beth had gotten used to seeing him in his police uniform, but today he sported old jeans and a gray T-shirt, covered by an open flannel. His freshly cut sandy-colored hair had darkened a bit over the winter, and he wore an eager expression.

"She's spunky, we have to give her that," Beth said.

"Don't get so swept up in this that you forget why you're here." Ben crossed his arms. "You're the brains. Be the brains."

"I could use another brain, you know. And some of your millions."

Ben laughed and started toward the house. "I don't have millions."

"But you have lots."

"So do you, Beth. Don't pretend you haven't been squirreling money away for the past ten years."

He didn't know the truth. No one did. They would be so disappointed in her. The smart one. The sensible one.

Hardly.

"It's not that simple," she said. "Molly's broke. I'm looking for a couple of investors. Of course, my first thought was you. I'm sure you agree we don't want to bring Mom into this."

Ben shook his head. "You're right about that."

"Even though she'll never use everything Dad left her," Beth muttered.

"No, we aren't dragging her into this. We don't even know if she's healthy yet."

"I know. And I agree." Beth frowned. "So it looks like we're on our own."

Her older brother looked the part of a rugged outdoorsmen, like he'd just stepped off the pages of an Eddie Bauer catalog. In fact, he fit so well in the great outdoors, Beth couldn't understand how or why he'd chosen to make a life in the city. He didn't care as much as she did what people thought of him, so what was it? Why was he so intent on staying away from Willow Grove?

"I'll look around and let you know what I think."

"And you'll help me come up with a plan?"

Ben met her gaze. "Isn't that what I just said?"

She frowned. "No. That's not at all what you said."

"I'll let you know. Just give me some space, you nutball." He walked away, pretending to be annoyed. At least Beth thought he was pretending.

As he disappeared behind the old barn, she did a slow turn around the property. What if this was another bad investment? What if this time, instead of being purposely swindled by a slick-talking salesman, she was accidentally swindled by a well-intentioned sister?

Beth had managed to save back up a little—enough to match Molly's investment, but not much more. What would she tell her siblings when they asked why she couldn't put more toward their new pet project? She certainly couldn't tell them the truth.

People bustled around the yard, hauling branches and piling garbage into the dumpster, all working diligently for the promise of something none of them could really deliver—pockets of peace in the middle of a much too busy life.

And it was all Beth could do not to wonder if she'd just sunk the last of her little nest egg into a project doomed before it started.

Chapter Ten

Outside, Drew watched as people gathered rakes and hoes and trash cans from their cars, each moving purposefully toward whatever task they'd been assigned.

He'd slipped out without a job, not quite ready to sign on to anything until he saw the old place for himself.

Fairwind had changed. Twenty years, what did he expect? Behind the main barn, he could see the roofs of the outbuildings, outlined by trees whose leaves had filled out nicely for spring. He walked the same path he'd walked so many times as a boy, only this time he walked it alone.

All those years ago, Jess had been right on his heels.

"Keep an eye on her, Drew," his dad had called after them. Drew had waved to let them know he'd heard. Of course he'd keep an eye on her; they weren't interested in anyone else on the farm—and he needed Jess to remind him where the best fishing spots were.

That's how they'd spent their days. Fishing in the lake. Catching grasshoppers. Hide-and-seek. Bonfires. Everything had seemed so simple back then, like something straight out of a fifties television show.

Drew's family stayed in the guest rooms inside the farmhouse, which didn't look so old and worn back then. For him, it was a treat—their own little getaway. And while his parents and Jess's parents did boring grown-up things during the day, he and Jess had played the summer days away in the fields and outbuildings—basking in the sun, fishing, hiding in the corn, dreaming in the rafters.

Drew rounded a bend, and a small red barn appeared in a clearing up ahead. He paused for a minute, willing himself to breathe.

He stopped. This was so stupid. What did he think he was going to find? Evidence? Would he just walk in and replay the entire event with stark mental clarity—all the missing parts from his dream neatly filled in and ready for a police report?

There was a reason he hadn't been back in all these years. The whole idea of it—his even being here—was absurd.

And yet, here he was.

He wanted the nightmares to stop. Wanted to get her face—the sound of her laughter—out of his mind.

Drew pushed the door open and stared inside the dark space. In a flash, he was ten again, hiding in the loft, the smell of hay and earth filling his nostrils. He could almost hear her voice cut through the black.

"Drew, no fair. You know I don't like this barn."

He did know. It was why he'd hidden there. She'd always had an unnatural fear of the outbuildings on the property, but especially the small red barn. As if she knew, as if something inside her had warned her to stay away.

And he'd been the one to lead her straight into it.

If he'd just hidden somewhere else—by the lake, up in the giant oak tree, in the bakery cooler—that day wouldn't have happened.

He closed his eyes. Felt the wet as it ran down his cheeks. It was a mistake, his being here, but he was frozen in place.

The sound of the car door echoed through the hollowness of his memory in the empty barn. The shadow slipped across the darkness. Drew's heart raced as he called out to her.

"I'm here, Jess! I'm right here." He stepped down off the ladder and onto the floor of the barn.

Then it all went to black.

It always went to black. Cut off, like his memory had been sliced in two. There had to be more. A smell. A voice. Something.

"Do you remember anything else, son?" They'd asked and asked and asked, but the answer was always the same. For a little while, he'd thought about making something up, just so he'd have something to give them. But even at ten he knew that was a bad idea. He'd disappointed everyone—let everyone down. Let Jess down.

Had he forgotten something important? He'd been reliving that day for twenty years. Where were the missing pieces?

His pulse quickened as he let his eyes refocus, panning the old barn, the remnants of life inside. A shovel hung on a rusted nail. Next to it, a large broom leaned against a weathered wall. Years ago, this barn had housed horses. They'd been out to pasture that day, but their presence was always known.

He picked up the broom and started sweeping the floor, kicking up dirt and pushing down memories. Distraction was the only way to keep himself sane.

Stay busy. Don't think. Just work.

It was what he'd always done to quiet his mind.

After he swept out the barn, he made his way back to the main parking lot, where Roxie waited for him in the truck. He let her out, commanded her to stay, fished out the toolbox he kept in the back, and then went to work.

For hours, he kept his head down. He cleared away debris, picked up sticks, hauled garbage. He checked off jobs that weren't even on the list, and he did it all without saying a word to anyone.

Around what had to be lunchtime, the smell of burgers on the grill stirred the emptiness in his belly. He finished repairing the back door on the main barn, then swung it open and closed to make sure the hinges were tight.

When he reopened the door, Beth stood in the doorway, looking at him.

"I don't think you've stopped working since you got here," she said.

He stuck his hammer back in his tool belt. "I came to work." And to remember. One of those things he'd mastered; the other continued to haunt.

She straightened. Something about him made her uneasy, he could tell. As if she hadn't made up her mind about him—but then, why would she? He was a stranger on a farm full of friends. He remembered the camaraderie of Willow Grove. The community had always been close-knit, bound together by something he hadn't understood as a child. It was even clearer now that he was older. Businesses that relied on tourism and local support gave them something in common.

But as a child, when he'd spent his summers here, he had always felt like he belonged. They'd been accepting, going out of their way to draw him in.

Exactly the opposite of how he felt now.

"I just wanted to thank you. And tell you to get some food before the vultures come in from the fields." She motioned to the grill, where a tall guy about their age flipped the burgers.

"Thanks. I can wait till everyone else has eaten," Drew said.

"Don't be silly. No one else is working half as hard as you are. I'm paying in food, so please." She started to walk away but stopped, turned back and regarded him for a few long seconds. "Why are you here?"

He wished he could tell her he was helping out of the goodness of his heart, but he knew better. He didn't do it to help anyone but himself.

"Guess I just wanted to be of some use," he lied. He had no real interest in restoring the farm. Not really. If he had his way, they'd bull-doze the thing and start over, burying every memory.

"But you work like a machine. Where are you from?" Beth's tone interrogated.

"I live in Colorado. Work on a ranch out there. I guess this is just my usual pace." Not a lie. Whenever his mind had something to work out, he used his hands to do it, and since he'd been working out distant pain for years, he'd become quite adept with his hands. He could fix almost anything. His pace was just a by-product of his desire to forget.

"Well, thank you."

Roxie edged forward, as if they'd been ignoring her too long.

"Does your dog want some water?" Beth looked at Roxie but didn't touch her.

Roxie whined.

"I guess she does," Drew said. "Do you have a hose?"

Beth frowned. "I honestly don't know."

"I'll find one."

She nodded and walked away.

Drew knew exactly where to find the water spigot out back. He took Roxie and let her drink. Moments later, Beth appeared at the back of the barn carrying a plate of food. He watched as she walked toward him. She wore a pair of jeans with holes in the knees, but he had the distinct impression it was fashion, not work, that had put them there. Her waterproof work boots looked brand-new, and he couldn't help but admire the way her dusty blue T-shirt hugged her curves. Her hair hung in a loose braid over one shoulder, strands falling out on the other side.

He didn't doubt she was a hard worker, but somehow he imagined most of her work was done indoors. What was a girl like her doing buying an old farm in rural Illinois? Did she feel as out of place here as she looked?

When she reached him, she held the plate out in his direction. "I didn't know what you'd like, so I kind of grabbed a little bit of everything."

He took the plate. On it were two burgers, a pile of potato chips, some sort of church potluck salad with broccoli in it, and three cookies.

"I thought you might rather eat out here anyway."

She was observant; he'd give her that.

They stood at the back of the farmhouse underneath an enormous oak tree, where a circle of folding chairs had been set up. "You don't figure me for the social type?"

There was something shy about the way she smiled. It contradicted what he'd seen of her so far. From what he could tell, she was confident, though maybe a little out of her depth. The farm didn't suit her. Not yet. But she wasn't the type to admit it.

"You've hardly said anything since you got here this morning. I guess it seems like you prefer to work alone."

Drew bit into one of the cheeseburgers and looked at Roxie, who begged with her eyes. He chewed, swallowed, thought about her comment. "I guess I do. I like the work."

"You seem to know what you're doing. You said you're from Colorado?"

"That's right."

Her eyes narrowed on him. "You're a long way from home."

He'd never said it was home. He didn't know if he'd ever feel like anywhere was home. He didn't respond.

She stood there for a few long moments, as if waiting for him to say something. When he didn't, she looked away. "You're not, like, a serial killer or something, are you?"

Drew nearly choked on the bite in his mouth. "Not that I know of."

He assumed she was kidding, but she looked him up and down one more time, as if making up her own mind. "Well, enjoy your lunch."

"Thanks."

He watched as she walked away. Was that the question she'd wanted to ask all along, or had he just done something to make her uncomfortable? He wasn't great at conversation. She'd probably sensed his uneasiness and taken it as a sign he wanted her to go away.

He didn't. Not really. And that was strange because, for the most part, he wanted everyone to go away.

Still, whatever message he'd sent her, he had a feeling it wasn't "hang out here for a while." He was an idiot.

Roxie plopped herself down in the grass at his feet and let out a groan.

Even the dog didn't approve.

Maybe it was better this way. Beth would keep her distance, and he could focus on making some sense of the past. He still had too many reckless emotions firing inside his mind, and nothing good would come out of making friends with a pretty girl. After putting in a full day of hard work, his unwanted emotions should be pretty well whipped into shape, giving him the clarity he needed to piece together whatever was missing.

But as he threw away his plate and went back to work, he had no confidence that any answers would come.

Chapter Eleven

Why did she even bother? Beth trudged back to the barn, feeling like an idiot for trying to talk to Mr. Fix-It at all. He obviously had the conversational skills of a monkey, but she'd kept asking him questions, as if at some point he'd quit with the perfunctory answers and actually share something about himself.

Beth made her way to where the crowd had started to gather around the food. They hadn't even rung a bell or anything; just the smell of the burgers lured people in from all different parts of the farm.

Callie met her by one of the food tables, eyes wide, waiting for some explanation. She'd been the one to talk Beth into taking Drew the plate in the first place.

So this was her fault, really.

Beth felt stupid. A serial killer? Really? Just because he was grumpy and reclusive didn't mean he was a sociopath. And even though she'd been half kidding, her sarcasm seemed lost in his reaction.

"No-go?" Callie followed her into the kitchen.

"What do you mean?" Beth reached into a bag of potato chips and took out a handful.

"He didn't want to talk? Tell you where he's from? Ask you to marry him?" Callie plucked a chip out of Beth's hand and popped it in her mouth.

"I just gave him lunch," Beth said. "Isn't that what you said I should do?"

Callie stared at her. "Yes, but I thought maybe you'd exchange a few words with the guy before you came back here."

"I did."

"So, what do we know about him?"

"I know he's working harder than anyone here." Beth glanced up and out the window to where Drew stood with his dog. He stared out toward the backyard, up into the orchard, seemingly unaware anyone else was on the farm at all.

What was he doing out there? What was he doing here, at Fairwind? And why was he helping them—two strangers—with an insurmountable task?

Callie stole another chip. "I resent that. Do you know how long it took me to bake all those pastries?"

"You know what I mean." Beth leaned against the counter. "It's like he's out there trying to prove something."

Callie waggled her eyebrows. "Who does that sound like?" She didn't wait for an answer. Instead, she walked out, leaving Beth with a handful of chips and an unspoken snarky comeback.

She spent the rest of the day avoiding Drew Barlow. Never mind that it made no sense he was there in the first place. Or that he didn't have good manners.

The guy never stopped—not once. Even when he took his dog out back for water, he still seemed to work, or at least calculate his work. He moved from job to job without being told, and as much as she hated to admit it, it became painfully obvious that she and Molly needed someone like him on the farm.

He fixed things she didn't even know were broken.

As the day waned, people began to leave, all dirty and tired but asking if they could come back the next weekend. The Whitaker sisters had free labor in droves and no idea how to put them to work.

Molly promised everyone another productive day next Saturday, but Beth knew better. Clearing the land of fallen branches and garbage was easy. But what came next? They needed someone to tell them.

Beth stood at the door of the main barn, watching cars kick up dust from the gravel driveway as they pulled away. Behind the house, Molly and Bishop had started a bonfire, having invited everyone to go home and change and come back for s'mores.

Sometimes Molly was such a kid. Sometimes that made Beth jealous.

"You need to hire that guy." Ben's voice pulled her out of her thoughts.

"What guy?" She knew what guy.

"The guy you've been pretending not to notice all day." He stood beside her, a foot taller and almost twice as wide. Her big brother—strong and athletic—had taken their father's place in so many ways. He had wisdom, and Beth admired that. She couldn't simply disregard his advice.

"I don't know what you're talking about."

Ben's disbelieving expression told her to stop lying. "I talked to him. He manages a ranch in Colorado. Manages people, takes care of animals, fixes whatever needs fixing. He's your guy."

"Well, what makes you think he'd take a job on a farm in Illinois?"

He shrugged. "Couldn't hurt to ask."

Beth sighed. "What else do you know about him?"

"Not much. He's not a talker, which is better for you."

Better for her? Hardly.

"I can tell by watching him that he knows what he's doing."

Beth followed Ben's gaze out to the parking lot, where Molly ran toward Drew and Roxie, undoubtedly begging them to come back for the bonfire. No way a guy like that had any interest in socializing with the Willow Grove locals.

Or with her.

Not that it mattered. What did she care if some grumpy cowboy wanted to talk to her or not?

She turned to Ben. "I agree, and I think we need someone to help us, but why can't that be you?"

Ben was safe. He was a well-known quantity—and didn't have the potential to break her heart.

He took off his baseball cap and ran a hand through his hair. "Honestly, I'm intrigued by the whole idea. I'm going to invest, but I'm two hours away, Beth. I can't get back here every day, and that's what this place needs if you have any hope of reopening in the next year."

She bumped into his shoulder with her own. "You're going to invest?"

He held up a hand. "On one condition."

"Uh-oh." She turned to him. "What?"

He nodded at Drew. "You hire that guy."

Beth watched as Drew turned and walked away from Molly, his dog close on his heels.

"We don't even know him, Ben. He's going to get in his old truck and drive away and we'll never see him again." She hoped so, anyway. Kind of.

"Then I guess you'd better stop him."

"Are you serious?"

"You need someone around here to spearhead this little project."

She knew there was nothing little about it. But this guy? Really? Couldn't they just find someone in town? Someone less attractive?

Beth took a deep breath but couldn't get her feet to move. "I'll think about it."

But they both knew he was right. They needed Drew Barlow if they had any hope of restoring Fairwind Farm and opening by fall. And the thought of needing any man—let alone a distant cowboy with bad social skills—didn't sit well with her at all.

Chapter Twelve

Beth's body was tired, but her mind worked overtime. The Community Work Day had come together quickly, and she hadn't sat down once. Her feet and back ached, and even though she'd washed her hands three times, there was still dirt underneath her fingernails.

The day had been a success. It was clear that, somehow, she and Molly had sparked a ripple of excitement in the hearts of the people of Willow Grove. However, it was also clear they were in way over their heads. And that continued to nag her.

Ben's ultimatum hung thick in the crisp night air above the bonfire, where several people huddled under blankets, toasting marshmallows and enjoying the songs strummed on Bishop's guitar.

Beth settled into the quiet away from the crowd as Molly attempted to wave her over. When Beth didn't respond, her sister strolled her way.

"You're missing all the fun," she said.

"I know," Beth admitted.

"Come hang out. Pretend you don't have anything to worry about." Molly grabbed her hand and tried to tug her up.

"Maybe in a few minutes," she said.

But an hour passed, and Beth still sat in her chair, away from the fray. They would probably say she was antisocial. She'd heard that one before, but small talk didn't suit her. She'd never been one for pointless conversation. Maybe that's why her attempted chat with Drew had gone awry.

Or maybe he was even worse with small talk than she was.

Beth glanced at Molly, her shoulder pressed up against Bishop's, oblivious to the way he looked at her as she led the group in some of her favorite songs. Everyone seemed to be having so much fun.

And then there was Beth, sitting several yards away in the same chair where Drew had eaten his lunch. Alone. Maybe the two of them had more in common than she cared to admit.

She'd watched him get in his truck and drive away, that big old dog's head sticking out of the passenger window, and a knot had formed at the center of her stomach. Ben had specified Drew was the guy to hire, and she hadn't even asked where he was staying. Was she sabotaging their efforts before they even started?

Maybe Ben would agree to hiring someone from town. There had to be someone who would put her brother's mind at ease. Surely Drew wasn't the only guy who knew how to work the land, repair old buildings and take care of animals.

But as she scanned the crowd, surveying the many able-bodied young men who stood around the bonfire, Beth knew none of them had the same qualities they'd all seen in the handsome stranger.

Few men did. Hard work seemed a thing of the past.

On the other hand, she knew all of these guys. She'd either gone to school with them or knew their families from church, or she'd babysat them (not that she'd readily admit that). They might not be work-horses, but they were familiar. Beth did better with familiarity than she did with change, which was, she supposed, why she had been running the office at Whitaker Mowers instead of hunting for a job in Chicago.

Maybe losing that job was all the change she could handle right now. Besides, what did they really know about Drew Barlow? The few details he *had* told them could, for all they knew, be fiction.

It didn't really matter anyway; Drew was long gone. Finding him again might be as easy as an online search or as difficult as locating buried treasure—who knew?

Thoughts of what to do next tumbled around in her mind, and while she wanted to relax and have fun like Molly, she seemed unable to turn her brain off.

Something wet brushed against her hand, and she quickly pulled it back.

"Roxie. Sit."

Beth looked up and saw Drew's silhouette cut through the darkness, dimly backlit by the fire.

"Sorry, she has no manners," he said.

What did they say about dogs resembling their owners? Her embarrassment came back in an unwanted wave.

He stood across from her for a long moment, awkward, as if he wasn't sure what he was doing there.

What *was* he doing there?

"Mind if I sit?"

Her body stiffened, but she managed to nod. Why did this guy make her so nervous? For years, she'd run an office full of employees. She'd stood in front of them every week and told them how to do their jobs better. She was good at running an office. She usually managed people well. But around this guy she was fourteen again, unsure of how to carry on a normal conversation.

She tried to tell herself he was just a guy. That it didn't matter that he looked like he'd stepped off a Times Square billboard advertising trips to Colorado. She even tried to tell herself his image on such a billboard wouldn't have had her booking the first flight to Denver.

She tried all of these things, but as soon as she dared a single glance in his direction, the bubbling nerves were back.

It wasn't on her to start a conversation with Drew. After all, she'd already tried that. And he was the one who'd shown up on *her* farm. The oddity of that didn't escape her.

After several long, tense moments, she realized he had no intention of talking. While she didn't much feel like talking either, the silence was a less desirable alternative to tortured conversation.

"I'm surprised you came back," she said at last.

"Me too," Drew said.

Roxie circled their chairs and finally sat down, her tail draped over Beth's feet. It was the smallest, silliest thing, but it caught her off guard. The dog seemed comfortable with her. Beth wasn't a dog person, yet something about that tail on her tired feet made her feel like she had a friend.

They sat in silence for several more minutes, Beth searching for something to say and Drew probably relishing the quiet.

"My brother wants me to offer you a job." It wasn't what she'd intended to say, but she blurted things out when she got nervous.

He barely reacted. "Really?"

She nodded. "Guess you made quite an impression. And Ben's not easy to impress."

He looked away, one side of his face in shadow, the other barely lit by the dancing orange of the bonfire in the distance. "I have a job," he said, his voice quiet.

"That's what I told him."

Beth's mixed emotions wrestled with each other. Part of her was happy he'd be on his way and her nerves could settle down already, and part of her was oddly disappointed. She told herself it was because without him, Ben might refuse to invest, but she knew better.

Her disappointment had nothing to do with Fairwind Farm.

She told herself to focus. The last thing she needed was a crush on a guy who couldn't even hold up his end of a conversation. Especially when she had to work so hard to hold up her end.

Michael had been great at talking. He wasn't like other guys that way. He enjoyed conversation, debate. He was smart, and he liked to show off. Too bad he pretty much only talked about himself.

"What's the job?" Drew leaned forward and stared at the fire, giving her another chance to study his profile. He carried something with him, something heavy. She hadn't noticed it before, but he'd either let his guard down or grown too weary to cover it up anymore.

He glanced at her, and she realized he'd asked her a question, but she didn't exactly know the answer. She hadn't thought of an official title, and she certainly didn't know farm lingo. What did they call the person who did everything they didn't know how to do?

Godsend?

"We need someone who understands how to restore old buildings and work the land," she said. "Molly has good intentions, and I understand business, but you can probably guess we're both a little . . ." She couldn't think of the right word to describe what they were. She didn't want to admit how ill-equipped they were for this job.

"A little . . . ?"

When she met his eyes, she suddenly felt silly for even bringing it up. "Never mind."

Roxie's wagging tail against Beth's feet comforted her. She'd never plunged headfirst into anything without a solid plan. A safety net. But she'd learned the hard way that even the sturdiest of nets could unravel.

Maybe it was her exhaustion, but in that moment, she thought she'd made a terrible, horrible mistake.

"I might be able to help for a little while," Drew said.

She looked at him, though he was still staring off into the distance. Why had her eyes clouded over? She wasn't a crier. Crying was another sign of weakness, and like her father had always said, *There's no place for weakness in business.*"

She cleared her throat and played it cool, thankful for the darkness. "That would be good."

The edge of his mouth pulled upward in a smile so slight she almost missed it.

No one else would ever guess that, deep down, she felt like a scared little girl, but Drew Barlow seemed to be on to her. She'd have to be extra careful around him—she couldn't let her guard down for one second with this man.

Remember what happened the last time you trusted a man, Beth.

"Would you want to meet me out here first thing Monday morning? We can go over what needs to be done." She leaned forward, elbows on her knees, hands folded in front of her.

Roxie's nose found Beth's hands, and the dog inched forward.

"Rox. Sit," Drew said. She obeyed.

"She's a good dog," Beth said. "Did you train her yourself?"

He stroked Roxie's head. "I did. She's a special girl."

Maybe his only friend?

"So, Monday?"

Drew nodded. "Sounds like a plan."

Beth stood, anxious to put some distance between her and a man far too attractive for his own good. But as she drove back to her mother's house, all she could think about was how many hours would pass before she'd get to see him again.

Chapter Thirteen

Sunday morning came hard and fast. Before Beth even opened her eyes, she could feel that the aches in her feet and back had traveled to all of her extremities. She did her best work behind a desk at a computer, not in a field hauling branches bigger than her.

She rolled over and let out a slight groan.

"Stinks to be out of shape, doesn't it?"

Beth opened her eyes to find her sister standing in her room with two steaming mugs of coffee that smelled like heaven.

"What are you doing up so early? And in my room? And dressed up?"

"It's Sunday. Church."

Beth rolled over. It had been their tradition for as long as she could remember, but somehow she'd thought she might get a free pass today—she wasn't sure she could move.

"Rise and shine, sleepyhead."

Obviously her sister had other plans.

Ever since Beth had moved back in with their mom, Molly had insisted on coming over early every Sunday morning. Even when their mother was nearly immobile, they found a way to cart her to church.

"I think I'm staying home today," she said.

"My eye. Mom's up and ready. We leave in half an hour." She set the coffee on Beth's nightstand. "Jesus is waiting for you."

"How do you know He's not waiting for me on the back porch?" She threw a pillow at her sister but missed.

The fact that Molly had this much energy and Beth felt like she'd been hit by a Mack truck was one of life's greatest injustices. She sat up and took a sip of coffee, determined not to rush around. Molly appeared again in the doorway, that *hurry up* look on her face.

"I'm coming," Beth groaned.

As she made herself presentable—a task that proved to be more challenging than usual—she imagined herself sitting in the church pew. She'd consulted God in every decision she'd ever made. Michael. College. Working for her father. She'd accepted that Michael had had his own free will, and though he'd broken her heart, she didn't blame God for that.

Her latest failure? She was having a bit more trouble being gracious with that one. She'd prayed every single day before going against her father's instructions. She'd taken a risk, but she had been certain it would save the company money.

She'd asked God to stop her if it was a bad decision.

But He hadn't.

And look what had happened. She'd never messed up like that before. And worse, she'd covered it up, and it had cost Beth her job.

Her dad had taken the blame for her error in judgment, but obviously there was still some trace of it or Darren never would've found out. He said he'd keep it to himself, but if it ever came out, nobody in business would ever take her seriously again.

Her dad had died before she'd had a chance to make him proud again. He'd died because of the stress she'd caused.

She had to believe God could've given her a heads-up. Something— anything—to keep her from making the wrong decision. She'd let everyone down. Why hadn't He stopped her?

It had been a long time since she'd really heard God's voice, yet for some reason that day, as she finished putting her mascara on, she felt like maybe she needed to break the ritual. Church was a tradition, but maybe she'd been going through the motions.

Maybe she needed to do something different today. She'd never really believed you could only find God at church, after all. How many times had she heard His still, small voice on her walks with Mom? Or in the shower or the car on the way to work?

She emerged from her room with time to spare, poured more coffee into a travel mug and met Molly in the driveway.

"You go ahead, Mol. There's something I need to do this morning."

Molly studied her, but uncharacteristically chose not to press. "Will we see you at church?"

"Maybe not," Beth said.

She frowned. "Is everything okay? You know we have these people to thank for a successful Community Work Day yesterday."

That was true. People would expect to see them there. Beth had built a life out of other people's expectations. Today, she needed to do something for herself.

"And we're partners, so you can thank them." Beth opened her car door and smiled at Molly as she got in. A part of her felt a little rebellious. Maybe she should do whatever she wanted more often.

Acres of newly planted corn and soybean fields stretched out on either side of the highway as she drove toward Fairwind Farm. In high school, she'd never appreciated the tremendous amount of work that went into making those crops grow. She'd never seen the beauty of the earth providing everything needed to create something new. Back then, she'd had only one goal: get out of Willow Grove.

The thought niggled at the back of her mind as she pulled into the parking lot at Fairwind and parked near the main barn. She hadn't done the one thing she'd set out to do. She'd missed the mark. She hadn't gotten out of Willow Grove, and now she'd made a decision that would anchor her to it for years to come.

She hadn't signed anything—she could still back out. But then, where would that leave Molly? Beth couldn't do that to her.

"Sometimes you have to live with the mistakes you make, Beth," Dad had told her when he'd finally found out what she'd done. "There's no getting out of it. You just get through it."

She could still see the look on his face. He'd been so disappointed. She could only imagine what he'd say now as she faced another potential disaster.

Was Fairwind something else she'd have to get through?

She stepped out of the car and walked around the large barn, impressed by how much better the place had already started to look. A patio at the back had been weeded and power washed and now looked like a passable place for a social gathering. Maybe not a fancy one, but something casual, like a birthday or graduation party.

Beth stopped to admire a row of lilac bushes that filled the air with their sweet fragrance. She inhaled the scent. How had she not noticed these yesterday?

She continued walking, drinking in the morning, almost forgetting the tired ache of a body that had been pushed to its limits the day before. The property they now owned seemed to stretch on forever. And she'd thought her parents' yard was big.

Instead of wondering who would take care of it all, she chose to focus on the beauty of it. The morning sunlight streamed through the trees, illuminating the path in front of her.

Off to the right was the orchard—rows and rows of apple trees, different varieties that all looked surprisingly healthy, not that she would necessarily know if they weren't.

Up and to the left was the Christmas-tree farm. Acres of various-sized evergreens stretched out in front of her, and she was instantly transported back to a simpler time when they'd all packed into the minivan, decked out in full winter garb. As soon as they'd pulled into the parking lot, even Beth, a moody teenager, had felt that Christmas excitement as clearly as the chill in the air.

All six of them had made their way past the barns and up toward the trees, determined to find one bigger and better than they'd had the year before. She could still hear her father's voice as he steered them toward the one her mom wanted, knowing that Lilian would defer to the kids. He'd always been so intent on making her happy.

That may have been the last year they were all together to go pick out the tree. Things had been easier then—why had she been in such a hurry to grow up and get out?

She walked up a hill near the end of the evergreens, and as she reached the top, something stopped her. Up ahead across a clearing, a small church building nestled back into the trees, almost hidden out of sight. She'd never had much freedom when they'd visited Fairwind Farm, so she'd had no idea it even existed. She stared at it for a few long moments. Standing like a lighthouse for weary travelers, it seemed to hold some secret promise for those who stopped long enough to pay attention.

Is this why You wanted me to come here today?

Despite its chipping white paint and obvious disrepair, the forgotten church shone like a beacon. She closed her eyes, and an image of what the church could be flashed through her mind as clearly as an actual photograph.

Walking around the church, she let her dream run off by itself for a minute.

She'd start with a fresh coat of white paint and then figure out what needed to be done to restore the steeple. She wanted it to stand tall and proud through the trees, the way it must have when the church was first built. She'd put window boxes on each of the windows—two in front and three on each side. Then she'd plant a lilac bush or two around the back to match the ones on the side, just because she liked lilacs. In the spring, their fragrance would fill the small chapel if the windows were open.

She walked through the brush toward one of the windows, cupped her hands around her eyes and peeked inside. Particles of dust floated through the air, caught by the sunlight streaming through the windows.

How many prayers had been whispered inside these four walls?

She made her way back to the front and walked up the few steps, stopping at the door. She pushed it, but it didn't budge. She pushed again, this time using her shoulder, but still couldn't get the door open.

How long had it been since anyone had been here?

Instinctively, she ran her hand along the top of the doorframe, surprised when something small and metallic fell off and clinked on the ground. A key. She bent and picked it up, turning it over in her hand.

A climbing vine had wound its way up around the old door, hiding the lock from view. She brushed it away, careful not to cut herself on the greenery, and forced the key inside the lock. Her tired muscles screamed at her as she attempted to push the door open. Finally, it gave, and she tumbled into the little chapel.

Light filtered into the small room from the skylight above and three windows on each side. She left the door behind her open and took a few steps inside.

Quiet filled the space.

Beth admired the exposed wooden beams overhead, still strong after all this time. She walked down the center aisle, rows of simple wooden benches on either side. At the front of the room, a small pulpit stood one step above the floor.

She sat on the front row and took a deep breath of silence. Somehow, in spite of it having been forgotten all these years, Beth sensed a holiness in the little chapel.

She knew only bits and pieces about Fairwind's former owners. She knew they'd lost their daughter. She knew the mother was said to have died of a broken heart. She knew the tragedy had pulled Willow Grove out of its utopian mind-set, putting everyone on high alert for too many years.

Sad how people were so willing to hurt each other.

She hadn't thought about it in years. But now, standing in the place they'd probably prayed desperate prayers, she could think of nothing else.

Beth stood and walked over to the small piano in the corner. She wished she'd learned to play. Her hands slid across the instrument, wondering how long it had been since it had made music. Whose piano had this been? What would this space sound like filled with worship?

She lifted the lid on the bench and saw a stack of sheet music, a hymnal and a little black book inside. She pulled them out, one by one, mesmerized by the history she held in her hands.

Fairwind had been owned by Harold and Sonya Pendergast, and before that, the farm had belonged to Harold's parents. They'd been the ones to turn it into a tourist destination. Harold and Sonya had carried on that tradition, working in the family business. Beth knew the pressure of that. How had Harold felt when he'd been unable to keep it going after his family died?

She'd never considered that. He had simply become a sad old man—a town fixture with a reputation that kept everyone away.

But his heart had been broken. Could any of them blame him for not being able to pick up the pieces?

She looked around, wondering how old the chapel was. She didn't know who'd owned the farm before Harold's parents—what if this building dated back to the original owners? Had they married here? Been buried here? Had they celebrated and mourned inside these four walls? Had Sonya stood in this very spot begging God to spare her daughter?

God, why didn't You spare her daughter?

Beth leafed through the hymnal, stopping to admire the lyrics of "How Great Thou Art," the melody floating through her mind. She set the hymnal down and picked up the little black book.

She opened it and quickly discovered it was some sort of journal. On the first page, someone had written an inscription:

Fill these pages with the prayers of your heart, for there is One who hears. One who listens. One who answers. If you find this book, you're welcome to use it, to capture the prayers whispered inside the chapel at Fairwind Farm.

As she carefully turned the pages, she saw each entry started with "Heavenly Father" or "Dear Lord," and not all entries were in the same handwriting.

It was more than just a journal—it was a prayer book.

She held in her hands the prayers of generations. How many people had taken the time to record their requests in this journal? How many tears had been shed over it—tears of joy and sorrow?

Beth sat on the old piano bench and started to read, feeling like she'd just entered a sacred chamber and praying she was welcome there.

Each entry had been signed and dated, and from what she could tell, the book had been left in the chapel, open for anyone who wanted to use it.

And it was well used.

Dear Lord,
How do I thank You for bringing us here? For giving us this land? For bringing us neighbors to help raise the barn? We are so blessed to have good crops and strong bodies to reap the harvest. Thank You for hearing our prayers, for sending the rain. The earth drinks in Your goodness, and so do we.
Your child,
Sarah

Beth read a few others but quickly became curious about the last entry. She flipped through the pages until she found a blank one and stared at the words on the page before. It was dated twenty years ago.

Dear Heavenly Father,

She's gone. Our little girl has been taken from us, and her case seems to have gone cold. Harold says he'll keep searching, that justice must prevail, but Lord, I know in my heart my daughter is with You. I don't know why You've allowed this to happen to us, but I will continue to praise You and believe in Your goodness and your mercy. I beg You to fill my husband with peace, as we may never know what happened to our Jessica. He is too intent on finding the truth. I'm worried about him, and I know I need to trust You. Bring us the closure we so desperately need, and if it's Your will, bring something to light so we can properly mourn the loss of our beautiful girl. Only one person can give us the answers we need, but perhaps he is too fragile to remember. Send peace to him, Lord.

I don't have the strength to carry on, not without Your help. Please be my source. I give Fairwind to You and ask that it will be what You've always wanted it to be——a place to restore families and remind people of Your goodness.

I'm sad and my heart is broken, but my life is now and always will be Yours.

Sonya

A small newspaper clipping had been stuck to the last page—an article about the missing girl, Jessica Pendergast. Beth tried to swallow the lump in her throat.

They'd been the same age, but Jessica had been homeschooled, and if it weren't for the photo in the article—a snapshot of the nine-year-old girl—Beth wouldn't have remembered what she looked like. She'd been taken from the property, but that was all Beth knew, thanks to overprotective parents who'd shielded them from the truth. She didn't know any details about what had become of her—no one did. The case had never been solved.

Now, reading Sonya's prayer, Beth wondered if anything she'd heard about the previous owners had been true.

Everyone said Mrs. Pendergast had died of a broken heart, but her words were peaceful, as if she'd accepted the outcome and reconciled her feelings with God.

Beth marveled at the idea. She'd been so heartbroken over Michael, so devastated by her own shortcomings, she'd been holding this grudge against God for years. How had Sonya Pendergast kept the anger away after the tragic loss of her only daughter? Beth had been angry at God for allowing her to fall in love with a cheater—Sonya had to have been angry at God for allowing her child to be taken from her own property, never to be seen again.

Hadn't she?

Beth's own betrayal, her heartache—they seemed so trite and pointless by comparison.

She ran a finger over Sonya's handwritten name, suddenly intrigued by the woman who might've sat in that very spot and poured out her heart to a God she trusted and loved, in spite of everything.

Beth wanted to live that way, certain of God's goodness and without a shred of doubt. She wanted all the anger and confusion to disappear, and she wanted her life to mean something. Even if she still lived in Willow Grove.

It was all she'd ever wanted. It was why she worked so tirelessly. Surely God saw the countless hours she put in to make sure she did her very best. That kind of dedication had to count for something—and yet, it never seemed to be enough. There was always more work to be done, always something else to prove—to herself, to her dad, to God.

It was like something deep down, some child trapped inside her, was asking, *Are you proud of me yet?*

But the person she'd wanted to please most had spent his final days trying to dig them out of the mess she'd made.

"I worked so hard to make sure you were always taken care of," her dad had said. "You know that, Beth. You've never done something so reckless before."

He was right. She hadn't. She'd never let him down so badly, and still, he'd never told a soul. Not even her mother.

As she sat there in the stillness of the old, holy chapel, two words echoed in the corners of her mind.

Trust Me.

And for a few welcome moments, all the stress of her situation, all the wrestling to figure out her next move, all her doubt and fear and worry and the staggering need to succeed fell away.

"It's not You I don't trust," she said. "It's myself." She was, after all, the one who'd picked the wrong man to give her heart to, the one who'd made the wrong business move. How could she ever hope to trust her gut instinct again? How could she trust that she was actually hearing God's voice when she'd been so wrong about hearing Him before?

Trust Me.

"I don't know how, Lord." The words shamed her. She should know this by now. She'd had twenty-nine years of practice. And yet, trust didn't come easily to her.

You know what to do.

Did she, though?

Her heart and head were at odds with each other.

She stilled, hands wrapped around the small black journal. There were so many emotions inside its pages—grief, gratitude, forgiveness. She could draw strength from the women who had gone before her. Even if the task of restoring Fairwind Farm seemed daunting. Even if she didn't know what she was doing. Even if she failed. Again.

Was it crazy that a part of her wanted to try?

At times, the fear was crippling—could she ever overcome that?

"Lord, I cannot fail again."

And yet, as she whispered the words aloud into the darkness, an inexplicable peace settled inside her. She had to believe that whatever decision she made, it would be okay. God wouldn't abandon her for making the "wrong" one.

Neither her head nor her heart had proven trustworthy, so what choice did she have but to follow Sonya's lead and turn all of it—every scary, overwhelming bit of it—over to God?

But as she left the little chapel, book carefully placed back inside the piano bench, Beth kept thinking the same thing: *I have no idea where to begin.*

Chapter Fourteen

Beth went to Whitaker Mowers Sunday afternoon and cleaned out her office, quietly leaving a resignation letter on Darren's desk. As she closed the door behind her for the last time, she was struck by an unexpected sense of freedom—not sadness—that she wouldn't be back.

After her time in the chapel, she felt more willing to jump into this renovation project with both feet . . . even if it wasn't the smart thing to do. Once she'd finished dinner that night, she and Molly retreated to Beth's room and ran through the "what was next" of the whole project, clarifying their roles and talking through their plans.

"How involved are you wanting me to be here? Do you want me to be a silent partner and just give you money?" Beth asked, surprised to find herself hoping that wasn't what her sister wanted.

"No way." Molly propped herself up on her elbows. "I want you to manage the whole project. You're the business mind. I'm just the looks." She sprawled out and purposely gave herself a double chin. "Ain't I purty?"

"You're insane." Beth threw a pair of socks at her sister and hit her in the face.

Molly tossed the socks back, and Beth sat down on the edge of the bed to put them on.

"I can tell you're excited about this," Molly said. "I think you're just scared."

Is it that obvious? "Scared of what?"

"Of me having a great idea."

"Don't be ridiculous."

"Fine. I'm ridiculous."

Beth sat for a few long seconds without saying anything. Molly was half-right—she was scared, but not of her sister being right about the farm. (That was more of a minor annoyance.) It was the fear of failing again that kept her up at night.

"So?"

Beth glanced at Molly, realizing her sister had just asked a question she hadn't heard. "So, what?"

"Where are you today?"

"I'm fine—I was just thinking. What did you say?"

"I asked what's next. Did you talk to Ben?"

"He said he'd only invest if we hired that guy from yesterday."

"That guy?" Molly smirked. "Like you don't know his name. "

Beth rolled her eyes and stood, ready to get outside for her nightly walk with her mom.

"I already asked him if he'd come work with us," Molly said, pushing herself to the edge of the bed.

Beth turned. "Weren't we going to consult with each other before making any decisions?"

Her sister stood. "Please. I know you're meeting him tomorrow to talk about a job. Pot, meet kettle. I think you know each other's color."

Molly walked out, leaving Beth standing alone in her childhood bedroom, wondering why her heart couldn't get on board with her head and kick this whole idea to the curb.

You should move to Chicago. You're not getting any younger. It's now or never.

The unwanted thoughts raced through her mind, but none of them seemed to stick. The only thing that did was *this could be my second chance.*

Monday morning, Beth awoke at dawn, showered, dressed and made her way to Butler's to pick up coffee and scones before heading out to the farm.

"That was something on Saturday," Callie said while she made Beth's much-needed latte. "It even made me want to be a part of your big Fairwind Farm project."

Beth felt her shoulders straighten as an idea hit her. "You should, Callie. You can run the bakery."

Callie's eyes brightened. "Really?"

"Would you ever want to do that?"

She laughed. "I've kind of been waiting for you to ask me."

"Sorry. I've been preoccupied."

"With anyone in particular?" Callie's eyes twinkled.

Beth groaned. "Not you too."

"Your sister told me you have a meeting with Drew Barlow this morning." She waggled her eyebrows.

"A meeting, Cal. Not a date."

"So this other cup of coffee—it's for him?" She held it as if it were a sacred treasure.

Beth only stared.

"Okay, then you need pastries." She shuffled around behind the counter for a few quick seconds. "Drew ate the cheese Danishes on Saturday, and I know you like my cinnamon scones."

"You noticed what kind of Danishes he ate?"

Callie shrugged. "I keep track of what people like, what can I say?"

Beth took a quick drink of her latte as Callie handed her the bag. "Thanks."

"So, it's just going to be the two of you out there, huh?" Callie grinned.

"This is strictly professional."

Callie pouted. "Well, that's boring."

"Boring is my middle name."

"True." She gave a soft sigh. "Is Ben going to help you guys out?"

Beth shrugged. "If Drew agrees, Ben said he's in. We need his money."

"What about his muscles?" Callie propped her elbow on the counter and her chin on her fist. "I could definitely use his muscles."

Beth rolled her eyes. "Why don't you say something to him already? Ask him to dinner?"

Callie groaned. "No, that would ruin the fantasy. At least this way there is still hope. If he turns me down, the sliver of hope is gone. Besides, I'm content to stare at him when he's not looking and imagine what our children would look like."

Beth covered Callie's hands with her own. "Do you think you'll ever get over him?"

"I was over him. Then I saw him Saturday."

"Did you talk to him?"

Callie frowned. "Of course not. I hid myself in the back room and stared at him from behind the safety of a cracked door."

Beth shook her head. "You don't give yourself enough credit. Ben would be crazy not to fall head over heels for you."

"Stop. I think you're forgetting who we're talking about here. Mr. Major League and the baker who still works for her parents." She glanced at Beth as if realizing she'd said something offensive. "It's not the same—you working for your dad's company. You run that place. I'm a glorified barista making lattes for cranky customers all day."

"Hey." Beth held up her cup.

"I didn't mean you. You seem surprisingly uncranky today."

"I'm not even going to ask what you mean by that. I have to go." Beth picked up her coffee and pastries and walked toward the door, guilt gnawing at her. She still hadn't told Callie the truth about her job.

How would she ever own up to it? She turned back before pushing the door open. "I'm serious about the bakery. You can work for yourself."

"Done. I'll give my notice today." She winked.

"Might want to wait a few more months before you do that."

"Have fun with your farmhand," Callie called out.

Beth glared at her and shook her head, aware that everyone in the diner had heard the remark. Her friend looked anything but apologetic.

When she reached Fairwind, her latte was half-gone and her nerves were shot, just like they'd been the first day at every new job, class or interview she'd ever had. Professional nerves were natural, though, right? It had nothing to do with the beautiful man waiting for her on the steps of the old house.

A glance at the clock told her he was early. She could appreciate that in an employee.

As she parked, he stood, and Roxie ran out to greet her. The German shepherd had a sweet way about her. Beth might even grow to like her, which was strange considering she had never been an animal person. Molly was the animal lover in their family—she'd have a houseful if her landlord would allow it. But Beth? She didn't want the hassle. Or the dog hair. Or the saliva.

Still, she rubbed Roxie between the ears when the dog reached her in the middle of the yard.

Drew wore jeans, a long-sleeved Henley and a plaid shirt with the sleeves rolled up. His tattered red ball cap sat backward on his head, and he seemed even better-looking than he had Saturday. How was that possible?

Somehow she didn't think this kind of assessment qualified as professional.

They met halfway between the parking lot and the house, and she handed him the coffee. "I didn't know if you'd have a chance to get breakfast."

He took it, then directed her attention to the porch where two Butler's coffees sat, a bag of pastries between them.

"I thought the same thing," he said.

"You brought breakfast?" It was thoughtful. So few people were thoughtful anymore.

He looked away, almost shyly. "I guess we can save some of it for lunch."

She laughed. "Great minds, right?"

"Only great if you got the best pastries." He turned toward the porch.

She fell into step beside him. "Cheese Danish."

"Oh, you're good." He sat down and took a drink. Roxie lay down in the grass at the bottom of the stairs. "Can I expect this kind of treatment every day if I take the job?"

She laughed. "Don't count on it."

A soft lull fell between them, and Beth realized it was her turn to talk—and not about pastries. A little playful banter was fine, but she needed to remember why they were there and act accordingly if she had any hope of winning this man's respect.

She'd been working for respect since the day she graduated college—and while nobody else knew about some of the poor choices she'd made, she knew. Which meant she'd been working overtime for respect the past two years. She had a lot to make up for.

She reminded herself that he didn't know any of that. He didn't even know who she was.

It's a second chance.

She pulled her portfolio from her bag and laid it on the porch between them. "Molly said you used to come here when you were a kid?"

He nodded. "Years ago. Haven't been back since, though."

"I'm not sure how much you remember." She leaned back on the porch railing, trying to figure out how to sit properly when conducting business on the wide, run-down porch of an old farmhouse.

He looked away. "Not much, I'm afraid."

She looked out across the acres. Knowing she could own a third of the farm still overwhelmed her. All that was left to do was sign the contract. This meeting might determine whether or not she did. She stood. "Maybe we should walk?"

"You're the boss."

She started off toward the barn and discovered he held back, just a few steps.

"Do you always walk this fast?"

She tossed a glance over her shoulder. "Do you always walk this slow?"

He caught up with her as they reached the barn.

"You've been in here," she said. "This is the main building, the big white barn. You probably remember this is where the store was. And the fudge counter. And the—"

"Bakery." He shoved his hands in his pockets. "I remember."

"The coolers are still here. I just don't know if they work. And of course everything needs to be cleaned."

"You want to get the store up and running right away, I'm assuming?"

Beth faced him. "I guess we do. We have a lot of ideas right now— we're still working on prioritizing them. My sister isn't exactly practical, so I have to lay out some clear guidelines."

He frowned. "Something got you worried?"

She must wear worry on her sleeve. "Look around. It all has me worried."

He nodded.

"Anyway, back here . . ." She walked toward the kitchen. "We're thinking a little bakery and restaurant." She'd been half joking with Callie about opening up her own business, but she actually thought it was a great idea. Could she get her friend to leave the comfort of working at Butler's? That remained to be seen.

Drew walked the edge of the barn, probably making a mental tally of the enormous workload in front of them.

"So, I'm thinking we'll need to talk about refinishing the floors, repairing the walls and roof, painting, getting the kitchen in shape, that sort of thing. We'll likely need new appliances, and it has to pass health-department inspection."

That sounded like she knew what she was talking about, right? Maybe this wasn't so very different from what she was used to. If she could run an office, she could do the same thing at Fairwind Farm.

Part of her wondered how long she'd need these daily pep talks.

He followed her out the back of the barn and onto the patio.

"They did a good job cleaning this Saturday," Beth said. "I want to make sure it's inviting. We want people to rent the space for family gatherings, weddings, reunions, parties."

"So, will you restore the little chapel on the west side of the property?"

Her eyes darted to him. He stared out in the direction of the church and didn't meet her gaze. "How'd you know about that?"

He shrugged. "Doesn't everybody?"

She studied him, suddenly aware of how little she knew about him and his connection to Fairwind. "I never did."

He took off in the opposite direction from the church, toward the outbuildings. "You gonna have animals?"

Was he changing the subject on purpose?

Beth groaned. "I guess. Molly wants them."

"Don't sound so excited."

"I'm not much of an animal person," she said. She glanced at Roxie. "No offense."

He looked at the dog, then at Beth. "She's tough. She can handle it." He stopped outside a small barn near the pumpkin patch, with rows and rows of apple trees behind it. "This is where the animals were, right?"

She nodded. "Petting zoo."

"Smart if you want kids to visit." He studied her. "Unless you're not much of a kid person either?"

Beth met his eyes. "I wouldn't say that."

"But you don't have any?"

For someone who didn't say much, he sure asked personal questions. "No. Do you?"

He shook his head.

"So, we'll want to repair this barn and make sure it's safe for animals. And then I guess I'll have to figure out what animals to put in a petting zoo. And where to get them. And how to take care of them."

He laughed. "Why'd you guys buy this place, anyway?"

The question took her off guard. But it was a fair one.

"You think it was a mistake?" She started past the animal barn toward two other outbuildings, neither of which she'd even been inside.

"I didn't say that," he said behind her.

"Despite what it looks like, this is a good investment." She tried not to sound defensive.

"For the right investor, sure."

"And I'm not the right one?" She turned and faced him. Only then did she realize he stood almost a foot taller than her. "You don't think I can handle this."

Calm down. Your insecurity is showing.

His eyes widened. "Not at all. I'm betting you can handle just about anything you put your mind to."

Why did that sound like an accusation when he said it?

"But?" she asked.

He shrugged, almost as if he couldn't be bothered. "You don't really seem like the farming type."

She hugged her portfolio to her chest. She'd read up on farming, orchards, what it took to restore old buildings. She'd crunched numbers and researched other businesses like Fairwind. Still, the fact was she was just as clueless as Molly, and Drew Barlow knew it. She didn't like that at all.

She could pretend to know the lingo all she wanted. That didn't make her an expert. Not yet.

"Is that right? What type do I seem like?"

He bent over and pulled a long blade of grass from the ground, then tore it into pieces as he spoke. "Bossy. Lots of money. Always in charge. You give the orders and people do what you say."

Bossy? Just because she was a leader didn't mean she was bossy. She planted her free hand on her hip.

His eyes narrowed. "But you don't understand this farm, and that's killing you."

"That's not true." She and this farm were starting to become friends—at least she and the chapel were.

"You're going to hire me to run the place, but I know more than you do, and *that's* killing you."

She turned away and started off into the trees. "You don't know what you're talking about."

"It's not a bad thing to admit you were wrong about something." He followed close on her heels.

"I can admit when I'm wrong." As she trudged through the trees, she thought about the last time she'd messed up and how she had yet to tell a single soul. By definition, she absolutely could *not* admit when she was wrong.

She moved forward, hoping eventually she'd land near one of the other barns she knew was back here somewhere. "I can admit I might have been wrong to assume you were the best person for this job."

After too many long seconds of silence, Beth realized Drew was no longer behind her. His idea of a joke, maybe? Let her get lost in the woods on her own property and force her to ask for help.

"Drew?" She stilled and listened, but all around her there were only sounds of nature. Two birds had a melodic conversation overhead. "Drew?" she called out again, but still no response.

Her heart raced as she turned back in the direction she'd just come from. All around, she searched for signs of where he might've gone, until finally, in the distance, she spotted a lonely old barn. Was this one of theirs?

If so, maybe he'd known about it and wanted to see how badly it was damaged. Leaving her alone in the woods might've just been thoughtless, though that seemed out of character for someone who'd brought her coffee and pastries.

Maybe she'd irked him enough to make him leave.

The air felt thick, like a heavy cloud had settled right over this barn and where she stood. She stared at it, heart still pounding too loud and too fast in her chest.

"Drew?" She called out again, moving around the corner of the building, where she found the doors open and Drew inside with his back to her. He stood, unmoving, at the center of the hollow space—a small, dilapidated barn with a rickety ladder leading up to what she could only assume was a very unsafe loft.

He was like a statue where he stood, and she wasn't sure if she should interrupt him.

"Drew?" She kept her voice quiet.

He turned, and for a brief moment, he looked like he didn't remember who she was, as if he'd been immersed in some other world.

"Are you okay?"

He looked away, still seeming lost in a distant fog.

"I guess this is one of ours too, huh?" She met him in the center of the space. "I don't know that this will be very high on the priority list, though. Doesn't seem like one we would need right away, does it?"

He shook his head, but said nothing.

"I wonder what they used this one for. Horses, it looks like."

135

Still, he didn't respond.

Unlike the other buildings, this one appeared to have been cleaned out, at least partially. Maybe one of the workers had stumbled in here Saturday and swept.

"Drew?"

Finally, he met her eyes, and she saw something behind them she didn't recognize. "Sorry," he said, then turned and walked out.

Back on the path, it was she who wondered why he was walking so fast. She struggled to keep up with him as he strode back toward the main barn, Roxie at his side.

When they reached the yard, Beth finally caught up with him—or he finally let her. "Is everything okay?"

"It's a lot of work," he said, avoiding her question as he trudged on toward his truck.

"Too much work?" She watched him, wondering why he'd gone from cocky and teasing to awkward and withdrawn in a matter of seconds. Maybe he didn't want the job after all.

"I'll have a detailed plan including an estimated budget by morning," he said, still avoiding her eyes.

"That would be good. Should we discuss payment?"

"I'm fine with whatever you decide."

Independently wealthy? He didn't dress it or drive it. "You sure about that?"

He nodded. "If we're done, I'd like to get started."

She hadn't expected that. What was he going to do out there by himself?

He waited several seconds, and when she didn't respond, he went around her and pulled tools from the back of his truck. He started off in the opposite direction, but stopped—abruptly—and faced her. "One more thing."

She looked at him, holding the gaze she'd been working so hard for, until he eventually broke eye contact.

"What are your plans for the house?"

Beth glanced beyond where Drew stood to the old farmhouse that had fallen into the same disrepair as the rest of the farm. Inside, it looked like it had been frozen in time, but it wasn't as bad as it could've been. She assumed Harold had maintained the house at least a little longer than he had the barns, but it still needed some major updates and a few repairs.

"What do you mean?"

He squinted in the sunlight behind her, then turned his hat around to shield his eyes. "You can pay me a lot less if you let me stay here in the house. I'll work on it in my free time, get it back in shape. Unless you planned to move in right away."

"I don't plan to move in at all."

"Ever?"

She hadn't even considered moving in. Would Molly want the house? Someone should live there if they owned it.

"I'm not sure."

"Well, let me know. The hotel guests don't like Roxie, so the owner said I need to make other arrangements." Roxie perked up at the mention of her name.

"By when?"

He glanced at his truck in the driveway. "Tonight."

Beth laughed. "I don't think you're going to want to stay here tonight. We haven't even cleared out the old man's things."

He shrugged. "I've stayed in worse."

Something about this felt horribly wrong, yet before he walked away, she heard herself tell Drew Barlow to go ahead and move his things into the house at Fairwind Farm.

Chapter Fifteen

Drew practically ran away from Beth, away from the house, away from the past. He'd seen the old barn in his dreams the night before. He could *smell* it, and when he'd woken that morning, a torrent of anger flooded his mind. Why couldn't he remember? What couldn't he see?

He'd spent hours sweeping and cleaning it out Saturday, and it had done nothing to stir the old memories. Today, walking through the woods, the barn seemed to call his name, begging him to come in for one more try.

Foolishly, he thought the past would give him the answers he'd been waiting for. But as he stood there, begging for the truth, his mind was blank.

Too much time had passed.

He'd felt like an idiot for trying. Why did he think he would ever find closure? In that moment, he'd considered leaving. He could get in his truck and drive back to Colorado. It would be like he'd never even come.

But something had gotten ahold of him—something wouldn't let him leave.

So, he took the job. If he had any hope of finding out the truth, he had to stay at Fairwind, and taking this new job gave him unlimited access to the farm—and the house—no matter how haunting.

Besides, he needed work if he wanted to calm his mind.

He'd called Elkhorn the night before to tell them he'd be gone a little longer than he'd thought. As expected, his boss wasn't happy, but Drew needed answers.

Jess deserved that.

He only hoped he could give her some.

Now, standing behind the main barn with his tools spread out on a picnic table in front of him, he forced his weary heart to stop racing.

"There you are!"

He spun around to see Molly walking toward him with a grin as wide as a jack-o'-lantern's.

"Heard you took the job."

Roxie ran to her, and she welcomed the dog with excited pats and a good, long ear rub. It struck him how different these two sisters were. Molly was open and welcoming. Beth was closed off and mysterious. He had a feeling that wasn't where their differences ended.

His pulse had returned to its normal rate—thankfully. "You heard right, I guess."

"Beth said you're going to put together a list for us?"

"That's the plan."

She stood in front of him now, squinting up at him in the morning sun. "She also said you're acting weird and wants me to make sure you're not a lunatic." Molly tilted her head and sized him up. "So, are you?"

Drew stared at her. "Am I what?"

"A lunatic?"

"I don't think so." Though his actions not long ago suggested otherwise. He'd frozen. Panicked. He didn't know how to manage the onslaught of emotions he'd been burying for twenty years.

"Good." Molly pulled her messy brown hair into a ponytail. "Now that we've got that out of the way, I have to show you something. I haven't shown Beth yet because she's going to kill me, but wait till you see." She walked around the east side of the building, putting the barn between them and the house and shielding them from her sister's sight.

They rounded the corner, and Drew couldn't help but notice the pride on her face.

"It's a sheep," Drew said.

"Her name's Bluebell. Blue for short."

The black sheep had been tied to an old pipe near the edge of the barn. She looked up, seemingly confused by her new living arrangements.

Drew ran a hand over his chin, made a mental note to shave at some point this week. "You bought a sheep?"

"Someone was giving her away. Do you believe it? Who would want to give away a cute little sheep?"

Drew watched as Molly approached the sheep as if she were a dog. Blue let out a disconcerted baa and hobbled away from her.

"What exactly are your plans for Bluebell?"

"Put her in the barn. Feed her. Let kids pet her when we open." Molly took another step toward the sheep, but Blue scurried away. "She's kind of shy."

"And your sister doesn't know about this?"

Molly shielded her eyes from the sun and stared at him. "We need to get something straight, Cowboy. If you're going to work here, we need to form an alliance."

"That right?"

"Beth has a reputation around here."

"Oh?"

"Not *that* kind of reputation. She's notoriously *not fun*." She said the words as if they left a sour taste in her mouth. "Going into business with her is smart, but if we want to have fun, there are going to be some things she can't know about."

He snapped his fingers at Roxie so she'd stop sniffing the sheep. "Pretty sure she's going to find out about this one."

"Right, but if we present a unified front, she won't be able to say anything about it." Molly pulled the bill of his hat down lower. "I'm counting on you."

Drew held his hands up in front of him. "I'm just the employee around here. I can't get in the middle of your family stuff."

Molly cocked one hip out and crossed her arms over her midsection. "You're not just the employee. You're the guy who understands how all this stuff works. If you say Blue gets to stay, then she gets to stay."

"And who takes care of her?"

Molly's eyes darted away. "We'll take turns."

"Uh-huh. Maybe we should go get your sister."

Molly turned away, startling the sheep, who hurried off in the opposite direction with enough force to pull her loosely tied leash from the pipe, sending her running off into the parking lot with Molly close behind.

Drew walked toward the lot and watched as Beth spotted her sister. Molly was now flailing her arms in an effort to capture the poor animal. Blue turned in circles, doing her best to keep away from Molly's grasp.

"What is that?" Beth ran toward them, face flushed and fire in her eyes. "Molly! Why is there a sheep out here?"

Molly continued chasing Blue, hollering at Beth to shut up and help her.

At Drew's feet, Roxie whined and inched forward, seemingly anxious to get in the middle of the ruckus, but he didn't release her. He was having too much fun watching the two women run in circles around the overgrown sheep. Each time one of them would get close, they'd pull back, unsure how to best wrangle the poor animal, who had to be terrified by all the commotion.

Finally, and only for the sake of poor, innocent Bluebell, Drew released Roxie. The dog ran out to the sheep and corralled her back toward Drew. He picked up the lead around her neck and led her back to the pipe, this time tying the rope tight enough so she couldn't escape. Roxie barked until Drew thanked her.

He turned, looked at both disheveled Whitaker sisters, called for Roxie and walked away.

Something told him this job was going to be quite the adventure.

Chapter Sixteen

"A sheep, Molly?" Beth stormed toward the farmhouse and followed Molly inside. "What were you thinking?"

"I was thinking this is a farm. It needs animals." Molly leaned against the kitchen counter. She ignored the piles of dishes behind her, which Beth had pulled out of the cupboards for damage assessment.

"We agreed we weren't going to make any decisions without consulting each other," Beth said. "That's the only way this can work." She pulled her yellow dish gloves back on and knelt down in front of the fridge.

Molly sighed. "I got a really good deal on her. I couldn't pass it up."

"How do you know what constitutes a 'good deal' on a sheep?" Beth took her frustration out on a nasty stain in the bottom drawer of the refrigerator. She'd moved her cleaning efforts indoors when she realized she didn't have the muscle strength to do any good outside.

"She was free. I'd say that's a pretty good deal."

"What are we going to do with a sheep?"

Molly reached into the Butler's bag on the table and pulled out half a scone. "Breed her? Get more sheep? Petting zoos always have sheep."

Beth sprayed the inside of the fridge with Clorox and starting scrubbing.

"There's a man a few miles away with a horse too. And I was thinking we should get a dog. I like that Roxie so much."

"Molly!" Beth threw her sponge into the fridge and stood.

"What?" Molly's eyes were wide, her mouth full of scone.

"We have to get the farm repaired. That's our first goal. We can't start boarding stray farm animals when we don't have anywhere to put them."

"You don't think Blue will be okay in that barn? Drew can whip it into shape today."

Beth frowned. "We have a prioritized list. That means there's an order to things. The petting zoo is not at the top of the list."

Molly swallowed her stolen pastry. "Maybe it should be."

Beth shut the refrigerator and sighed. "I don't think you have any idea what we're up against here. There is so much work to be done, and we really don't have the money for it."

"What about Ben?"

"What about him?"

"You said we have no money. With him on board, we have more than we had yesterday."

"Nothing is certain yet, you know that," Beth said. "I left Ben a message this morning when Drew took the job, but even if he invests the same amount as us, we're still going to come up short."

"Do you know that, or are you just being your usual negative self?" She took another bite.

"I've been doing some figuring." Beth opened her portfolio. She'd been "doing some figuring" for days now. Drew would bring her his list of repairs, but Beth had already started one of her own. She'd contacted a few local businesses to get rough estimates, and after her walk around the property with Drew this morning, she'd added a few more things she hadn't thought of before.

This way, when he brought her his proposed budget, she'd know if he was doing his best to save them money. That had been important to her dad, and it was important to her.

"You can learn a lot about a person by how he spends someone else's money," he'd told her.

What did the way she'd spent her father's money say about her?

Molly stared at the figures Beth had scrawled on her legal pad. "You really think it's going to cost this much?"

"No, I think it's going to cost more. These are very rough estimates."

Molly sat down in the rickety chair at the end of the kitchen table, a defeated look on her face. "I don't have any more money."

"Well, don't freak out yet. I've got my share plus whatever Ben invests."

"What about Mom?"

Beth blew a stray hair out of her eye. "No. We talked about this. We're not getting Mom involved."

"Beth, she's got money."

Ben and Beth had both agreed. Mom's money was hers. They had to respect that. "No, Molly. Let's leave Mom out of this."

"What about Dad's business?"

Beth frowned. "What about it?"

"Is there any money there? Dad was always investing and making tons more than he put in."

Beth's fingers went cold. Whitaker had barely bounced back from her mistake. "I think that's a dead end."

"Why? It's our family's company. If there's money just sitting there, shouldn't we get it?"

"There's not money just sitting there, Molly. It doesn't work that way." *Thanks to me.*

"Fine. It was just an idea." Molly finished the last of Beth's scone. "So we can't ask Mom. The business doesn't have anything. What other choice do we have?"

Beth had been racking her own brain with the same question, though she didn't like to think about it. She had her trust, but that was like her security blanket. She never touched it. But with her savings spent on the purchase of the farm and still not built back up to where they were before she'd tried to bail the company out of the mess she'd made, she would have to get into it. Otherwise, she didn't have her share of the money at all.

But she wouldn't tell Molly that.

"Let me talk to Ben. And after Drew gives me his list, I'll have a better idea. I think we prioritize and do what we can, then worry about raising the rest of the money."

"There was someone else interested in the property," Molly said. "A real estate investor or something."

"What do you mean?"

"Last week, a couple of days after the auction, this really tall guy I'd never seen before came up to me and handed me a business card. He said to call the number when I realized I was in over my head—his employer would take the place off my hands. Made me kind of mad, actually. I told him I was doing just fine, *thank you very much*, and tried to hand him his card back."

"And?"

"He said, 'Keep it just in case.'" She did her best impersonation of a cranky man.

"You're just mentioning this now?"

"I didn't want to tell you. I was afraid you'd call the guy and sell the place out from under me."

"I probably would've."

"And see all the fun you would've missed out on."

"Are you kidding? I would still be sheepless."

"Exactly my point." Molly grinned.

"Who was this guy?"

"No idea. After he gave me the card, he walked over to a black Cadillac and talked to someone sitting in the back seat. The tall one glanced back at me, said something else to the mystery man, got in the car and drove away."

"Did you see the guy in the car?"

"Just for a second as he rolled up the window."

"What was his name?"

"Davis something. Davis Biddle?"

Beth jotted the name on her legal pad. She'd have to look him up when she got home.

"That doesn't make any sense. If he wanted to buy Fairwind, why didn't he just come to the auction? He could've bid one dollar more than you and been the new owner."

"He was vacationing in the Caribbean. That was the other thing the tall guy said." Again, she put on a male voice, only this time, she sounded snooty: "'My employer would've bought the place himself if he'd known about the auction, but he was vacationing in the Caribbean.'"

"Was he British?"

Molly looked confused. "No, why?"

"Your impression of him sounded like a cheeky British guy."

"Funny. Maybe he'd invest? Another silent partner—like Ben."

Beth didn't like the idea. Ben was their brother. This guy would come in and tell them what to do and how to do it. And even if that was exactly what they needed, she didn't want a boss right now. "I don't know, it all seems a little strange to me."

Molly shrugged. "Yeah, and a little creepy. Not the right kind of person to buy Fairwind—even if he could probably bankroll the whole thing."

A silence fell between them.

"It's too bad Seth's not around," Molly said.

"I'm sure his money is long gone," Beth said. Their youngest brother had cashed out his trust the day he turned twenty-one, and they'd hardly seen him since. He'd breezed in for Dad's funeral, acting unfazed as usual, and the next day he was gone.

None of them even knew if Seth was in the country right now.

Molly sighed. "I really wanted this place to be ours. A family affair." She sat up straighter and looked around the kitchen, which, Beth had to admit, looked a lot worse than when she'd first started cleaning. "What are you doing in here anyway?"

Beth went back to the refrigerator. "I'm cleaning."

"But there's so much to do outside. Isn't that the priority?" she mocked.

Beth scrubbed at the stains on the fridge's shelf. "It all needs to be done."

"But no one lives here. Can't the house wait?" Molly balled up the empty Butler's bag and tossed it in the garbage can. "Beth?"

"Mm-hmm." If Beth put her head any farther into the refrigerator, she'd freeze her nose hairs.

"What aren't you telling me?"

The side door opened, and Drew walked in. At the sound of him, Beth startled, knocking her head against the shelf. When she finally extricated herself from the appliance, she could already feel a knot forming. "Hey."

Very cool. Very nonchalant.

Drew's eyes darted from Beth to Molly and back again. "You don't have to do this."

"It's a mess." And so was she.

Molly cocked her head to one side, a playful smile spreading across her face. Beth pretended not to notice but prayed that for once her sister chose not to embarrass her. "If I'm going to stay here, I can clean it up." He turned on the water faucet and filled up his water bottle. "And how many guys do you think we can hire to help me outside?"

Beth left the refrigerator open and moved away from it. She sprayed the only small patch of counter that wasn't covered with dishes, and scrubbed, aware that Molly's playful smile had vanished. In its place a death glare now lasered in on the back of Beth's head.

Drew turned the water off and turned around, suddenly looking caught.

"What's he talking about?" Molly asked.

"Did I say something wrong?"

"It's not your fault, Drew. Beth has a policy about us not making decisions without consulting each other first." Molly said this in her throw-it-back-in-your-face tone.

"He needed a place to stay," Beth said, finally facing her.

"And you didn't think you might want to *consult* me about that first?" Molly had dug her heels in. Beth wouldn't be able to say anything to appease her. "Do you see what a ridiculous double standard this is? You haven't even officially signed any papers. You're not even an owner yet."

Again, Beth closed the refrigerator, still wearing her yellow dish gloves, which carried the faint smell of bleach and dirty sponge. "I know, Mol, I . . ."

What could she say? She hadn't even considered consulting Molly first, but it made good business sense to pay Drew less and allow him to live in their unoccupied house.

"I bring a harmless *sheep* to live here and you fly off the handle. You bring a *man* to live in *my* house and I'm supposed to act like it's no big deal? What if I wanted to move in here?"

"Do you?"

"Of course not, but what if I did?"

Molly wasn't going to let her off the hook. She had a point to make, and she would make it. And it really irritated Beth to know she owed her sister an apology.

"He's staying here as a trade for work," Beth said. "It was a smart business decision."

"So is collecting animals for our petting zoo, Beth. Especially when they're free."

Beth peeled off the gloves and tossed them in the sink. "I'm not going to talk to you until you calm down."

Molly turned to face her. "You know I'm right. You did the exact same thing I did. You made a decision without talking to me, only your decision is a whole lot riskier than mine. A sheep isn't going to set fire to our farm. Or slit our throats when we aren't looking."

They both looked at Drew, who stood wide-eyed, like the collateral damage he was.

"I don't really think those things about you. I'm just making a point," Molly told him. He nodded. "Good to know."

"What do you want me to say?"

Molly narrowed her gaze, locked tight on her sister. She raised one eyebrow in a challenge. A challenge Beth recognized instantly. "You know what you need to say."

Beth crossed her arms over her chest. "We're really going to do this now?"

Molly's only reply was to cross her arms over her own chest and stare Beth down.

"I think I'll excuse myself," Drew said.

"No, stay," the sisters said in unison, neither of them looking away.

He froze. "I can find another place to sleep."

Molly's eyebrow popped upward ever so slightly. "Well, that's up to Beth."

Beth didn't know when this ridiculous game had started. Maybe it was right after Molly'd had the brilliant idea to let her hamster "sleep" in her underwear drawer. Or maybe it was after she'd dropped out of college, throwing a full year of work—not to mention money—straight down the toilet.

Somewhere along the way, Molly had begun taking great pleasure in pointing out every single time Beth was wrong—payback, of sorts, for all the times Beth had pointed out one of Molly's blunders. The difference was, Beth wasn't trying to be mean or condescending. She was trying to be helpful. What was she supposed to do? Let Molly carry on as if nothing was wrong?

If Beth hadn't intervened, who knew where her sister would be right now?

That didn't change her current situation, however. Beth saw that familiar twinkle in Molly's eye. Right now, there was only one thing her sister wanted from her—and she wasn't going to stop until she got it.

There were three little words that would make this all go away. Three words that had Beth wishing this standoff hadn't happened in front of the handsome stranger from Colorado.

For the sake of the farm, Beth pressed her lips together and took a deep breath. "I . . ."

Molly leaned a little closer. "Yes?"

"I was wrong." In her periphery, she saw Drew's eyebrows shoot up in surprise. A contented look settled on Molly's face.

"Can you say it one more time, please? I didn't quite hear you."

"Don't push it, Molly."

"It's just music to my ears. I mean, it's not often I'm the smart one around here."

"That's a fact," Beth said.

"Does this mean I can stay?" Drew asked.

"Of course, Cowboy," Molly said, her false anger dissipating. "I just wanted Beth to admit it out loud. Very hard words for her to say."

"When are you going to grow up?" Beth threw a dish towel onto the counter, genuine anger building inside her. Sure, Molly may have been half kidding with her, but Beth didn't like feeling stupid, especially not in front of her employees. As she opened the back door, she heard Molly say to Drew, "I told you we have to stick together."

The screen door slammed behind her, and Beth picked up her pace, her mind spinning. They wouldn't have enough money to complete the repairs on the farm. They didn't have enough help to get any substantial work done. And now they had a sheep and a boarder with a big German shepherd.

The words *I was wrong* had never echoed so truly in her life.

Chapter Seventeen

Drew's first night sleeping in the farmhouse was restless and strange. His mind played tricks on him in the darkness, and the house creaked in the wind. In the morning, he'd given his chore list to Beth and went outside to work while she looked it over.

She'd brought coffee and pastries again, and he thanked her, unsure how to process her kindness.

He'd started the week expecting Fairwind to yank away every brick he'd carefully built around his heart, but as the days wore on, something unexpected happened.

Yes, the nightmares still plagued his sleepless nights, and yes, he spent too much time trying to force the memories he'd worked for years to forget, but his days weren't spent in quiet solitude the way they usually were.

At Elkhorn, he'd been pretty much left alone, with the occasional interaction with guests or other ranch hands. Here, though, there were always people around. Molly, Beth, their friends.

By the end of the week, he knew all their names. They drank coffee and ate scones before spending their days or evenings tackling the chores he'd listed out and prioritized. At night after he finished working, despite his sore muscles, he walked the perimeter of Fairwind with

Roxie, surprised to find an unexpected peace strolling through the rows and rows of trees in the orchard.

Now a full week had passed, and while he'd originally been driven by an aching need for closure, he'd found a different purpose in the work he was doing. For the first time in his life, he felt like he was a part of something—he hadn't even realized that was something he wanted.

Tonight, before he started his walk out toward the orchard, he admired the work they'd accomplished on the main barn. Both he and Beth agreed it was the top priority, and after just a week of volunteer labor, they could see marked improvements.

Maybe they had a shot at making that open-by-fall deadline the Whitaker sisters had given him after all.

He whistled for Roxie, who fell into step beside him, and started walking toward the orchard by way of the woods behind the house.

Once upon a time, the creek that ran through the property had been a great little fishing hole for two adventurous kids, and while that memory would've upset him only weeks before, he'd begun to make peace with the place that had stolen his friend.

The weight of his burden hadn't lifted, but he'd still found a way to enjoy his new surroundings—despite the fact that if he stayed even one more week, he'd likely be replaced at Elkhorn Ranch.

Maybe that was okay.

Maybe it was worth it to see the progress he made in bringing the old farm back to life. Maybe that was the way to make amends with his past. Do good in the present.

Or maybe he simply liked the view.

He turned back and allowed himself a few stolen seconds, watching as Beth swept the wraparound porch of the old farmhouse. She wore a pair of khaki shorts and a bright-pink tank top with flip-flops, of all things. The woman baffled him. Too sure of herself in unfamiliar surroundings, she was full of business sense but just naïve enough to have no idea just how much work was still ahead of them.

They'd talked over the numbers. She had her own estimates, proving she didn't quite trust him yet—but when she'd seen his figures were lower than hers, she seemed grateful.

"That's really good," she'd said to him the previous afternoon. "Sounds like you've got it figured out."

"That's what you hired me for." He'd leaned back in the chair at the kitchen table and watched as she shuffled through the papers spread out in front of her. There was a heaviness on her.

"Why are you doing this, really?" he'd asked.

She'd met his eyes, surprise on her face.

"I mean, you seem especially driven." He could tell she was passionate about the whole project, but he wasn't sure what it was that drove her.

"I just don't want to lose a bunch of money, that's all."

He didn't buy it. Maybe one of these days he'd earn her trust, and he'd learn what it was that really made her tick.

Guilt poked at him. What would she think if she knew his real reasons for being there? He'd kept his identity, his connection to the farm a secret. It was a harmless secret, and it was his, but would she see it as some sort of betrayal?

He shook away the nagging thoughts. She hadn't exactly opened up to him; why should he feel guilty for keeping a few awful things to himself?

He focused on the list of things left to do, which played on a continuous loop in his mind. So far, he'd repaired broken boards, reinforced the beams, refinished the floors and put a fresh coat of paint on the interior of the main barn. He'd tackle the exterior with hired help next week. Ben had sent over a landscaping plan, and when it was time to add plants, Drew knew that old barn would look better than it ever had.

He'd make sure of it.

Somehow he felt like he owed it to Harold.

Or maybe to Beth. Which was crazy because he didn't owe her anything. Except that she'd given him this job—a job that allowed him to keep searching for the thing that had brought him here in the first place. A job that provided the distraction he needed to keep his mind from going to a dark place.

Maybe he did owe her.

He made his way up a hill surrounded by trees and saw the little chapel in the clearing. It seemed magically illuminated by a ray of sunlight shining through two clouds overhead. Roxie ran in front of him, leaving Drew alone with the tiny church, a place where he and Jess were never allowed to play.

"Why do you have a church in your yard?" he'd asked her after a rousing game of hide-and-seek.

"It was built before the house," she answered. "I'm going to get married there someday."

She lay down in the lush grass and stared at the sky overhead.

"Why would you want to do that?" Drew asked, sitting down beside her.

She picked a dandelion. "Because my mom did." She handed him the weed in flower's clothing. "You can be my husband, if you want."

He took the dandelion with a shrug. "I guess so."

She sat up then, put her face right in front of his. "Really?"

"Sure. It's not like you're a real girl anyway."

She gave him a shove. "That's not a very nice thing to say."

"I meant it as a nice thing. Girls are boring." He popped the head off the flower, and she laughed.

"That's true." She plopped back down, hands under her head. "I'm glad you don't think I'm boring."

He lay down next to her, and they stared up at the clouds. "I think you're awesome."

They'd spent that afternoon finding shapes in the clouds until their parents called them in to eat.

Now, the air was filled with the smell of lilacs from the bushes all along the side of the chapel. She would've been married there. Someone would've loved her till death did them part.

But she'd never gotten the chance.

Was he to blame? Could he have stopped what happened to her? If he'd hidden in a different spot that day, would Jess still be alive? Would her parents have lived full, happy lives?

His pulse quickened at the thought, and he started off in the opposite direction from the chapel.

Beth had given him a clear deadline. He hadn't told her he'd be leaving as soon as he got what he needed from this place. He also hadn't told her there was a chance they wouldn't get the farm up and running by late August and she might have to wait another season before they could open at all.

Instead, he kept his head down and checked things off the list.

She showed her gratitude with home-cooked meals and morning coffee deliveries. And the absence of questions, which he appreciated more than any wage.

He walked along the back of the property, forcing himself not to linger at the abandoned barn, willing away unwanted emotions, the same ones that still woke him every night.

Regret. Shame. Sorrow.

He'd never been allowed to grieve. Not really. There had been too much commotion. Too many questions. An ambulance had rushed him off to the ER, where his scalp was treated with four stitches where he'd been struck from behind. Before they'd even finished stitching him up, a detective pulled a stool up next to him and started with the questions.

They came at him fast, making it impossible to remember what had really happened.

He'd been struck. He heard a scream. Jess. He blacked out. He woke to the panicked voices of his and Jess's parents, begging for answers, but none came.

His dream told him there was more, but his mind never uncovered the foggy, faded details, and he vowed not to talk about it out loud. Ever.

The doctors tried to get him to open up. He sat on their couches staring at the wall until the hour was up. One by one, the therapists told his parents that his subconscious had buried it to protect him, and when he developed signs of post-traumatic stress, they stopped prodding him. Finally, his parents left him alone.

He'd been alone ever since.

Up ahead on the east side of the property was one more outbuilding. As far as they knew, it had been used only for storage, so clearing it out didn't even make his list. Only now as he walked toward it did he realize there might be things of use inside.

He whistled for Roxie, and she met him on a path that took him off to the left toward the barn. But before he cleared the trees, the sound of someone singing halted his steps.

"Rox," he hissed. The dog circled around, then sat at attention.

He stilled, listening closely, wondering if he'd imagined it. Great. Now he was losing what was left of his mind.

But after a few seconds, a woman's voice rang out, cutting through the silence of the woods at dusk.

He glanced at Roxie as if the dog could tell him how to proceed.

He took a few steps closer and realized the voice came from inside the outbuilding—a barn where Harold had stored his tractors. Smaller riding mowers were kept in a shed near the house—he knew because he'd had to stop work to show Molly how to mow the lawn. Twice.

The voice seemed to come from the second story. He glanced up at the windows lining the top of the structure. What would someone be doing out here in this old building?

For a split second, a wave of fear washed over him. But he quickly reminded himself that no woman, no matter how off-key, could really do him any harm.

Unless she, say, knocked him on the back of the head with a shovel.

He quietly pulled open the door, took a garden rake off a nearby hook and motioned for Roxie to stay close.

As he looked over the open space in front of him, a memory flashed in his mind. He'd been here before. He couldn't wrap his mind around when or why, but as he inhaled the musty stench of dirt, familiarity washed over him.

The barn door opened directly underneath the second-floor loft, which covered only the right side of the structure. Dust particles danced on the waning light that filtered in through the windows, crisp and clear to match the outdoors.

The singing started up again. He startled, then inched to the left, hoping to catch a glimpse of whoever was up there before whoever was up there caught a glimpse of him.

As he inched into the room, eyes scanning the loft above, he saw easels and artwork lining the ledge built around the loft space. The smell of bubblegum flooded his senses, and he closed his eyes for a long moment, trying to place the whirl of memories that assaulted his mind.

Nothing.

He dared a step farther into the barn, the only way to get a better look above. A wooden staircase jutted out in front of him, and he leaned in closer.

With one foot on the bottom step, he drew in a breath, preparing to intrude on whoever was up there, but before he could make a move, a woman's face appeared at the top of the stairs.

"Hey!" she yelled as Roxie started barking. The chaos and surprise of the entire scene sent Drew backward, where he landed on the ground with a thud.

"Who are you?" the old woman shouted. She bounded down the stairs and stood above him, her frizzy red hair springing out in all directions. She wore a long robe of a dress. Strands of beads were piled around her neck, clanking together as she swung a long plank of wood around her head, agitating Roxie, who would attack if Drew gave her permission.

He wouldn't.

"Roxie," he said. The dog let out one more bark as if she couldn't help herself and then stood, unhappily waiting for Drew to release her.

"Answer me," the woman said.

"I work here." He pushed himself to his feet, ignoring the pain that shot down his backside. "I think a better question is: Who are you?"

The woman's jaw went slack, and she gripped the wood plank a little tighter.

He grabbed the end of it. "Can you put this down?"

Her shoulders slumped as she sighed, allowing him to remove the plank from her clutches.

"Fine. You caught me. Call the cops." She turned and walked back up the stairs, leaving him staring at Roxie, unsure what to do next.

"I can start packing now, I guess," she called down.

He started up the stairs, cautiously. For all he knew, she was waiting above, ready to smack him on the head with another wood plank. He inched in carefully.

As the loft came into view, he saw a makeshift art studio filled with paints, canvases, paintbrushes and a wall of finished artwork. Drew was no art lover, but judging by what he saw in front of him, the old lady wasn't half bad.

She stood at a desk, filling an oversized bag with paint supplies from the drawers.

"What are you doing?"

"I knew it was just a matter of time until someone found me out here," she said, her voice rough and low, like she'd smoked a lot of cigarettes in her day. "I've been waiting for you to come and kick me out."

Drew stood awkwardly in the center of her space. "Back up. Why don't you tell me who you are?"

162

Her head tilted to the side as she sized him up. "I'm sure you've heard the stories. What are they saying about me these days?"

He shrugged. "I'm not from here."

"Oh. Well, there are plenty of stories. The government has a whole file on me." She rushed over to him, invading his personal space, wagging a finger in front of his nose. "Don't believe any of those lies they feed us on the television. We're supposed to keep buying into whatever they're selling. I've got a bomb shelter at my house, filled with supplies. When it all breaks loose, you come find me."

He could only stare.

She stuck out a bony hand with three rings on it. He looked at it.

"People your age don't shake hands anymore when they meet someone new?"

"Oh." He took a step back and shook her hand, surprised by her firm grip.

"I'm Birdie."

"Drew."

"Good to meet you." She let go of his hand and grabbed a little jar off her desk. "Bubblegum?"

As she took off the lid, the smell of Bazooka Joe wafted up, and the flash in his mind reappeared. Had he met her before?

"Go ahead. It's not sugar-free, but one piece won't kill ya."

He pulled himself together. "Thanks, I'm fine."

She shrugged. "Suit yourself."

"How long have you been using this space?" A loaded question, given his ulterior motives, but as an employee of Fairwind, he considered it fair.

She waved her hand in a circle near her head. "I lost count. Twenty-five years?" She took a step closer, squinting at him. "What'd you say your name was?"

"Drew."

"Hmm." She gave him a once-over, as if she was trying to make up her mind about him. "You say you're not from here."

"No, ma'am. I'm working on the farm."

She locked her eyes onto him like a missile onto a target. "I know. I've seen you from the windows. You never stop working, do ya?"

He looked away from her too-curious eyes. "There's a lot to do."

"Oh, it's more than that. You only work as hard as you do if you're trying to avoid something. There's pain on your face—I can see it plain as day. Same as that blond girl who's always around. She never slows down either. But the brunette one? The one with the sheep. She seems like a riot."

Well, she had them all pegged.

She walked back to her easel and picked up a brush. On the canvas, she'd painted two oversized flowers. Turquoise, orange and red, with accents of yellow. Gaudy colors, but they suited her. "Can't figure out why kids your age refuse to sit still. What is it you're running from?"

He didn't like where this was headed. "Why don't you tell me what kind of arrangement you worked out with the previous owner?" *And what else have you seen from the windows of your loft?*

She propped a pair of reading glasses on her face. "What do you want to know?"

"Do you have anything in writing?"

She cackled. "Don't be ridiculous. Harold, Sonya and I were practically family. Sonya had big dreams for this old barn. This one was hers. She wanted to turn it into an art barn, a place that brought people together to create. They asked me to help."

Had Sonya been an artist? He wouldn't have noticed back then, but maybe some of the pieces hanging in the farmhouse were hers.

"So what happened?"

Birdie stilled. "Life happened."

"But you stayed—all this time?"

She came alive again. "Look at the light in this place. I knew I'd hit the jackpot. Plus, painting here got me away from my husband, and that was a very good thing."

Drew laughed.

"What'd you say your name was again?"

Third time's the charm. "Drew."

"You remind me of a little boy I knew once. Used to give him bubblegum too." Their eyes met, and he quickly looked away.

"I assume you're not paying rent?" He walked to the other end of the loft, anxious to put some distance between them before the woman pieced together who he was—and yet, after two decades, how could she?

"He had a little scar on his chin."

Drew resisted the urge to touch his chin. A fall off his bike had left a permanent mark on his face, barely noticeable anymore but still there if someone looked hard enough.

He was thankful he hadn't shaved that morning.

But when he turned and found her standing inches away, staring at him, he wondered if the scar was more visible than he'd thought.

"I didn't expect you to ever come back here."

He put on a confused face. "I don't know what you're talking about. I've only been here a week."

"Mm-hmm."

She wasn't buying it. Why would she, when he'd done such a rotten job selling it? "The rent?"

"No rent." She turned back toward her easel, giving him a split second to catch his breath. "Why'd you wait till Harold passed to come back?" She poked her brush into a blob of yellow paint and dotted it onto the canvas at the center of her weird-looking flowers.

"Sorry, lady, I think you have me confused with someone else."

"I never forget a pair of eyes. Or a scar." She raised an eyebrow as she looked at him. "Don't worry, kid, your secret's safe with me."

He eyed her for a long moment, wishing he didn't have a secret at all. Why hadn't he just told Beth and Molly the truth about who he was?

Because he didn't want the questions. He didn't want the pitying or judgmental looks. He didn't want to be reminded he hadn't done right by Jess. And now he looked like someone with something to hide.

Because he was.

But Birdie knew the truth. She'd made him, so what was the point in trying to lie to her?

He sat on the odd-shaped sofa in the corner, sinking down farther than he wanted to and wishing he'd never strolled into the barn in the first place. "I don't remember you."

A satisfied smile graced her lips, and she returned to her artwork. "I knew it was you. Something about the way you walk around here. I've seen you every night. Got a clear view of the old barn where she went missing. You go in. You stay a while. You come out."

"Observant."

"I am now. Wish I had been that day."

Me too. He watched her poke dots of paint onto her canvas haphazardly, like a child in art class.

"They said you were the key to finding whoever it was that did this. They said you saw the guy." Birdie plopped the paintbrush into a mason jar of cloudy water and looked at him.

Drew didn't respond. He didn't remember. Sometimes he thought there was a face in his dream, but maybe his mind had just filled in the blanks where there were no real memories. Maybe he was using the face of a newscaster or the checkout clerk from the grocery store or the last person to serve him coffee. Anything to give him the illusion of an answer that could help.

When he woke up, his mind was always blank. No faces ever stayed with him. There'd been a time he was thankful for that.

"You were so young. No one should ever have to witness something like that." She held her brush in midair and watched him for too many seconds.

He scooted up in the sofa and stood. "I'll make you a deal. You don't tell anyone about me, and I won't tell anyone about you."

She tilted her head and regarded him where he stood. "What are you hiding from, little Drew?"

Even a rhetorical question could elicit unwanted answers in a person's mind. He forced himself to focus on Birdie. "Do we have a deal?"

"Fine," she agreed. "I'll keep sneaking around until you're ready to admit to everyone, including that pretty blonde, who you really are."

"I'm serious. If anyone finds out I was there that day, you'll have to find a new way to get away from your husband."

"Oh, he's long gone. It's just me now. But I take your point. I like my natural light."

"Good."

"I've got about another hour of daylight, so I'm going to use it. You can stay if you want to."

"No, I should get back."

"Suit yourself."

She didn't say goodbye or show him to the door. But when he got out into the yard and turned back to look at the windows, he saw her up there, watching him go.

What if he wasn't the only person who might have information about what had happened to Jess?

She disappeared from the window, and he turned around, an uneasy feeling settling on his shoulders.

As he and Roxie headed through the trees and into the yard, he caught a glimpse of Beth up near the house. Birdie was right: she never stopped moving. And while he'd never considered it before, he began to wonder if he wasn't the only one trying to make amends by keeping his head down and breathing new life into an old farm.

Chapter Eighteen

It had been a week and a half since Beth and Molly hired Drew, and he'd been working with a skeleton crew of volunteers who showed up when they could. Still, he'd made considerable progress on the main barn and inside the farmhouse.

Every morning when she arrived with coffee and Danishes, Beth knocked on the side door and he let her in. She set up a makeshift office in the kitchen, giving her a somewhat obstructed view of the yard, where she could watch him work.

He never stopped.

Even when the volunteers stopped, he kept going. He hardly even took a lunch break. As an employer, she was thrilled. As a person, she was concerned.

She'd start on paperwork, but she almost always ended up in the yard, though she often felt a little useless out there.

Now, she sat in the kitchen with papers spread out across the table. Numbers stared back at her, daring her to calculate them again, as if they might give her a different answer this time.

She'd taken Drew's estimates and run them by Ben, surprised and thankful he'd found better prices than she had.

That said something about him.

But the numbers were still daunting. They'd finished all the contracts, making her an equal partner with Molly and Ben, but even with Ben's investment and her own, they still didn't have enough money for everything that needed to be done on the farm.

Worse, she hadn't even had someone out yet to survey the condition of the orchard. Those trees were their bread and butter, and while they still seemed to be thriving, she was no tree doctor. For all she knew, they could be infected with some rare tree virus or something. Was there such a thing?

Daily, she wrestled with the idea that the only second chance Fairwind Farm would bring her was a second chance to fail.

And that wasn't something she was anxious to do again.

She closed her eyes and rubbed away the dull ache in her temples.

Behind her, Drew cleared his throat. She'd been so lost in thought she hadn't heard the screen door open.

She startled.

"I'm sorry," he said. "I didn't mean to scare you."

"I was just spacing out for a minute." She looked at the papers and empty coffee cups strewn across the kitchen table. "I'm sorry. I made a mess of your kitchen." He'd been nice enough to let her work in here—and this was how she repaid him?

Drew's gaze fell to the table, where papers surrounded her calculator and notebook. "You're an artist."

Beth glanced down at her notebook and saw a sketched image of Fairwind staring back at her. She'd been so caught up in her daydream, she hadn't even realized she'd been drawing.

"Your heart shows up in your art," her favorite professor had always said. *"So if you're having trouble finding your way, sit and sketch for a while. Your way will find you."*

Her father hadn't agreed. Said he knew from the time she was very young that business was her only path. "You can't waste that mind on art, Elizabeth. You can draw in your free time, but it's not going to pay the bills."

So she'd majored in business, yet still found ways to sneak in art classes. She was convinced it tapped into a part of her brain that no business class ever could. She missed out on studying it, though, the way an art major would. Instead, she spent most of her college days learning how to convince people they needed whatever she was selling, then later vying for a coveted position at one of Chicago's top firms.

A position that had gone to Michael.

A position that had ruined her life not once, but twice.

She'd spent the next several years convincing her father that she hadn't wasted her college education. Until recently, it had been years since she'd sketched, drawn or painted anything.

Suddenly embarrassed, Beth picked up the notebook and turned the page. "I just doodle."

"If you say so." Drew smirked at her, catching her lie.

How many angst-ridden arguments had she had with her parents over studying art? She'd been convinced it was her destiny, and yet she'd given it up without a real fight. A part of her always knew she'd abandoned her biggest dream in favor of the practical path.

It felt like a lifetime ago. Odd how that part of her was creeping in now when it had been suppressed for so long.

Drew turned the chair around and straddled it, meeting her eyes. She'd found ways to ignore his attractiveness over the last week and a half. She wasn't finding that so easy now.

"What's all this?" he asked.

She focused on the paperwork in front of her—anything to avoid his eyes. "Finances."

"You don't look happy."

She shrugged. "It is what it is." No sense telling him they wouldn't have money to do half the things on his list.

171

"You know, I was looking at the numbers myself." He pulled a folded sheet of paper from his back pocket.

"That's not part of your job." She already felt like they were taking advantage of him.

"Saving you money is part of my job."

She watched as he scanned the paper where he'd scribbled notes to himself. "Why are you here?"

His eyebrows shot up.

"That came out wrong."

He took off his ball cap and set it on the table between them.

"I just meant we're hardly paying you. You said you liked your job on the ranch. I've been trying to figure out why you would stay here, unless you've got some kind of hero complex and feel like you need to save us."

He held her gaze for a long few seconds. "I'm here to help. Does it matter why?"

She'd noticed all the work he'd done in the house. If she had to guess, this man slept a total of two hours a night. But maybe he was right—maybe it didn't matter *why* he was here. Just that he was. And she should shut her mouth and thank the Lord.

But she couldn't. It wasn't in her nature to leave things alone.

"Where's your family?" She chewed the inside of her lip.

"My parents retired near Denver, but they're all over the place. Last I heard from them, they were in San Diego."

"Siblings?"

"One sister. Sharly. Pain in the neck."

"I know something about that."

His smile was so faint she almost missed it. "Your sister's okay."

"But you have to admit, she's a pain in the neck." Beth set her pencil down. "She bought a goat, for Pete's sake."

Drew laughed. "It's a sheep."

"Same difference." Wasn't it?

Drew looked like he wanted to correct her but didn't.

"You're a hard one to figure out," she said. "I feel like you could be making more money anywhere else."

"I could say the same about you."

Beth's shoulders stiffened.

Yet it wasn't an indictment. It wasn't an accusation. He wasn't saying someone like her shouldn't be here in sleepy Willow Grove, just that she didn't have to be.

Drew looked away. "I'm not here for the money."

"Obviously." She waited until their eyes met again. "So?"

He ran a hand over his chin. "Sometimes you just need a change." He stared at her as if he knew she could understand. After all, wasn't that why she was here too?

That and her second chance.

She watched him for a few long moments, but he seemed to be done talking. At least about this. She'd already pushed him enough, so she decided to let it go.

She stood and pulled his house to-do list off the refrigerator, noting all the tasks that had already been checked off. "You've been busy."

He put his baseball cap back on his head.

"Do you sleep?"

He laughed. "Not well."

"Well, you've made a lot of progress. Don't kill yourself on it, though—I don't know if anyone's going to live in it for a while."

"You're not moving in?"

She shrugged. "I don't know. My mom had a stroke about ten months ago, so I moved back in with her."

"I didn't know."

She sat back down across from him. "How could you?"

She read over his list. Each room still needed painting. The hardwood floors needed refinishing. He'd made several notes about the kitchen, depending on the budget. She looked around. It did need attention. New appliances, new cupboards, a new floor. In her mind, she heard the dinging of an imaginary cash register.

"Thanks for putting this together," she said. "I know it's about the last priority, but it's good to know what we're looking at." She hadn't expected him to work on the house. The fact that he was, that he seemed truly invested—well, she didn't know what to do with that.

"When I was younger, they had something called the Fairwind Farm Market. Were you ever here during one of those?"

He shook his head.

"Maybe we could raise some more money for renovations if we organized one for this summer. We could invite local vendors—artists and makers—to come out and sell their stuff, and we could scour the house for stuff we could sell ourselves. Maybe have a booth with apple-cider donuts—sort of a tease of what's to come."

Thanks to the Internet, it wouldn't take long to compile a list of midwestern vendors. Many of them might even remember the Fairwind Market.

"Sounds like a lot of work."

"Yeah, but at least it's work I understand. Do you know how many times I've swept the porch or weeded the flower beds? There's only so many ways someone like me can help around here."

He eyed her for a long moment. "I didn't have you pegged for the kind of person who underestimates herself."

She started to respond but snapped her jaw shut. He had a point.

"How much money do you really think you can make hosting something like this?" He looked skeptical.

"I'll get back to you on that." Maybe it was crazy. Maybe it wouldn't be worthwhile. But it was the best idea she'd had so far. If it helped keep Fairwind in their family without having to find an outside investor, it was worth a shot.

Never mind that part of her knew it might be their only solution if they wanted to open before she and Molly turned into two old biddies shuffling around on the porch.

"Maybe we should see what's upstairs," Beth said, feeling excited for the first time since this crazy Fairwind adventure had begun.

Drew stood and started for the door. "Why?"

"There might be furniture up there we can sell. I'm betting it's all vintage. Isn't it?"

"I haven't been up there yet, but take a look and let me know what you find." Another tug on his baseball cap, and he was out the door before she could respond.

He'd been living there for over a week and he hadn't gone upstairs? *What are you hiding, Drew Barlow?*

Beth took her notebook and walked up the creaky staircase to the second level. While a barn sale might not be a huge moneymaker, every little bit would help, and the Pendergasts did have a lot of nice furniture. Old, but nice. People loved old, nice furniture. And it could be great publicity for the orchard. They'd get all that foot traffic out here to see what they were up to. The sooner they could get people thinking of the farm, the better. Her marketing mind had already started spinning with ideas.

As she reached the top of the stairs, she turned into the first bedroom. It seemed to be a guest room, with a small table in the corner that held a sewing machine. Unlike the downstairs, the upstairs seemed to have been carefully preserved. Everything in order. Almost untouched. The large wooden four-poster bed was made, and the room looked staged, like something you'd see in a magazine. A soft rug covered perfect hardwood floors. With the exception of a significant layer of dust, the room was still beautiful.

The two levels of the house seemed like polar opposites. How could one floor be in such disarray while the other was so pristine?

Beth imagined they could get a fair price for the bed—and the wardrobe at its side was a beautiful piece, though it wasn't her style. She had no attachments to anything inside the house, so it would be easy to sell it off. Especially if it helped get them closer to opening the orchard.

Across from the guest room was another bedroom. Stepping across the threshold was like stepping into a time warp.

Thick white woodwork around the windows popped off the pale blue-gray walls. Not a cheery blue, but not depressing either. White eyelet valances covered only the tops of the three windows overlooking the yard. Beth loved the natural sunlight that poured through the windows, making the room appear larger than it was.

Sketches of farm animals hung all around. She touched the image of a horse, squinted at the detail. Not bad. Especially for a child.

So, the Pendergasts' daughter had been an artist.

On the distressed white dresser sat a framed photo of the Pendergast family—all three of them. Happiness danced in their eyes. Beth hated that the end of their story didn't reflect that same emotion.

A chill shot through her as she opened the closet door and saw all the little clothes, neatly folded on shelves or hanging up on the rack. Little shoes met her where she stood.

The tragedy of Fairwind rushed back. The girl—Jessica—had gone missing the day after the Whitaker family had been at the farm for the Fairwind Market. She could still remember her parents discussing it in hushed tones while she and Ben pressed their ears to the door of their bedroom.

"They don't have any leads at this point," her father had said.

"This is just terrible. Who would do such a thing to a little girl?" her mother asked, her voice cracking with empathy for poor Mrs. Pendergast.

"They've got search parties going 'round the clock," her dad said. "I'm going to see if I can help."

Her mother must've made a face, the kind her father could read without any words. "What is it?" he asked her. Beth imagined him sitting beside her on the bed.

"That could've been one of our girls." She'd cried then, and Beth had decided she'd heard enough.

For weeks, volunteers had gathered near the old farm, searching for the little girl who'd been kidnapped from her own yard. Fairwind had shut down for the rest of the summer, and the newspaper ran stories for weeks speculating on what might have happened to Jessica Pendergast.

But to this day, no one knew.

Beth shuddered now, remembering Sonya's prayer carefully, probably tearfully, written in the old prayer book. She couldn't imagine what that poor couple had gone through, to one day have a daughter and the next day—not. No wonder the farm hadn't survived many more years after that.

God, why?

Beth tried not to obsess over questions that had no answers. Questions like *Why would Michael destroy what we had?* Or *Did he ever love me at all?* Or *Why did You have to take Daddy before I could make things right with him?* But this new question begged to be asked. How could a loving God allow something like this to happen to someone who obviously loved Him so much? Sonya's words were faith-filled and peaceful. She hadn't deserved this ending. How many people had this tragedy destroyed?

Several years after Jessica had gone missing, Sonya passed away. The town cried, "Death by a broken heart," but maybe she'd been sick. Whatever the case, after her death, Mr. Pendergast became a shut-in— and not a very nice one, though who could blame him? Beth didn't imagine she'd be very cheery either if the two people she loved most in this world died so many years before their time.

According to local gossip, Harold never recovered. Visited the police station once a week with new theories and "evidence." Everyone brushed him off like he was crazy.

And maybe he was.

But wasn't anyone sympathetic to what the man had been through? It didn't take long for the stories to spread—for him to be painted as a wildly crazy man stuck in the past.

Beth wondered if anyone had shown him kindness or empathy.

Or had he spent years wondering why the entire town of Willow Grove—a place that was supposed to be safe and welcoming—preferred to forget what had happened, as if it were a blemish on an otherwise spotless record?

Mr. Pendergast had become the butt of a town joke. Shame settled on Beth's shoulders. Why had this never occurred to her before? She'd been every bit as guilty as the rest of them, wanting nothing more than to pretend something so tragic had never happened. Not in her hometown. Not here.

The pain of that betrayal was almost palpable. They'd all let this family down.

On the top shelf of the closet, Beth spotted a little wooden box. Overcome with curiosity, she stood on her tiptoes and pulled it down. Inside she found a heart-shaped rock, a friendship bracelet and a faded photograph of a little blond girl with long braids standing next to a dark-headed boy. Both grinning, both holding freshly caught fish.

She turned the photo over. *J + D.*

Beth stared into the little girl's eyes. As if she might be able to tell her something the police didn't already know.

"What happened to you, Jessica?" Beth whispered.

Footsteps on the creaky staircase drew her attention to the hallway, quickening her pulse, as if she should be afraid of getting caught. Molly appeared in the doorway, and Beth released the breath she'd been holding.

It wasn't like she was trespassing—why did she feel like she was?

"What are you doing in here?" Molly's eyes widened.

"Snooping."

"Is this the little girl's room?"

"Yeah, look." She handed her the photograph.

Molly studied it with sad eyes. "She was beautiful. Who's the boy?"

Beth shrugged. "Not sure." Had the photo been special to Jess? Had she carefully placed these items in the box for safekeeping?

"They look so innocent." Molly plopped down on the bed and took the rock from the little box. "It's a heart." She held it up.

"I saw."

"She would've been around our age."

Beth remembered thinking the same thing all those years ago when the girl had disappeared. She'd known every other kid in town except Jess Pendergast. No one had known her. She'd been homeschooled and spent all her time on the farm. When the Whitakers visited Fairwind, she would see the little girl running around in the yard, often on the perimeter, keeping her distance from all the visitors. Did they felt like intruders to Jess? Was she a fan of seclusion, or did she enjoy the company? Did she take to the shadows and make up stories about the families that descended on her home?

In all the time they'd visited Fairwind, many weekends for several years, Beth had never spoken to Jess. She regretted that now.

"I could ask Bishop." Molly carefully put the rock back in the box.

"Ask him what?" Beth asked.

"If he'd let us see the case file."

Beth took the box from her sister. "I don't even think that's legal."

"Couldn't hurt to ask."

"To what end?" Beth turned the friendship bracelet between her fingers.

Molly sat down on the bed. "To figure out what happened to her."

"Molly, the case went cold. If the police and detectives and her own father couldn't figure it out, what chance do we have twenty years later?"

"No one ever found her, Beth. What if she's still alive? Can you imagine your only child being taken right out from under your nose and never knowing by who or why?"

Beth shook her head. "No. I can't. But this is a job for someone else. Someone who doesn't have an entire farm to restore."

"I just want to look at the case. I want to know what happened on our property all those years ago. Tell me you're not curious."

"Molly. Let it go." But one look at Molly, and Beth knew her sister had already decided exactly what she was going to do. Beth sighed. "I'm not going to be able to change your mind on this, am I?"

"Nope. I'll check the public record, but Bishop might have access to the case that we don't."

"This is a bad idea."

"Your position has been duly noted." Molly started for the door. "Oh, and Beth?"

Beth glanced up.

"We got a dog."

Chapter Nineteen

Monday morning, the beginning of their fourth week of work, Beth sat in her car in the parking lot of Willow Grove Community Bank, replaying the meeting she'd just had with Linda Dorset, the loan officer she'd been working with for years.

A loan officer who knew her personally as well as professionally—Whitaker Mowers did a lot of business with the bank. Why, then, had Linda chosen now as the time to get stingy?

While a loan was just about the last thing in the world Beth wanted, she'd owed it to herself to at least explore the possibility—only she'd discovered it wasn't one at all.

Drew had been working at the farm for two full weeks, and he'd done just about everything he could on his own. They'd had a steady stream of volunteers, but he'd politely asked for skilled help. She'd agreed, and as with everything else he did, Drew wasted no time assembling a crew of possible workers, many of whom she knew.

But she had no idea how she would pay them. And no idea how to break it to Molly that while Jerry had given *her* a loan, Beth couldn't get another one for the same project. "Too risky," Linda had said. "We just don't see it as a good investment."

Beth's heart had plummeted as Linda spoke her greatest fears aloud.

To make everything worse, Beth seemed to have been bitten by the frivolous-dreamer bug. (Too much time spent with Molly, perhaps?) Instead of coming up with easier and quicker ways to raise money, she'd become obsessed with the idea of bringing back the Fairwind Market.

She drove to the farm and knocked on the kitchen door, the same way she had every day since Drew had moved in, but when she pushed it open, she found him standing at the refrigerator wearing nothing but a pair of jeans frayed at the bottom.

"Morning." He pulled a carton of orange juice out and shut the door.

She tried not to notice that his hair was still damp and he smelled clean, like soap. Nothing fussy about this man. He hadn't even shaved. Probably in a couple of days.

It suited him.

"Morning." She handed him the coffee. It had become a ritual.

"You know you don't have to bring me coffee every day." He set it on the counter. "But thanks." He picked up a soft gray T-shirt that was draped over one of the kitchen chairs and pulled it over his head, covering his muscular torso and tanned skin.

She was relieved—seeing him shirtless was incredibly distracting.

She set her slouch bag down on one of the kitchen chairs and found her idea notebook lying open on the table. Somehow in the last two weeks, her portfolio had been replaced by an old sketch pad. Somehow in the last two weeks, her usual thoughts had been replaced by daydreams. She'd tried to deny it, but her mother wouldn't let her.

"I never thought I'd live to see the day when you were researching how to build a chicken coop," she'd said, reading Beth's computer screen over her shoulder.

"I don't seem like a chicken kind of person?"

Her mom had laughed and made her way to an armchair on the other side of the living room. Beth half watched until she was settled, content that her mom didn't need her, and went back to browsing about coops.

"It's nice to see you passionate about something again," her mom had said, as if it were just a simple observation.

"I'm not passionate about chicken coops, Mom."

"That notebook begs to differ."

Beth glanced down at the pad, full of plans and ideas. She wasn't sure when it had happened, but these days, instead of spending her evenings poring over market research, she was tearing photos out of *Country Living* magazine and stapling them into her sketch pad.

The notebook was more than a place to record facts and figures about their renovation—it was a place to dream about Fairwind. And she'd carelessly left it here over the weekend.

She'd mostly saved magazine cutouts and Pinterest links of things she eventually wanted to do at the farm. The picnic area she wanted to create underneath the old oak tree, with white lights dangling in the soft spring air. The quirky hand-painted wooden signs to direct their visitors around the property. The garden she dreamed of tending in the large open space behind the house.

A few of the articles she'd torn out were spread out across the table—"What to Plant and When." "Raising Backyard Chickens." "How to Build Raised Garden Beds." She picked them up and tucked them back inside the book, wrapping the attached elastic around it to hold everything in place, feeling a bit exposed knowing that he'd likely leafed through her ideas.

Even admitting she wanted to learn about something so far out of her comfort zone was hard for her. All it did was take her further away from her life plan. And yet, she couldn't help herself.

"I was looking for this notebook yesterday. It's not like me to leave something like this behind. Sorry about the mess."

"If you call a notebook with a stack of magazine articles in it a mess." He leaned against the counter and took another drink.

"Well, it's nice of you to let me work in here. I don't want to take advantage of your kindness."

He raised a brow. "You own the place, and I stay here for free. You can leave a notebook on the table." He pushed himself away from the counter. "Hey, can I show you something?"

"Of course." She followed him out the side door, across the patio and into the yard. It still amazed her that all this land was partly hers. Never in her wildest dreams had she ever expected to be part owner of a farm.

He led her out toward the huge old oak tree, the one practically begging to be strung with white lights. On the other side of it, next to the shed where they kept the mowers and other small lawn tools, he stopped.

She followed his gaze downward and saw three good-sized raised garden beds, filled with fresh soil. Raised beds that looked exactly like the ones in the article she'd saved.

"Eventually, I think we could clear this whole area for a garden. If you like it, I mean." Drew waved a hand across a section of grass tucked behind the farmhouse and directly in the sun. "But I thought it might be good to start with these. Fewer weeds to deal with in a raised bed, but we'll have to water them like crazy."

Beth stared at the scene in front of her. "When did you have time to do this?"

"Yesterday."

"Sunday."

"Yesterday was Sunday." He smirked at her.

"This was a lot of work. I read the article. I got overwhelmed about three sentences in."

He stuffed his hands in his pockets. His feet were still bare, his hair still damp. His eyes were bright blue in the morning sunshine. And he looked perfectly at ease. She knew he wasn't—no one who worked this much could be—but in that moment, he almost looked peaceful.

184

"Are they okay?" He looked across the beds, as if double-checking his work. "I didn't mean to snoop through your stuff—I just saw the article and thought they'd be great out here."

He'd turned one of her wishes into a reality. But why?

She wasn't sure anyone had ever done something so thoughtful for her. The realization of it hit her all at once, but she swallowed it and forced herself to smile. "You know there's a really good chance I'm going to kill every plant we put in these."

He smiled back—a real one—with his eyes. "I know. I'll keep an eye on them."

"Thanks for the vote of confidence," she said with a laugh.

"You'll be fine. I've got more soil in the barn. We just need to decide what you want to plant, and we can get started."

She waited until he met her gaze. "Thank you for this."

He waved her off. "It was nothing."

But it wasn't nothing. It was the first indication she had that Drew might actually be paying attention to more than just his job. Why did her stomach somersault at the thought?

She chewed the inside of her lip, suddenly nervous. He probably expected her to have some idea of what she wanted to plant. She didn't. Not yet, anyway.

Hadn't she read something about what to plant in raised beds? "I was thinking maybe some tomatoes? And peppers?" She tried to keep the sound of not knowing what she was talking about out of her voice.

"That'd be a good start," he said.

She gave a nod that was much more confident than she felt.

"And maybe some cucumbers and squash?" he said. "If there's room, we could do green beans too."

"Sure."

"All right. I've got some seeds in the barn. I'll go get what we need. I think there are some gardening tools and gloves in the house."

"I'll go get them."

When she returned, he was standing beside the beds. He'd put his work boots on, along with a ball cap he pulled down low over his eyes, the sun growing warmer as the day wore on. "Have you planted anything before?"

Her grimace gave her away.

"I'll take that as a no." He motioned for her to join him at the edge of the soil. "We're just going to create rows, like this." Using his hands, he dug a little trench in the dirt, dropped the seeds in and then covered it back up. "Wanna try?"

As she leaned in to clear away a spot for more seeds, he didn't move, forcing her to stretch across him to scoop the dirt out and to drop the seeds in. He reached down to help her, his hand brushing hers and sending a warm tingle down her spine.

She smoothed the dirt over the seeds and patted it down.

"Good. Once you're done, you'll want to water them all." He stood, hands on hips and nodded. "You can do this. I'll come back and check on you."

She pulled on a pair of gardening gloves she'd found in the house, along with a floppy gardening hat. Sonya's, most likely. Then she did exactly what Drew had shown her. She arranged her seeds in rows, not too close together, and covered them with the soil.

By the middle of the morning, the new crew had arrived. She watched as they met Drew in the main barn, where he gave them a rundown of their jobs. He'd hired them all last week after placing an ad in the *Willow Grove Sentinel* and putting up a sign at Butler's advertising exactly what they needed: able-bodied, skilled workers.

As Beth watched them filter in, she resisted the urge to tell him the best way to motivate these men. The truth was, she didn't know if her methods would work with such a different group of people. She found her confidence lacking as she went back to planting her seeds.

After a few minutes, the men were out in the yard, working. That was fast. She stood and did a quick glance around the farm, impressed that everyone seemed to know exactly where they were going and what they were doing. While up, she stretched her aching muscles, then took a moment to admire the whole first bed, completely planted.

"You taking a break?" Drew called out to her from several yards away.

"Just stretching,"

"You look proud of yourself." He smiled at her. He had a nice smile.

"Well, proud of us. I couldn't have done this without you."

"That doesn't suit you, you know."

"What doesn't?"

"Doubting yourself."

Hard to be sure of herself in such unknown territory. Before she could respond, an unfamiliar car—a silver Lexus—pulled into the parking lot.

Beth shielded her eyes from the sun.

"Expecting company?" Drew asked.

"No. You?"

The door of the Lexus opened, and the driver emerged. Beth's heart sank. "Oh no."

Dina Larson, with her long, wavy blond hair, got out of the car. She wore a pair of jeans, a cream-colored button-down shirt and a camel-colored suede jacket. Her heeled booties and checkered scarf made her look out of place at Fairwind Farm. She could've been a supermodel.

Beth wiped the sweat from her brow, spreading dirt across her forehead. She glanced down at her ripped jeans and old Cubs T-shirt. She was still wearing the floppy garden hat, and she looked—she was sure—like an absolute mess.

Dina waved as soon as she spotted them, then veered in their direction. She stumbled slightly as her heel sank into the grass.

"You know her?" Drew moved to Beth's side.

"Unfortunately," Beth said dryly.

That wasn't quite fair. Dina Larson had been one of Beth's friends—on the surface, anyway. They'd had so much in common and were in the same circle, and yet, there had always been a wide gap between them. That gap had only widened as they'd gone their separate ways.

Beth did her best to put herself back together, but she knew it was hopeless. She'd been working in the sun for hours, and under her hat, her sweaty hair had matted to her head in ways nothing but a shower could fix.

Dina stumbled again.

"She's going to break her ankle wearing those shoes out here," Drew said.

"Beth!" Dina called out with another overzealous wave. "Hey, stranger!"

"Dina, what are you doing here?" Beth tried to keep her tone light. Inside, her mind was reeling.

"I came to see you, of course." Dina gave Drew a once-over. "Now I see why you've taken such a liking to farmwork."

Beth glanced at Drew, who looked as uncomfortable as she felt.

"Drew, this is Dina Larson. We went to high school together," Beth said, patting her warm face dry with a gloved hand.

"You make it sound so clinical, Beth. We weren't just classmates—we were besties." Dina flashed her perfectly white smile as she reached out to shake Drew's hand.

Besties. Beth shuddered at the word. It sounded so juvenile. They were grown women, for Pete's sake.

"We're friends," Beth said.

Drew shook Dina's hand. "Good to meet you." He turned to Beth. "I'll let you guys catch up."

As he walked away, Dina gave Beth wide eyes while mouthing *O-M-G* like a teenager.

"He works for me." Beth stuck the trowel into the raised bed and clapped her hands together to remove the dirt from her gloves.

"Uh-huh. Send him my way when you're done with him," Dina said, watching Drew walk away. "Just kidding. I'm a married woman. But, good gracious, he is a fine-looking man."

"Dina."

She peeled her eyes away from Drew and turned to Beth, then burst out laughing. "You look so ridiculous right now."

"Thanks for that."

"Sorry." She laughed. "It's just quite the getup. Hold on, let me take a picture." She took her phone out and snapped a photo so quickly Beth couldn't have hoped to protest. "Nobody will believe you're out here digging around in the dirt on your little farm." She laughed again—loudly.

Beth pressed her lips together to keep from saying something she'd regret.

"So, how's it been going out here? Seeing you like this, I'm starting to wonder just how brilliant this idea actually was. I mean, I was all for it—you know that—but I guess I didn't realize how run-down this place had gotten."

Beth didn't dare tell her what it had looked like just a few weeks ago.

"It's going well, actually. Slow, but we're making progress."

Dina's smile looked forced. "Isn't it funny?"

"Isn't what funny?"

"How everything turned out. I'm living downtown with Harrison, running our own ad firm, and you're . . . doing this. It's exciting, right?"

Was it her intention to condescend?

Beth took off the gloves and laid them on the side of the garden. "Do you want some lemonade?"

Dina's face brightened. "Sure."

In the kitchen, she poured two glasses of lemonade and handed one to Dina, feeling uneasy about her being there at all. She was embarrassed for Dina to see the farm like this. To see her like this. Dina represented everything Beth had tried—failed—to achieve.

Beth shook that thought off. She shouldn't blame Dina for making something of her life.

She sat down at the table across from Dina, a stunted silence hanging in the air between them. They'd competed all through high school, always under the guise of friends, even if not "besties." But they hadn't kept in touch—so why was Dina here now?

She searched for something to say. Came up empty.

"I heard you have big plans for this place," Dina said. "And you want to be open by this fall. That's quite an undertaking."

Beth took a sip of her lemonade, noticing her hands were still dirty despite having washed them before she'd sat down. "We have a good team. A solid plan."

It was partly true. They did have a good team. Beth was still working on the plan part.

"I'm sure. You only surround yourself with the best." She smiled. Her words were complimentary, yet somehow Beth bristled at them, expecting criticism.

Dina took another drink. "The ad agency is doing really well."

Beth should've asked. She didn't have to, though, because Dina's grandmother Ginny had already told her—ad nauseam—how well Dina's business was doing. "That's what I've heard. Congratulations. You've done everything you set out to do." Her lack of enthusiasm resonated in her tone. Beth heard it loud and clear; she could only assume Dina had too.

This unspoken competition between them had always been there, simmering below the surface, pushing Beth forward in an effort to outdo, out achieve, out win. But now, it had turned into something even uglier.

Beth shrank under the weight of Dina's stare.

"Will you be ready to open by August?" Dina turned the glass around in her hand.

Beth glanced out the window and saw Drew in the yard with a few of the workers. She hadn't asked about the timeline lately. Part of her didn't want to know. "I hope so."

"I've already planned to bring Harrison back here when you're open. We really want to support you however we can. Maybe we can talk about an ad campaign—you know, when you're ready?"

"I doubt we can afford you."

Dina flicked the air. "I'd give you the best-friend discount."

For the briefest moment, Beth saw a glimmer of sadness behind her eyes. It skittered away as quickly as it had come, but it was the first indication that there was more to Dina than flashy cars and beauty-queen fashion.

"You've been back in Willow Grove a lot lately," Beth said.

Dina studied her glass. "I have. Thought I'd use the chance to check up on you. I have to admit, I never thought I'd see you on a farm, covered in dirt, but I guess things change, don't they?"

Beth looked away.

"I admire you for doing something like this—completely unexpected. It's hard to break out of the mold everyone else puts you in. Especially when that mold turns out to be different than you thought."

What was she saying? That she resented her successful company, gorgeous husband and wealthy way of life? Didn't she know she was living the dream? Beth's dream.

"It's just . . ." Dina's eyes found hers.

"What?"

"You're not hiding out here, are you? I mean, this *is* what you want, right?"

She sat with that for a moment. "Hiding from what?"

"I saw Michael's engagement announcement in the newspaper this morning."

Beth's heart dropped. "Oh."

She hadn't seen it. She'd been too busy digging around in the dirt.

"You hadn't heard?"

She shook her head. "But I'm not surprised. I wish him nothing but the best." How many lies could she tell in one day? She didn't wish him the best. She wished him the same heartache he'd caused her. That made her an ugly person, and she knew it.

"I'm sorry to be the one to tell you." Now it was Dina who lied. She was probably thrilled to dole this kind of news out to her high school frenemy. Beth wanted her to leave. She wanted to get back to her gardening, to something soothingly monotonous that took her mind off everything else.

"To be honest," Dina said, "I always kind of thought you two would get back together."

To be honest, so had Beth. The realization of that stabbed at her.

"You always were everyone's favorite couple. And when I saw the two of you at the reunion—well, there were still sparks."

Beth remembered. Michael had walked in wearing that custom-tailored suit, and Callie had let out a low groan. "Why does he still have to be so good-looking?" she'd said. Beth had waved her off, but as soon as she saw him, her heart flip-flopped and she was sixteen again, out on their first date, wondering if he was going to hold her hand during the movie.

Their life together flashed in front of her. High school sweethearts. Homecoming royalty. They'd gone to the same university and made plans together. Future plans. They were supposed to live happily ever after in a city apartment overlooking Lake Michigan. Ten years after graduation, they'd start their family. Two kids. House in the suburbs.

But he'd ruined it. He'd taken all of those years they'd spent together and turned them into wasted time.

Why, then, had she agreed to dance with him at the reunion "for old times' sake"?

He'd slipped his hand around her, placing it on the small of her back as if he were comfortable with her, familiar with the curves of her body. Because he was. In a way nobody else was.

That night, as he held her on the dance floor, she looked up into his eyes, searching for a sign that he regretted what he'd done.

"You're still so beautiful, Beth," he said. "We had so many good times."

She could smell the alcohol on his breath as he pulled her closer. "That was a long time ago, Michael."

"But we were good together, weren't we?"

She didn't respond.

"We could be good together again—just for tonight." He turned his face into her neck, lips brushing against her skin. "I have a limo." His hands had crossed out of comfortable and into intimate. He held one of her hands to his chest, while his other one skimmed the outline of her body. "I know you miss me. I can see it in your eyes."

Beth inched away from him and forced his gaze. "Is this what you've become?"

He loosened his grip on her, but only slightly.

"Or is this who you've always been?" Had she been too blind—too lovesick—too caught up in her perfect plan to see it?

"I don't know what you mean."

Her eyes scanned his, and she marked the moment in her mind. "I hope you have a wonderful life, Michael," she said, severing the connection between them. "I really mean that."

"Where are you going?" He had tried to pull her back, but she'd remained—as she always would—just out of his reach.

It was the closure she'd needed. And yet now, sitting across the table from Dina, her heart still ached knowing there was someone else in his life, someone he loved enough to spend forever with.

"Well, I'm glad to know this whole renovation thing is working out for you." Dina's words pulled Beth back to the here and now.

"You said yourself it was a brilliant idea." Beth hated that a lump had formed at the back of her throat.

"It's charming, I'll give you that."

"But you don't think it's brilliant anymore?"

"I didn't say that." Dina leaned back slightly in her chair. "Are you guys okay for money?"

"We're fine," Beth said—a little too quickly. Dina was the last person she wanted knowing about their financial struggles.

"Good. I'm glad." She smiled again. Why couldn't Beth find any trace of condescension on her face? Dina was famous for that. "You've sure got the town talking. Everyone is really excited about what you guys are doing for the community."

The thought made Beth nervous. What if she let them all down? Again?

"Well, I should go. I have a meeting in the city this afternoon." Dina scooted her chair back and stood up, lingering for a few long seconds, as if she didn't want to leave.

"Thanks for stopping out."

"Of course. And I'm serious about the ad campaign. Turns out, I'm pretty good at those." Dina opened her sleek designer bag and pulled out a small white card. "Here. Call me when you're ready, and we'll put something together."

"Thanks." Beth took the card, hating that it was Dina whose kindness made her feel like a charity case.

As they stood on the front porch, Dina turned toward her. "Good luck." She opened her arms, and Beth stepped into a quick but awkward hug.

Dina's phone rang. "I need to go. See you soon!"

Beth leaned against the railing and watched as the reminder of the life she wasn't living tiptoed through the grass, got in a sleek silver Lexus and drove away.

Chapter Twenty

Evenings at Fairwind Farm were too quiet. Drew had spent the last three weeks surrounded by people—volunteers, and now his crew of guys—but when the sun went down and the place was covered in moonlight, that's when his mind played tricks on him.

That's when the real nightmares started.

He'd cleaned the old farmhouse, repaired broken doors and cabinets. Two nights ago, he'd fixed the downstairs toilet, and next week, he'd paint the walls, then refinish the floors.

Now, with another day waning, he used the old hand-pump well behind the farmhouse to clean up. Beth stood off in the distance, watering the seeds she'd planted in the raised beds.

She wore cutoff shorts, a white tank top and a button-down shirt tied in a knot at the side. And that goofy-looking garden hat she'd found in the house. He couldn't decide if she looked ridiculous or adorable.

He'd seen the magazine clippings in Beth's notebook on the table when his mind had been especially anxious. He'd needed a project, so he'd built the beds. He hadn't expected they would make her so happy.

After seeing the way her face lit up, he wanted to figure out a way to do it again.

How long had it been since he'd made another person happy?

Still, he found it nearly impossible to talk to her about anything other than planting seeds or repairing barns. He wanted to, though, for maybe the first time in his life.

Oh, he'd had plenty of girlfriends, but he always broke things off before they could become too serious. He'd never wanted to talk about himself the way a woman always seemed to want a man to.

But there was something different about Beth. He wanted to know her. Was it because he had the impression that maybe she was hiding something too? She was hard to know, which made her all the more intriguing.

She was all business. Very professional. But he didn't care about any of that—he wanted to figure out who she was. He knew that wasn't going to happen, though, so he settled instead for making her happy from a distance.

It didn't take much. A new mailbox. A vase of freshly cut lilacs on the kitchen table where she worked. And maybe next week he'd have time to work on a chicken coop.

Anything to make her smile.

If he wasn't careful, he'd convince himself that making her happy around Fairwind Farm was the same as making her happy in her life.

It wasn't. And he'd be smart to remember that.

What was it about her that made him want to be known?

She glanced up and found him staring. He was caught, but he couldn't look away—not yet. He just wanted to see that smile dance around in her eyes. To think—even for a misguided second—that he'd somehow caused something so pure and beautiful? It was enough to keep him going for another week.

Her face softened and she waved, smile playing at the corners of her mouth.

What would she say if she found out the truth about him? That he was a coward—a disappointment?

Being "known" was out of the question, and he'd accepted that a long time ago. So he'd have to be content making her happy from the sidelines. That's what was best, for both of them.

As the sun disappeared behind the cornfields in the west, Drew made his way out to the barn he'd discovered the week before. He had to hand it to Birdie—she might be old, but she was stealthy. Even though he knew she was there, he'd seen her only when he'd gone looking for her.

And he'd gone looking for her more than once, drawn back to her, to the possibility that something she said or did would provide the answers he'd been searching for.

He walked inside the barn and called out, though he had a feeling she'd seen him coming from her window.

"I haven't had this much company in years," she said without looking at him.

"Am I bothering you?" He stopped halfway up the stairs.

"Are you kidding me? Half the town has decided I'm a tinfoil-hat-wearing lunatic, and the other half just doesn't like me. I could use a friend." She eyed him from behind her easel. "Something tells me you could too."

"Nah, friends are overrated." He climbed the rest of the stairs and sat down on a too-soft purple velvet sofa.

She shoved the jar of bubblegum at him. "Here."

To be polite, he took a piece and unwrapped it, then popped it in his mouth. While he didn't consider Birdie a friend, it was nice to have a conversation with someone who actually knew who he was.

"Have you told the blonde the truth yet?"

He met her eyes but didn't respond.

"I see." Birdie took the pair of reading glasses that hung by a chain around her neck and propped them up on her nose, squinting at something on her easel. "What are you waiting for?"

The taste of bubblegum exploded in his mouth. "I don't want her to know about any of this."

"Why in heavens not? Maybe she can help you."

Drew blew a bubble, let it pop, feeling like a ten-year-old again. Some vague part of him remembered sitting in here with Birdie and Jess. "What's she going to do, crawl inside my head and figure out what's broken?"

Birdie plunked her paintbrush in the water jar. "Did you ever think maybe you didn't see the man? Maybe you don't have a single answer locked inside your mind."

Drew shook his head. "There's something there. I can feel it."

"Why? Because some adults told you there was."

He didn't want to talk about this.

"Maybe the adults got it wrong, kiddo. And telling that pretty girl the truth isn't going to run her off."

"I lied to her, Birdie." He couldn't tell Beth the truth now. They'd been working together for three weeks—he'd missed his window. Besides, he didn't want people knowing he was the reason Jess's case had gone cold. What would they think of him then?

She took the glasses off and stood, still behind the easel. "Well, then unlie to her."

He leaned forward, elbows on his knees. "It's not that simple."

"That girl cares about you. She's not going to hold it against you that this terrible thing happened to you when you were ten years old."

He spit the gum into the garbage can. You could only chew Bazooka Joe for so long. "How do you know she cares about me?"

And why did his pulse race at the thought?

Birdie sat back down on her stool. "A woman knows."

"She just needs me to get the farm ready."

"Keep telling yourself that, sonny."

Birdie was obviously seeing things that weren't there. She glared at him. "I think you need to realize you didn't do anything wrong here."

The words hung there, thick and heavy, the way dense fog hung over the meadow in the cool mornings.

"You were as much a victim as Jess was. And shame on those adults for not making sure you realized that."

"I'm not a victim." He stood.

She walked over to him, standing at least a foot shorter, and stuck her bony finger into his chest. "You were just a boy. You shouldn't have had to carry the weight of any of that. And you're still carrying it—I can see it on your face. I could see it the first day you walked in here."

"I'm fine, Birdie."

"Then why did you come back?"

He swallowed the lump that had formed at the back of his throat. It caught him off guard, this rare, unwanted emotion that proved she was right.

"I'm here to restore an old farm," he said.

"Oh, honey," she whispered, taking a step back, obviously aware of his pain.

"I have to go." He started down the stairs. "I'll see you later."

She didn't respond, and he didn't look up at the window as he walked through the yard toward the farmhouse. Instead, he wrestled with the pain that jabbed at the back of his mind, begging for his attention.

As he approached the house, the windows on the second level caught his attention. For three weeks now, he'd slept on the couch in the living room, memories flooding his mind. But he'd never stepped foot on the second floor.

He hadn't been ready for what he might find up there.

Remnants of Jess.

Their second-to-last summer at Fairwind. He'd been nine and complained the entire drive. He hadn't wanted to spend a whole month on a stupid farm with no one to play with but some dumb girl.

But Jess had surprised him. She wasn't like the girls he knew back home. She'd grown fearless. She'd jump into the creek fully clothed if it meant catching a frog. She'd pick up garter snakes by their heads and fling them out into the cornfield. She'd ride the horses and complain when her dad wouldn't let her go faster.

He'd been so intrigued by her. Maybe even smitten, as much as a nine-year-old could be.

They'd become friends that summer. Good friends. And the next year, he couldn't wait to get back to the farm. They fell back into their comfortable friendship almost immediately, but only a few short weeks later, Fairwind was filled with police officers and search and rescue teams. And people ordering him to remember.

"You must've seen something out there, son," one cop had said. "Nobody can hurt you now. We need you to be brave and tell us what you saw."

He'd searched his mind for something—anything—that would help them find Jess. His own parents begged him to remember something. A sound. A smell. A face. But he came up empty.

His silence had made them think he was traumatized or hiding something. Their constant prodding had made him question himself. So here he was, trying to do what he should've done all those years ago. Trying to remember. He awoke in the middle of every night disoriented and drenched in sweat, having relived another nightmare that refused to tell the whole story.

Drew moved quickly through the kitchen and living room, straight to the stairs before he lost his nerve. Night had fallen, and he knew he couldn't wake up panicked one more time.

Desperation propelled him up the stairs, light from the moon filtering in from the window in the hallway above him. When he reached the top, he stopped and drew in a deep breath.

He noticed the door to Jess's bedroom was partially open, and a picture formed in his mind. On the rainy days, they'd sprawl out on her floor looking at her bug collection. She'd speak with such excitement, showing him the new bugs she'd found down by the creek. Jess had found each one in her encyclopedia, labeling them one at a time.

He squirmed over the assortment of dead insects, but Jess was downright thrilled by them. She loved learning new things. She'd always had such a sense of wonder about her. Some people probably thought she was weird, but Drew liked her for it.

He moved in silence past her room, careful not to glance inside. What if it looked exactly the same? Or worse, what if the Pendergasts had changed everything—wiped away every shred of evidence she'd ever existed?

He wasn't ready to find out.

Instead, he moved into the master bedroom and flipped on the light. It looked just as he'd remembered it. The only time he'd been in here was during a rainy-day game of hide-and-seek. He'd found Jess underneath the sleigh bed, which had felt so monstrous when he was little.

"Found you!" He'd tugged at her foot underneath the bed frame.

"Only because I didn't hide in my best spot." She scooted out from her hiding place and sat cross-legged in front of him.

"Where's your best spot?"

"It's a secret," she whispered.

"Show me."

She got up and checked the hallway, he assumed for their parents. When the coast was clear, she motioned for him to follow her.

He did as he was told, but when she led him to her parents' walk-in closet, he let out a groan. "A closet isn't a great hiding place."

She pushed the clothes out of the way and revealed a small door hidden at the back of the closet.

"Whoa."

"Told ya." She slid the door open and led him inside. "It's a secret room. Isn't it cool? When I grow up and live here, I'm going to make this my dream room."

"What would you do with a dream room?"

"I'd dream, you dork." She had laughed then. "We should get out of here. My parents don't like it when I play in here."

He'd looked around and seen nothing important, only boxes, but he'd done as he was told. If Jess's parents hadn't wanted them in their secret storage room, he wouldn't argue.

Now, standing just outside the closet, he wondered if the room was still full of boxes. He knew Harold had obsessed over Jess's case. There was no sign of that obsession anywhere else in the house, but Drew had a strong suspicion he'd kept it all behind this door.

He switched on the closet light and pushed a hanging row of women's clothes off to one side, searching for the door Jess had shown him all those years ago.

He found it and slid it open. Inside, a light bulb hung from the ceiling. He pulled the string, and the bulb cast dim yellow light on a wide-planked table built into the wall. Above it, newspaper clippings, articles and random notes were pinned up in haphazard fashion. He recognized so many of the headlines. He'd clipped most of them himself. Unlike Harold, though, he hadn't put them on display. Instead, he'd shoved them inside a notebook, which he'd stuffed underneath his mattress, then tried to forget about.

He'd done a good job for the most part, especially once Harold's notes had stopped coming.

But that notebook had found its way to Fairwind with him. He hid it underneath the seat in his truck, not ready to face the fact that maybe this case had the power to unravel him the way it had unraveled Harold.

What if the two of them weren't all that different, both one newspaper clipping away from crazy?

On the wall, he saw his own name scribbled on a piece of paper, circled with a question mark beside it. Drew took the pin out of the paper, wadded it up and stuffed it in his pocket. Then, he surveyed the board, begging a God he hadn't talked to in years to give him the miracle of a memory.

But nothing came.

He read familiar headlines on yellowed newsprint, reliving the dreadful days following Jess's disappearance. He hadn't been able to speak since he'd woken up on the ground in that barn, bleeding and disoriented. But he could hear the conversation in the next room.

When Drew hadn't been able to provide them with a single clue, one of the officers coldly suggested, "Maybe the kid was in on it."

"Don't be ridiculous," someone else said. "He's a kid."

"With a huge gash on the back of his head," said another. "What do you think, he somehow sliced his own head open with a shovel?"

There was a pause before the first officer spoke again. "Maybe he agreed to lure the girl into the barn. Maybe he didn't know it would get out of hand."

"That's insane," his mother said. "Drew would never, ever do anything to hurt Jess or anyone else."

Another pause.

"Sonya, you can't believe this." His mom sounded afraid. Drew remembered because he wasn't used to hearing fear in his mother's voice. "You know Drew."

"Of course not," Jess's mom said. "Of course he wouldn't."

The next morning, his parents packed up their things and left Fairwind Farm.

He didn't say a word the whole way home. So began his pattern of speaking only when he had something to say. And that wasn't very often. Regret twisted its way into his belly. They had all been counting on him, and he'd let them down.

Harold and Sonya Pendergast had died without an ounce of closure— no closer to finding out what had happened to their daughter than the day she'd gone missing. What made Drew think he was entitled to something they'd never had? He'd been running from that day since he was ten years old; like a soldier gone AWOL, he'd abandoned his post.

And he hated himself for it.

He sat at the little table in the hidden room, poring over the clippings, rereading every article and Harold's handwritten notes in the margins. He picked up a small photo of Jess, running his finger over the frozen image of her face. She'd tucked a flower behind her ear, and her smile was so full of life. What kind of dreams would she have whispered in the quiet of this room?

"I let you down, Jess," he said quietly. "I won't do that again."

She hadn't gotten to see a single one of her dreams come true, and someone should pay for that. He should make sure someone paid for that. If it meant spending every night in the little room and every day reliving her disappearance from the old barn, then so be it. Otherwise, it wasn't right that he was here, playing house in the very place Jess should be living. He didn't get to think about his future—it wasn't fair to her.

It had to stop. He had to remember so he could move on with his life. And while he knew he'd never forgive himself, it was time to take action.

He wouldn't be a coward anymore.

Chapter Twenty-One

At the beginning of their fourth week of working together, Beth arrived at the farm with coffee and pastries, but Drew was already out in the field, working.

She watched for chances to talk to him throughout the day, but he seemed to purposely make himself scarce. By the time she left that evening, she'd given up and left him a note with questions about the orchard and when they could meet with an expert, something that had been near the top of their list since they'd started.

The following morning, she arrived with Molly and Callie, who'd agreed to help with the Fairwind Farm Market. When she knocked on the side door of the farmhouse, there was no answer, and she could only assume Drew was already outside somewhere. Never mind that up until yesterday he'd always waited to get to work until they touched base in the mornings.

She'd grown to enjoy their little tradition. What had changed?

She pushed the door open. "Why don't we get started in here?" she said to Molly and Callie, hoping her disappointment didn't show on her face.

"As long as I get the apple fritter," Callie said.

Beth set the bag of pastries down on the table and glanced out at the yard. No sign of Drew, only the crew who'd started to wander in from the parking lot.

"I've got some creamer in the fridge," she said. "Let me get it." She pulled it out and was closing the refrigerator door when something in the trash can caught her eye.

The note she'd left the night before about the orchard.

It had been pulled off the fridge, crumpled up and discarded, like a nuisance. Not that she'd expected him to pin it up to his bulletin board like some keepsake, but seeing it in the trash like that put Beth right back in the conference room at Whitaker Mowers, desperately trying to sound like she knew what she was talking about, that she deserved respect.

She'd been striving to prove that she was more than just Jed Whitaker's daughter since the day she'd graduated college. She'd known she'd never accomplish everything she was meant to if she wasn't able to make these people take her seriously.

She brushed the thought away. This wasn't that. Drew was hardly the staff at her dad's company, and a crumpled-up note was hardly a brush-off. She knew a brush-off. Being asked to resign from your own father's company—now *that* was a brush-off.

"Beth?" Callie's hand on her shoulder pulled her back to reality.

"Sorry," she said. "I've got a lot on my mind."

"Well, let's get to work, then."

"I've been doing a lot of research," Beth said, sitting down at the table across from them. "There's a whole community of artists, makers and vintage vendors with huge followings."

"Duh." Molly took a bite of one of Callie's freshly baked apple fritters.

"You knew this?"

"You didn't?"

Beth frowned.

"You've spent way too much time in your office."

"How's that going, by the way?" Callie broke a piece off an apple fritter and popped it in her mouth.

"Work?" Beth's stomach dropped. *Can we not talk about work?*

"Yeah, how are they handling it with you out here every day?"

Beth met Callie's eyes. She should've told her the truth. Should've told Molly. She'd made this whole thing worse. It was humiliating.

"She took a leave," Molly said. "I'm sure they don't mind. They're probably just so happy you're still on their staff."

I. Was. Wrong.

The words echoed through Beth's mind. Why was saying it aloud still so difficult?

"Well, that's true." Callie laughed.

Molly smacked her hand down on the table. "So, the Fairwind Farm Market."

"Right." Beth opened her laptop. "I didn't realize these markets could be such a draw. But we have the perfect venue to make this a huge success."

"I'm starting to realize what I've gotten myself into," Callie said. "I forgot you don't do anything small."

That included making mistakes.

Ugh. What was wrong with her? Why did a crumpled-up note in a trash can have this kind of effect on her?

"I think we can really create an event that will put Fairwind back on the map," she said, forcing the ugly thoughts out of her mind. "That means a whole lot more work than we anticipated."

"Sounds good to me," Molly said. "It's not like we can do much else around here. There's only so many times I can mow the lawn and you can water your vegetables."

"I resent that," Beth said. "If we had time, we could learn to do all this stuff."

"Oh, I forgot. You're all 'I am woman, hear me roar.'" Molly rolled her eyes.

"You forgot that?" Callie asked. "She came out of the womb roaring."

Molly laughed. "That's true. Who needs a man? Not my sister! They'll just get in her way."

Beth straightened. "That's not true."

Molly's eyes widened. "Beth. Please. Do you know yourself at all?"

She looked away. "We need to talk about this sale. We need to make it the event of the year. I was thinking of asking Dina Larson for some help."

Both Callie and Molly stopped moving and stared at her, wide-eyed.

"I'm sorry, what?" Callie set her muffin down. "Dina Larson?"

"She was out here last week. Said she'd help with advertising for the farm. I'm sure she'd help with this too."

"We can't afford her," Molly said.

"She said she'd give me the best-friend discount."

"She's not your best friend." Callie sounded defensive.

"I know," Beth said. "But she offered."

Callie took a bite, chewed it slowly. "It would probably be good for her, I guess."

Beth frowned. "What do you mean?"

"I hear things sometimes," she said. "At work."

Molly's eyes darted to Beth, then back to Callie. "And?"

"I heard her husband is leaving her. Her grandma Ginny told my mom."

Beth's shoulders slumped at the news. What if Dina hadn't come out to Fairwind to rub her success in Beth's face at all? What if she'd simply needed a friend? Beth hadn't been what she was looking for, she was sure. She'd been far too untrusting to see Dina's actions as anything other than patronizing.

What if Dina Larson's perfect life . . . wasn't?

"I'll reach out to her," Beth said. "And I'll work on a website. Molly, can you reach out to vendors, since you seem to understand the way this world works?"

"Sure," she said. "I'll start today."

"Okay, but I need a list of everyone you contact."

Molly shot her an exasperated look. "I can do this, Beth. I promise."

"All right, let's go outside and map out where we want everything," Beth said, gathering her notes. "That way, if there's something we need cleaned or repaired before the day of the event, we can let Drew and the other guys know."

Saying his name aloud made her feel naked, like it was some sort of admission that she spent more time than she should thinking about him.

The three of them headed out toward the barn, Beth's uneasiness bubbling inside of her. After their day planting the garden, she'd expected her friendship with Drew to settle into a nice rhythm, but the opposite had happened. She hadn't thought it was possible, but he'd grown even more withdrawn than before. She didn't like that he seemed to have any hold over the way she felt, but between the note in the trash and the obvious distance he'd put between them, she could tell something was wrong.

Why did she care? He was her employee, not her boyfriend.

Even the thought of that sent heat to her cheeks.

"How do you get anything done with all these hot guys around all day?" Callie watched as two of Drew's guys walked out of the main barn.

"Oh, Beth only has eyes for one hot guy," Molly said.

Beth stopped walking and stared at her sister. "What? No, I don't."

Molly waggled her eyebrows in typical kid-sister fashion. "She's in denial."

"I am not," Beth said. A few more of the crew strolled around the property as if they had all the time in the world. "Don't they know we're on a really tight deadline?"

"Maybe they're on break," Molly said. "They get those."

They came up to the main barn, and she saw more men sitting around. Laughing. Taking it easy. Perhaps she'd put too much faith in Drew's ability to manage these men. All this time, she thought he'd insist on them working at his pace—not a snail's.

Inside, another small group stood in a circle shooting the breeze. Not a single one of them seemed to notice she was there. Shouldn't they at least pretend to be working, considering she'd be the one who signed their paychecks?

She scanned the barn for Drew, but he was nowhere to be found.

"Unbelievable."

"Beth, let's let Drew handle the staff," Molly said.

"That's what I thought we were doing," she said.

She and Molly deserved their respect too, and they clearly didn't have it. Beth had to prove herself competent, even if she felt anything but.

"Excuse me?" Her voice did nothing to end the chatter. If anything, the volume of their voices increased, swallowing hers up.

"Excuse me?" Louder and with more authority.

Acknowledgment rippled through the group at the same pace the men seemed intent on working. Slow and steady. Eyes finally turned on the three of them.

"Beth, this is a bad idea."

"Relax, Molly," she said quietly. "Someone has to show these guys who's in charge."

"Does it have to be you?"

"I assume you all know who I am," Beth said, ignoring her sister. "But if not, let me refresh your memory." She stood taller, remembering the importance of looking the part. She might be shorter and smaller than every man who now gave her his full attention, but she'd make sure her presence outweighed them by one hundred pounds. At least.

"I'm the one responsible for this farm. I pay the bills. I sign the checks. So when I come out here and find you all sitting around, chatting and laughing like a group of friends on a camping trip, you can imagine it doesn't sit well with me. In case you missed the memo, guys, we've got a deadline. And it'll be here before we know it. But none of you seem at all interested in working today, so what do you think I should do? Send you all home and find a crew who is actually interested in earning their money?"

Kent Tanner took a step away from the crowd. He still had the same cocky attitude he'd had back in high school; Beth could see it in the way he looked at her now. "Well, look at that, boys. Guess we've been told."

Beth stiffened and reminded herself not to lose her nerve. She should've known there would be at least one.

"It's true what everyone says about you, isn't it?" Kent took a step in her direction, towering over her. He weighed at least twice as much as she did.

She lifted her chin and narrowed her eyes, part of her wishing she'd stayed in the house. "Do you really think I care what anyone around here says about me?"

She did. Did it show?

He smirked, moving in on her. "I heard you're even more uptight than you were in high school. But then, you always did think you were better than everyone else."

"Dude, back off." Molly took a step closer.

Kent didn't pay attention to her, eyes still locked onto Beth.

"Crying shame you're so stuck up too. You turned out pretty hot." He walked around her, eyes full on her in a way that sent a chill straight down her spine.

"Kent, knock it off." Molly grabbed his arm, but he shook her off.

He leaned in close to Beth so the others couldn't hear. "Maybe you just need a real man to show you what you're missing." He took a strand of her hair and tugged it.

"Tanner!"

Beth turned, still aware of Kent's unnerving nearness, and saw Drew standing in the doorway.

"Boss." Kent took a step away, hands on his hips.

Drew looked at Beth, who quickly looked away, embarrassed.

Molly grabbed her arm and pulled her away from Kent.

"Miss Whitaker wanted to know why none of us were at work." Kent's glare was full of contempt.

"And you told her that I went to get the dirt and mulch and asked you all to be back at the barn at eleven to help unload, right?" Drew glanced at Beth again.

Was that worry in his eyes?

"Nah, Boss, I was just messing with her." Kent laughed.

"Messing with her?" Drew glared at him.

"Yeah, we go way back, me and Whitaker."

"She's your boss."

"You're my boss."

"Well, she's my boss, so you do the math."

"Dude, relax," Kent said.

Beth, Callie and Molly watched Drew, wide-eyed. The calm, even-keeled cowboy looked a little like he might explode.

"Drew, it's fine," Beth said, taking a step toward him.

He held a hand up to warn her not to come any closer, eyes still fixed on Kent. "You can go, Tanner."

A soft murmur of surprise wound its way around the circle of men.

"You can't be serious," Kent scoffed.

Drew walked over to him, fire behind his eyes. "Get out."

Irritated, Kent shifted his weight, as if unsure of his next move. Finally, he broke his stare, walked off to the side of the barn and picked up his jacket and a lunch box. "Yeah, okay. You all stay here and take orders from the Ice Queen." He walked toward Beth—stopping right in front of her. Too close. "You happy, Princess?"

She glared up at him, and then, without thinking, Beth hauled off and punched him in the face.

Unlike in the movies, Kent did not fall to the ground. In fact, he barely lost his balance. Beth pulled her hand back and watched, eyes wide, as he covered his nose with his hands, turning away from her.

"You're crazy!" he shouted, followed by a string of swear words. "What is wrong with you?" He turned back and fixed his glare on her, and she quickly took a step back, grateful when Drew grabbed him by the shirt and dragged him out of the barn.

Molly let out what sounded like an involuntary laugh. "Holy cow! You just punched a guy."

Beth looked at her hand, which screamed in pain. "I know. It hurt."

"But it felt good too, right? He deserved it." Molly held up Beth's arms like she'd won a boxing match. "In this corner, weighing hardly anything, my sister, Beth Whitaker, the reigning champion of Fairwind Farm."

Beth pulled her arm away. "Molly, please."

"What? These guys probably all think you're totally cool now."

"These guys have a truck to unload," Beth said, loud enough for them to hear.

In seconds, the barn emptied.

"I'll go get you some ice for your hand," Callie said, running off toward the house.

"I want to help these guys unload," Molly said. "I'm feeling pumped up after that fistfight."

Beth watched from inside the barn as Kent's ratty old truck pulled out of the parking lot, and she tried not to let his insults bother her.

The Ice Queen.

They'd always said she thought she was better than the rest of them. She'd been so intent on getting out of town, they'd said she looked down her nose at everyone who wanted to stay. And maybe they were right. Maybe she had.

And now look at her. She was one of them.

"You okay?" Drew walked toward her, concern on his face. He took her hand and carefully turned it over, brushing her knuckles with his thumb. She grimaced. Punching someone in the face hurt.

"You need ice." He moved into the empty barn.

"I'm fine." But even as she said the words, her eyes clouded over, and she begged herself to keep it together at least until she could lock herself in a bathroom.

Drew slipped his hand into hers. "Can you squeeze my fingers?"

She blinked and, to her dismay, a tear fell down her cheek, but she did as she was told and squeezed his hand. Pain shot through her fingers, concentrated around her knuckles.

"They aren't broken." Drew kept his voice quiet. "You clocked him pretty good." He sounded amused. With his free hand, he reached over and wiped the tear from her cheek.

She stiffened at his touch, but he didn't move away. Instead, he searched her eyes as if still deciding if she was okay.

She took a deep breath and tried not to let her nerves show. It made her mad she'd let Kent get to her. Even madder that she'd let herself cry—even for a moment. No matter what happened, she was stronger than that. "I've never punched anybody before."

"I'd say he was a good first punch." Drew smiled, then covered her hand with his other one, held it for a minute and, as if he'd come to some unspoken conclusion, let it go.

"Thanks for sticking up for me," she said, the words hard to form around the knot in her throat.

"Anytime." He said it like he meant it, and his kindness only made the knot bigger.

Her attempt to gain the workers' respect had backfired in the worst way. Why hadn't she just kept her mouth shut? She started for the door.

"Beth?"

She stopped but didn't turn around. The tears were too close. Drew walked toward her—didn't he know she needed to hide?

He moved around in front of her and stood for a long moment. She kept her eyes down, not wanting him to see her humiliation.

He probably thought she was a frigid ice queen too.

Gently, and careful not to disrupt her swollen hand, Drew reached strong arms around her and pulled her into a safe hug. And while everything within her screamed that she should run the other way, Beth resisted the urge and sank a little deeper into his embrace.

In that moment, her strong façade crumbled, and she realized the burden she'd been carrying around, feeling like this farm restoration was all on her. It was her second chance, and she'd been acting like she was the only one who could make or break it.

But what was it her father used to say? *"If you're going to be strong, you've got to learn to ask for help."* Jed Whitaker had said that more than once and in many different ways.

A lesson she'd never really learned.

Standing there in the empty barn, hand in pain and ego bruised, she wondered if Drew could be the first person she asked for help.

He held her until the tears stopped but didn't say a word. And when she was ready, he knew it and released his hold on her.

But as she walked back to the farmhouse, still aware of his watchful eye, she had a sinking feeling he'd never release his hold on her heart.

Chapter Twenty-Two

"Well, that was hot." Callie handed Beth a bag of ice for her throbbing hand.

"Me punching a guy in the face?"

"No, Drew saving you like that." She let out a breathy sigh, walking just a few steps behind Beth on her way back to the farmhouse.

"He didn't save me," Beth said. "I'm the one who punched that loser."

Callie jogged ahead of her and opened the side door leading back to the kitchen table, where they probably should've stayed put all along. "He's the one who got him out. For you. I think he likes you."

"I'm sure he would've done the same thing for any of us, Callie. He's a gentleman."

"Yeah, but he wouldn't have had that look in his eyes if it were me or Molly."

"What look?"

Callie's brows raised. "You must've seen it. I think it can only be described as passion."

Beth rolled her eyes. "You read too many trashy romance novels."

"I'm telling you. There's something there."

"Well, I disagree. Can we get back to work?"

Callie reluctantly agreed, and they spent the rest of the day figuring out the details of the barn sale and avoiding Drew and the rest of the workers. The only thing that mattered now was keeping her head down and getting stuff done.

Two more days went by. Drew had continued to cross chores off the list. Yesterday, Beth had worked at a table on the porch, as the floors on the main level had been sanded and stained and needed to dry. She couldn't be sure, but she thought Drew might've pitched a tent out back and slept in the yard. They'd barely spoken since the moment in the barn, though he'd asked her twice about her hand.

She'd assured him it was fine, though she had to admit, it still hurt. She'd wrapped it tightly in white medical tape, but she'd bruised it pretty good.

And for what? Pride?

It hadn't changed anything between her and Drew. Despite that hug, he was still as standoffish as ever, so she'd decided her best course of action was to treat him exactly the same way. Their interactions had been short, her tone purposely clipped.

It was the only way to protect her heart. She didn't like the way his long embrace had knocked her off-kilter, and while she appreciated him coming to her aid, she couldn't allow herself to revel in delusions of anything more than a professional relationship.

Even if she'd caught a glimpse of him working outside with his shirt off in the light of the late-afternoon sun. He'd looked like something out of *Legends of the Fall*. Her gaze might've lingered a little longer than it should've, but she knew there was nothing between them. She'd been misguided to even toy with the idea in the first place.

She considered her options and decided to spend less time at Fairwind. There wasn't much she could do out here anyway, and her mom had made more than one passing comment about how little she'd seen of Beth lately.

She would become a silent partner, like Ben.

It was best.

Distance between her and Drew was best.

Should she tell him or just let him realize she wasn't working from the kitchen table anymore?

She gathered her things and was heading out for the car when she spotted Roxie near the well, probably desperate for something to drink. The afternoons had grown warm as spring began its final curtain call and summer tried to come onto the scene early.

She slung her bag over her shoulder and headed out toward the well. The dog ran over to her, and Beth rubbed her head the way she knew Roxie liked.

"You thirsty, girl?"

Roxie turned in a circle. As Beth pumped water for her, Drew emerged from inside the small garden shed.

He lifted a hand, and she waved back, surprised when he started walking toward her. Her pumping slowed down at his approach. Standing in front of her, he almost looked like he didn't know what to say.

"Good day?" She righted the bag on her shoulder.

He nodded. "We got a lot done."

"Good."

Awkward silence hung between them.

"I did some digging on the orchards, like you asked."

The image of the crumpled note rushed back at her. She'd thought he'd forgotten all about that.

"Our trees actually look pretty good to me," he said, "but apple trees aren't my area of expertise."

"Mine either." She would hardly be able to tell a healthy tree from a dead one.

He kicked at the dirt underfoot.

She squinted up at him, took a fleeting moment to admire his well-defined cheekbones. She hadn't thought real people had cheekbones like that, only Greek gods and marble statues.

"I set up a meeting tomorrow with a tree guy. Can you be here first thing?"

"Of course." She gave him a curt smile, then stopped pumping the well. "Is that all?"

He took a step back and shoved his hands in his pockets with a nod. He'd done so much for them; he didn't deserve her coldness.

But it had to be this way. "See you tomorrow, then."

◆ ◆ ◆

That night, Beth scattered receipts and papers all around her on her mother's living-room floor. Her mom sat quietly in her favorite armchair, ignoring Beth's heavy sighs.

She'd just written a big check for lumber so Drew could repair the stalls in the petting-zoo barn. She had to wonder if it would've been cheaper to tear the whole thing down and start over.

Beth threw her pencil down on the notebook filled with figures that weren't adding up.

"When are you going to ask me?" Her mom turned the page of her book.

"Ask you what?" Lilian had a way of needling Beth, making her think about things she'd rather not discuss.

"For money." Her eyes stayed on her book, but Beth knew she wasn't reading.

"Never." Beth gathered the paperwork, regretting her decision to work on the budget here. She could feel her mother's eyes drilling into her. Finally, she looked up.

"What if I want to be a part of this new adventure?" Lilian set her book in her lap. "Would you really deny me that joy?"

Beth thought about their options. The barn sale would bring in some money, and she'd asked Ben to kick in a little bit more. She hadn't been able to get the loan, but she had her trust fund—she could pull from that if they needed to.

Her eyes found Davis Biddle's business card clipped to the inside of her notebook. While she was curious about the man, she'd yet to reach out to him. Even if he did want to buy the farm or become a silent investor, the thought of taking it outside the family still didn't sit well. And they knew almost nothing about this man.

"Your health is the most important thing right now, Mom." Beth neatly stacked her pile of papers on the coffee table.

"No, my kids are the most important."

Beth looked at her, sitting in that chair with the afghan over her legs, book in her lap. Would her mom feel that way about Beth if she knew her actions had led to her dad's heart attack?

"Beth?"

She made eye contact but said nothing.

Her mom gave her a kind smile. "You're not as alone as you think you are."

A lump swelled in Beth's throat. She looked away. Finally, she gathered her pile, kissed the top of her mother's head and retired to the solitude of her room.

Would the guilt ever go away? When would she be able to sit back and say, "Now I've done enough to make up for the pain I caused"?

Another year? Two? An eternity?

In the morning, as she drove out to Fairwind for her meeting with Drew and the tree guy, Beth tried not to think about the tears she'd shed in the dark of night. Her mother's love was almost too unconditional. Beth certainly didn't deserve it.

She pulled into the same space she'd parked in since day one. The farm looked pretty today, bathed in the morning sunlight.

She'd gotten a late start but still managed to pick up coffee for Drew. And when she met him on the front porch, Roxie at his side, she could see he needed it.

"Hey." He wore gray cargo pants and a red T-shirt with that same baseball cap and five o'clock shadow he wore every day. His eyes looked tired.

"Did you get any sleep last night?" She handed him the cup.

"Is it that obvious?" He took the coffee, drank. "Thanks for this."

"The bags under your eyes are a dead giveaway." She wanted to ask him why he never slept. Why his bedding was folded neatly on the end of the couch in the living room rather than in one of the bedrooms upstairs. Why he seemed intent on using work to distract him from whatever it was he didn't want to think about.

Instead, they drank their coffee in silence.

Silence, they were good at.

Moments later, a white Ford F-150 appeared on the gravel road. Roxie sat at attention.

"What do you know about this guy?" Beth stood.

"Not much. He called me. He must've heard we were asking around about the trees."

Beth frowned. "That's odd. Why wouldn't he call me?"

He smirked.

"What?"

He crossed his arms over his chest, sending the faint smell of his musky soap in her direction. She'd have to ignore that.

She watched the truck park next to Drew's. Roxie barked.

"You think he called you because he heard you were the brains out here," Beth said, keeping her tone light.

"No, he heard I'm the brawn."

Her attempt to hide her smile was unsuccessful.

"Haven't seen one of those in a while." Drew stood. "The smile, I mean."

She faced him. "I could say the same to you." His stony expression had come to define him in her thoughts. In all the time he'd been there, she'd hardly seen any genuine happiness in his eyes. Instead, he always seemed to carry a burden just a little too heavy for his shoulders.

"If I looked as pretty as you do when I smiled, I'd probably never stop."

Her jaw tensed as she forced herself not to babble the first thing that came to her mind, which wasn't difficult, as one quick search revealed her mind was hopelessly empty.

When he walked away, Roxie followed, leaving Beth speechless on the porch.

He thinks I'm pretty.

Reminding herself to remain in control, she stopped the nonsensical ideas from filling her head. He worked for her. In the business world, she could be sued for even looking at the man.

And she'd never admit how much looking she'd actually done.

She strolled toward Drew, Roxie and an older man wearing tattered jeans and a threadbare maroon T-shirt that fit snugly over his round midsection.

"Thanks for meeting us out here," Drew said. "Beth, this is Walter Sherman."

Beth shook his hand.

"I understand you're the new owner?" Walter asked.

"My sister and I." Molly had declined the meeting in favor of taking her new dog to the vet now that the puppy was ready to come home. Last Beth heard, she was trying to land on a name for the animal. Beth imagined they'd end up with a black Lab called Sparkles.

"Good to meet you. You've got yourself quite a project." Walter surveyed the farm, taking in the barns, the acres, the work left to be done.

Beth hated the way he'd said it, like they'd bitten off more than they could possibly chew. And they had. She just didn't like the reminder.

"We want to get a handle on the orchards," Drew said. "I've done some reading, and our trees actually look pretty good."

Beth admired the way he took ownership of the farm. Her dad would be impressed by Drew's solid work ethic.

And he thinks I'm pretty.

"They should," Walter said. "I've been pruning and harvesting them for years now."

Beth looked at Drew, who appeared as surprised as she felt. "You have?"

"Harold probably didn't leave much information behind, did he?" Even this early in the season, the man's dark skin suggested hours of work out in the sun.

The photograph of Jess and the little boy sprang to Beth's mind. "Actually, he left plenty, it's just that we're still sifting through everything."

"That's a job, I bet," Walter said. "We've been caring for the trees going on twenty years now."

Just after Jess had gone missing.

"Even after the farm closed?" Beth asked.

"Sure. After that, we harvested the apples for Sonya. Made a nice profit selling them at the farmers' markets and the like. I imagine those apples kept them afloat for a while."

"And after Sonya passed away?" Beth imagined all the prayers Sonya hadn't written down but simply whispered into the wind. Had she strolled through the orchards, begging God for answers?

Why, God?

"Same thing. We've never stopped with the orchards. They're valuable."

"I'm surprised Harold kept up with your bills," Drew said. "From what we can tell, he let everything go."

"Oh, he didn't pay us."

"Well, that doesn't make sense," Beth said. "Did you take your pay out of what the apples made at the markets?"

Walter's face warmed into a tender smile. "No, Harold and Sonya weren't the ones who hired me." He pulled his wallet from his back pocket and pressed a business card into her hand. "This man hired me to take care of the orchards for them. I'm not sure they ever even knew."

Davis Biddle.

"This man approached my sister," Beth said. "Does he want to buy the farm?"

Walter's smile broadened. "I don't know about that, but Mr. Biddle has always had a soft spot for Fairwind. Or maybe for Mrs. Pendergast, but you didn't hear it from me."

Beth glanced at Drew, who said nothing.

"So he took care of the farm all these years because he was sweet on Sonya?" Beth asked.

Walter scratched the side of his mustache. "I couldn't say for sure, ma'am. But he and Sonya were high school sweethearts."

"Why didn't he just buy the farm after Harold died?" Drew asked.

"He was in the Caribbean," Beth and Walter said in unison.

"You say this started about twenty years ago?" Drew asked.

"Just after the girl went missing. Mr. Biddle got a bad reputation. He's a shrewd businessman, and people don't always understand his choices. He's not known as a compassionate man, but when he heard what happened, he wanted to help."

"There must've been something in it for him, some financial motive," Beth said.

"Maybe he really loved her," Drew said.

"So he spent twenty years taking care of her land? Even after she died?" she asked.

"People do crazy things for love," he said.

Had Drew ever done something crazy for love?

"Maybe there was money in it for him," Walter said. "I couldn't really say. I don't ask Mr. Biddle questions, I just do what he tells me."

"I did a little digging on him when Molly gave me his card," Beth said. "He owns property that meets up with ours."

"I take care of his property too," Walter said. "He's hardly ever there—always traveling for business."

Maybe that's why Beth didn't know the man. Willow Grove was a small town; if Davis Biddle had spent any amount of time there in the last ten years, Beth would've known him.

"He doesn't talk about it," Walter added. "So, keep this between us, if you don't mind."

Nothing about this made sense.

"Should we take a walk through the orchards?" Drew asked, probably tired of Beth's suspicions. They were here to talk about trees.

"Sure. And I'll tell you what it takes to keep it going, write you up an estimate just in case you want to keep us on, at least till you get your bearings." Walter followed Drew toward the main barn, Beth and Roxie bringing up the rear. "Don't worry, I'll give you the family discount," he said over his shoulder. "I love this old farm."

Apparently, for some unknown reason, so did Davis Biddle.

And something about that didn't sit right with Beth.

◆　◆　◆

Drew drove a golf cart he'd found in the garage from the main barn to the orchards, with Roxie running close behind. He'd seen the business card on the table among Beth's mess of papers, but the name hadn't meant anything to him until Walter said it aloud.

Davis Biddle.

If he had a bad reputation—if he'd been Sonya's high school sweetheart—maybe Drew had overheard his parents talking about him. Maybe Drew had even seen him at Fairwind sometime.

Or maybe Beth's suspicious curiosity had rubbed off on him.

The only thing he knew for sure was that the name struck a chord in his gut—a chord telling him to pay attention—and left him wondering if Davis Biddle might be the key to filling in some of the blanks in his spotty memory.

Chapter Twenty-Three

Downtown Willow Grove bustled with activity on Saturday morning. The high school's senior class was throwing their annual school carnival and bake sale, the last big event before tourists took over their little town. Locals came out in droves to support the event, partly for nostalgic reasons and partly to raise funds for whatever the graduating class decided the school needed most.

This year, they wanted a new scoreboard for the football field.

Beatty Park, with its open fields and ample shade, had proved to be the best place in town for an event like this, complete with carnival rides, games and local food vendors who showed up early to aid a worthy cause.

Though Beth was exhausted, she knew showing her face at the carnival was important. These were the same people she hoped would support not only their barn sale, but the farm itself. Besides, she couldn't miss the carnival. It was a tradition.

She loved the artistic spin the Willow Grove locals put on a school fund-raiser. Off to one side of the park, artists set up easels to demonstrate their skills, surrounded by displays of the original artwork they had for sale. Beth always stopped to browse the paintings, the art lover in her wishing for the chance to hold a brush again.

After days of long hours and sore muscles, Beth told herself she wouldn't rush through the morning the way she usually did. She'd go slow, talk to the people she knew, people who had come out to volunteer their time and manual labor in an effort to get the farm off the ground. She owed them so much.

Today, she promised herself she'd enjoy the day off.

And true Saturday enjoyment started with coffee.

Up ahead, she spotted the red-and-white gingham bunting of Callie's bakery booth. She hoped her friend charged a fair price for her pies and pastries. Knowing Callie and her big heart, she was probably giving everything away. But—Callie would have coffee. And right now, that's what really mattered. Beth made her way through the crowd, and as she finally reached the booth, she saw a familiar profile in line behind an old couple.

Drew.

He glanced her way. She smiled. Her efforts to maintain a professional façade around him had been valiant but flawed. Because everything inside her turned to mush as soon as she saw those eyes.

"You're out early," he said as she reached the line.

"So are you. You didn't want to sleep in?" She knew better. He probably hadn't slept at all.

Roxie sat beside him, her leash wound through Drew's strong hands. The dog stood to greet Beth, but one tug from the leash and she sat back down. "She's not used to being around so many people."

Beth knelt down and rubbed Roxie's ears, avoiding the thick tail that pounded the ground beside her.

"Hey, you two," Callie said, clearly assuming they'd come together. "The usual?"

Drew nodded. "And two apple fritters." He glanced at Beth. "Unless you're not hungry?"

"I am, actually." She rarely allowed herself pastries, but lately she seemed to be living on them. Thank goodness even her simple farm chores burned lots of calories.

Drew took a twenty-dollar bill from his pocket and set it on the counter.

"Let me," Beth said.

"Not a chance."

Callie gave him his change and grinned at Beth. "Your sister was here already with her new dog."

Beth groaned. "I hope she had it on a leash."

"I think it might've been the other way around," Callie said. "But she left me some postcards for the Fairwind Farm Market." She patted the stack on the counter. "I'll make sure everyone gets one, and I'll talk to the vendors I know—some of them came out for this."

"Thanks, Cal."

A man walked up behind them, and Drew moved out of the way.

"I'll stop back before I leave," Beth said.

Callie smiled, waved goodbye to Drew and then waggled her eyebrows at Beth.

"You guys seem like good friends," Drew said.

"The best."

Drew followed her to one of the many picnic tables set up all around the park, opened the bag and took out the apple fritters, setting them on the paper between them.

"You're lucky." Drew took a swig of coffee.

She picked at the glaze on the fritter. "You must have some good friends back home."

"Well, let's see. There's Mabel. I guess I'd call her a friend."

Beth swallowed the bite in her mouth. "Oh."

"Course, she's a horse, so I don't know if that counts."

She glanced up just in time to see his smile skitter away. "Funny." A quiet lull fell between them.

"I feel like you know a lot about me," Beth dared. "But I know almost nothing about you."

"You know plenty about me." He tossed a piece of apple fritter in his mouth.

"You worked at a ranch in Colorado—a ranch that has a web page that doesn't list its staff, by the way."

"You checked?"

"Course I checked. The only reason I didn't call your boss is because I didn't want to get you in trouble."

"You're thorough, I'll give you that." He smiled.

Oh, that smile. It was something.

"There's really not much to tell," he said.

"Did you go to school?"

"I did."

"For what?"

"Agricultural sciences."

"For real? No wonder you know how to do everything."

He laughed. "Well, working at the ranch taught me most of what I know—more than school in a lot of ways."

"So you have a degree from . . . where?"

"Colorado State."

"Colorado State, and you're doing this kind of work?"

He shrugged. "I like it."

She eyed him for a long moment.

"What about you?"

She took a drink of her coffee, wishing that if they were going to change the subject, they could focus on something other than her. "What about me?"

"I assume you have a degree."

"I do."

"In?"

"Business."

"I can see that. And, what, you just love Willow Grove so much you came back home after college?"

She laughed. "Can we walk?"

He balled up the fritter wrappers and tossed them in the garbage can. "Let's walk."

She kept her eyes ahead as they wandered down the makeshift rows of carnival games and food booths, smiling at the occasional passerby. He was quiet, most likely waiting for her to elaborate, yet she wasn't sure how much she wanted to open up to him.

He was her employee, after all.

She glanced at him. His eyes were focused in front of them, leading Roxie through the crowd that had started to gather.

"I actually kind of hated it here." She kept her eyes straight ahead. "I talked a lot of trash about this town. I guess I just wanted a different life. I mean, did you ever feel like there was something more you were supposed to do? Like you should've done it by now?"

Somehow, his silence encouraged her to go on.

"I went to college in the city, and by my senior year, I had this great internship with my dream company. I was in the running for a full-time job there after I graduated, but the job went to someone else."

"Guess it wasn't your job, then."

She frowned.

"I mean, if the door didn't open, it wasn't your door."

She laughed. "Did you read that in a fortune cookie?"

"I might have, actually." He tugged Roxie away from a box of popcorn someone had dropped on the ground.

"I didn't see it that way. I was crushed. I graduated and came back here, you know, to figure out my life, and I've been here ever since."

"You might've skipped a little bit in there."

"Like what?"

"Like, why didn't you go back to the city and get a different job?"

She pressed her lips together, figuring out how to reply. "My dad had a great business here—a manufacturing company. They make two specific parts for lawn mowers. Doesn't that sound glamorous?"

The corner of his mouth turned up in one of his trademark nonsmiles.

"I worked there in high school, just in the office, so after college, I took a very temporary position. That was seven years ago."

He didn't respond, not that she thought he would. What was he going to say—"Wow, that's kind of pathetic?"

"I was the office manager." *I almost destroyed the whole business.*

"Was?"

"I haven't told anyone, but they asked me to resign just after Molly bought the farm."

More silence.

"The truth is, if this Fairwind thing hadn't come along, I don't know what I would've done." She stopped at a game booth, the one where she could throw baseballs at jars and win something if she knocked them over. It was humiliation, not a desire to play the game, that compelled her to stop there.

She gave the kid at the booth a dollar in exchange for three baseballs.

"Miss Whitaker, let's see that arm," he said.

She squared off with the jars, drew in a breath and threw the ball as hard as she could. It smacked against the back curtain with a thud, leaving the tower of milk jars standing perfectly still.

Sighing, she lined herself up again, threw the second ball and got the same result.

She glanced down at the third ball in her hand, turning it over. As she stood there, she replayed the day her father had learned that she'd gone against his wishes and it would cost them dearly, and her eyes clouded with fresh tears. She blinked them back, determined not to let herself cry again in front of Drew.

He put a hand on her back and wrapped his free hand around the baseball she held. "Let me."

She stared at his strong hand wrapped around hers, their skin touching on the edges around the ball. She didn't know how to let anyone do anything for her—but standing there, next to him, she wanted to try.

She released her grip on the ball, and he inched it out of her hand. "Here, take Roxie."

He handed her the leash, and the dog sat at her feet as Drew stepped up in front of the booth. He lined up with the jars, threw one pitch and knocked all of them down.

"You're not as alone as you think you are."

Her mother's words rushed back at her, but she didn't know how to make sense of them. She *was* alone.

Drew took a small stuffed-animal prize from the kid manning the booth and handed it to Beth.

"Thanks," she said.

As he took Roxie's leash from her, her fingers brushed against his, and her whole body was aware of the touch.

He continued walking in the direction they'd been going before she'd stopped. "What happened? With your job, I mean?"

She looked away. She'd sworn she'd never tell a soul.

Why, then, was she actually figuring out how to put it into words?

Beth weaved in and around people walking in the opposite direction until finally Drew took hold of her hand and pulled her off the path and toward the band shell, where only a few other people sat.

He sat down and ordered Roxie to do the same.

"It's nothing, really," she said.

"It's not nothing."

She let out an exhausted sigh. "I was wrong."

His eyebrows shot up.

"I was really, really wrong." Slowly, she sat down in the chair next to him. "My dad had been running his business for years. It was doing really well—like, really well." She glanced at him. She saw no judgment, only a willingness to let her talk.

235

"Like I said before, we manufacture lawn mower parts. I thought I'd found a less expensive way to make this one specific part. I went to my dad and told him about it, and he wouldn't even hear me out."

She'd been so excited—so sure she'd found something that would save money. They'd streamlined the material, made it more affordable so shops like theirs didn't have to pay as much. The best part was they wouldn't have to change what they charged because nobody would ever know the difference.

She worked for two weeks straight on a presentation to take to her dad. Now that she was managing the office, keeping costs within their budget was something she was responsible for, and she wanted nothing more than to do him proud.

She'd hardly gotten through the opening paragraph of her presentation when he held up a hand and stopped her. "No."

She stood, slack-jawed, in front of his desk. "You haven't heard what I'm going to say."

"I know where this is going. I'm not changing the materials in our parts. Our customers rely on us. They know they're getting the best. This stuff"—he waved a hand across her paperwork—"is not the best."

"It could save us a lot of money."

"And it could ruin our reputation. I appreciate your work on this, Beth, but the answer is no."

She recounted the conversation for Drew, then paused to take a breath.

"It might've been the first time in my life I didn't do what my father said." She stared at her folded hands in her lap. "And I should have. About six months later, customers started complaining. Because of the change, our clients' mowers were defective, and three of them got together and sued my dad's company."

Beth could feel the tears building behind her eyes. Drew hadn't moved a muscle the whole time they sat there. He only listened. She supposed men who hated talking were good at that.

236

"I'd never seen my father so angry," she said. "Especially at me. At my brother Seth, maybe—but me?"

Beth had been so ashamed. Whitaker Mowers was being sued for the first time, and it was because of her. She'd tarnished the reputation of the company her father had tirelessly worked to build.

"The worst part was that he took the blame." She wiped a traitorous tear from her cheek and stared at the ground. "He never told anybody it was my fault. And neither did I." Of course Darren Sanders had found out—a paper trail tattled on her. When he'd confronted her on it only a few weeks ago, she'd almost felt relieved.

Almost. As far as anyone in her family knew, she was still working at Whitaker. How was that for shameful?

"Is that why you work so hard? You're trying to make it up to him?"

She shrugged. "He died before I could. He had a heart attack. I can't help but think that was my fault too. I caused so much stress. I broke his heart." Another tear slid down her cheek. "But a part of me has always felt like I had something to prove."

"Right, because you're supposed to do something more."

She stilled. "More than Willow Grove? Yes. Great dreams don't come true in places like this."

"Sometimes they do."

Slowly, she found his eyes.

"Mine don't. I'm not like the people who live here. People like Callie. She never had big dreams like I did. She likes this small town. She bakes pies for a living—and she loves it. The only thing missing from her life is a husband and a carload of babies. Once she has that, she'll never wish for anything else the rest of her life."

"And that's not okay?"

"It's great for her." Beth wiped her palms on her jeans. "Not for me." She paused. "I just thought I'd be closer to my goals by now, I guess."

"You do realize you are one of the people who live here, right?"

She frowned, then looked away.

"And there's nothing wrong with that."

He didn't understand. How could he? He hadn't grown up here.

He took another drink. "Did you ever think maybe the something 'more' you were supposed to do is exactly what you're doing right now?"

She didn't even know how to answer that. Renovating an old farm was hardly in her ten-year plan. She was supposed to do *more*. Didn't he get what that meant?

Drew's stare, a little too intent, rattled the cage around her heart.

"You know, for a guy who doesn't say much, you sure have some smart things to say."

He hitched two fingers underneath her chin and flashed that lazy grin she'd come to crave. "You can't corner the market on guilt, you know. We've all done things we regret."

A quiet beat passed between them. "So what's your story?"

He pulled his hand away and wrapped it around the disposable coffee cup. Something in him shifted.

Perhaps they were more alike than she'd thought.

"Ah, well, that's a story for another day." He swallowed his last swig of coffee, then stood and threw the cup in the tall metal garbage can behind them.

She sat, unmoving, feeling like she'd said too much. She didn't make a habit of unloading her regrets on people—especially strangers—but there was something safe about Drew. Or at least there had been until he'd reciprocated nothing.

Maybe opening up to him had simply been another in a long line of bad choices.

Chapter Twenty-Four

So she was human.

Drew had started to wonder.

Listening to Beth unload the baggage she'd been carrying around had been a sort of therapy for him. Somehow, knowing he wasn't the only one with massive regret weighing him down had done him good.

It would probably do her good too, to know that she wasn't alone, but he just couldn't go there. Not yet. Probably not ever.

Not only had he kept the truth from her, but the truth was awful. Working didn't dull the pain of it anymore, not the way it used to. What would he do if he couldn't find a way to keep the thoughts at bay?

He'd spent hours in Harold's hidden room. He'd read and reread every scrap of paper the old man had collected over the years.

Nothing but nightmares came.

Now, standing in the seats outside the band shell, waiting for Beth, he wondered if it was time to get back to his real life. Back to Colorado, where at least he wouldn't be faced with the memory of Jess every time he walked outside.

"Do you have time to walk around for a little while?" he asked, hoping he wasn't stepping out of line. Somehow he didn't feel right about leaving her alone.

She looked genuinely surprised he'd asked.

She finished off her coffee and threw her cup away. "Sure." She ran her fingers through her hair, shaking it out behind her and just about driving him nuts in the process.

If he wasn't careful, he could fall in love with this girl. And that couldn't happen. He needed to stay focused—if happily ever after was not in the cards for Jess, it wasn't for him.

"Do you think less of me now?" she asked, avoiding his gaze.

He grabbed her arm and stopped. "Beth, no."

She wouldn't look at him.

"I'm glad you told me."

Finally, he had her eyes—she looked like she wanted to say something, but apparently thought better of it.

"I mean it," he said.

She gave one quick nod and started walking again.

"So, tell me about this big barn sale you're going to have." He hoped the change of subject would lighten her mood.

Thankfully, she smiled. That smile he'd started to dream of.

They started walking, Roxie between them. She told him about the old days when the Fairwind Farm Market was the biggest event in town.

"They did it in late spring, but I think we can get away with doing it in the summer," she said.

"So it's like a big rummage sale?"

She stopped walking and glared at him. "Seriously?"

He shrugged. "This whole thing sounds really girly to me."

She shoved him in the shoulder, and he held up his hands in mock surrender.

"Molly's done a really good job securing vendors," she said.

"What kind of vendors?"

"All kinds. Art, jewelry, handmade signs. Like the stuff you see here. One couple makes and sells organic dog biscuits. You should get some for Roxie."

"And how do we make money on this?" He realized his mistake as soon as he said it. "Sorry, I meant you. How do *you* make money on this?"

"I actually like the way you talk about the farm, like you're a part of it. My dad always said the best employees are those who take ownership of their work."

"Sounds like my kind of guy."

"You would've liked him." She smiled. "He would've liked you."

Why did he feel like he'd just passed a test he didn't know he was taking?

"To answer your question, all vendors pay a fee to be part of the event, and then we charge admission. Plus, we'll sell what we can from the farmhouse."

"And you think it'll be profitable?"

"I think it could be amazing."

With her in charge, he had no doubt.

"Maybe next year I'll even be able to sell my own vegetables there. I mean, I haven't managed to kill anything yet."

No, but it had been close. She'd nearly flooded the raised beds twice.

"I appreciate you sharing your knowledge with me. I've never had much of a green thumb."

He glanced at her. "Or maybe you don't like dirt under your fingernails?"

Her eyes went wide. "Are you saying I'm prissy?"

"I'm not saying a word." He couldn't help but smile.

"Someday maybe we'll clear out that whole section of land and turn it into a big garden," Beth said. "Don't tell Molly or she'll rent one of those Bobcat things by Monday just because she thinks it'd be fun to drive."

"Speaking of Molly."

Beth followed Drew's gaze to the end of the row, near Dickerson's Produce, where a black Lab lumbered toward them, dragging Molly behind.

"Twenty bucks says she asks you to train that dog," Beth said, keeping an eye on Roxie, who sat at attention as Molly and the other dog approached.

"Daisy. Sit." Molly had done her best to sound commanding, but the puppy continued to circle around them.

"Need some help?" Drew handed Beth Roxie's leash and commanded his dog to stay, then took Daisy's leash and gave it a tug. With his free hand, he pushed Daisy's hind end down to the ground. "Sit." She sat for a split second, and he pushed her backside down again. "Sit."

The dog finally obeyed, but they knew it wouldn't last long.

"You gotta help me with this dog, Drew," Molly said, trying to catch her breath.

Drew met Beth's eyes, and she mouthed the words *twenty bucks*. He rubbed Daisy's head. "She's a good girl," he said. "She's just a puppy."

Roxie whined.

"I've been handing out barn-sale postcards since I got here," Molly said, thrusting a stack of them at Beth. "You can do the rest." She pulled her hair into a ponytail and wrapped an elastic around it.

"I designed them. You were supposed to hand them out." She handed them back.

Molly frowned. "Do you know how hard it is to talk to people with this dog?"

"Maybe you should've left her at home."

Daisy sniffed Roxie, who looked irate but didn't move.

"That's the other thing," Molly said.

Beth glared at her. "*What's* the other thing?"

"My landlord said no dogs. She's going to have to live with you and Mom."

Beth said nothing.

Drew looked at her, then at Molly and back to Beth. "She can come live at the farm."

"Yes!" Molly practically shouted.

"No!" Beth crossed her arms over her chest. "This is exactly what I was talking about, Molly."

"Not now, Beth. I have good news." She took a step closer. "I talked to Bishop about that case."

Molly's train of thought looked a lot like the inside of a pinball machine.

"He's pulling the file and bringing it over tonight. We're going to look through the entire thing."

Beth shook her head. "He could get in trouble for that, couldn't he? Showing you a case file?"

Molly ignored her. "I went to the courthouse yesterday and had them print out everything that's public record, but maybe Bishop's file can fill in the holes."

Drew gave Daisy's leash a firm tug and stood. "What are you talking about?"

"Oh, gosh. You probably don't even know!" Molly said. "Twenty years ago, there was a kidnapping on our property. The owners' only daughter." She pushed a postcard into the hands of a passerby.

For a moment, Drew lost his breath, as if all the oxygen had been sucked out of his lungs by a high-powered vacuum cleaner.

Beth drew in a deep breath. "Can you keep your voice down, Molly?"

"It's not a secret." Molly looked around, like she was only just that second aware they were in public. More postcards into more hands.

They were digging around on the case? Why? And why was this the first time he'd heard anyone mention it?

A bohemian-looking woman in a long purple skirt stopped beside them and looked at the glossy card. "You're the Whitaker girls."

"That's right," Beth said. "I'm Beth, and this is my sister, Molly."

The woman turned her gaze on Drew. "And you are?"

"Drew Barlow." He shook her outstretched hand, jangling the bracelets halfway up her arm, but his mind was elsewhere.

"He's not from here," Beth said. She glanced at him, and he got the impression she thought she was protecting him from something.

The curiosity of nosy townspeople, maybe? Beth had deduced how much he didn't enjoy small talk—he appreciated the gesture, though it did little to calm his wary nerves.

"You can call me Cricket," the woman said.

"Cricket?" Molly smiled brightly. "I love that."

"It's a nickname," Cricket said.

"Because your last name is Chirper." Beth must've heard of her.

"That's right," Cricket said. "Everyone knows the crazy Chirper family. We're the ones with the pink house out on the edge of town."

"I love that house." Molly could win an award as the most easily excited person Drew had ever met. He knew it annoyed Beth, but he found the younger Whitaker amusing.

"I love this barn sale idea," Cricket said. "I'd love to bring my jewelry out there, especially if it supports Fairwind Farm. You girls have been so kind to allow my mother to continue to use her art space. I know she's thankful."

Beth's jaw went slack as she turned to Molly, seemingly expecting her sister to connect the dots, but Molly shrugged—she clearly had no idea what Cricket was talking about.

But Drew did.

His heart sank.

"Oh, no," Cricket said, assessing their faces. "You didn't know she was there."

Beth looked at Drew. "Did you?"

His eyes widened. "What now?"

He couldn't lie—not to Beth—not when he'd withheld so much from her already.

Cricket closed her eyes and let out a long sigh. "I'm so sorry. After the auction, I told her to contact you girls and find out if she could continue to rent the barn loft. I saw her last week, and she told me she'd had it all cleared with you."

Beth's smile looked forced. "She's using one of our buildings?"

"I would go drag her out myself right this second, but I'm manning a booth in ten minutes."

Molly simply shrugged again. "Well, if she's not hurting anything—"

"Why don't I go talk to her?" Beth cut in.

Cricket grabbed Beth's hand. "Go easy on her. Birdie is a good, old soul. She's just always been off in her own world."

Possible that ran in their family.

"She loves that space so much," Cricket said. "She and Harold had an arrangement."

"Do you know the terms?"

"Not really. Just that Harold allowed Birdie to paint in the loft of one of his old barns. They'd been friends for years, all of them. Birdie was nice to Harold when no one else was." A soft smile warmed Cricket's face. "And I think Harold was nice to Birdie when no one else was too."

"Don't worry," Beth said. "I'll talk to her."

"I'll go with you," Drew said.

Cricket nodded and thanked them, then walked away, leaving the trio and two dogs.

"Since you're both going out there," Molly said, "can you take Daisy?"

Beth glared at her sister, who grinned and walked away, pushing postcards on everyone she passed.

Chapter Twenty-Five

"I really can't believe this woman would continue to use the barn knowing there were new owners. It's just common sense, really. And how did she stay hidden this whole time? We're out in the yard nonstop. What barn is she using?" Beth prattled on as Drew drove in silence, two barking dogs in the bed of his truck. He wished he had a way to warn Birdie she was about to be evicted, though he had reason to believe the woman would not go quietly.

And if she let on that he knew she was there, what then? Would Beth kick him out too?

His mind spun with excuses. He should just come clean. He should tell her everything—that he knew about Birdie but didn't have the heart to make her leave, partly because she was the only person he'd met who'd been around at the time Jess went missing.

But an admission like that would require the whole truth—not just about Birdie, but about why he was there in the first place.

And he wasn't ready to get into all of that. He didn't want to show her the secret room in Harold's closet or the bulletin board he spent his evenings studying. He'd even added to it: Davis Biddle's business card. The wrapper from a piece of chewing gum he'd swiped off Birdie's desk. Photocopies from his own collection of articles—anything that might help jog his memory.

So far nothing had.

"I just can't believe the nerve of some people. If she wants to pay rent, maybe we can talk—we could use the extra income. But to have someone out there not paying a dime? That's just not how it's done." Beth crossed her arms over her chest, working herself up with every mile marker they passed.

Drew half listened. His mind raced through something—anything—to justify his keeping this from her. It was a small thing, really. Why hadn't he just told her the truth? Was trusting her that difficult?

They reached the gravel road leading to Fairwind, and Beth finally quieted.

"Maybe you'll like her." Drew tried to sound optimistic.

Beth scoffed. "She's a thief."

He snapped his mouth shut.

"Sorry. I'm just a little bent out of shape." She glared at the road in front of them.

"Maybe I should talk to her."

She glared. Wrong thing to say?

"Why, because you're a man?"

"No, because you've practically got steam coming out of your ears."

She crossed her arms again and harrumphed back onto the seat. "You think I'm overreacting."

He tapped the steering wheel with his thumb but didn't answer. He did think she was overreacting, actually, but only because he'd met Birdie. She'd grown on him. Their early evening chats had become a semiregular thing, and though she was certainly in her own world, he'd begun to enjoy the moments she invited him to be a part of it.

"I am. I know. I'm just stressed out," Beth said. "The money thing, it's—well, it's really hard to manage this place. Right now we can't afford to give anything away for free."

"Then maybe you shouldn't go in there half-cocked. Maybe she'll be a great tenant." He knew better, but what else could he say? There was always the off chance that Birdie loved the natural light enough to pay for it.

They ambled up the gravel road in silence, giving his mind room to roam.

They'd been interrupted, but knowing Molly was digging into Jess's case only added more stress to the morning. He'd been assured his own record would be sealed, but the longer he stayed at Fairwind, the harder it would be to keep his identity under wraps. Between Birdie and the cold-case files, it was just a matter of time.

Tell her, you idiot.

He glanced at Beth, who was still worked up over the "thief" in their barn. It wasn't the right time. Yes, he would tell her, but not right when she was already upset about something else. She needed him at the farm. Maybe she'd overlook his dishonesty? Or maybe something would finally fall into place and he'd get the answers he needed so he could go back to Colorado, though judging by the unanswered voice-mails on his phone, he was pretty sure he'd be looking for a new job once he did.

"I'm guessing she's probably in the old barn on the east of the property," Beth said. "Have you been in that one?" She didn't let him respond—thankfully. "I haven't. It wasn't important because I knew we didn't need it ready by fall. Obviously that was a mistake. Why didn't I walk through every single inch of the property before I signed those papers?"

"That would be quite a walk."

"Still."

Drew drove out onto the grass, stopping near the would-be art barn. He'd grown so familiar with the space and with Birdie. He liked her. Maybe because she was full of conspiracy theories and no ability to censor herself. It was hard to find people who said what they really thought without any concern for how it sounded. Plus, she'd known Jess. She'd mourned her death and still thought about what had happened to her. They had that in common.

Beth pushed the door to the barn open, and he listened for Birdie's music. Instead, all he heard was silence. Good, maybe she wasn't even there. He stood back while Beth explored the dark space. It felt more honest than pretending he hadn't been there before.

Who was he kidding? He was up to his neck in dishonesty. Why pretend otherwise?

Beth started up the stairs, and he followed, thankful that unless the old woman was sleeping on her sofa, she wasn't in the barn.

When he reached the top, he let out a sigh. "No one here."

Beth studied the art supplies haphazardly strewn across the two long tables against the wall. She moved on to the artwork, some hung, some propped up, some still waiting to be finished on easels in the center of the room.

"Wow," Beth said quietly. "I'm almost jealous."

He watched as she leaned in closer, studying the piece of art Birdie had been working on the day he'd discovered her. Abstract flowers that looked a little bit incredible now that they were done.

"This is an amazing space," Beth said.

He nodded, looking around, wondering if there was any evidence he'd ever been there. When he turned back, she stood with a faraway look in her eye. "What is it?"

"The art. It feels like we're reading her diary or something."

"You would know, being an artist."

She laughed. "I traded in my paintbrushes a long time ago."

"For business?"

When she nodded, she almost looked sad.

He shoved his hands in his pockets and watched her, trying to focus on what she said instead of the way she looked when she said it.

He didn't talk much, but that gave him plenty of time to listen—and the guys he'd hired had plenty to say about Beth Whitaker. Homecoming queen. Voted Most Likely to Succeed. To hear them talk, it seemed she'd always been out of this town's league. He could see why.

Her blue eyes alone could make a man forget his own name.

Maybe that's why she'd always felt she was supposed to have done more than what she had—because everyone told her she should. Same way everyone had told him he should remember.

Did she feel like a disappointment?

He knew a little something about that.

Maybe that's why Kent Tanner had gotten under her skin like he had. Maybe what he'd said spoke to some part of her that thought he was right. Maybe some part of her believed, after the things she'd done, that she was unlovable.

Drew had practically dragged the guy out into the yard, and when he had, he'd made sure Tanner knew never to step foot on the property—and never to insult Beth Whitaker—again.

"Are you into her?" Kent had let out a wry laugh. "Unbelievable, man."

"Shut it, Tanner—just go."

Kent stumbled away from him. "Don't get your hopes up, buddy. That chick is now and always has been a prissy little princess who thinks she's too good for guys like us."

Drew stormed toward Kent, grabbed him by the collar and rammed him into the nearest vehicle. "That's because she *is* too good for us, you idiot."

Kent squirmed from Drew's grip, shouting and cussing all the way to his car. Drew stood outside, calming himself down and waiting until Kent's truck drove away.

When he'd gone back into the barn, he'd found Beth broken and near tears. And he'd had the impression he was seeing her in a way very few people ever had.

She wasn't bulletproof. What Kent said had hurt her, and when Drew saw her hurt, something inside him ached. He wanted to take all of the pain away. Maybe it was leftover guilt from not being able to save Jess, but there wasn't much he wanted more than to pull Beth into his arms and keep anything—or anyone—from ever hurting her again.

"You look like you're somewhere else." She turned to him from the other side of the loft.

Drew shook himself back to the present. Now was not the time to leave his thoughts unattended. "I was just thinking you should ask the old lady to have a booth in your barn sale."

Beth's eyes scanned the finished pieces along the wall. "She is really good."

"Maybe you could go easy on her."

She eyed him. "You think I wouldn't?"

"Well, the way you were talking before we got here—it was kind of icy." He'd meant it as a joke, but by the look on her face, he could tell she hadn't found it amusing.

She pressed her lips together and lifted her chin.

"I didn't mean—"

She held up a hand. "No, I get it. It's fine."

"Beth."

But she'd already turned away and started down the stairs, done with the conversation. Done with him.

And he supposed it was probably better that way.

Beth didn't even know why she was upset.

Maybe his use of the word *icy* had set something off inside her. The Ice Queen lives again.

Why did she care so much what Drew Barlow thought of her? Why did it matter if he looked at her the way everyone else did—like a cold rule-follower who couldn't admit when she was wrong? Why did it matter if he looked at her at all?

Maybe because she'd opened up to him. She'd let herself feel naked and vulnerable, and now she wished she could take it all back. She shouldn't have told him about any of that. She knew better than to let her guard down.

But Drew was different.

She watched him working sometimes. Stood behind the sink in the kitchen and stared out the window while he cut and stacked wood, dragged branches to the burn pile or pulled the weeds behind the main barn. It embarrassed her how many times she'd admired his shirtless figure as he tirelessly worked to save them from financial ruin. If they survived this restoration, it would be only because of him.

They'd spent weeks together now. Sometimes they ate together. Sometimes they sat on the porch at the end of the day and went over the plan for the morning.

Always businesslike and professional.

But always, always, she hesitated to say goodbye.

Oh, she played it cool and pretended not to notice when his hand brushed hers as he took his morning cup of coffee. She even whipped out her professional voice every chance she got, but inside, when he looked at her, she went weak.

And she hated being weak.

Now, as they sat in his truck, headed back to get her car in the high school parking lot, she begged herself to let go of this stupid insecurity.

"You're quiet." He tapped the steering wheel with his thumb.

"Am I?" She stared out the window.

"I didn't mean to offend you back there." His eyes stayed on the road.

She waved him off. "It's not a big deal."

Drew pulled into the lot across from Beatty Park, where the carnival was now in full swing. He parked alongside her Audi.

"It's a big deal to me." He put the truck in park.

When he looked at her, her breath caught in her throat. "It shouldn't be. I think I'm just tired. I'm not usually oversensitive." She gripped the door handle. "Thanks for taking me out there and driving me back." She didn't want to leave. When had this happened?

Hadn't she told herself she'd never do this again?

"You have plans for lunch?" Drew folded his hands on top of the steering wheel.

She begged herself to play it cool. "I don't, actually."

He stared out the front window. "We could cook out?"

She watched him, smitten with the twitching in his jaw. "We could do that." She kept her tone nonchalant, but inside, her stomach bounced like a kid on a trampoline.

Drew looked at her. "Race you there?" His eyes glimmered like a child's.

She studied him. "Are you challenging me?" Did he know how competitive she was?

"Scared?"

"Not a chance, buddy." She opened the door and got out. "Wait till I get in."

He grinned. "What, do you think I'm a cheater?"

She shut the door, threw her purse in the passenger seat and started her engine, hoping, probably a little too much, that Drew Barlow was not, in fact, a cheater.

And devising a solid plan to leave him in the dust.

Chapter Twenty-Six

Beth sat on the steps, trying to calm her competitive self down after the adrenaline rush of racing Drew back to the farm. If she could look like she'd been waiting a while by the time he finally arrived, all the better.

When his truck appeared on the gravel road, she steadied her breathing, certain it would be her last chance to do so until she left the farm that night.

"What kind of crazy driver are you?" He flashed one of his rare, genuine smiles. A part of her felt honored he'd saved it for her.

Unlike Beth, who was serious by nature, Drew had a playfulness about him. She saw it sometimes in their back-and-forth banter, but he always seemed to catch himself and shut it down. Like he didn't think it was right to show her (or anyone else) that side of himself.

But then, didn't she do the same, always insisting on being professional and proper? Hadn't that earned her the Ice Queen nickname? She drove people away.

"My dad used to drag race." Beth attempted to keep her tone light. "You challenged the wrong girl."

"I guess so." He stopped when he reached her, hands on his hips, and took a moment to size her up. "You knew a shortcut, didn't you?"

Beth couldn't keep the grin from spreading across her face. "Who knew being a hometown girl would have its advantages?"

He shook his head. "I want a rematch." He stepped closer, as if challenging her to a duel.

She steeled her chin, stubborn as she was. "Anytime."

His eyes searched hers, then found her lips, sending a rush of nerves through her entire body. She hadn't dated anyone since Michael. Told herself she preferred it that way, but the truth was, she was scared. She couldn't go through that kind of heartbreak again.

Then there was the fact that nobody had asked her out.

Molly said it was because she was too intimidating, but Beth had begun to wonder. Was she really so unlovable?

Not the time to think about that. She should worry about much more important things, like whether or not she even remembered how to kiss—because she very much wanted to kiss Drew Barlow right now.

But as the thoughts swirled around in her head, he looked away and started toward the house. "Burgers okay?"

She swallowed her disappointment.

Get it together, Beth.

"Sounds good to me." She followed him inside.

There, she watched Drew wash and dry his hands, then begin preparing the burgers for the grill.

"Do you like roasted vegetables?" she asked, begging the heat in her cheeks to cool down.

He glanced at her, but his smile seemed forced. "Sounds great."

An awkwardness passed between them. Did he regret asking her to lunch? Why did she have to overanalyze this? Why couldn't they be friends and be fine with that? Did it matter that she'd never in her life had a male friend she was so attracted to?

Maybe that was the problem. She needed to figure out a way to be less attracted to him.

"I'll get the vegetables." She made a beeline for the refrigerator. Her mind searched for something wrong with him. Something that would make him seem less perfect. There had to be something.

She peeked into the living room, hoping for a mess, but everything was in its place. At the kitchen window, where she washed and peeled potatoes and carrots, she caught a glimpse of him standing at the grill. Chiseled features. Dark hair. Blue eyes. And then there was the way he'd listened as she'd unloaded her whole humiliating admission.

He now knew more about her than her own family.

And that scared her to death.

Because while a part of her seemed to need this man—something she absolutely hadn't planned on—a part of him still seemed so far away.

"You okay?"

He'd come back in through the side door. She looked down and realized she'd been standing in the same spot, holding the same potato for probably two full minutes.

"Fine." She hurried up and peeled the rest of the vegetables, cut them, tossed them in olive oil, salt and pepper, then spread them out on a cookie sheet to bake.

Drew leaned against the counter, finished off a bottle of water and tossed the empty container in the garbage can.

"I wanted to thank you for all the work you've been doing around here," Beth said, anxious to fill the silence.

"You've thanked me plenty. I'm happy to do it." He looked comfortable with his arms crossed in front of him, his worn gray T-shirt fitted enough to show the definition in his arms. Silence didn't seem to unnerve him the way it did her. In fact, he seemed to prefer it.

Maddening when she wanted nothing more than to hear what he thought about as he was hauling, painting, finishing, restoring . . .

She shifted, uncomfortable under the weight of his gaze. "I'm trying to be better about appreciating people who deserve it."

He studied her, almost too intently. "Better than what?"

She swallowed. This was called stupid conversation. She didn't need to get into every single one of her fatal flaws in the same day.

He waited until their eyes met again. "I feel appreciated."

She nodded, searching for something—anything—to say, but the only question she really wanted answered was one she wouldn't ask again.

Why are you here?

He'd tell her when he was ready.

Or maybe never.

Either way, she couldn't force him to trust her with whatever it was he wouldn't say. Some things a person had to work out on their own. Even if they didn't know it at the time.

And some things, a person didn't want to admit to, no matter how much time passed.

Drew seemed to understand that. He never made her say more than she was ready to say. She would try to offer him the same courtesy.

"The grill should be hot enough," he said, interrupting her thoughts. "I'll get the burgers on." He vanished onto the patio through the side door, giving her a few minutes to compose herself. She pulled two plates down from the cupboard, gathered silverware and two cans of Coke and headed outside.

"I thought we'd eat out here?" Beth stood on the patio, wondering if Drew knew how handsome he was or if he was one of those guys who didn't think about it. It all seemed pretty effortless—his clothes, his hair, his five o'clock shadow.

A refreshing change.

Michael had been so into his looks, sometimes she felt like he was the girl in the relationship.

"It's a nice day for it," Drew said. "Though it feels like rain."

"I would never wish away the rain," Beth said, thinking of the orchard, "but I'd be awfully happy if it held off till after we ate."

"Agreed." Drew returned to the grill while Beth set the little café table on the patio with the plates and silverware, suddenly aware that this meal felt more formal than their usual grab-something-from-the-fridge-and-stand-on-the-porch-to-eat-it meals. Typically, they talked business as they ate thrown-together sandwiches and chips straight from the bag, and often, they were surrounded by other people.

There she went, overthinking again. What difference did it make if they sat at a table to eat? This was just lunch with a friend.

A very, very good-looking friend.

When the oven timer went off, she pulled the pan of vegetables from inside, sprinkled them with Parmesan, dumped them into a serving bowl and grabbed a container of potato salad from the refrigerator. She came back outside and found Drew standing at the table, a plate of burgers in his hand.

"It smells good," she said.

They sat down, and she became even more aware that they were now expected to carry on a conversation until the food in front of them was gone.

How was she going to do that?

The lunch started off quiet, and Beth searched her mind for topics he might not find eye-gougingly boring, surprised when he cleared his throat and started the conversation himself.

"You still thinking about an investor?" he asked between bites.

"Only if we have to. I'm trying to set up a meeting with this Davis Biddle guy so I can figure out what he really wants." Beth had spent too many hours pondering why someone like Davis would pay for the upkeep of the orchard, and when she came up empty, she'd decided to set up an appointment and ask him outright. No sense speculating when he kept popping up in their plans.

Drew swallowed a bite of his first burger. "I'll go with you."

She paused midbite. "You will?"

"If it's okay with you."

"Of course, but it's not necessary." Beth knew she needed Drew on the farm, but the business side of things she could handle.

"I know it's not," he said. "But I'd like to size the guy up for myself, if it's all the same to you."

She laughed. "Don't trust my judgment?"

"Don't trust him."

Beth watched as Drew started in on his second burger. "You don't?"

He shrugged. "Something doesn't sit right about it, is all. I kind of feel invested in this place myself, but I won't give you my opinion unless you ask for it."

For the first time in her life, it didn't bother her one bit that a man insisted on protecting her. She found something about it rather charming, actually. Chivalrous.

"You're a walking mystery," she said before she could stop herself.

He met her eyes. "Funny, I've thought the same thing about you."

She took a sip of her soda. "You have?"

"When I first got here, you seemed kind of out of place on the farm."

She swallowed her bite. "That's an understatement."

"But now, I don't know, something about it suits you."

When had she turned into this person? Someone who admired chivalry in a man and whose big dream was to plant her own vegetables? Was this really who she wanted to become?

This thing they were doing, restoring this farm—could Drew be right? Could this be the "more" she'd been searching for?

He picked up her hand and stroked it with his thumb. "And you've got a mean right hook."

She was keenly aware of his skin on hers.

Drew set her hand down, but kept his eyes on her. "Kind of seems like you found whatever it was you were looking for around here."

She forced herself to hold his gaze. He already knew so much about her. By comparison, she knew so little about him.

"What is it you're looking for?"

He looked away, silence hanging between them. In her mind, she willed him to answer her—to trust her enough to let her in on the thing that made him work so hard.

Instead, he pushed himself away from the table. "I'll get these out of the way."

She stayed still as he cleared the table and disappeared into the kitchen.

Was he kidding?

She'd told him everything—things Callie didn't even know. Did he think it was easy for her to open up about any of that?

Before she gave it too much thought, she stood and walked into the kitchen, where she found him rinsing dishes at the sink.

"Do you know how frustrating you are?" The words came out angrier than she'd intended.

He turned off the water and looked at her, but she didn't give him a chance to respond.

"You've been here over a month, and I know as much about you today as I did the day you got here."

He dried his hands and leaned back against the counter, facing her but still quiet.

"I've never told anyone what happened with my dad or my job. Nobody knows about any of that stuff, Drew. Do you know how hard it was for me to tell you that?"

Never mind the relief she'd felt as soon as she had. She'd been holding it all in far too long—but he didn't need to know the gratitude she felt for his willing ear.

"You can't answer a single personal question. You change the subject or, worse, you get up and walk away. I'm trying here, Drew, but it seems like you don't want me to know you at all."

"Are you asking as my boss?"

"What difference does that make?"

"Didn't know an employer needed all that personal information, is all."

It stung. She tried to keep her face from crumpling, from letting her weakness show. Her eyes found the floor. "I get it."

She'd misinterpreted everything. Let herself daydream one too many times.

Straightening, she lifted her chin and met his eyes. "I get it," she repeated softly.

He watched her, a little too closely, shaking her resolve.

"I should go."

But as she turned toward the door, he grabbed the sleeve of her sweatshirt, pulling her toward him. Her breath caught in her throat, and his hands found the sides of her face. Drew's eyes searched hers, and she could see it then—he *was* looking for something, but he didn't know what it was. A desperation there gave him away—he was lost.

"Drew, I—"

He inched closer, brushed his thumb over her bottom lip, silencing her. "I'm not very good with words."

In that moment, the world went quiet, and it was just the two of them, standing in the kitchen, their bodies only inches apart. He pulled her in, closing the gap between them, and kissed her—the kind of knee-buckling kiss she'd replay a thousand times.

He stopped abruptly and pulled back, looking into her eyes again. "I don't really want to be polite."

She swallowed, her lower lip trembling. "Then don't be."

With her hands pressed on his chest, she could feel his heartbeat, racing to match her own. He moved away from the counter, leading her backward until the wall behind her stopped them.

Her breaths came more quickly now. He leaned into her, hands pressed against the wall behind her, and she wrapped her arms around his neck, pulling him closer, wanting his lips on hers.

He kissed her again, anxious and hungry, leaving her breathless and bewildered. Then he pulled back, giving her time to recover, to inhale the scent of him, to wish he'd go back to kissing her.

"Why are you really here, Drew?" The words came without her permission.

He rested his forehead on hers, lips close enough to be kissed.

"What is it you're looking for?" Maybe she could help him. Maybe she could carry some of his burden—if only he let her in.

He straightened, still studying her face, but said nothing. He couldn't tell her. Whatever it was, it either didn't have a name or he hadn't found a way to put it into words. She should've kept her mouth shut. Pressing him had only forced him to retreat back into himself.

And now it was too late.

She swallowed, her throat suddenly dry. "I'm sorry."

He shook his head. "You don't have anything to be sorry for." He wrapped his arms around her, kissed the top of her head. "There's something I need to tell you."

Finally.

Please don't let him be a serial killer. Or married. Please don't let him be married.

But before he could get a single word out, the sound of tires on gravel pulled their attention outside.

"Are you expecting someone?" she asked.

"I don't know anyone here, remember?"

She went to the window and saw Molly's VW Bug speeding toward them—really, much too fast. "It's Molly." Beth looked around, tidying up the kitchen, as if there was evidence of what had just happened between her and Drew all over the room.

"What are you doing?" He watched her, looking perfectly calm.

She could feel the blood race up her neck and across her cheeks.

Before she could answer, Molly barged into the house, and Beth said a silent prayer of thanks it wasn't three minutes earlier.

"Beth! You are not going to believe this."

Bishop trailed close behind her. He stuck a hand out toward Drew, who shook it.

"Good to see you again, Mr. Barlow," Bishop said.

"You too, Officer."

"Will you guys stop with the niceties?" Molly said. "This is important." Molly waved a stack of manila folders in the air, then slammed them down on the table. "Guess what the newspapers forgot to report?" She opened the top folder.

"Molly, what are you talking about?" Beth's face had to be flushed—she still felt the heat of what had happened between her and Drew, whose eyes she now completely avoided.

"Jess Pendergast."

Beth dared a glance at Drew. His face had gone blank. Was he regretting that kiss? Or, like her, wanting to get rid of Molly and Bishop so they could do it again?

Molly stared at her, awaiting her response.

Anything to get rid of them. And fast. "Okay, Molly, what did you find?" Beth stared at the case file. "What am I looking at?"

Molly pointed to a sentence on the page. "Juvenile male witness. No memory of attacker. Taken to hospital; treated with stitches and released." She tapped on the table forcefully, as if she'd just proven herself right about something tremendous—like life on another planet or something. "There was a witness no one ever knew about because he was too young—another kid."

Beth frowned. "Do you think it was someone local?" They hadn't heard anything about a witness, and while her parents had shielded them from much of the tragedy, surely someone would've mentioned if a little boy had seen Jess taken.

"Doubtful," Bishop said. "It's unlikely it wouldn't have come out by now. You know how people in this town like to talk."

Beth pressed her lips together. "So, is the boy's name in here?"

"No, and his records are sealed, but Bishop thinks we can get it."

"How?" Beth asked.

"My dad was friends with one of the detectives who worked the case. He retired to Florida, but I think I can track him down."

"Is this even legal?" Drew's tone had an uncharacteristic edge to it.

"If Bishop handles it, it will be." Molly paused. Squinted at Beth. "Wait a minute. What are you guys doing out here? I thought you were working, but this doesn't look like work."

Beth glanced at Drew, then at the floor.

"Is this a date?" Molly folded her arms over her chest and cocked her head, waiting for a satisfying reply.

Beth couldn't find a single coherent sentence running through her mind.

"Oh, my gosh," Molly said. "You two?" She turned to Bishop. "I told you she liked him." Back to Beth. "I told him. He said you were too focused to think about romance and to stop trying to play matchmaker, but I told him." Over to Drew. "She does have very good taste."

He managed a soft laugh, but Beth could feel the heat as embarrassment radiated through her body. She picked up the folders and pushed them back into Molly's arms, shoving both her and Bishop toward the door.

"I get it," Molly said. "You guys want to be alone. Geesh! All you had to do was say so."

"Since when do you listen to anything I say, Molly?"

Before leaving, Bishop turned to Drew. "Sorry, man."

Drew raised a hand as if to tell him it was okay, but Beth slammed the door shut before Bishop had a chance to see. She faced the door, willing them off the porch, into the car and miles away from the farm. "I'm so sorry," she said, still not looking at Drew.

"What are you sorry for?"

She turned around. "You like to keep your personal business personal. I didn't think you'd want anyone to think . . ." The words got all jumbled up before she could even finish the thought.

"I don't care what people think, Beth." He walked toward her, meeting her in the entryway.

When she met his eyes, she knew he meant it.

"I like you," he said. "I'm not embarrassed by that."

She looked away but couldn't hide her smile. He pulled her to him and held her for a long moment, then kissed her again. "I've got some work to do outside."

Her heart sank. Disappointed to leave him and, more importantly, disappointed that he didn't want to tell her whatever he'd planned to say before Molly had barged in.

She wouldn't push him. "See you tomorrow?"

"You know where to find me."

As she drove home, mind spinning, lips tingling from his kisses, Beth replayed the entire day in her head. Her cheeks flushed with something she could only describe as passion—she was anxious to see him again.

She'd done her best to strengthen her resolve around Drew Barlow, but her resolve had failed her in every possible way.

That night, she fell asleep well after midnight, praying she could relive their first kiss over and over in her dreams.

Chapter Twenty-Seven

What had he done?

Drew closed the door behind Beth, wishing he could pull her back inside and tell her everything. Every moment he stayed quiet only put more distance between them. He knew it, so why hadn't he just explained everything?

He had much more to lose than he'd thought he did.

Birdie had seen it—why hadn't he?

"When are you going to tell her how you feel?" She'd dotted her paintbrush on the canvas in front of her.

"About what?"

She'd tossed the brush into the jar of paint water and glared at him over the top of those reading glasses she wore. "Don't play dumb with me."

"She's my boss."

"And?"

"I don't have feelings for her. I respect her, but that's all."

"You're either lying to yourself or lying to me or both." Birdie had shaken her head, tsk-tsking him as she did. "I just hope you wake up before it's too late. That girl won't be around forever."

Maybe he'd been chewing on the whole idea a little more than he should've been. As it was, Beth was just about the only good thing he had in his life. He watched her sometimes, amused by her stubbornness. The woman would try the same thing ten times and never ask for help. Usually, he'd wait for her to leave and then fix whatever it was she'd been trying to do without a word.

One of these days, maybe she'd get used to needing someone else, but so far that hadn't happened. It was one of the things he liked about her.

One of many things.

Seeing her all fired up today—it set something off inside him. He'd gotten under her skin, and he loved that he had.

He more than liked her.

He spent the rest of the day working monotonous chores and trying to forget, but his mind wouldn't let him.

Finally, after a full evening of not forgetting, he dropped onto the couch with a heavy sigh. Now that Molly knew there had been a witness to Jess's kidnapping, it was only a matter of time until they found out it was Drew. Beth deserved to hear it from him, not from some retired detective who'd worked the case two decades ago. That knowledge, coupled with the memory of the way her body felt in his arms, kept him staring at the ceiling throughout the night.

He'd missed her as soon as she'd walked out the door, and he hated himself for it. Hated that, after everything, he was still a coward.

Morning came too early and he awoke, certain he'd been dreaming again. He lay still for a few long moments as his mind tried to recall the faintest detail—anything that might give him insight into what had happened in the barn that day. But, like a misty fog hugging the morning, it dissipated as soon as he realized he was awake.

His cell phone buzzed on the table beside him. The clock read seven, and the caller ID read *Beth*.

The memory of her kisses raced to his mind.

"Hey." He tried to sound more awake than he felt.

"Did I wake you?" Her tone apologized.

"No, I'm awake. Just not up."

A quiet pause made him imagine the look on her face. He ached for the moment he could kiss her again.

"I'm sorry to call so early. I had a message from Davis Biddle on my phone this morning."

"Oh?"

"Well, from his assistant. He has a male assistant. Is that weird?"

Drew laughed. "I don't think so."

"He asked if I could meet Mr. Biddle today at eight. I thought I'd call and see if you were serious about coming along."

He'd suggested it for two reasons. One, like he'd said, he didn't trust Biddle. And he supposed a part of him wanted to protect Beth, just in case. But two—and this was the part that grated on him—the name was familiar. Maybe seeing the man in person would rattle something loose.

"Of course. Should I meet you?"

"No," Beth said. "I'll come to you since he lives just down the road from there."

And maybe that's where the familiarity ended. Maybe he'd heard his parents or Jess talking about Davis Biddle. Maybe Davis had nothing to offer Drew's spotty memory at all.

But there was only one way to find out.

Beth arrived at the door forty-five minutes later, coffee in hand.

"You knocked." He stood in the doorway, taking her in.

"I felt like I should."

She'd probably been trying to process what had happened between them. Why couldn't they just leave it undefined? They'd kissed—was that a big deal?

His gaze fell to her lips.

Yeah, it was a big deal. Because he hadn't stopped thinking about doing it again since she'd left yesterday afternoon.

"Can I come in?"

He laughed. "Of course. Sorry. What time did you get up?" He led her into the kitchen.

"Early." She ran a hand through her hair. "I didn't sleep well."

"You too?"

She watched him. The expression on her face said nothing and everything at the same time. She wanted answers—he'd only made things more confusing with that very not-polite kiss.

But he didn't have words for any of it. "We should probably go."

She looked away with a quick nod and walked outside to the car, with Drew following close behind. The entire silent car ride, he tried—failed—to think of something to say. He had to find a way to tell her how he fit into Fairwind's sordid past, but every time he looked at her, he lost his nerve.

It was stupid, but he didn't want to lose her. In his entire life, he'd never felt for anyone the way he felt for Beth. He'd never let himself. He'd been stuck in the past since the day Jess went missing. Thick, heavy, painful memories had kept him grounded, and the longer he stayed at Fairwind, the more he realized that wasn't going to change.

They arrived at the gates in front of the Biddle estate, and Beth waited to be buzzed through. His silence had to be killing her, yet he had no words to remedy that. Instead, he reached over and took her hand, hoping that she'd somehow understand what he couldn't say.

Forgive me.

She glanced at him, probably confused by the mixed signals he sent, but he kept his gaze steady on the house in front of them.

When the gates opened, they passed through and drove up the driveway to the mansion at the back of the property.

"I did some research," Beth said. "He built this house about thirty years ago and lives here with his son. No wife. I think she passed away a long time ago."

"So it's just him, his kid and his money."

She turned off the engine. "And I imagine a whole staff of people to answer his beck and call."

"Let's go find out."

The stone fountain at the center of the circle drive shot water into the air, making the grand spectacle that was the Biddle estate even grander. The mansion itself may've been Fairwind's closest neighbor, but the two homes couldn't have been more different. While Fairwind had farmhouse charm, the cover of ancient trees and green earth, the Biddle estate had an elaborate and stately appeal.

Drew waited for Beth to comment on the two-story stone structure in front of them, but even as a man let them into the entryway, complete with marble floors and a winding staircase, she said nothing.

The man led them into a study. "Have a seat. Mr. Biddle will be with you shortly."

On one side of the room, a large fireplace with a thick white mantel held professional photos of a man who must have been Davis Biddle, shaking hands with important politicians and professional athletes.

After ten quiet minutes of watching Beth push buttons on her phone, Drew finally let out a sigh.

"Bet you wish you'd stayed behind," she said without looking up.

Was she mad at him? He couldn't blame her, as silent as he'd been. It wasn't right to kiss a girl the way he'd kissed Beth and then refuse to talk about it the next day. He could've at least greeted her with a kiss this morning—anything to let her know he didn't regret how things might've changed between them.

He only regretted that he'd allowed their relationship to grow under false pretenses.

Before he could say anything—as if he would've said anything—the oversized wooden door opened, and in walked a sturdy-looking man dressed in a neat suit and tie. He wore an indifferent expression on his face, like he might or might not have been aware of their presence in his office.

Drew waited for something about the man to strike a chord of familiarity, but nothing came. If he'd ever met Davis Biddle before, he certainly didn't remember him now.

"I assume you're Beth Whitaker?" The man sat in the chair behind his desk and looked at Beth.

She inched forward and stuck her hand out to greet him. "I am."

He shook it—one firm shake—and then glanced at Drew. "I didn't know you were bringing a guest."

Beth tossed a glance in Drew's direction. "He's not a guest. He's my grounds manager."

Had she just made that title up on the spot? She didn't even stutter. Something in her had changed, as if she'd become a different version of herself as soon as the man had entered the room. Maybe this was the Beth he'd seen traces of over the past few weeks. She had professionalism and confidence written all over her.

"I see." Davis regarded Drew long enough to make him uncomfortable. "And your name?"

"Drew Barlow." He stuck out a hand.

Davis paused for too many seconds before reciprocating the gesture. He hesitated before finally turning his attention back to Beth. "So you've considered my offer."

Beth frowned. "Sir?"

"My assistant spoke with your sister after the auction."

"She told me. And I suppose, yes, I am here about that, among other things." Beth leaned forward in the chair. Drew couldn't help but notice she looked stunning. She'd pulled her hair back and dressed up for the meeting, he assumed to impress the powerful man on the other side of the desk.

He tried to focus on her words instead of the way her black dress pants hugged her hips or how her sleeveless blouse dipped at her chest, showing a simple silver necklace with something he couldn't read engraved on it.

"What kind of other things?" Davis folded his hands on the desk and stared at Beth. She stared right back. Drew felt like he was sitting too close to a Mexican standoff.

"I was told you had interest in investing in Fairwind Farm." Beth crossed her legs and leaned on the arm of her chair.

Davis chuckled. "Is that what you heard?"

She frowned. "Have I been misinformed?"

Drew waited for her cheeks to heat red like they usually did when she was embarrassed, but she maintained complete composure.

"Yes. I'm in real estate, Miss Whitaker. I know a lemon when I see it. I respect your sense of nostalgia, but surely you must see this project is doomed. What I'd hoped my assistant conveyed to your sister is that, when you both realize you've had too much of this, I'll take the old place off your hands."

Beth pressed her lips together. "I see."

"I would've purchased the property myself if I'd been in town when Harold died. My lawyer was supposed to alert me of any change in the property. He didn't. He's no longer my lawyer." Davis smiled.

"I understand."

One of his eyebrows hitched up. "I'm happy to get you out of this mess, though, if you're in over your head. I just don't see it as a wise investment unless I have complete control."

"From what I understand, you've been investing in Fairwind for years."

Drew wasn't sure if Davis was surprised or impressed with Beth's straightforwardness. Drew was both.

"Unless you *didn't* hire someone to maintain the orchards?" she continued.

"Walter."

"Yes, Walter. He said you've been paying him regularly for twenty years. That's a long time to invest in a property you don't control."

He drew in a slow breath, smile holding steady on his face. "I made Harold an offer years ago. The land backs up to my property, and there is value in those apple trees. He wouldn't sell, but we did eventually work out a deal."

"What kind of deal?" Beth stared at him.

"I hired Walter to handle the orchards, and we split the profits."

"Why would you do that?"

"Call me a Good Samaritan."

Beth folded her hands in her lap but said nothing. Drew wondered if she was remembering the rest of their conversation with Walter. According to him, Biddle wasn't making a penny on those apples.

"Look, you seem like a smart girl." Davis opened his portfolio, scribbled something on the pad and tore out the sheet of paper. He folded it and pushed it across the desk. "My offer."

Beth glanced at the paper but didn't pick it up.

"You won't get a better one."

"Why is that farm worth anything to you? You have a whole estate here. Don't tell me you need more land."

Davis shrugged. "I have my reasons. Now, if you'll excuse me, I have other business to attend to." He nodded toward the folded piece of yellow paper. "Be sure to take that with you."

After the door closed behind him, Beth snatched the paper off the desk, shoved it in her purse without looking at it and stomped out the door.

Chapter Twenty-Eight

The nerve of that guy.

Beth stormed out of Davis Biddle's ostentatious mansion—which had no business in Willow Grove at all—and drove in silence back to the farm.

This man, this cunning businessman, had a reputation of brilliance. Why then would he want to buy Fairwind but not invest in it, especially when, as she saw it, he'd already invested so much in the upkeep of the orchards all these years? It didn't make sense.

To make matters (and her mood) worse, Drew hadn't said a word about yesterday. And he'd given her no indication that a kiss like that would ever happen again.

The thought of it lodged a lump in the center of her throat.

They pulled into Fairwind's parking lot and found Molly sweeping out the main barn, no doubt preparing for the Fairwind Farm Market, which was now only a few weeks away.

They'd begun collecting items from the house and other barns, and soon they'd assemble it all together in a nicely ordered booth for people to browse.

"How'd it go?" Molly looked up when they approached, eyes darting from Beth to Drew and back again.

"Something is weird about that guy," Beth said.

"So, not an angel investor?" Molly leaned on the broom.

"Definitely not."

"Bummer." She went back to sweeping. Something about her non-chalance, coupled with Drew's silence and Davis Biddle's insinuation that they were doomed to fail, set something off inside Beth.

"Do you have any idea what we're up against here, Molly?"

Her sister stopped sweeping and stared at her, wide-eyed.

"He wants to buy the farm when we fail. Not *if* we fail—when."

"Okay, well, he's going to be out of luck, then, isn't he?"

Molly had no idea what any of this was actually costing, the dire straits they were in. Secretly, Beth had been hoping her meeting with Davis Biddle would go well enough to at least convince him to continue taking care of the orchards—just for a little while.

But that wasn't going to happen, heaping another huge expense straight into her lap. Not Molly's—hers.

Beth dropped her purse on the table. "Why did I ever let you talk me into this?"

Molly crossed her arms over her chest and watched Beth pace. "What's your problem?"

"Are you kidding? Ever since we started this, I've been out here every single day clearing out the house, cataloging the furniture, promoting the barn sale, trying to raise money."

"Well, you're not doing it by yourself." She shot a look in Drew's direction.

"No, but I'm not doing it with *you*. You've been off chasing leads in a twenty-year-old kidnapping case and buying dogs and goats and—"

"You're always so negative, Beth. I wish you could open your eyes to how much we've accomplished."

"It doesn't matter, when we have so much more to do." Beth sighed. "We aren't going to have the money. We need to be logical here and at least consider this offer." She pulled the paper from her bag.

"I don't even want to see that, and I can't believe you would think twice about this." Molly turned away.

"Molly, I'm trying to be practical here." Was she? Or was she looking for a way to escape? She glanced at Drew. Her heart ached for him. She wondered if she'd be so intent on considering Davis's offer if Drew hadn't been so cold that morning.

Of course she would. This was about the farm, the lack of money and a clear way out of what might've been an even bigger disaster than the one at Whitaker Mowers.

"What's happened to you?" Molly put her hands on her hips and leveled their gaze. "The Beth Whitaker I know would never just lie down and let this guy walk all over her. She'd take his words as a challenge, and she'd say, 'You don't think I can do this? Watch me.'" She shook her head. "Where's *that* girl?"

Beth steeled her jaw, biting back words that would only do harm.

Out of the corner of her eye, she saw an old lady wearing a long, draping dress and carrying a box, canvases in several sizes sticking out the top. *Birdie.* "What is she doing here?"

"She's going to have a booth at the barn sale." Molly cocked her head to one side.

"You can't be serious."

"She's a sensational artist. You'd like her. We're going to turn her barn into an art barn. Host community art events."

"*Her* barn?" Beth did a slow turn toward Drew, as if to ask for help, but he stood, hands in pockets, with a confused look on his face. So much for being invested in Fairwind. So much for being invested in *her.*

"I told her she could stay," Molly said. The slight lift in her chin told Beth her sister had just issued a challenge. And this one was even worse than making her confess she was wrong.

This one was crossing a line.

Birdie set the box on a nearby table. "So sorry we're meeting under tense circumstances," she said as she approached Beth. "I understand you're an artist too?" Her singsong voice trilled through the tight air.

Birdie took both of Beth's hands in her own and led her over to the box of artwork. "Perhaps you can tell me what you think of my work?"

Beth swallowed, her mouth dry. "I'm sorry, I need to talk to my sister."

"Of course."

Beth turned, but Molly and Drew had both gone. She faced Birdie. "Molly and I will have to discuss the terms of your agreement with us. My sister likes to make decisions she's not really capable of."

"Of course, dear." Birdie picked up a canvas. "Do you like this one?"

Beth looked down at the painted flowers covering the canvas. Rich, bold colors melded together like a garden, deep with unspoken emotions, the kind that couldn't be talked about, only painted. Somehow, it moved her. "I like it very much."

Birdie stilled. "Flowers have such strength, don't they?"

Beth found kindness waiting in Birdie's eyes. "I've never thought so."

"Those are gladiolus. They're known as sword lilies. Tell me there's something stronger than a gladiator flower."

Beth knit her brow. "I don't think that's what it means."

"Look it up, smarty." Birdie took the canvas. "You're not a flower girl, I can tell."

Beth crossed her arms over her chest. "What makes you say that?"

"I've seen you in the garden." Birdie picked up another canvas, this one covered with deep-red poppies.

"I guess I don't have much of a green thumb."

Birdie let out a deep laugh. "No, you certainly don't."

Beth turned away. She'd thought she'd been doing a good job in the garden. Drew had probably gone behind her, making sure those plants grew.

Birdie peered at her over a pair of gold-rimmed reading glasses on a long gold chain. "What is it you're hoping to prove with all that work?" She stepped closer. "What is it you need?"

Beth inched away, but Birdie wouldn't let her off the hook.

Under other circumstances, Beth would've called security to remove an unwanted nuisance, but when she met the old woman's eyes, something told her Birdie wasn't asking to be nosy.

But then, sometimes people asked questions they already knew the answers to. Birdie sat in the chair beside the table and pulled on Beth's arm until she sat beside her.

"I've seen you down here, running around with your clipboard and your cell phone, trying to make sense of a world that doesn't make sense to you. I can't help but wonder what you hope all that work will accomplish." Birdie waved a stray hair out of her eye, the sound of jangling bracelets filling the barn.

Beth pressed her lips together. "We can't reopen the farm without all that work." Wasn't that obvious? Did she dare point out that some days she felt like the only one with any sense of urgency around here?

"Yes. That's true. Hard work is an important thing." She paused. "But it's not the only thing."

"Well, of course it's not."

Birdie raised an eyebrow. "This farm was built slowly and with a whole lot of love. Do you even take time to enjoy any of it?"

"Sure I do."

"I don't think so. You try to force those plants and flowers to grow, and it's never going to happen. Just water them. Give them light. Eventually they'll shoot up out of that soil like the gladiators they are. They do it because it's what they were made to do."

"What are you saying?"

"I'm saying if you do what you were made to do, then you'll find the peace you've been looking for. You can't work for it, you know. You just have to rest in it." Birdie's words wove an invisible thread between them.

Beth studied her hands, folded in her lap.

Birdie leaned in, as if to share a secret. "Just like you can't earn love. Or forgiveness. Or grace. Those things are gifts. You just have to reach out and take them." Birdie covered Beth's hands with her own. "You don't get to be my age without a few lessons along the way." Her smile was sympathetic, like the smile of a person who actually understood.

Beth stilled.

"It's awful tiresome, if you ask me." The woman pulled her hands away and slumped in her chair. "I mean, why work for something you already have?"

The words radiated into Beth's weary soul.

"I heard a quote once: 'The two most important days of your life are the day you were born and the day you figure out why.'"

Beth met her eyes.

"Find your 'why' and the rest of it—that will fall into place. And it'll let you off the hook. All the things you thought you *should* have done—if they aren't part of your 'why,' then they don't matter anymore."

Beth sat silent for a few long seconds. "I have a 'why.'"

"Having a 'why' isn't the same as having something to prove."

Beth frowned.

Birdie glanced at the canvases on the table in front of her. "You know, once upon a time, all I wanted was a gallery showing in New York City." Beth's face must've shown her surprise, because Birdie laughed. "I know, can you believe it? Me in a New York City gallery? I worked tirelessly to make that happen. I thought once it did, I would finally— finally—be somebody. I'd be respected and well-thought-of and *known*."

Birdie pulled her stack of paintings from the box.

"There's something deep down within us, isn't there, that just wants to be known?"

There was. Beth had felt that longing many times.

"Anyway, I had my gallery showing in the city."

"You did?"

"Don't sound so surprised, kid. I'm a sensational artist." Birdie winked at her. "And you know what? My heart never settled into it. I started painting what the gallery owners and my manager told me to paint, instead of what my own soul wanted to paint. They wanted me to wear stuffy clothes and look professional, and I wanted to be my hippie-dippy self."

"So what did you do?"

"I left."

"Just like that?"

"Packed up my brushes and moved to this little hole-in-the-wall town in Illinois, where I met my husband, who gave me the very best life I could've ever imagined."

"Here?"

"Yes, right here in Willow Grove, hometown girl."

"You didn't feel like a failure for not going after the big dream?"

Birdie waved her off, her bracelets clanging together halfway up her arm. "Are you kidding? This *is* the big dream!" She let out a loud laugh. "I started to love painting again. I was creating whatever I wanted—nobody got to tell me how my art should look or what the people would buy. I didn't care. I just did it because I loved it."

Beth stilled.

"You get to decide, Miss Whitaker, what 'the big dream' is for you. And it's okay to want a simple life. It's even okay to admit that you kind of love it here—that this place is your 'why'—at least for right now. I mean, look what you're doing—bringing people together. Fairwind Farm is a connector of people. We need that around here."

Beth was skeptical. Birdie Chirper was a crazy old lady who really needed to pay them rent if she wanted to continue to paint in their barn, but she made a lot of sense.

Could Beth ever be that brave—that comfortable with her own choices that it didn't matter what anyone else thought?

Birdie stood. "I've got more paintings to cart down here." She turned to Beth. "Unless you don't want me to participate in your sale?"

Beth shook her head. "Of course you should participate."

She smiled. "Of course I should."

Beth watched as the old woman left, resting in the words imparted by a perfect stranger and begging God to show her how to rest in the gift of His "why."

Chapter Twenty-Nine

The next day, when she arrived, Beth knocked on the front door again. Drew had made up his mind not to be so distant with her today—even if it seemed awkward. Yesterday had been brutal, and not knowing where he stood with her was killing him.

He'd figure out a way to tell her who he really was tonight. He owed her that much.

He pulled the door open and found her eyes, which asked permission to come in. One look at her and his self-control unraveled.

"Good morning." She shoved a coffee at him.

"Good morning." He took the cup.

"Listen, can you tell me what's going on here?" She motioned at herself, then at him. She'd taken on her business tone, same one he'd witnessed when she talked to Davis Biddle. He watched her for a few long seconds until she looked at him again. He couldn't help it—he smiled.

"You're smiling."

"You're cute when you're confrontational."

She gave his shoulder a shove, and he held on to her wrist, pulling her close.

"I'm serious," she said. "I can't figure you out."

"I like you, Beth Whitaker," he said.

She let out the slightest sigh (of relief?) and sank into him. "I like you too."

He kicked the front door shut with his foot and kissed her the way he'd wanted to ever since their first kiss. When he pulled away, he found her breathless and beautiful.

"I know I was weird yesterday," he said. "I'm sorry."

Her face fell. "I want you to know you can trust me. You can talk to me."

He brushed a stray strand of hair away from her eye, tucking it behind her ear. "I know. Let's talk—tonight? Dinner?"

"Yeah?" She smiled.

"Yeah."

"Deal."

He stared at her for a few long seconds until she remembered there was work to do.

"Okay, today I'm going to start hauling stuff from the second floor down to the barn for the sale," she said.

He frowned. "By yourself?"

She cocked her head to one side. "I'm a perfectly capable woman, Mr. Barlow. I can haul a few boxes out of the house."

He nodded. "Noted."

"But I might need help with some of the really heavy stuff, so I'll let you know."

He laughed, kissed her again and headed outside. His crew had been roped into helping set up for the barn sale, but thankfully no one had complained.

Drew stepped back to admire the progress so far. He'd focused most of the last few weeks on that barn and it showed. The place looked better than new. Once they had inventory, they could turn it back into a store.

He'd fixed the checkout counters—all eight of them—as well as the shelves that would hold whatever Beth and Molly decided to sell. In the back near the coolers was the apple-cider donut counter, and across from that were open rows perfect for bushel baskets and bags of apples. It had all been cleaned and repaired. Just off to the right of the entrance, the fudge counter had been rebuilt and new cases installed.

It looked better than it ever had, and he was proud of his guys. Proud of himself. He felt like he'd made a real contribution—and more importantly, it would make Beth happy.

If Walter was right about the orchards and the trees were in good shape, there was a chance they really could open by fall. They wouldn't have everything finished, but they could certainly get the store and bakery up and running. He relished the sense of accomplishment for a long moment, then picked up his toolbox and moved outside.

The guys had this under control. Today, he had another project for himself—the petting-zoo barn, which didn't need as much work as he'd originally thought. A few days—a week, tops—and he'd have that one sealed up.

It felt good to cross things off his list. It felt good to go to Beth with visible progress.

Maybe it would ease the worry in her mind a little.

He found Roxie lying in the shade of an old oak tree while Daisy ran in circles around Blue. He hadn't had much time to work with Molly's dog, and she went rogue every chance she got. Eventually, she would have to be trained.

But not today.

Drew walked through the petting-zoo barn, assessing the damage to each stall. He'd have to pull out rotted wood and start over with the new lumber he'd purchased last week. An old radio hung from the corner. He flipped it on and found the nearest station without static. An oldies station. It would do.

He found a sledgehammer in the bottom of his toolbox. He'd start by clearing away the rotten wood. When he rebuilt the stalls, he'd create some order in the barn—judging by what was there now, this setup had been a last-minute hodgepodge of cagelike stalls that Harold had built as they'd procured more animals.

He didn't know what kind of animals Beth and Molly intended to put in their petting zoo or when, but it didn't matter. It felt good to slam the hammer into the wood, to knock out the old in favor of the new.

Normally, when he worked, it was to drive away some kind of aggression. Today, he worked to work, as if something had taken the edge off his sorrow.

There was only one thing that had changed. Beth.

She made him happy. How long had it been since he'd felt that way?

An image of two kids rolling down a huge hill at the back of the Fairwind property raced through his mind. Had it been that long?

A part of him still felt guilty for enjoying what Jess couldn't. But he tried to focus on nothing but the task at hand. As he worked, the radio blared songs from the fifties and sixties, most of which Drew knew from his own childhood. It's what happened when a kid took long road trips with parents who insisted on listening to Chubby Checker and Buddy Holly.

He pounded at the wooden stalls, some sections more rotten than others, all of it easy to remove. He stacked the garbage wood in a neat pile just outside the barn, doing his best not to think about the fact that he'd told Beth they'd talk tonight. *He'd* talk. He'd tell her the real reason he was there—all of it.

Bishop would likely uncover it all in a matter of days, and Drew couldn't let her find out from anyone but him. He knew there was a chance it would make her mad—she did have a temper—but he hoped she would understand.

She could tell him to leave, and he wouldn't blame her, but it wasn't what he wanted. Not only because he still had no answers, but because he thought he might love her. Leaving now—after he'd finally admitted it to himself—how would he live with that?

More pounding, more hauling.

"Surfin' USA" by the Beach Boys rang out through the barn. The upbeat music reminded him of Jess. Years ago, the jaunty melody would've suited Fairwind, but now? The two seemed a complete contradiction.

The song ended, and the DJ's voice interrupted Drew's thoughts.

"And now we've got a special treat—a one-hit wonder by fifties doo-wop group The Chords. Let it take you back to a time life really could be a dream. Here's The Chords singing 'Sh-Boom.'"

A familiar tune bounced through the air, filling sad space with another fun melody. Four men sang harmonies that begged feet to move, a song that enticed even the most conservative listeners to dance. It was a playful tune that touted the ironic idea that life could be anything other than painful—that it could, in fact, be a dream. And as the words filled the barn, Drew's mind drifted back years, setting him right there in one of the stalls beside Jess.

He stilled, marveling at how he could hear the smile in the lead singer's voice, but as he rose to his feet, his mind spun with decades-old memories, the kind that turned his dreams into nightmares. He closed his eyes, watching the memories spill in front of him like a movie on a theater screen. Vivid and bright, he saw Jess dancing at the center of the barn.

"You're going to hurt the animals' ears," Drew had said, wishing he could be as free as she was.

Jess shook her body and laughed. "They love this song."

He sat on a bale of hay.

"Dance with me, Drew!" Her voice matched the song's tone, happy and exuberant, buoyant like a raft tossed down the river.

He hesitated, feeling self-conscious and unsure what to do with a girl dancing next to him, but nothing about Jess suggested anything but innocence. Dancing made her laugh, and when she was happy, she wanted everyone else to be happy too.

He obliged her with a few quick moves, and she threw her head back, hooting as she imitated him. Soon, the two of them were in the middle of the barn, twisting and spinning and giggling in the quiet country air.

Drew watched the shadow of his memory as it tried to fade, but before it did, before the song ended, his ten-year-old self glanced up into one of the back stalls, and in that moment, he remembered they weren't alone. Someone sat there against the wall, watching the two children play.

Drew spun Jess around with a laugh, looked up and met a pair of angry eyes staring straight through him. He'd gasped, stopped dancing and moved in front of her.

The song came to an end, and Drew shook himself back to the present, the memory—and fresh tears—stinging his eyes. He closed them tightly, his breathing labored, and fell to his knees, the image of the face still fresh in his mind.

Why hadn't he seen it before? Why hadn't he remembered this man until now? Why had this song triggered a memory that should've been there since that very day?

What had they done that day in the barn? Why hadn't he told his parents someone had been watching them? Why had they continued to play in the barns without an adult, as if they were invincible?

Drew closed his eyes again, pressing his knuckles into them. He could still see the man's face, vivid as a photograph. But he didn't recognize him. He had no idea who he was or if he'd played a role in the single event that had shaped Drew more than any other.

How could he get the image out of his mind and into the hands of the police? It had been two decades, but maybe someone would recognize him.

Drew stood, unsteady on weak knees. He leaned against the only stall he'd yet to tear out, the one at the back, often shadowed and hard to see into. The man had been in that very spot only days before Jess had disappeared. That couldn't be a coincidence.

All those years he'd been right. He hadn't seen anyone the day Jess went missing, but he had seen someone two days before.

He had the answer he'd been looking for.

He dropped the hammer back into his toolbox and started toward the house. He might not be able to get the image out of his mind, but he knew someone who could.

Beth's art was different from Birdie's, clothed in realism. He wished for a fleeting moment it was the other way around. Birdie already knew who he was. Asking her would be easier.

Asking Beth had all kinds of ramifications. But he'd never be able to love her the way she deserved if he didn't finish this.

Time to stop being a coward.

He passed through the commotion in the main barn. When he didn't see her, he headed straight for the farmhouse.

Inside, it was quiet.

"Beth?" he called out, but the only reply was silence. "Beth?"

After checking the main floor, he started upstairs. He moved quickly, trying to hold on to every shred of the image he'd seen, though he was pretty sure he couldn't forget that face—those eyes—if he wanted to. He finally had something tangible, something that could lead them to Jess's kidnapper. Even the possibility of it quickened his pulse.

"Beth?" Still nothing. He checked each room, wondering if she'd gone or if she was outside somewhere and he hadn't realized it.

A quick glance in Jess's room. Empty. Guest room. Also empty. The bathroom door stood wide open, with obviously no one inside.

The master bedroom. She was probably cleaning out the closet.

Oh, no. Drew's heart sank.

What if . . . ?

"Beth?" His voice was quiet now as he entered the bedroom and moved toward the closet. The door was open, and all the clothes had been cleared away, revealing the door to the hidden room, which now stood open and exposed like a gaping wound in need of stitches.

Inside, under the dim light of the single hanging bulb, Beth sat at the table, studying the clippings and photos on the bulletin board.

She turned, tears in her eyes, holding a small photograph Drew recognized almost instantly. Him and Jess at the creek, proudly holding the fish they'd caught that morning. Jess's mom had snapped the photo, and he'd found it tucked behind an article on the bulletin board.

"Beth, I—"

"It was you." Her voice shook as she slowly faced him. "You were the witness. You know what happened to Jess Pendergast."

Chapter Thirty

Drew stared at her, pain radiating behind his icy blue eyes. He looked at her, then at the photo in her hands, then to the room where she sat—a tiny room she hadn't intended to find. When she'd cleared away the clothes, there it was—and what she saw inside looked like the work of a madman.

"This is why you're here."

He turned away, took his hat off and raked a hand through his hair. "This isn't how I wanted you to find out."

"You could've told me weeks ago." She scanned the wall of photos, newspaper clippings and random scribblings on napkins. Most of the items were old and weathered, undoubtedly the work of Harold Pendergast. But some of those things, like Davis Biddle's business card, were brand-new.

Those things told her Drew not only knew about the secret room, he knew about the wall. He'd contributed to it.

Was he a madman too?

Beth waited for an explanation, but as usual, Drew seemed unable, or unwilling, to speak.

She stood and walked toward him. "Drew, what's going on?"

He finally turned toward her but kept his eyes down, like someone with something to hide. He'd heard them talking about the case more than once yet never said a word. Was he protecting someone? Protecting himself? What if *he'd* been the reason Jess went missing? What part had he played in her disappearance, and likely, her death? Was that why he'd been so silent?

And if he was guilty—then why was he here at all?

"Did you have something to do with her disappearance?"

His face went pale, his skin white. "You can't be serious."

Beth paced across the room, trying to piece it together. "Was it an accident? Did you hurt her? Is that why you told the police you couldn't remember?"

"I can't believe you'd even ask me that."

She spun around. "Then tell me." She held up the photo, a copy of the one they'd found in Jess's closet. "Tell me what happened that day."

The air thickened between them.

She dared a step toward him. "Drew, you were a kid. A young kid. If you did something that led to her death—they wouldn't have held it against you."

Slowly, he lifted his gaze to hers, and for a moment, she thought he might actually explain. Instead, he looked away. "I'll go."

Her stomach dropped. "You're leaving?"

His face fell. "I can't stay here if this is what you think about me."

"Tell me what to think. For once, just tell me the truth."

He looked at her then, his eyes steady but so sad. Her heart broke for the pain she saw there, years of bottled-up angst with nowhere to go but in. Whatever had happened that day clearly still haunted him.

Could she blame him if he couldn't talk about it?

He took her hands, brought them to his lips and held them there for a long moment. "Please know I never meant to hurt you. That's the truth."

"Drew, please." A lump formed at the back of her throat as he let go of her hands.

"And I didn't hurt Jess," he said. "I would never hurt anyone." His blue eyes had gone distant.

"I know you wouldn't." Her words came out as a whisper, too quiet and too late.

He stayed still for a while longer, then headed down the stairs. Beth watched through tear-filled eyes out the second-story window as Drew Barlow exited her house, duffel bag slung over his shoulder and German shepherd close on his heels. He threw the bag in his truck, let Roxie in the front seat and pulled away.

Sobs overtook her body, and she sank to her knees, still holding the photograph of a little boy with the same kind eyes as the man she loved.

Chapter Thirty-One

The emptiness of the farmhouse seeped into the loneliest parts of Beth's soul. After too many long minutes crying on the floor of the hidden room, her phone rang, forcing her to pull herself together. A number she didn't recognize showed up on the caller ID.

"Hello?"

"Beth? It's Dina. I just got your email about the barn sale."

Beth had sent that email weeks ago.

"It got lost in our server—long story—anyway, I had my team work something up. A logo, a website and an ad campaign. Look it over and send me the names of the vendors so I can put the finishing touches on it and make it live. I would say send me your changes, but the sale is in just a couple of weeks. We should probably just go with it as it is."

"Dina, you shouldn't have gone to all that trouble." She thought about the gossip she'd heard and wondered if it was true. And if Harrison was leaving her, how was Dina handling it?

Her own heart ached at the thought of losing Drew—and their relationship had barely begun.

"I told you, I think it's brilliant what you're doing. I want to help if I can."

"Well, thanks. I haven't had much time to put anything like this together."

"You want me to handle it?"

Beth straightened. "Handle?"

"All the advertising. The whole thing. I'll get the word out for you. We'll pack that place."

Beth didn't know how to respond. She wasn't good at asking for help—especially from someone like Dina.

"It would mean a lot to me if I could help with this, Beth. No charge."

She heard the sadness in Dina's voice. She needed something to keep her mind occupied—to help her stop thinking about her impending divorce.

Beth's thoughts turned to Drew, the way he'd worked around here as if his life depended on it.

And maybe it did. Maybe he needed this place as much as it needed him.

Had she taken that from him?

"Beth?"

"What? Oh, sorry. I would really appreciate your help, Dina. I'll look at what you sent over, and if you could get the word out, well, we'd be really grateful."

"Anything for Fairwind Farm. I mean it. Think of me as your in-house ad agency. I'm here whenever you need me. Once you guys get up and running again, we can discuss pricing and I'll work with your budget, I promise." Dina sounded happy—and Beth had to admit, genuine. "Thanks, Beth."

The words hung between them—simple, yet so full of meaning.

"No, thank you," Beth said.

After she hung up, she set her phone down and walked outside. The day had turned gray. Clouds hung low and dark in the sky.

Good. Rain was just what the ground needed.

A clean, fresh start would be good for them all.

She did a quick survey of the barn. They'd made so much progress. The new and improved Fairwind Farm Market would be a huge success. They might even open this fall. All thanks to Drew.

And she'd driven him away.

She trudged through the open field toward the little chapel at the back of the property, turning over unwanted thoughts in her mind.

Why hadn't Drew just been honest from the start? Why couldn't he have told her who he was instead of waiting until she'd found out, searching in the old man's closet?

It was humiliating that he didn't trust her when she'd shared so much with him.

Life had her head all turned around. What was she doing here? How could *this* be the "more" she'd been looking for? How could an old run-down farm be her "why"?

Birdie was wrong. Beth didn't belong here at all. She wasn't a home-town girl.

Why am I here at all, Lord?

She unlocked the chapel with the little key above the door and went inside just as a rumble of thunder made its way across the vast midwestern sky. Beth closed the door and inhaled a deep, lonely breath.

Why had she come here? What did she hope to find waiting for her? Birdie's words filled her mind:

"There's something deep down within us, isn't there, that just wants to be known?"

She sat with the memory for a moment.

Had she ever let anyone know her?

She'd been too afraid. All this time, she'd hidden the truth from her family the same way Drew had hidden it from her, because she didn't want them to think less of her. She was ashamed, and she didn't want to admit any of it to the people she'd hurt. But even before that—had she ever let anyone know her for who she really was?

I know you.
The words welled up from the depths of her soul.
You are known.
He knew her. He knew her and He loved her anyway.
"Having a 'why' isn't the same as having something to prove."
Birdie's words echoed in her mind again.
"You can't earn love. Or forgiveness. Or grace. Those things are gifts. You just have to reach out and take them."

Beth opened the prayer journal and turned to the last page, where Sonya had written the most stirring prayer about her daughter, about the peace she'd found in spite of her circumstances. Beth had asked for that peace, and she supposed she'd expected God to wave a magic wand over her, granting her wish.

What if Birdie was right? What if peace and forgiveness and love really were gifts? What if God had been waiting for her to reach out and take them this whole time?

Could it really be that simple?

Beth stared at the blank page near the back of the journal. Did she even know how to accept something she hadn't earned?

She picked up the pen tucked inside the worn book. Somehow, adding her own handwriting to this precious journal made her nervous. Like she didn't deserve to be part of the group of women who'd already breathed their hearts' desires onto its pages. She poised the pen over the paper.

Heavenly Father,

She'd start her prayer the same way the women before had started theirs. Had Sonya stopped at this point, taken a moment to breathe in the weight of her own prayers?

I'm not like the other women who've sat in this little chapel and shared their prayers on the pages of this sacred book. I'm much more flawed. I realize now, in my thirtieth year, that I've wasted so much time on things that have no real value. I've worked and strived and tried so hard to become who I thought I was supposed to be, but really, in doing those things, I lost myself.

I know peace and unconditional love——they're gifts You've given us.

She stopped and stared at the words she'd written, pen still at the ready. She crossed out the word *us* and changed it to *me*, then read the last sentence aloud.

"I know peace and unconditional love—they're gifts You've given me." She paused to let the words permeate her soul. Tears sprang to her eyes, as if she'd realized the statement's value only in that moment. She continued to write:

Help me receive the gifts You've given without feeling so unworthy all the time. I want to be known. I want to know that I'm loved. And I want to give love as freely as You do, without expectation. Genuine and real.

Her pen stopped moving, as if on its own.

She didn't know how to receive love, and she didn't know how to offer love as a stringless gift. Look at how she'd driven Drew away. She'd been so selfish, she hadn't even seen his pain.

Pain that had been so evident from the first day he'd started working at the farm.

He'd been looking for the same thing she had been—a second chance. He'd felt, like she had, that he could do more.

And now he was gone. Because of her.

Lord, let me love the way You've loved me. Even in my ugliest, darkest moments. Even when I don't deserve it. Show me the way to offer that kind of love.

Show me my "why," Lord. I have a feeling it's not at all what I thought it was. Maybe I am meant to be here——at least for now——living a simple life and connecting people. Is that what You want from me? For Fairwind?

My life is Yours. This beautiful farm is Yours.

Help us to make it what You want it to be.

Amen.

As she put the pen back inside the book, the thunder rolled outside, the storm approaching much more quickly than she'd expected. Rain pounded on the chapel roof, and Beth sighed, knowing she'd have to wait it out or get soaked. She opened the door, leaning over for a glimpse of the driveway, but hers was the only car she could see. Everyone else had gone.

The wind kicked up, yanking the door out of her hand. She grabbed it and pulled it closed. The room that had felt like a sanctuary now felt like a prison.

Maybe she wasn't finished here.

She sat down on one of the wooden pews. As the trees behind the church brushed across the windows, Beth whispered a prayer for Drew. He hadn't been able to talk about whatever it was he'd seen that day, but she understood a little bit better now. Like her, he'd been working for the one thing that had already been given—forgiveness.

"Use me to help him see that, Lord."

Beth closed her eyes, listened to the rain and let peace wash over her, believing for the first time ever that everything just might be okay—whether she worked for it or not.

Chapter Thirty-Two

Drew sat in a folding chair across from Bishop's desk at the Willow Grove Police Station, waiting for the officer to return from patrol.

Four desks were positioned in haphazard fashion around the room, and he was pretty sure the woman who'd escorted him back here still stared at him from her desk at the entrance, but he pretended not to notice. She seemed to think Bishop would be right back, but Drew had already been waiting fifteen minutes, and there was no indication Bishop even knew he had a visitor.

Every so often, the police scanner came to life. In the time he'd been sitting there, he'd heard reports of a stray dog running down the highway and the ice cream truck's new route. This place likely never saw much excitement, but he supposed that's how most of the people who lived here preferred it.

Outside, the sky had grown dark, no trace of blue underneath the thick gray clouds.

"Hope your windows aren't down," the woman called back. She stood at the front window.

Drew joined her just as big, full drops of rain started to hit the pavement. Roxie stood on the front seat of his truck, barking out the partially cracked window.

"Someone doesn't like storms," the woman said, watching the dog.

Drew sighed. He never should've stopped here. It wasn't like Willow Grove had a sketch artist anyway.

Behind them, garbled voices sounded on the police scanner, and the phone rang.

"People get so upset whenever there's a storm." The woman plodded back to her desk. "You wouldn't believe what they're like when it snows."

She picked up the phone. "This is Nancy."

Nancy. He'd forgotten her name, too distracted by the hive of red hair atop her head.

"Slow down," Nancy said into the receiver. "Are you sure?"

The scanner went off now in a steady stream, like audible commotion. Drew listened more carefully.

"A tornado has touched down just west of Willow Grove. I repeat, a tornado has been spotted on the ground just west of Willow Grove."

Drew glanced at Nancy as the color drained from her cheeks. She hung up the phone. "We need to take cover."

Outside, a tornado siren went off.

"Get your dog, and let's go to the basement," she said. "They're going on the airwaves now to tell everyone to get underground."

Drew's thoughts spun back to Fairwind. He'd left in such a hurry, he hadn't cleaned up any of the rotted wood outside the barn where he'd been working earlier that day. If the winds were strong enough, those beams could destroy the main barn.

Whether he wanted to admit it or not, he'd been honest when he'd said he was invested now. Not only because of all the time he'd spent on the place, but because he'd fallen hopelessly in love with its owner.

Beth. Did she even know about the tornado?

He fished his cell phone out of his pocket and dialed her number. After five rings, it went to voice mail.

"We should go." Nancy stood near a door at the back of the station.

"You go ahead," Drew said. "I need to go check on someone." Fairwind was on the east side of town. If he hurried, he could beat the storm. Maybe.

"Are you crazy? This isn't a drill. We have a confirmed twister on the ground. It's headed straight for town."

"I know." Drew hit "Redial" on his phone. "I need to hurry. Thanks, Nancy."

Still no answer on Beth's phone. Where was she? This wasn't the best time for her to be stubborn and refuse his calls.

He rushed out to his truck and pulled himself inside, rain dripping off the ends of his hair and onto his jeans.

Roxie barked, riled up from the thunder.

"I know, Rox. We've gotta hurry."

He drove the now-familiar highway toward Fairwind, trying not to think about the fact that Beth could still be sorting through clothing and linens on the second floor of the farmhouse. She could be in the yard, pulling in the lawn chairs. She could be in real danger. And it was possible she had no idea. Out there, she wouldn't have heard the tornado siren.

He mentally beat himself up for leaving the way he had as he listened to her outgoing voice-mail message for the third time.

Rain came down in sheets now, forcing him to slow down. Behind him, the sky had turned an ugly shade of green, the color of an old bruise.

And it didn't look good.

"Come on, Beth." He dialed again as Roxie whined in the passenger seat. Beth hardly ever went anywhere without her phone. What if something had happened to her? What if she'd gotten hurt and there was no one there to help?

He tried not to think the worst and focused instead on the dark road in front of him. When he finally made the turn that led to Fairwind, his heart kept time with the frantic windshield wipers.

Maybe she'd lost service. That was possible. He glanced at his own phone and saw four bars. His heart dropped.

Beth's car still sat in the driveway, the same place it had been when he'd left earlier that day. Maybe she'd taken cover in the cellar? Drew pulled his truck alongside Beth's Audi and killed the engine. He pulled his hat down lower and turned to Roxie.

"Ready, girl?"

As he opened the door, the rain, which now came down diagonally, instantly drenched him on one side. He hurried the dog out of the truck, slammed the door and ran toward the farmhouse, the wind whipping torrents of rain against his face and body.

He raced to the porch and pushed open the front door, slamming it closed behind him. He ordered Roxie to stay in the entryway—no sense in both of them drenching the place.

Inside, the house stood quiet.

"Beth?"

No answer.

"Stay here," Drew said to Roxie as he started checking every room of the house, calling Beth's name in each one. In the master bedroom, he tried not to replay the conversation they'd had earlier that day.

He'd hurt her—and then he'd left, like the coward he was.

When will you ever do the hard thing?

He opened the door of the hidden room, just to be sure. Beth's phone sat on the table, displaying several missed calls. He took it, then checked the dusty old basement in the hope that she'd been smart and taken cover.

There was no sign of her. Panic settled in his heart. He would never forgive himself if something happened to Beth.

Drew called Roxie into the kitchen, where she turned in circles, her wet fur dripping on the linoleum floor.

"Where is she, girl?"

He rushed outside and scanned the yard. A quick pass through the main barn told him it was secure, but that pile of rotted wood behind it was still a huge concern. He couldn't stand the thought that the mess he'd left behind could damage the buildings they'd worked so hard to restore.

He raced back behind the main barn, but Beth was nowhere to be seen.

"Come on, Beth, where are you?" He tapped his hand on his thigh, staring out across the yard. She had to be out there somewhere.

He hurried on into a clearing at the back of the property. The little chapel came into view. If she was upset, it made sense she'd go there. To get some perspective. Maybe to pray. He ran toward the church as the wind whipped through the trees, and the rain seemed to fall from every direction. He kept his head down and followed the sound of Roxie's barking. Thunder and lightning erupted overhead, and he could think only about the muffled voices on the police scanner.

What if a tornado whipped through Fairwind? It could take the entire farm all at once. And if Beth wasn't prepared for it—it could kill her.

He had to find her. He had to keep her safe.

Roxie reached the chapel before Drew. She stood outside the door and barked. Beth had to be inside. He reached the door just as hail started pelting the rooftop. On the ground, golf-ball-sized bits of ice bounced into the grass. Drew pulled open the door, fighting against the force of the wind. He motioned to Roxie to go inside, though he knew the chapel was hardly a safe place to weather a storm this powerful.

The door slammed open for the second time since Beth had taken cover underneath a pew at the front of the little chapel. She'd left her phone back in the house, but she'd lived in Illinois long enough to know this was no ordinary storm.

Twice, she'd almost made a run for it, but the thunder, lightning and wind forced her to stay put.

Outside, another crash vibrated the floor. What had started as a calm retreat from the day had turned into a white-knuckled hideout, reminding her of all the times she and Molly had hidden under their covers with flashlights, waiting for storms to blow over.

"Beth?"

Drew's voice cut through the silence. She crawled out from under the pew and met his eyes. He stood in the doorway, rainwater pooling beneath him, his face, arms and hair wet.

"What are you doing here?" She stood.

His breaths came quick. He'd been running. "There was a tornado on the other side of town."

"Is anyone hurt?"

"I don't know," he said. "Are you okay?" He moved toward her, holding up her phone. "I've been trying to call you."

The sky outside flashed with the kind of lightning that didn't have to pause for effect. Thunder followed immediately.

"I'm fine," she said, assuming he meant physically. "You're drenched."

"It's raining out," he said dryly. He watched her for a long moment, and she saw the relief loosen his shoulders. "You're okay." He took another step toward her, cautious, as if asking for permission.

"I'm fine." Beth stared at the floor. "Are you okay?"

He must've felt the distance she put between them. He dropped onto the back pew and rubbed his temples, eyes closed. "I will be."

She wanted to help him—to let him off the hook for not telling her everything right from the start. Any shred of suspicion or anger had been pulled out of her and replaced with understanding.

Outside, the sound of wood cracking and splitting drew them both toward the window. Drew got there first and quickly shoved Beth behind him. "Get back."

More cracking wood, more vibrations from the thunder.

He stepped back from the glass. "I think we just lost a tree."

Beth paced. "Tornado?"

He turned. "I'm not sure. But it's not safe in here. This is the oldest building on the property."

Roxie barked.

Fear rose inside her. "What do we do? We can't leave."

"I know. We have to wait it out." He strode back toward Beth. "Move to the center of the room, away from the windows. Back under the pews."

Beth did as she was told while Drew tried to calm Roxie down, pulling her underneath the wooden benches.

When he settled in, he was lying on his side, facing her, one arm propping his head up off the ground. He took her hand, and somehow that simple gesture made her feel safe. As if he'd just pledged to keep her that way.

Outside, the storm raged, but Beth's fear had faded. She'd given her life, this farm, Drew—all of it to God. That meant He was in control of whatever happened.

She'd spent too long being angry with Him; it was time to let it all go. To lay it down. To find her "why."

To rest in the peace that He promised.

Drew had a faraway look in his eyes—so close, and yet still just out of reach. She studied his face, his ice-blue eyes, the scar on his chin. She wanted to know how he'd gotten it. She wanted to know how often he shaved and if he used an electric razor. She wanted to know how he celebrated Christmas and when his next birthday would be. She wanted to know everything about him, and she'd wait as long as he needed her to.

Because words weren't easy for this man.

But loving was. He was good and safe and kind.

She never should've implied otherwise.

Lying on the floor of the old chapel in the woods, it was as if God was giving her a picture of the lonely life Drew Barlow had led, carrying a guilt that was never his to bear.

She saw that ten-year-old boy in the man at her side, and she knew what he needed was unconditional love. He needed the reassurance that when the storm that raged inside him finally ended, leaving the grass greener and the flowers a shade more vivid, she'd still be there. No judgment. No questions.

The same kind of unconditional love she'd been given. It was a gift—and she wanted to learn to give it freely.

To be known and still loved without question. *Isn't that what we all want?*

Beth had been staring at Drew's chest, aware he wasn't avoiding her eyes. She felt his gaze on her. Another crash of thunder shook the chapel, but she barely noticed. Slowly, she lifted her eyes to meet his. She reached out and let her hand rest on Drew's stubbled cheek, certain that somewhere within him was the heart of the boy who'd lost hope all those years ago.

And she loved him. Deeply and without strings. Even if it made her weak. Even if he didn't love her back. Even if he hadn't told her every single secret he kept.

And she left the rest in God's hands.

Chapter Thirty-Three

After half an hour underneath the pews, Beth could tell the rain had mostly stopped. The thunder and lightning seemed to have moved on, but neither she nor Drew moved.

At some point during the storm, he'd pulled her closer, enveloping her in his arms, and now, still lying beside him, hand resting calmly on his chest, she wished they could continue to hide away.

But they had to face reality at some point.

"I suppose we should go check on the farm." Dread resonated in his voice. All that work—his work—was on the line. "Not knowing is worse than facing it."

Somehow she had the feeling he wasn't talking only about the damage from the storm.

She drew in a deep breath, then inched her way out of his arms. "I guess you're right."

He scooted out from under the pew and stood, staring at her.

They'd hardly spoken since he'd arrived, opting instead to listen to the storm as it beat on the sides of the chapel, praying the roof wouldn't cave.

But now, when she looked at him, she saw him more clearly than she had before. "I'm sorry, Drew."

He held up a hand. "I'm the one who's sorry."

She wanted to say more. To ask questions and make sense of the burden he carried, but she knew that wasn't what he needed right now. Instead, she wrapped her arms around him in an apologetic hug, wishing she'd been more understanding from the start. He held her for a long moment, then slipped his hand in hers and led her out of the church, Roxie close behind.

They started toward the farmhouse, walking through the wet grass, rain still dripping from the leaves overhead. Branches were down all over the yard, and the Adirondack chairs they'd set up around the bonfire had been blown out into the cornfield.

"Looks like we did lose a couple of trees." He pointed off to the right where the tree line met the cornfield.

The potential devastation of a storm like this began to sink in. They'd worked tirelessly for weeks—what if everything they'd accomplished had been undone in a matter of minutes?

Drew squeezed her hand, leading her toward the main barn. They both knew this building was the most important. They could reopen the farm without any others, but this one housed everything they needed for the fall, not to mention the barn sale only a few weekends away.

Beth's stomach lurched as they maneuvered through the downed branches and debris scattered across the yard.

Drew led her around to the front of the barn, which from this vantage point seemed undamaged, but when they opened the doors, they saw a gaping hole in the back corner where the roof had torn away. Several inches of water stood in a puddle, ruining their newly finished floor.

Without the roof intact, the storm had ripped through the building, tossing tables and breaking glass. Branches, leaves and dirt had collected all across the floor.

Beth stood at the center of the barn in a puddle of water, and hopelessness washed over her. "It's ruined."

Drew started around the perimeter, assessing the damage the same way he'd done his first day on the job. Birdie's artwork and several pieces from the farmhouse had been drenched—probably ruined. The overturned tables that had been collecting barn-sale items looked like remnants of a riot, their contents in piles all over the wet floor. Two sets of shelves they'd installed had been torn away from the wall, and the glass cooler was broken.

At the back of the barn, Drew stopped, his face looking every bit as forlorn as Beth felt. For once, she didn't mind that he had nothing to say. She didn't need words to know what he thought.

Her cell phone buzzed in her pocket, and she went through the motions of fishing it out and answering.

"Miss Whitaker. Davis Biddle."

She nodded, as if he could see her through the phone.

"We just drove by Fairwind and saw the damage. Looks like the cleanup and repairs will be extensive."

Why was he calling her to tell her what she already knew?

"Just wanted you to know my offer is still good."

Her eyes found Drew, who watched her as she listened to the man on the other end. Was it some sort of sign that it was time to let go of this crazy idea once and for all? Had she been wrong—again—about what God wanted her to do? She'd been so sure when she'd gone against her father's wishes, so sure when she'd devoted so many years to Michael. She'd thought this time was different.

She'd thought Fairwind was her "why."

She'd even begun to think that living here, in Willow Grove, wasn't a consolation prize. It didn't make her a disappointment—it was a gift, like Birdie said.

How could she have been so wrong?

"Miss Whitaker, I'm sure you're in shock right now, but believe me, this is nothing I can't handle."

If Davis bought Fairwind, it wouldn't be a community gem anymore. It wouldn't be a tourist attraction or a place for families to reconnect. It would just be a memory of what used to be.

Is that what You really want, Lord?

She looked down at the water pooling around her feet, thanked Davis and hung up, avoiding that earnest expression on the face of the man she loved.

She'd have to find a way to explain to Drew that all their hard work might have been for nothing. They might have to sell the farm to Davis Biddle—whether they wanted to or not.

Chapter Thirty-Four

Beth stood on the porch, watching as Ben's truck pulled into the parking lot next to her Audi. Moments later, Molly's VW Bug appeared at the farm's entry.

A Whitaker family meeting was in order, and Beth had a feeling it wouldn't go smoothly.

Yesterday's storm had upended their plans, and her brother and sister needed to see it for themselves. She and Drew hadn't discussed the future of the farm. He'd spent every waking minute since they'd left the chapel clearing away the debris that had rained down on their beloved Fairwind. Never in her life had she known someone to work with such diligence, especially for something that wasn't his.

Why couldn't they just crawl back underneath the chapel pew and pretend none of this was happening?

Molly and Bishop got out of the VW as Ben opened the door of his truck. Under different circumstances, it might have been a nice gathering.

Beth greeted everyone, the mood decidedly somber. "I asked Callie to join us too," she said, watching her old friend's car pull into the parking lot. "The bakery was one of the areas hit the worst." She hated that she'd talked Callie into coming on this grand adventure with her and everything had fallen apart.

"I'll show you guys the damage."

They reached the main barn and took turns marveling at the harm the storm had done. Thankfully, most of the other outbuildings, including Birdie's art barn, were unscathed. Beth would cling to that small miracle every time she looked at the hole in the main barn's roof.

They stood in the doorway looking at the destruction as Drew cleared away all of the branches that didn't belong indoors.

"Thank God you weren't hurt, Beth," Callie said.

"I'm fine. Drew's fine. Even the animals are all fine," she said. "But we have a lot of work to do."

"I don't know if that's a good idea," Molly said.

Beth's eyes widened. "What do you mean?"

"I mean, I know Davis Biddle called you."

Beth's heart lurched. She could feel Drew's eyes on her. Why hadn't she told him about the phone call? Because she was actually considering taking the offer or because she didn't want him to tell her to consider taking the offer?

It was an impossible decision.

"Who's Davis Biddle?"

Beth couldn't believe what she was hearing as Molly filled Ben in on Davis's offer. Clearly her sister—the one who'd once fought tooth and nail for this farm—had given up.

Just like that.

"I can't believe you."

Molly turned to her. "What?"

"You think we should sell."

"Of course I do, Beth. Look around."

Beth could feel the slack in her own jaw. What had happened to Molly's insistence that this was their second chance? Didn't her sister understand how much Beth had grown to love this farm?

The realization wove through the back of Beth's mind.

She loved this place. And she'd fight for it—even if her sister wouldn't.

"No. Fairwind is not for sale." Beth squared her shoulders.

"The way I see it," Molly said, "we didn't have enough money before the storm, but now? All the work we've already done is ruined."

"We can fix it," Beth said.

"Not for free." Molly shook her head. "I think maybe you were right from the beginning. It might be time to admit that we're in over our heads."

"So, what? We're just supposed to pack it all up? Sell the farm to a man who'll turn it into God only knows what?"

"What do you suggest, Beth?" Ben asked coolly. "We've sunk about as much as we want to into this place."

He was right. She had nothing more to give. She'd practically drained her trust on repairs for Fairwind Farm. But this couldn't be the end. She couldn't give up on her "why" just because she didn't see a way out of this right at that moment.

Sunlight streamed in through the gaping hole in the roof.

"Just let me think for a minute," she said.

"There's nothing to think about." Molly crossed her arms.

"Then what am I supposed to do now?" She was horrified when her eyes filled with tears. Behind her, Drew stopped moving, gaze fixed on her.

"Beth, you can go back to your job at Whitaker Mowers, and it'll be like none of this ever happened," Molly said.

"I can't." The words slipped out before she could catch them.

"Of course you can. They've probably been bugging you for taking so much time off."

Beth's eyes fell to the ground at Molly's feet. "No, they haven't. They asked me to resign."

"They what?" Ben asked.

She looked up. Found their eyes, full of confusion. Drew took a step toward her—for moral support?

"I made a mistake. A big one. It cost the company a lot of money." A knot caught in her throat. "Dad found out about it, and he covered for me, but after he died, I knew it was only a matter of time before someone else connected the dots."

"Beth," Molly practically whispered.

"How bad was it?" Ben asked.

"Bad." Shame wound its way through her belly. "It was really bad. And Dad told me it was bad before I did it, but I thought I knew better."

"Why didn't you say anything?" Molly asked.

A tear streamed down Beth's cheek. "Are you kidding? And admit that I was wrong?" She wiped the tear away. "What would you have thought of your big sister then?"

"Um, that she was human?" Molly reached over and tugged on Beth's hand. "It's okay, Beth. We all mess up."

"I know that now. And I know that keeping it to myself only made it worse, but I was afraid of letting you all down. Especially Dad. I thought if I could make a go of this—make it work somehow—I could prove that I wasn't a total disaster."

She glanced at Drew, who watched her, his strength and support the only thing enabling her to continue.

"I know it doesn't work that way. Dad forgave me. I guess I just needed to forgive myself."

"That sounds like a smart idea," Molly said.

"But you can understand why I can't let you sell the farm to Davis Biddle."

"You can start over, Beth."

"She's right," Ben said. "If this guy wants the farm as much as he says he does, we've got some leverage. We can make sure we all get out of it what we put into it." Ben had always been the voice of wisdom, and Beth always agreed with him.

Until now.

"What about your mom?" Callie asked, eyes hopeful. "I mean, it doesn't change much for me, but I feel so bad for you guys. I loved your plans. Everyone in town loved your plans."

"We agreed not to bring our mom into this," Beth said. "Because of her health."

Callie stilled. "Well, what do you think, Drew?"

Drew stood on the outside of their circle, arms crossed. "I think it'll be hard to get everything repaired by fall."

"But not impossible, right?" Beth could hear the naïve hopefulness in her own voice. Somehow Molly had become the voice of reason, and she'd become, well, the deluded one.

Drew looked away.

Not him too.

"It doesn't seem like we have a choice." Ben shook his head. "We don't really have any reason not to sell to this guy."

Beth caught a glimpse of Drew, who looked like he might choke on whatever words he wasn't saying.

"What is it?" She turned to him.

His eyes widened.

"You have something to say, I can tell."

He shook his head. "I don't."

She stared at him. Didn't he know she'd been watching him swallow his thoughts for weeks now? Usually she let him off the hook, but not this time. "Tell me."

"You're just as much a part of this as the rest of us, man," Ben said.

"You're more a part of this than the rest of us," Beth said quietly.

Drew shook his head, as if silently making a decision. "We're not going to land on the same side of this one, Beth. Just let it go."

"Why?" She felt like she'd been punched in the stomach. "You don't want to fight for everything we've been working for?"

"Of course I do." He kept his voice calm and even as always. "But you're more important. You've got a chance to get out of this without losing everything. You should take it."

Beth looked around the circle of sad faces that all told her the same thing. No matter how much she wished it, the only way to save the farm was to let it go.

None of them saw any other choice. And as much as she hated to admit it, neither did she.

Their dreams for Fairwind Farm had washed away in the storm.

Chapter Thirty-Five

Beth sat in one of two Adirondack chairs she'd salvaged after the storm, staring at the empty fire pit and trying to figure out how to let the farm go.

Why had God chosen to take this away from her, just when she'd begun to love it?

She didn't understand it, but she chose to trust He had a plan. In the past, she'd been so angry when things didn't go her way—if she'd learned anything, it was that anger had turned her into someone she didn't want to be.

Her phone rang, and she saw Dina's name on her screen. Beth hadn't told her the barn sale was off. And she'd probably been working round the clock to spread the word.

Beth let out a heavy sigh, then clicked the phone on. "Hey, Dina."

"Beth, have you had a chance to check your email? I'd love to know what you think of the mock-ups. And you'll be happy to know *Midwest Living* and *Country Life* agreed to promote the sale online in exchange for advertising, which I'd be willing to donate."

"Dina, you don't have to do that."

"It's already done. Someone will be calling you this week. They're excited. They might even send someone out to the sale."

She sounded so happy. In spite of everything, she'd been a good friend to Beth. It felt terrible to let her down. "You haven't talked to your grandma, have you?"

Dina paused. "No, why? Is she okay?"

"She's fine, but the farm isn't. There was a tornado." That stupid lump was back in her throat.

"Oh, no, Beth. I'm so sorry."

"It looks like we're going to have to sell. We don't really have another choice." Even as she said the words, Beth thought of a hundred other choices—though she had to admit, most of them resulted in their financial ruin.

"So what's next for you, then?" Dina asked after a pause.

Beth swiped a tear before it could slide down her cheek. "I haven't figured that out yet."

"Come work for me."

Beth laughed. "What?"

"Come on, Beth. You'd be amazing. I know we were always a little competitive in high school, but we're past all that now—and my team could use a great leader like you."

Was she serious?

"So, what, I'd move to the city?"

"Sure, why not? Isn't that what you always wanted?"

"Yeah, I suppose it is." Or at least, it had been.

"Think about it. Let me know. I'll hold on to the advertising and leave the magazine interviews in place for a couple more days. Maybe there will be some sort of miracle."

"I hope you're right. And Dina?"

"Yeah?"

"Thanks."

She hung up, a familiar hollow feeling returning to her gut. After everything they'd invested in Fairwind, she was sick to think of walking away from it now.

A stick cracked behind her, and she turned to find Drew standing there. How long had he been there?

"You're leaving?" Even in the shadow, she could see his disappointment.

She looked away. "Aren't you?"

"Haven't decided yet."

She stood and faced him.

The ten-year-old boy in the fishing photo popped into her mind. Anger rose within her. Why hadn't anyone done a better job making sure he was okay? If they had, maybe he'd be able to talk about it now. Instead, he stood there, the truth trapped inside him.

She didn't know how to let him go. She didn't know how to give him the space she'd promised. Not when she wanted to know every-thing about him.

"You gave me something," she said, "and I don't even know if you realize it."

His eyes held hers, unmoving.

"A safe place. I didn't even know I needed it. I was so ashamed of everything that happened at work, but the day I told you, it was like it lost its hold on me. I realized life isn't about how much I've accom-plished or what I've done. It's about who I've loved and how well I've loved them."

He didn't say anything, but then, that didn't surprise her.

"Do you know how hard it is to love someone who doesn't let you in?" Tears returned to her eyes, but she forced herself to keep going. She moved over to him, reached up and touched his face. "It's safe here."

Finally, he looked at her, and in that moment, she saw the fear that tormented him. The pain of a past that wouldn't go away. For years, he'd lived with the memory of something that he'd likely had no control over, something he probably blamed himself for, and it had held him hostage—a spectator in his own life.

"You've got to let this go."

Drew closed his eyes, as if wrestling again with a demon that had him by the throat. He started to speak but quickly closed his mouth.

Beth could see it now—he wasn't unwilling to open up, he was unable. Had he ever talked about that day to anyone?

He inched away from her, again just out of reach. Turning in a circle, he raked his hands through his hair, then put the ball cap back on his head. He glanced at the side door of the house—the nearest escape—but stopped before going in.

"If you leave, what happens to us?"

The question took her off guard. How should she respond? He'd told her she didn't have another choice but to sell—he had to know she'd get another job. And yet, from where he stood, it probably looked like she was walking away.

Leaving him with the exact opposite of a safe place.

How could she expect him to do anything but run?

He didn't give her a chance to respond. The sound of the slamming screen door punctuated the end of their conversation.

◆　◆　◆

Drew stormed through the house, out the front door and back out to the barn, stepping over debris that made the farm look worse than it had the day he'd arrived.

Anger stuck to his thoughts like static cling.

Why was this so hard to talk about? He wanted to tell her everything, but every time he started to, something stopped him.

A thick barrier of shame.

He moved toward the tree that had sliced through the roof, and started hauling the mess away. Each downed branch gave him something else to throw. He cut through the larger sections with a chainsaw and hauled them out to the burn pile. He swept shattered glass into a dustpan and threw it in the garbage.

He worked angry.

Beth was right. He had to let this go. It was killing him—yet he didn't have the right to wish for a peaceful life.

Not until he found peace for Jess.

He picked up a fallen table and slammed it back where it belonged. He did the same with the other tables, then the chairs.

His pulse raced, and his face heated. He wanted to punch something. Hard.

Drew picked up an old wooden chair and threw it against the wall. The chair fell in pieces onto the ground. He picked up another one and did the same thing.

Jess's laugh echoed in the emptiness of the barn. Seconds later, the buoyant melody of "Sh-Boom," the song he'd heard earlier, filled his thoughts. He tried to shake them away, but scenes from his nightmare played out in front of him.

Dancing with Jess. Her singsong voice calling his name. The face in the shadows. The icy realization that something was wrong. Crawling out of the loft. A blow on the back of the head. Darkness.

He had answers to questions no one was asking anymore. He had to tell someone.

He had to find a way to make himself talk.

It was why he'd come here in the first place—to finally, finally put this thing to rest.

He looked at the wooden chair he was clutching in his hands. Slowly, he set it down, pulse still racing as he fell to his knees.

He hadn't prayed in years. All the time his parents had forced him to go to church, he'd sat with a chip on his shoulder, angry at a God who would allow something so tragic to happen to Jess. To him.

Something tragic had happened to him. And he'd never made peace with that. He'd never cried for Jess. He'd never cried for himself. For the loss of his childhood.

Now, in the silence of a broken barn, Drew allowed himself to feel the painful burden he'd carried for so many years.

It wasn't fair, what happened to her, God. I'm angry at You for letting it happen. I'm angry that I couldn't stop it. I'm angry that nobody protected me.

It had shaped his life, this pain he couldn't carry anymore. It had left him alone, unable to let anyone in.

I want to let this go, God. You've got to take this from me.

Drew pulled himself up and looked at the mess he'd made, evident even with all the storm damage. He'd clean it up. If he was going to say goodbye to Fairwind, he was going to do it with a clear conscience.

He walked outside and started for the house—but stopped at the sight of the squad car in the driveway.

Chapter Thirty-Six

Beth had been sitting in the kitchen when she saw the squad car pull in. She imagined Molly had hitched a ride out to the farm, but when Bishop got out of the car alone, she realized this wasn't a social call.

She met him on the porch, noticing the manila envelope in his hand.

"What's wrong? You look freaked out." Beth moved aside so he could come in.

"Remember how there was a witness to Jess's kidnapping?"

He knew about Drew. Beth took a deep breath. "I already know, Bishop."

"And you didn't tell me?"

"I've been a little busy with a tornado and the crushing of my dreams." She sat down at the table.

"Well, now you just sound like your sister."

Beth rolled her eyes. "What is there to tell? He witnessed something terrible twenty years ago. He was a kid."

"So why's he here now?"

Beth had wanted that question answered so many times, but this time, she chose to trust. "I don't know yet."

"I think I might." Bishop was paid to be suspicious. "He was at the station the day of the tornado. Nancy said he acted nervous. I think maybe he had something to confess."

"Confess what? He was ten years old." Beth thought about his face when she'd accused him of exactly what Bishop accused him of now. He'd been hurt by her betrayal. She had to believe the best about him.

"I don't know. What if he was messing around and he accidentally knocked her on the head or something? People have died that way." Bishop rested his hand on his holstered gun.

"I think he was a victim. A scared little kid who saw something terrible."

"Then why would he come to see me?"

"I don't know. You'll have to ask him."

"Ask me what?"

Beth turned and found Drew standing in the doorway behind her, eyebrows knit.

He'd entered through the side door. Beth sat at the table, her back to him, and Bishop stood, hat in hand, leaning against the sink opposite her.

They both turned and looked at him.

"Hey, Bishop." Drew's attempt at lightheartedness fell flat against the tension in the room.

Beth looked away.

"What's going on?" Panic simmered inside him.

Bishop twisted the hat around in a circle between both hands. "Nancy said you were waiting to speak to me at the station. Before the storm."

"That's right."

Bishop pushed himself to a full standing position and crossed his arms in front of him. "Care to have a conversation about that now?"

Drew's eyes narrowed. Beth still avoided them. What was going on here? Did they think he'd gone to the station to confess his guilt?

Fists formed at his sides. "If you don't mind, I'd like to talk to Beth first."

Bishop glanced at her as if asking permission. She gave a slight nod.

"I'll wait on the porch." He left the two of them alone in the weighty silence of the farmhouse kitchen.

Beth stood and smoothed her white button-down over her jeans.

"Beth, what are you thinking?"

Her eyes darted to his, then back to the floor.

"I didn't hurt her, if that's what you think."

Beth shook her head. "I know, Drew. I know you didn't."

He let out a sigh of relief. Thank God. "I wanted to tell you, I just . . . couldn't."

She crossed her arms over her chest and gave him her full attention.

It was time to let it go. Time to lay it down. And he knew it. He drew in a deep breath. "They never looked at me as a suspect. Not really. I was a kid. And I was knocked out cold."

"Was it an accident?" Beth's eyes searched his.

"No." Drew took off his hat, ran his hand through his hair, then over his face. As if anything could stop the pain that pulsed through his body now. "I came up here to tell you. I just . . ."

He turned away, but before he could move, he felt her hand in his.

"I'm listening." She sat down at the table and pushed out the chair across from her with her foot.

After a long moment, he sat. Wished he could leave. But one look at her told him he couldn't. There was too much at stake.

He didn't want to keep anything from her anymore.

"I was there," he finally said after several silent seconds. "We were playing hide-and-seek." He closed his eyes and, just like that, he was there, climbing the ladder to the old barn loft.

"It smelled like springtime. Hay and dirt and maybe an animal or two." The loft had been off-limits, but Drew was old enough. He'd been on dozens of ladders.

Beth watched, eyes intent. Safe.

"I heard her come in. She'd been yelling my name." He smiled at the memory. "I hid from her in the place I knew she'd be too scared to look. She hated that loft." His smile faded. "But after a few seconds, I could tell something was wrong. I heard someone else in the barn. I knew right away she was in trouble."

Her quiet expression urged him to go on.

"I wasn't fast enough. I wasn't smart or strong enough to help her."

He hurried through the rest—coming down off the ladder, feeling the crack of metal on his skull, getting knocked out. Then, waking up to voices and stitches and questions from the police. "Everyone was convinced that, because I'd been in the barn, I'd seen his face. I was the only one who could help find Jess." His eyes clouded then.

Beth reached across the table and covered his hands with hers. "That's a lot of pressure for a little boy."

He pushed his fist into his eyes and forced himself to hold it together. "The trouble was, I didn't remember seeing anyone, but for days, cops were out here, pacing the floor, setting up interviews with therapists. One of them even tried to hypnotize me." Drew only just remembered that.

"The worst part was knowing that I was letting my own parents down. And Mr. and Mrs. Pendergast."

"Why didn't you say anything—when you first got here?"

"I was such a coward, Beth." Drew pulled his hands back into his lap and stood. "I should've come back years ago. Harold called me every year begging me not to give up trying, but I didn't want to relive any of it." He stood at the sink and stared out the window across the cornfield. How could there be so much peace here, in a place of so much tragedy? "It was selfish of me not to do that for him. For Jess."

"It was wrong of them to put all that pressure on you," Beth said. "Even adults wouldn't be able to process what you saw. Did anyone tell you it wasn't your fault?"

Her words stopped his breath for a split second.

She came up behind him, wrapped her arms around his chest and laid her head on his back. They stood like that for several seconds until finally the weight of his burden began to fall away.

He turned around and pulled her close, letting his chin rest gently on top of her head. He inhaled her, charmed by her sweet vanilla scent.

"I'm sorry I didn't tell you sooner."

"It's okay. I know it wasn't easy."

No. It wasn't. And yet, he felt a sense of relief having gotten it all out. He inched away and studied her face. "There's something else."

"There is?"

"The day you found the room in the closet."

Beth nodded, pulling just out of his grasp.

"I remembered something. A song came on the radio outside, and it was like I was there. I was ten years old again."

Drew recounted the man in the stable. He'd seen him. He remembered him, but he didn't recognize him. "What if this is the man who took Jess? What if Harold was right, and I've had the answer all along?"

She shook her head. "Don't do that to yourself. You remember now."

"I need you to help me with something."

She raised her eyebrow. "Anything."

Drew picked up her notebook and handed it to her. "I need you to sketch his face."

Beth took the notebook, and for a second, she looked like she didn't recognize it, didn't know what to do with it. "You want me to draw the man in your mind?"

"That's why I went to Bishop. To see if they had someone who could sketch it for me."

Beth frowned. "I don't think they do."

"I didn't think so, but I didn't want to leave town without at least trying."

"You shouldn't have been leaving town at all." She smirked.

He tugged at her hand. "You thought I was guilty. I thought I'd lost you."

"I'm sorry for that." Embarrassment whisked across her face.

"Will you help me?"

Beth stared at the blank paper. "I'll try," she said. "But I can't promise you it's going to come out right."

Drew pressed his lips to her forehead. "It doesn't have to be perfect."

Her eyes found his. "And neither do you."

Simple words had never spoken so deeply to his soul.

Chapter Thirty-Seven

"Was his face long or round?"

Drew squinted. "Round. Pudgy. And he had freckles across the top of his nose and cheeks."

Beth sketched, feeling rusty. "I feel like someone else would be better at this."

"It doesn't have to be perfect, remember?"

But it felt like it did. There was so much riding on this.

She listened closely as he told her what he remembered. Every once in a while, he'd get quiet, lost in a memory. She'd wait patiently for him to continue, praying this brought him the closure he needed.

"Have you ever told anyone about any of this?" She kept her gaze on the sketch pad as she shaded the man's left eyebrow.

"No."

The one word said so much. He'd bottled it up all these years, but he'd trusted her enough to break his silence. "I'm glad you told me."

"I am too."

She prayed he saw that self-preservation, not cowardice, had driven him to bury these memories. That lie he'd believed had robbed him of years of living.

Beth stopped shading the face of a pudgy man, young, maybe late teens, with a stout nose and thin eyebrows.

"Are you sure the expression is right?" she asked. The man she'd sketched didn't look angry, but sad. It took a special kind of evil to harm a child—maybe Beth had gotten it wrong.

Drew took the paper and studied it. "No, this is right. He looks mean to me. You don't think so?" He turned the drawing toward her.

Drew saw the man differently. Like a child might. Beth stilled, but before she could respond, the front door opened. Bishop still stood on the porch. It had been over an hour since he'd gone outside to give them some time alone.

Oops.

"I assume you've had enough time to chat?" he asked, hands on his hips, looking a bit disheveled.

"Bishop, I'm so sorry you've been out there this whole time." Beth stood. "Come in."

He shuffled through the door and turned his attention to Drew. "Do you want to tell me now why you were down at the station yesterday?"

Drew stood and handed him the drawing. "I remembered something."

Bishop studied the paper, eyebrow raised, but no recognition on his face. "Who's this?"

"Was hoping you could tell me." Drew shoved his hands in his pockets.

Bishop took another look, then shook his head. "Doesn't look familiar, but I can show it around. Who is he?"

Drew explained his memory of the man hiding in the stables and watching him and Jess, and Bishop agreed he was certainly a person of interest.

"It's hard to say whether or not anyone will recognize him now. It's been a really long time." Bishop must've caught the look of despair on Drew's face, because he quickly added, "But this is the first solid lead we've ever had in this case. Good job, man."

A commotion on the porch drew their attention outside, where Birdie was stumbling up the stairs.

"Oh, thank heavens, you're okay. I just heard about the damage from the storm." The poor woman looked terrified.

"We're fine, Birdie. I suppose we should be thankful no one was hurt." But even as she said the words, Beth felt anything but thankful. She was happy no one was in the barn when the tree went through the roof, but not happy at the decisions ahead of them or the knowledge that she was about to lose the life she'd grown to love.

"Did you just find out about the storm?" Drew asked.

"Heavens, no. I was in my fallout shelter." She looked at Drew. "I told you I was stocked up. I enjoyed myself so much down there, I just came up an hour ago. Cricket had left frantic messages on my machine. The whole town's buzzing about the damage to your farm."

Beth could imagine. The people of Willow Grove had been as excited about their grand reopening as she and Molly were. Selling to Davis wasn't only a letdown for her, but for the whole town. Beth hated that.

Birdie turned her attention to Beth. "What a mess. I suppose we'll move the sale to the art barn, then? Use the great outdoors a little more than we wanted to?"

Beth looked at Drew. Neither of them had even considered moving the sale. It was like they'd both been completely defeated from the second they'd seen the main barn, but most of the work was still done, including Dina's advertising campaign.

"I never thought about that," Beth said. "I suppose it could be like one last hurrah for Fairwind."

Birdie frowned. "What are you talking about?"

"It's a long story." Beth couldn't bring herself to get into it, but one glance at Birdie told her she'd lost her attention anyway. Instead, the old woman seemed captivated by the paper in Bishop's hand.

"Birdie? What is it?"

"Did you draw this?" Birdie took the paper from Bishop.

"Yes." Beth felt suddenly self-conscious of her work.

Birdie turned to Drew. The two of them exchanged a sort of rare, knowing glance, the kind that told Beth she recognized the man in the sketch. The kind that told her Birdie understood what Drew had been through to get that image out of his mind and onto the paper.

"Who is he?" Drew asked, his voice low and quiet.

"You don't remember," Birdie said.

He shook his head.

"It's Monty. He worked here that summer. Harold felt sorry for him, so he gave him a few odd jobs around the farm. No one ever considered him a suspect, because he'd been out of town that week." Her fingers met the edge of the paper. "Or at least that's what everyone thought."

"I saw him two days before Jess went missing," Drew said. "I know he was here."

Birdie fell onto the chair and covered her mouth with her hand. "The answer was there all along."

"Let's not jump to conclusions," Bishop said. "All we know is that we need to question him—nothing more."

"He was a troubled kid. Sweet, but troubled." Birdie seemed lost in her own world.

"Birdie, how can we find this Monty now? Does he still live in Willow Grove?" Bishop asked.

She slowly met Drew's eyes, as if what she knew would cause him pain. "He's right next door, Bishop. That's Monty Biddle. Davis's son."

Chapter Thirty-Eight

Birdie's words hung in the air.

Beth paced the kitchen floor, feeling like they had to piece together puzzles from two separate boxes. She recounted her conversations with Davis to Bishop, who scribbled notes in a little black notebook he pulled from his back pocket.

Molly showed up at the door, confusion all over her pale face. "Bishop said you were all out here. Why didn't you call me sooner? Was there a break in the case?"

Beth ignored her. Not the time to be dramatic.

"Why are we just standing around?" Drew paced the same six feet of the white linoleum, his brow knit.

"I want to have all the facts so we don't barge in half-cocked," Bishop said. "Molly, I need you to tell me everything that happened the day Davis Biddle's assistant gave you that business card."

Molly went over it again.

"He obviously wants this property for something," Beth said. "He's gone to a lot of trouble to make that clear." He'd made offers before and after the storm. Good offers that any sane person would take. He wasn't backing down.

Molly shrugged. "Is it possible he doesn't know about Monty? Maybe his son never told him what he'd done? Maybe he wants the land because it's valuable—and so are the orchards."

"I don't think that's it," Beth said. "I mean, we all see the value in this old farm, but I can't help but wonder if his motives have nothing to do with money at all."

Birdie let out a soft sigh.

"What is it?" Beth asked.

"I don't know why I didn't put it together sooner, but Monty stopped working here after that weekend. I've only ever seen him a handful of times since, but as far as I know, he still lives with Davis."

Concerned looks crisscrossed the room. Had something happened to Monty that day too? Maybe Davis wanted the farm because he—not his son—was the real criminal. Maybe there was still evidence on the property, or he was one of those creepy serial killers who kept trophies of his victims.

Was Fairwind his trophy?

"He's a special kid, Monty," Birdie said quietly. "He was always very sweet, but he was behind the rest of the kids. Got picked on a lot. Davis hired tutors for him so he wouldn't have to deal with all the bullies."

"And you're sure he still lives at home?" Bishop asked. "He'd be in his late thirties by now."

"I'm not sure of anything." Birdie's bracelets jangled as she stood. "And there's no sense speculating. We should just go over there and ask."

Bishop shook his head. "*We* aren't going anywhere. Monty needs to be questioned, I agree, but that doesn't involve any of you."

"Yes, it does." Drew glowered in the corner. "You're not going without me."

After some hesitation, Bishop agreed, out of common sense or fear, Beth didn't know. But she wasn't about to let them go without her either.

"What if I go?" Beth asked, ignoring Molly's slack-jawed expression.

"We can't roll up there with an entourage, Beth," Bishop said.

"But he thinks we're selling him the farm." She paced. "Maybe I can find out more. Do a little digging about why he's really interested in this old place."

"All due respect, Beth, I'm not sure he'd open up to you. And I'm not sure we need his life story." Bishop snapped his notebook shut and put it back in his pocket.

Beth chewed the inside of her lip. "I understand." She didn't really. She wanted to know the man's endgame. What did he think? That he could bring down Fairwind one barn at a time? That he could destroy what they'd restored and just walk away?

"I think Beth should come," Drew said. "It might be easier to get him talking if we go in to discuss business. We've already been there once. It can't hurt."

Bishop didn't look impressed. "I'm not interested in his shady business deals, you guys. If he or his son had something to do with Jess Pendergast's disappearance, that's all I care about."

Molly put a hand on Bishop's shoulder. "He's been out to steal Fairwind from us since the beginning, and from what we've heard, he doesn't like to take 'no' for an answer." She met Beth's eyes. "We almost forfeited our farm to that man."

If anyone could change Bishop's mind, it was Molly. He'd pull the moon down for her if she asked.

"This goes against every bit of police training I have," he said. "But I'll give you a few minutes alone with him before I come in."

Beth nodded a thank-you to Molly and then turned to Drew. "Are you sure you're going to be okay?"

He held her gaze for several seconds. "Positive."

Chapter Thirty-Nine

Beth called Davis and asked to see him right away. She explained that they were desperate and had made a decision, but they had a few questions before they could finalize the deal.

As expected, he invited her right over. She and Drew arrived ten minutes later, with the understanding that Bishop would come after twenty minutes. Knowing Molly, she'd likely sneak into the back seat of the squad car when he wasn't looking—to her, this was all terribly exciting.

To Beth, it was nauseating. Her stomach rolled as Drew shut off the truck's engine.

"You okay?" he asked.

"Shouldn't I be asking you that?"

"I'll be okay," he said. "Long as you're okay."

"What if Monty was a tool his father used?" Beth asked before they got out of the truck. "What if Monty delivered Jess to his father?"

Drew looked away. Thinking about it had to hurt. Walking in there, asking questions—all of it would hurt. She hated that he had to go through this.

They walked to the door, which opened before they could knock. Davis's assistant welcomed them in, ushered them into the office and left them alone.

Beth's eyes scanned the framed photographs on the mantel, the desk, the wall. "Don't you think it's odd that he doesn't have a single picture of his family? If I didn't know better, I'd have no idea Davis had a son at all."

"Yeah," Drew said. "It's odd, just like everything else about this guy."

But he wasn't odd. Not really. Davis Biddle was a little arrogant, but otherwise a completely normal guy.

Minutes later he entered, walked straight to his desk and sat down. "I hear you've come around, Miss Whitaker. It's nothing to be ashamed of, really. Farmwork isn't for everyone." He smiled. He was almost charming. "If I didn't have the money to hire out all the work, I probably wouldn't take it on myself."

Beth pressed her lips together. "If you don't mind me asking, what are your intentions for the farm?"

Davis laughed. "This is a piece of land, Miss Whitaker, not a daughter I'm trying to marry off."

"It's more than a piece of land to me," Beth said. *It was supposed to be my second chance.*

"I understand the sentimentality of a place like Fairwind Farm, Miss Whitaker. I really do."

"So are you going to restore it and reopen it?"

"I don't want to mislead you." He folded his hands on the desk.

"So you're going to buy it and level all the buildings?"

"That's more likely. Though, the orchards are producing well. Walter tells me they're worth keeping. Probably worth expanding. We get the outbuildings out of the way, we can give ourselves a lot more room for the orchard."

"Seems like small-time for someone like you," Drew said.

"I guess I'm just trying to get back to basics, Mr. Barlow. Maybe you'd be interested in staying on as the grounds manager?"

Drew's jaw twitched.

"It's interesting you said you worked out an agreement with Harold about the orchards," Beth said.

"Why is that interesting?"

"Because it's a lie."

Surprise skirted across his face. "What makes you say that?"

"Walter told me. It made me wonder why a man like you would go to all the trouble of pouring his hard-earned money into a local apple orchard for no return. Especially the same year the owners' daughter went missing."

"That's not a secret," Davis said.

"Were you just being a good neighbor, or did your sudden generosity have something to do with your son?" Beth pulled the sketch from her notebook and slid it across the table.

Davis looked at it, then slowly met her eyes. "What is this?"

"It's a sketch of a man who was at the farm around the time of Jess's disappearance."

Beads of sweat gathered on Davis's upper lip. "Of course he was there. Monty worked for Harold and Sonya. What's your point?"

"He was seen hiding in one of the stables, watching the little girl play," Beth said. "And a tenant in one of the barns remembers him. She never saw him working on the farm again after that day."

"Is that Mrs. Chirper?" Davis said, his brows drawn down. "You can't trust anything that woman says."

"Oh, I don't know. I think she makes a lot of sense." Never mind that Birdie was known for her conspiracy theories. She'd interrupted her share of city council meetings with her outlandish speculations—from chemicals in the water supply to toxic birds with cancer in their waste.

"Well, nobody in their right mind would believe her."

"Maybe not, but they'll believe me," Drew said.

Davis narrowed his gaze, focusing on him. "I was wondering if you were the same Barlow who was there that day."

"Does that make you nervous?"

"Of course not. I have nothing to hide." Davis leaned back in his chair. "That case is twenty years old. Why drag it all back up now?"

"Because nobody ever paid for what they did to Jess," Drew said. "And it's about time someone did."

Davis's eye twitched—so slightly Beth almost missed it.

"Maybe we could speak with your son, Mr. Biddle?" she asked. "Do you know where we could find him? We're told there's a chance he still lives with you."

Davis waved her off. "Not possible."

"Why not?" Drew looked like he might come unglued.

"He's not here."

What if Davis was telling the truth? What if something had happened to Monty—would anyone in town even know?

The doorbell rang.

Bishop. He'd have other officers with him and a search warrant.

Beth took out a small photograph and slid it across the desk.

When Davis looked at it, irritation flashed across his face.

"That's Jess," she said. "She was nine when someone grabbed her out of her own yard, and her body has never been found."

"I remember, Miss Whitaker. Why are you telling me what I already know?"

"I want you to remember her face. I want you to do the right thing. Tell us what happened to Jess."

Davis pressed his lips together. "I can't help you."

"Sir, I'm sorry to interrupt." Davis's assistant appeared in the doorway, but before he could continue, Bishop pushed through, followed by three other officers.

"Mr. Biddle, we've got a few questions for your son."

Davis stood. "He's not here."

"I'm sure you won't mind if we take a look around."

"In fact, I do mind, Officer—what did you say your name was?"

Bishop took out a document and handed it to the other man. "I have a warrant, sir. I'm afraid you'll have to stay in here while we conduct our search." He must've caught the glance passing between Davis and his assistant, because he grabbed the assistant by the arm and ordered him to sit on the couch in the office. Before he left, he told one of the other officers to keep a close eye on them both.

Drew and Beth followed Bishop out into the entryway, mostly because they didn't want to sit in the same room with Davis Biddle, but also because they were curious. Was Monty hiding somewhere in the house? And if so, what skeletons was he hiding in his closet?

Bishop jumped into action. "Let's start in the kitchen. You guys stay here." They watched him and the remaining officers disappear down a long hallway and through a door.

Drew stood in the same spot for all of five seconds before he inched away from her, looking up the grand staircase, which no doubt led to the bedrooms.

"Maybe he's upstairs," he said.

"Bishop said to stay here," Beth whispered.

Drew held a finger over his mouth to silence her, then started up the stairs.

She leaned around to look down the hallway. When she saw the coast was clear, she—against her better judgment—followed Drew.

"You know the odds of us finding anything up here are really slim." Beth hated the way her nerves had kicked up. Hated that they'd only ever find out the truth if Monty confessed.

And after twenty years of silence, why would he do that?

Uncovering the truth might be impossible at this point.

◆ ◆ ◆

Drew opened a door at the top of the stairs. He then opened each door down a narrow hallway. Powder room. Linen closet. Guest bedroom.

They moved down the corridor. "Everything is so perfect," Beth said.

"Too perfect, if you ask me." Drew closed the door to another guest room. "This place is so sterile it's creepy." He pulled open the door to another linen closet. "I mean, look."

The sheets and pillowcases were expertly folded. Pristine white towels were stacked next to each other, perfectly symmetrical. Two small canvas baskets were at the bottom of the closet, holding extra toiletries.

Drew closed the door and moved toward the last room in the hallway. "Maybe we should wait for Bishop," Beth said.

He'd been waiting two decades for answers. He wasn't waiting another minute. He turned the doorknob and pushed the door open.

They walked inside what looked like two large bedrooms combined into one spacious loft-style apartment. An old episode of *The Andy Griffith Show* played on a large-screen television that hung on the wall.

On either side of the TV, rows of books and DVDs were neatly arranged on shelves. A couch and a recliner faced the television, and hanging all around the room were old, framed movie posters. Behind the recliner was a collection of Superman paraphernalia—posters, books, figurines, toys.

"What in the world?" Beth's eyes settled on the recliner, where a man sat, engrossed in the TV show.

Monty. He'd aged, of course, but he still had the same round face and wide nose he'd had back then.

Beth reached over and put a hand on Drew's arm. He was okay. He just wanted to get this over with—once and for all.

Drew moved toward Monty, who wore a blank expression and seemed unaware they'd come into the room. Drew cleared his throat, and the man startled.

Monty's face went pale. "Who are you?" He held his hands up in front of him, as if to protect himself.

"Monty?"

He covered his head with his hands. "Not here."

Now Drew remembered him. When Birdie said Monty had been behind the other kids, she'd meant he had a severe mental disability. It was why kids had made fun of him, why Harold had tried to help him. It was why he still, after all these years, seemed like a child.

But Monty was harmless—wasn't he?

"I like your room," Beth said, walking toward him. "This used to be one of my favorite shows too."

"*Andy?*" Monty looked up at her.

Beth nodded.

Monty laughed.

So, it was Beth—not Drew—who should ask the questions. She must've sensed it too, because she sat down next to Monty and took the lead.

"You live here?" she asked.

He nodded. "My apartment." Snapping the recliner to an upright position, he stood. "My TV." He pointed to the television. "My kitchen."

"It's very nice," Beth said. "Do you like Superman?"

Monty nodded, moving over to the collection behind the recliner. "Superman."

"What do you like about Superman?"

He picked up one of the toys, a Superman action figure. "He can fly."

"Yeah, that's pretty cool." Beth picked up another toy.

Monty eyed her, and for a split second, Drew wasn't sure he was going to let Beth get away with touching something from his collection.

But she met Monty's eyes and smiled, and the man relaxed. He towered over her—at least a foot taller and a hundred pounds heavier. Drew moved closer, just to be safe. What if Monty had a temper?

"You know what I like about Superman?" Beth asked.

Monty shook his head, still eyeing the toy in her hands.

"I like that he saves people." She reached into her pocket and pulled out the same small photograph she'd shown his father.

"Monty, do you remember this girl?" she asked quietly.

He took the photo, and his brow furrowed as he looked at Jess's face staring back at him. "Jess."

"Yes, Jess Pendergast," Beth said.

"My Jess." Monty nodded. "Not supposed to talk about Jess." His head moved in quick pulls, back and forth.

"Do you want to help Jess, Monty?"

He looked up at Beth.

"Like Superman helps people?"

Monty nodded. "Help Jess."

Bishop appeared in the doorway and shot Drew an irritated look, but Drew held up a hand to tell him to wait. Bishop stayed where he was, but pulled out his phone, most likely to record whatever conversation was about to take place.

"A lot of people have been looking for Jess, Monty," Beth said evenly. "Did something happen to her?"

Monty's nods were quick, his eyes blank, as if replaying a distant memory. "Yes."

"Can you tell me what happened to her? We'd really love to help her if we can."

"My Jess." Monty started crying, as if the memory tore the stitches from a long-abandoned wound.

"It's okay, Monty. We just want to help."

"I didn't mean it."

"No, of course not." She glanced at Drew quickly, then back to Monty.

"That boy came. He came, and I lost her. I saw them laughing. I had to get her out." Monty's eyes went dark as his memory wandered back. "The boy fell down. I took my Jess."

Drew swallowed, his throat dry. His eyes welled, his heart sank.

"I took her home. She screamed at me." Monty stared out into nothing, still holding the Superman action figure. "I told her it was okay. It's okay, Jess. It's okay." He pulled the toy closer and rocked back and forth. "She was my friend. It was okay."

His voice grew louder, his eyebrows knit into one straight line.

"Quiet, Jess. Be quiet or Daddy will hear you." His hands shook as he held the toy even closer, rocking it in his arms. He grew agitated, rocking faster—face angry, hands shaking. "Quiet, Jess. Quiet! Quiet!"

The toy snapped in his hands.

The image of Jess's frail, lifeless body in Monty's arms sprang to Drew's mind. Beth covered her mouth with her hand.

"Quiet." Monty looked at the toy, broken in two pieces.

No one moved for a long moment. No one could.

Monty had killed Jess.

Drew closed his eyes and let his head fall forward into his hands. It had been an accident—a case of Monty not knowing his own strength.

Slowly, Beth took the toy from Monty and ushered him back to the recliner.

"Monty is sorry." He sat down, broken, a man who'd relived unbearable pain.

Drew knew a little something about that.

"Monty, do you know where Jess is now?" Beth asked.

He wiped his nose on his sleeve. "Outside. Daddy put her in a deep, deep hole. She's sleeping now. I can't see her anymore. I'm not allowed to see her anymore. Monty did a bad thing. Monty is bad."

So Davis did know what his son had done. He not only knew, he'd covered it up. Drew's sorrow dissipated, and anger moved into its place. Maybe Monty couldn't be held accountable for his actions, but his father certainly could.

Because of him, Harold and Sonya had gone to their graves still unsure of what had happened to their daughter. Because of him, Drew had lived with the ache of a million unknowns.

He had the answers he'd come for, yet part of him wondered if things had been better before he knew.

Footfalls in the hallway pulled their attention. Monty's father appeared in the doorway. Drew turned and faced him, daring Davis Biddle to say a single word in his own defense.

"You can't talk to my son without my permission." His eyes fell on the large man in the recliner, who slowly rocked back and forth, a blank stare on his face. "Monty . . ."

"It's too late, Davis," Bishop said. "Both you and your son need to come with me."

Davis turned in a circle like a caged animal, then rushed over to his son, kneeling down beside him. "Monty, are you okay?"

"Monty is bad." The man didn't look at his father.

"No, Monty. You're not bad. It's going to be okay, I promise." He ran a hand through his gray hair and stood. "Please. He didn't mean to hurt anyone."

"A little girl is dead, Mr. Biddle," Bishop said.

Davis covered his face with his hands, and Drew watched as the grief of the past spilled out of him. He'd been carrying his secret for twenty years too, and it had taken its toll.

He sat down on the couch across from Monty, who still quietly rocked back and forth. "You have no idea how hard this has been."

Heat shot through Drew like a dart, but before he could put the man in his place, Davis continued.

"I know it's been harder for you, son." He didn't look at Drew. "And I know—" His voice cracked. "I know how hard it was for Harold and Sonya."

"Then why didn't you come forward?" Beth asked.

Davis looked at them, tears in his eyes. "He's my son."

Drew glanced at Monty, unsure whether the man was even aware of what was happening in his own room.

"I found him in the garage, holding her—neck snapped, arms and legs draped over him like a rag doll." Davis looked at Monty. "It was my fault. After Monty's mother died, I worked all the time. I was never here for him. He roamed around outside, and I guess Harold felt sorry for him and gave him a few things to do around the farm. But if I'd been here like I should've been . . ."

Drew didn't have words to comfort this man. He was right. It was his fault that Jess was dead. His fault that Drew had spent his entire life shouldering the weight of his guilt.

"He wouldn't have gone to prison," Bishop said. "If you'd just turned him in, he would've been committed to an institution."

"Monty's mother was the love of my life. She made me a better man, and she was adamant that Monty live here with us, not in some institution with strangers. I made her a promise."

"So you kept Monty here," Beth said.

"He has twenty-four-hour care. He's never alone. He's not allowed out of the house by himself. When I go out of town, he doesn't go out of the house at all."

Drew glanced at Monty. In a way, he'd been in prison his whole life.

"I made sure another accident could never happen." Davis reached over and clasped a hand on Monty's shoulder. "My son is a good boy. He never meant to hurt the little girl."

"Where is the body?" Bishop asked, the question coming out cold. It hurt Drew to hear them talk about Jess like that—as if she weren't a person but a case to be closed.

Davis looked away. "I buried her out back on the hill underneath my wife's favorite tree. I know how difficult this must've been for you, son, but I want you to know a week hasn't gone by that I didn't put fresh flowers on her grave."

A thoughtful sentiment. Drew wished it were enough.

Chapter Forty

Drew stood in the driveway of the Biddle estate, watching as officers led Davis and Monty to squad cars whose lights shined flashes of red out into the darkness. He was weary and worn, and Beth was at his side, where she'd been the entire night.

She wound her arms around his waist and let her head fall to his chest. "It's over."

He liked the way she fit perfectly in his arms, as if they'd been made to go together.

Could he ever let her in the way he wanted to?

He kissed her forehead, and she lifted her chin, found his eyes. "What is it?"

He supposed he shouldn't be surprised she could sense that he was still unsettled. He loved her for that. He loved that he wanted to tell her instead of burying his feelings, giving them the ability to haunt him later.

"All this time, I knew Jess was gone," Drew said. "I guess I just expected to keep on hating the man who killed her. But now that I know who he is—I sort of feel sorry for him."

Beth leaned into him and wrapped her arms more tightly around his torso. "Then maybe you can finally let it all go."

How did he begin to do that? How did this singular event simply fall by the wayside, a remnant of something he used to know?

Anger. Pain. Sadness. Those things made sense to him.

But after seeing Monty's face—hearing why Davis had done what he did—the anger had dissolved, leaving Drew with feelings he didn't know how to process.

Beth led him back to the truck, where he went through the motions of getting in, buckling his seat belt and driving back to the farm.

Inside, he fell onto the couch, conflicted by the sorrow he felt over the lives affected that day. It wasn't just Drew or Jess or the Pendergasts whose worlds had been turned upside down, but Monty's and Davis's as well.

All those lives torn apart by a secret hidden for too many years.

Had it lost its power now that it was out in the light?

Did he really have the closure he'd been searching for?

The next morning, sunlight poured in the living room window, waking Drew from the soundest sleep he'd had since he was ten years old. Not a single nightmare had shaken him from sleep. He'd forgotten how it felt to be rested.

He didn't remember lying down last night, but someone had covered him up, given him a pillow, taken off his shoes. Someone had taken care of him.

Probably the same someone who'd brewed a fresh pot of coffee in the next room.

After brushing his teeth and splashing cold water on his face, Drew made his way to the kitchen.

He watched Beth as she stood over the stove, cooking bacon and eggs. Unaware of his presence, she moved without any trace of self-consciousness, humming along with the tune playing from the portable speakers connected to her iPod. He watched her from the doorway, trying to find words to thank her for everything she'd done for him. She might not know it, but because of her, he wanted to move beyond his past for the first time in his life.

Because of her, he could.

Words didn't come—he supposed some things would still take time. It didn't change the way he felt about her. Every part of him wanted her, and he wanted her to know it.

He ran a hand through his mess of hair and cleared his throat.

She met his eyes and smiled. "Hey."

"What time is it?"

"It's ten." Another smile. "You obviously had some sleep to catch up on." She poured him a cup of coffee and handed it to him.

"Where'd the coffeemaker come from?"

She flipped the fried eggs onto a piece of buttered toast, then added bacon and cheese. "My mom's. I had an extra from when I lived on my own. I figured it was smarter to have one here since this is where most of the coffee-drinking happens. Makes it feel a little bit more like home, don't you think?"

Home. He didn't know how that was supposed to feel.

Beth set the plate on the table. "I hope you're hungry."

"I'm starving."

"Good. It's one of the few things I know how to cook. My dad always made the best bacon-and-egg sandwiches."

"It looks good."

She sat with him while he ate, drinking a cup of coffee and studying him. It might've been the first time in his life he felt perfectly comfortable under someone else's gaze.

After he finished eating, she stood and reached for his plate, but he pulled it away from her. "I can clear my own dishes. But thank you for breakfast."

He took his plate to the sink, rinsed it and set it inside.

"I want to show you something," Beth said, a sparkle in her eye.

He followed her out the door and onto the front porch, where he saw a parking lot filled with cars and trucks. All around the yard, people moved quickly, some hauling garbage. Some carrying tools into the main barn. Callie walked around handing out pastries.

"What's this?"

"This is Willow Grove," Beth said, her voice shaky. "Molly put in a call to Pastor Harker's wife, and word just spread. All of these people believe in Fairwind Farm. So they came here to put the place back together."

Drew watched the scene in front of him. The organized chaos of a community connected by a common love for what the farm and orchard had come to mean to each of them.

"The damage isn't as extensive as we first thought. We're moving the Fairwind Farm Market to the other barn. Birdie was thrilled."

"She's staying, then?"

Beth smiled. "She agreed to our terms."

"What are they?"

"She can stay and paint, but once a week, she has to give me art lessons."

He raised a brow as he regarded her from the side. "Is that right?"

She shrugged. "Turns out, I kind of miss that part of my life."

He loved the thought of Beth out in that barn, painting in what Birdie called "glorious light." It suited her.

"Also"—her eyes filled with excitement—"it looks like our little barn sale is going to be a really big deal. We've already sold five hundred tickets, and we have over a hundred vendors."

"Is that good?"

"You're such a guy." Beth swatted him on the shoulder. "Yes, it's really good. Dina thinks we'll get over a thousand presale tickets sold."

He did quick math, knowing the admission price. Beth had been right—it would be a nice little moneymaker for the farm.

"The main barn will take a bit more time to repair, but I actually feel like everything is going to be okay."

"Better than okay," he said.

Her smile was soft. "Better than okay."

He put an arm around Beth's shoulder, both of them quietly staring out over the busyness of another Community Work Day. This one, though, felt more like a rescue—everyone chipping in to pull them back onto solid footing.

"So, what about you?"

Beth turned to him. "What about me?"

"Didn't Dina offer you a job in the city?"

Her eyes scanned the scene in front of them. "It makes about as much sense as buying a summer home in Antarctica, but I'm committed to this place now. I think it's my 'why.'"

He didn't understand what that meant, but it sounded important to her, so he smiled. "And the money?"

She looked away. "I don't know. I can't explain it—on paper, none of this makes sense. But I've decided not to worry about what I can't control."

He brushed a stray hair away from her face. "Sounds like a really good idea."

She lifted her chin to meet his eyes. His breath hitched for a quick second as he realized his feelings for her had gone deeper than even he'd known.

"And what about me?" He felt vulnerable asking.

"What about you?"

"What if I invested in Fairwind?"

She pulled out of his embrace, eyes locked on his. "I could never ask you to do that."

"You're not asking. I'm offering." He stared out over the barns, the fields, the plans for the farm ingrained in his mind. "I built those fences. I tore out the rotted wood on the small barn out back so Blue and whatever other animals Molly brings home can have a safe place to live." He turned, then held her gaze. "Feels like home for me here."

Did she know how hard it was to say? To admit he'd wandered through life feeling lost and alone? To admit he didn't want to live that way anymore?

Of course she didn't know how hard it was. He'd never told her. But he needed to—he wanted to let her in.

Before he could, she asked, "What about your job in Colorado?"

"I called them yesterday. Told them what they already knew—that I'm not coming back."

Her shoulders sank ever so slightly. "Why?"

"Because I am stupidly in love with you, Beth Whitaker." He took her face in his hands and brushed a tear from her cheek with his thumb.

He kissed her forehead, then each cheek, then finally let his lips find hers. She kissed him back, arms wrapped around his neck and standing on her tiptoes. Her kisses began to chip away at the bricks encasing his heart.

And he didn't even try to stop it.

She leaned back and watched him. "How much money are we talking about here?"

Drew laughed. "Enough."

"How?"

"I never made much money, but I didn't spend anything. My room and board was always included in my job—what else did a guy like me need?"

"So you've just been saving it all?"

He shrugged. "For a rainy day."

"Are you sure you want to do this?"

He kissed her again. "I've never been so sure about anything in my life." For the first time, he didn't feel like he was watching his own life from the sidelines. He was an active participant in the world around him—and this farm, this woman, had everything to do with that.

He pulled back and studied her face, her lips, her eyes. She saw him even when he didn't want her to, and she hadn't run away. No one had ever loved him like that before—without condition, without permission.

And he vowed in that moment to return that love every day for the rest of his life.

Chapter Forty-One

Two Fridays later, the day before the Fairwind Farm Market, Beth awoke early. Her nerves kicked up when she realized the weight of what lay in front of her. Today would not be like every other Friday. This weekend would not be like every other weekend.

Special moments deserved to be amplified, so Beth made a conscious effort to do that.

Every day that week, members of the Willow Grove community had joined them on the farm, rebuilding what the storm had stolen and helping them set up for the sale. She'd been woefully absent from the preparations, deciding instead to focus her attention on something possibly even more important than saving their dreams for Fairwind Farm.

Still, sacrifices were being made on their behalf—the weight of that didn't escape her. She'd become a part of this community, not because she was a disappointment who had no other option, but because she loved it here. This was exactly where she belonged.

Now, she walked practically on tiptoes, careful not to let her heels sink too far into the earth behind the old farmhouse. Up ahead, the chapel stood underneath one divinely placed beam of sunshine. Beth stopped to breathe it in, certain God had positioned the light just so and just for her.

She opened the door to the chapel and looked across the rows of wooden pews, light filtering in through the skylight and windows. At the front of the space, on the tiny platform, a large photo stood on an easel she'd found in Birdie's art barn.

The faces of Harold, Sonya and Jess Pendergast smiled back at her, radiating life and hope and promise. Their dreams had been dashed by an inexplicable accident, an accident that robbed them of their chance at ever having a proper goodbye.

That would change today.

She turned at the sound of footfalls entering the small church and found Drew standing in the doorway.

He, like the rest of them, had spent the entire week working non-stop on the farm, but he'd taken frequent breaks to check on her, talk to her, steal kisses from her. Something inside him had shifted, and she sensed he'd found exactly what he was looking for here at Fairwind.

Funny, she had too.

Her heart leapt to think she could be a part of his prize.

At the sight of her, Drew stopped moving, as if he needed a moment to drink her in. "Is it wrong for me to really love the way you look in that dress?" His mouth pulled upward in a crooked smile.

She smoothed her hands over her simple black dress, tapered at the waist and fitted perfectly to her body. She wore a small strand of pearls around her neck, and she'd pulled her long hair up into a simple, messy bun.

"If it's wrong, then we're both guilty," Beth said, eyeing him in his dark jeans and a blue button-down that skimmed his body in all the right places. "You clean up nice."

His smile dangled there for a few long moments, and then he drew in a deep breath, as if he'd only just remembered why they were there. "I never thought this day would come."

She glanced at the photo of the Pendergast family, then back at Drew. "I hope you're still feeling okay about a memorial service."

"I am. And it'll be good to lay Jess to rest here with her parents."

They would bury Jess at Fairwind, in the family cemetery behind the chapel. Sonya and Harold had been buried there, and beside their graves, a small stone had been placed in Jess's memory. Now, thanks to Drew, they'd be able to reunite the little family once and for all.

At the sound of approaching voices, Beth started toward the door, but Drew grabbed her arm, stopped her. "Beth."

She met his eyes.

"Thank you."

"I didn't do anything. You did this."

"No." He looked away. Words still didn't come easily for him. And that was okay. He needed to know it was okay.

"It's okay, Drew, I—"

"You gave me a safe place," he cut her off. His blue eyes looked even brighter in the light of the chapel, or maybe a shadow had been lifted, making everything clearer, crisper. "I've never had that before."

Beth wanted to wrap her arms around him, to hold him forever.

In a way, he'd given her a safe place too. A place to be herself, even if that wasn't who she'd expected it to be. He'd loved her without condition, in a way that didn't make sense to her, and she prayed in that moment she'd be able to do the same for him—for as long as he would let her.

Molly appeared at the doorway, with their mother and Bishop close behind. Beth gave Drew one last knowing glance, then moved toward the door to meet her family as Drew went to the front of the chapel.

She reached her mother, who pulled her into a gentle hug.

"You're doing a wonderful thing here," Lilian said.

Beth smiled. "Thanks for the push, Mom."

Her mother's eyebrows shot up. "Me? I had nothing to do with this. This was all you girls. And that handsome man up there, from what I'm told."

Beth followed her gaze to Drew, who stood near the front of the chapel, looking over his notes. "Yes, I'll introduce you. After. Go find a seat."

Her mom studied her for a moment. "You seem happy."

"And you seem healthy."

Her mother squeezed Beth's hands and walked off with Molly, leaving Beth in the doorway. She greeted familiar faces—Birdie, Callie, Ben, even Dina had made the drive—while Bishop strummed hymns on his guitar until everyone was seated. There weren't enough seats, but nobody seemed to mind standing.

Everyone wanted to say goodbye to the little girl who had gone too soon.

Beth walked to the front of the church and took a seat next to Drew. He reached over and took her hand as Pastor Harker stepped onto the platform and met their eyes. He gave them a warm smile and then opened his Bible.

◆ ◆ ◆

Pastor Harker read from Ecclesiastes, familiar words about a time for everything under heaven. When he finished, he asked Drew to join him on the stage.

Drew's throat was dry.

He must not have been thinking when he'd agreed to this.

"It has to be you, Drew," Birdie had said. "You knew her best."

And he knew she was right—but as he stood behind the small pulpit, feeling too clumsy and too big, he looked out over the crowd of now-familiar faces looking back at him.

"Just talk to me," Beth had said.

As if that had ever come easily to him.

His eyes found her, sitting in the front row looking stunningly beautiful, hair pulled away from her face, bright eyes startling life into his bones.

She gave him a warm smile.

"The day Jess went missing was the worst day of my life," Drew began.

The crowd stilled.

"A lot of people thought I had answers. Some even thought I had something to do with what happened to her. I spent a lot of years wondering if they were right. Got pretty mad at myself when I couldn't give everyone what they wanted."

His eyes fell. "I had a lot of nightmares, and after a while, I started to hate all of my memories of Fairwind Farm.

"But today, I realized something. I realized I had more than nightmares of this place. I also had the memories of a girl who had the loudest, funniest laugh. A girl who loved to hunt for frogs and bait hooks for fishing out back in the creek. And if you tried to do it for her, she'd slap your hand away." He laughed at the memory. "I can still hear her singing in the barn—completely off-key—just because she loved the song so much."

He pulled his gaze from the podium to the audience. "Yeah, something terrible happened that day. And I was a witness to it. But I was also a witness to something pretty amazing too. Jessica Pendergast's life."

He took a moment to hear her voice in the shadow of his mind, then looked at Beth. "Man, I wish you'd all known her. She would've cracked you guys up."

Tentative laughter trickled through the room.

"Jess was what you'd call spunky. If you told her she couldn't do something, it only made her want to do it more." Another glance at Beth. "I suppose you two had that in common."

Beth smiled.

"I came here looking for something—I don't even think I knew what it was," Drew said. "But I didn't expect to find what I did. While I'm now able to turn the page on one chapter of my life, a new one has already begun. And I owe that to the people in this room."

He drew in a deep breath. A breath that washed new life over him, giving him permission to put his shame to rest alongside Jess Pendergast.

"I just want to thank you all." He turned to Beth. "Especially you. For accepting me into this family." His voice caught in his throat. This was more talking than he'd done all year. "Just, thanks."

Drew walked off the platform and into the reverent silence of the room, certain that he'd never be able to properly convey to the world, or to Beth, the way her love had saved him. Now, on the other side of his pain, he could see that he'd been a walking shadow of a man.

But never again would he be haunted by the darkness he'd carried for so many years. Instead, he'd stepped out of the shadows to live in the light.

They stood in the family cemetery behind the small chapel as Pastor Harker prayed one final prayer and Jess's small white casket was lowered into the ground. The people of Willow Grove had donated money for a new headstone for the little girl, one that included both the day of her birth and the day of her death along with the following words:

The earth laughs in flowers.

Beth brought a rose to her face and inhaled its glorious aroma. While she'd once believed a love of flowers made a girl weak, she now saw them for what they really were—a beautiful gift bestowed on all creation by a kind, loving Creator. The kind of gift that didn't need to be earned, the kind given to anyone who stood with arms stretched up to heaven in surrender.

Today, and every day, Beth decided to live with her arms open, welcoming every lavish gift God wanted to give her.

No matter how unworthy she felt.

And as they followed the rest of the group away from the gravesite, Drew's hand firmly pressed into her own, Beth inhaled a deep prayer of thanks for the gift she'd grown to love most of all.

A beautiful, broken soul with pitch-dark hair and stunning blue eyes. A man she'd decided to love without condition, the way God loved her. She slowed their pace, putting distance between them and the others.

"How are you feeling, really?" she asked when everyone had moved along.

He squeezed her hand. "Better than I think I ever have."

"I liked what you said in there." She brushed a stray hair back into her messy bun. "I was just wondering, this new chapter you were talking about . . . am I in it?"

Drew stopped walking and looked at her, doing a poor job of hiding a smile. "On every single page." He took her face in his hands and kissed her—wholly, sweetly and wonderfully kissed her.

With her arms around his neck, she leaned back and met his eyes. "You are the best gift of all."

He answered her with another kiss.

Another reminder that the best gifts are given freely and without strings.

And for the first time in her life, Beth Whitaker decided not to ask questions, but instead opened up her heart, outstretched her hands and received.

AUTHOR'S NOTE

Dear Reader,

I love writing stories. I love everything about it except the parts where I get stuck. I love dreaming up names for people who will become so real to me in my own mind, I almost forget they don't live next door. I love creating a new town and filling it with people, and I especially love pulling in elements from my own life along the way.

I first had the idea for *Hometown Girl* when I was visiting an apple orchard about an hour from my hometown in Illinois. I'm a Midwest girl through and through, and apple orchards are a staple in my world. Every fall, we make at least one trip to the orchard for cider and apples and our favorite, apple-cider donuts. If you've never been to an orchard, you may not be able to fully appreciate the ridiculously delicious taste (and smell) of an apple-cider donut, but truly, there is nothing like it. And if you can get it warm and fresh—well, you might as well just freeze time right there.

I loved the idea of exploring family relationships set against the backdrop of a place like the ones I love so much, and I am thrilled to have the opportunity to share it with you. Beth's journey, especially her spiritual one, is not unlike my own. We both have trouble asking for help and feel we should have everything figured out. We're both stubborn and sometimes take on way too much. We both need Jesus with every breath we take. Maybe you can relate?

I'd love to invite you to join my newsletter mailing list for superfun exclusive giveaways, freebies and prizes, as well as all the latest from my neck of the woods. Even more than that, I'd love to hear from *you* and the latest from *your* neck of the woods.

You can do all that by visiting my website, www.courtneywalsh-writes.com, signing up for my newsletter or dropping me an email at courtney@courtneywalshwrites.com.

Thank you again for taking the time to read this story. It means the world to me, and I'm so very grateful for you.

Courtney Walsh

ACKNOWLEDGMENTS

It's with the utmost gratitude I offer thanks . . .

To my sweet family, who cheer me on, celebrate my successes and don't complain too much when I announce it's "fend-for-yourself night" for dinner. Again.

To Adam, you are everything. It's your creativity that inspires me, your encouragement that pushes me forward and your kindness that makes me better in every way. Thank you for loving me.

To my kids, Sophia, Ethan and Sam. I just love you all with every fiber of my being. And I'm so thankful I get to be your mom.

To my parents, Bob and Cindy Fassler, who still pray for me and who have always taught me so well.

To my sister, Carrie Erikson, who helps me learn more about Jesus just by living her life. I'm so grateful for the uncontrollable belly laughs (you are the loudest!), the violent sneezes, the encouragement and the wisdom you share with me. I am grateful to have you for a best friend.

To the Emenecker family: Trent, Natalie, Alex, Addison, JT and Tyler, for answering questions about life on a farm you didn't even know I was asking. Also for opening your Fairwind Farm to people like me who seek a bit of solace in a busy, busy world. You never fail to remind me what's really important, and I'm so grateful for your friendship.

To Natasha Kern, my agent. Thank you for finding a home for this book, which otherwise would've sat in a drawer. I am so grateful to you for believing in me and for helping me on this journey.

To my writing friends Deb Raney, Katie Ganshert, Becky Wade, Melissa Tagg and the Grove Girls. I am so, so grateful that even in this solitary world we've created for ourselves I still have the friendship of so many beautiful souls. I count you among my greatest blessings.

And to you, dear reader. Thank you for picking up this book and going on this journey with me. You're on my mind often, and I'm so thankful for you.

ABOUT THE AUTHOR

 *New York Times* and *USA Today* bestselling author Courtney Walsh is a novelist, artist, theatre director, and playwright. *Hometown Girl* is her seventh novel. Her debut novel, *A Sweethaven Summer*, was a Carol Award finalist in the debut author category. She has written two additional books and a novella in the Sweethaven series, as well as three small-town romance novels: *Paper Hearts*, *Change of Heart*, and *Just Look Up*. She lives in Illinois, where she and her husband own a performing arts studio and youth theatre. They have three children. Visit her online at www.courtneywalshwrites.com.